Evelyn Hood                                              An
ex-journalist, she has been a full-time writer for several
years, turning her talents to plays, short stories,
children's books and the novels that have earned her
widespread acclaim and an ever-increasing readership.
For more information about Evelyn and her books,
visit www.evelynhood.co.uk

*Praise for Evelyn Hood*

'Immaculate in her historical detail'
*The Herald*

'Quite simply, I couldn't put it down. A rich and
rewarding read'
Emma Blair

'Evelyn Hood, with her ever-distinctive style, has the
ability to make her characters come alive'
*Historical Novels Review*

'Highly entertaining'
*Manchester Evening News*

'Bold and compassionate'
*Liverpool Daily Post*

'One of Scotland's most prodigious writers'
*Scottish Daily Record*

# EVELYN HOOD OMNIBUS

# Birds in the Spring
# The Silken Thread

SPHERE

This omnibus edition first published in Great Britain in 2010 by Sphere

Copyright © Evelyn Hood 2010

Previously published separately:
*Birds in the Spring* first published in Great Britain in 2007 by Sphere
Paperback edition published in 2008 by Sphere
Copyright © Evelyn Hood 2007
*The Silken Thread* first published in Great Britain in 1986
by William Kimber and Company Limited
Paperback edition published in 1997 by Warner Books
Copyright © Evelyn Hood 1986

A CIP catalogue record for this book
is available from the British Library.

ISBN 978-0-7515-4481-7

Printed and bound in Great Britain by
Clays Ltd, St Ives plc

Sphere
An imprint of
Little, Brown Book Group
100 Victoria Embankment
London EC4Y 0DY

An Hachette UK Company
www.hachette.co.uk

www.littlebrown.co.uk

# BIRDS IN THE SPRING

This book is dedicated to
Aileen Mitchell Cowie,
who has always been there for me.
And, I know, always will be.

# Acknowledgements

My thanks to bridal fashion designer (and friend) Sharon McPherson for allowing me to 'borrow' her young daughter, award-winning Irish dancer Cavan, as a character in this book.

Cavan, I hope that you approve of your name-sake.

On every other night of the year the Paisley streets would have been deserted when the town hall clock struck midnight. But this was no ordinary night; it was the moment when Hogmanay, the last day of the year in Scotland, gave way to Ne'erday, the magical moment when an old year passed away and a new year came blinking and squalling into the world.

A special new year, this one. It was 1920, the beginning of a new decade; the opportunity for those who had survived the horrors of the Great War to start again. The streets of Paisley were filled with men, women and children celebrating the new year and new decade of peace. Celebrating, too, the fact that even though most of them had lost at least one loved one to the war they were finally beginning to look forward and not back – towards a future that would surely be better than ever before.

Caitlin and Mary Lennox eased their way through the crowds, their small niece Rowena tucked securely between them. Murdo Guthrie, Caitlin's fiancé, and Lachie MacInnes, Mary's young man, were a few steps behind them. 'Just think,' Mary said, 'we're standing in the middle of history here! Rowena . . .' she put an arm around her niece '. . . you must remember this time because one day when you're a very old lady you'll be able to tell your grandchildren about tonight.'

'I'll be able to tell them about backsides and bellies, because that's all I can see,' ten-year-old Rowena complained, then gave a short squeal as she was suddenly swept into two strong arms and lifted off the ground.

'There now, is that better?' Murdo said into her ear.

'Murdo, put me down, I'm no' a wee wean!'

'Mebbe not, but you're too wee to see over folks' heads, so you might as well stay up here with me and enjoy yourself,' the big Highlander said, so she gave in, cuddling against his broad shoulder to keep warm. Caitlin tucked her hand into the crook of his free arm and let him help her, too, to forge a way through the crowds.

The mood was jubilant, and it reminded her of the night just over a year ago when the Great War came to an end. Then, as now, the people had poured from their homes, desperate to be with others as they celebrated the end of four terrible years.

Somewhere in the crowd an accordion broke into 'Keep the Home Fires Burning', and a singer joined in almost immediately. His voice, affected by drink, leaned heavily on the notes instead of lifting with them, sometimes not even managing to get close enough to lean. Others joined in, each bringing his or her interpretation, until the song turned into a cacophony of discordant sounds and the accordion could scarcely be heard at all. As Murdo and Caitlin moved on, with Mary and Lachie following, the singing died away behind them.

Most of the people tonight were in a good mood, but there were always those who had started to celebrate early in the town's public houses before weaving their way out into the streets, unsteady on their feet, and with heads fogged by alcohol. They met up with one such reveller a few minutes later, a small man who almost lost his balance as he passed them, staggering into Mary and sending her reeling. She might have fallen if Lachie hadn't caught and steadied her.

'Sorry, hen, jist a wee accident.' The man caught her other arm, peering closely into her face. Mary, who couldn't stand the smell of strong drink, pulled back against Lachie, almost choking on the whisky fumes. 'Here, have a drink,' the man urged, pushing his opened bottle at her.

She wrinkled her nose and shrank away from him. 'I don't want any of your drink. Will you just go away from me?'

'What's the matter, hen? Too proud tae drink wi' an ordinary workin' man like me? A man that fought in the war tae keep the likes o' you safe?' His voice was suddenly belligerent.

'Go away and stop bothering me!' Mary could put on an icy voice, and she also had a glare that could normally quell the strongest of men, but for once neither worked.

'I'm no' botherin' ye, I'm askin' ye tae drink tae the New Year wi' a soldier back from the wars. Nae need tae get so nebby. Think ye're better than me, is that it?'

Lachie MacInnes pushed past Mary. 'You heard the lady – she doesn't want a drink,' he said in the lilting accent of folk more used to speaking Gaelic.

'So that's the way o' it? Now she's walkin' oot wi' the likes o' you she thinks she's better than a decent Paisley man?' the drunk sneered, squaring

4

up to Lachie, who was only a little taller than he was, and slightly built. 'Well now, laddie, this is my toon, no' yours, so why don't ye get the hell oot o' it and crawl back where ye came from? Away an' live wi' the sheep where ye—'

The words ended in a gurgling sound as Lachie gathered up the thin scarf about the man's throat in one fist.

'Leave him, Lachie, he's too drunk to know what he's saying. Don't argue with him – you're just showing us up in front of all these folk.' Mary put her hand on Lachie's arm but he shrugged it off, pushing his face into the man's.

In the light from a street lamp Caitlin saw that his familiar features, normally easy-going and cheerful, were set into a scowl so menacing that she felt the blood chill in her veins.

There was a crash of broken glass as the man's bottle fell from his hand. His eyes began to bulge as Lachie's fist twisted, tightening the scarf. Mary caught hold of Lachie's arm again and pulled at it with all her might, but he continued to tighten his grip. The drunk clawed weakly at his own throat, then began to sag to the ground. Around them, the revellers continued to sing and dance and shout, oblivious of the drama unfolding only inches away.

'Murdo . . .' Caitlin turned to see that he was

already letting Rowena slide to the ground. He pushed the girl close against Caitlin's side before stepping forward to say something swiftly and urgently in Lachie's ear. When the younger man ignored him he spoke again, in his native Gaelic tongue, at the same time taking hold of Lachie's wrist and tightening his grip until the other man's fingers were forced to open.

As the drunk fell to the ground, released, Lachie whirled on his friend, his face still set in its menacing scowl, his eyes blazing hatred. Murdo caught him by the shoulders, holding him still and talking to him until the heat began to leave Lachie's eyes. Then he said to Caitlin and Mary, 'Take him away from here. I'll follow you in a minute.'

Mary seemed too stunned to do as she was told, so it was left to Caitlin to take Lachie's arm and lead him away. To her relief, he went with her, seemingly too spent to protest.

Murdo caught up with them when they were halfway down Causeyside Street. Rowena, who had been unusually quiet on the journey home, immediately slipped her free hand into his, while Lachie hurried ahead to join Mary, who was stepping out so fast that she was almost running. In the normal course of things the two of them would be arm in arm, but once he had caught up with her Lachie walked apart, staring down at the pavement while Mary talked. They were too far ahead for the others to catch any of her words.

'Was that man hurt?' Caitlin asked quietly over the little girl's head.

Murdo threw a brief, reassuring smile at her. 'He's fine. All it needed was some money to buy another bottle.'

'What got into Lachie? I've never seen him lose his temper like that.'

'The war can change men,' Murdo said, his face suddenly grim. 'He's all right now.'

They were going against the flow now, easing their way through crowds of people hurrying to get to the Cross in time for the bells that would bring in the New Year. Murdo raised his voice, smiling down at Rowena. 'I'll be glad to get back indoors, nice and warm and away from all these folk. We promised your gran and grandda that you'd be home before the bells, and we'll just about manage that.'

Alex was looking tired, Rose thought, glancing across the table at her husband. He paid no attention to the conversations going on around him and his long, lean face had a closed-in look, while his fingers played restlessly with a corner of his starched linen napkin.

Rose's heart went out to him. She knew that if

there was one thing that Alex detested above all others, it was having dinner with her parents. Normally she tried to avoid her mother's invitations, but this was New Year's Eve (her parents never referred to it as Hogmanay, considering the word too lower class for them), and like all married couples at this festive time of year she and Alex were obliged to spend some time with each family. Dinner tonight with her parents, lunch tomorrow with Alex's father and sister in Glasgow, and then the part they both looked forward to – a Ne'erday dinner in Espedair Street with his mother and stepfather. She cheered up a little at the prospect, but then her shoulders sagged slightly as she thought again of the formal obligations to be gone through first.

Her gaze drifted back to Alex, and this time he glanced up as though sensing the butterfly-soft brush of her eyes against his face. He smiled at her and, as always happened, for that brief moment it was as though the table with its delicate china, sparkling glass- and silverware, and snowy cloth had disappeared, taking with it her parents and her two elder sisters, two brothers-in-law and seven nephews and nieces, leaving only the two of them, alone together.

She smiled back, while her gaze took in the bruised shadows beneath his blue eyes and the downward turn at the corners of his mouth. He had not long recovered from the results of the terrible influenza that had decimated soldiers and civilians alike at the end of the war, and he still tired easily.

Her mother was not pleased when, as she summoned her daughters and grandchildren and prepared to move into the drawing room, leaving the menfolk to their brandy and cigars, Rose announced that she and Alex were going home.

'But you're all staying here for the night so that we can go to church tomorrow morning and then exchange our New Year gifts!'

'I'm sure that you will all enjoy it just as well without us,' Rose said firmly, 'and we'll leave our gifts to you and take yours home with us to open tomorrow morning. We've had a lovely meal and a lovely time, but now I feel tired and I want to go home – if you don't mind, Alex.'

'Not at all.' Her husband leaped to his feet with ill-disguised enthusiasm.

'Rose, you are never tired,' Mrs Hamilton said, and then, with a sudden lift to her voice, 'Oh, my goodness, you're not—?'

'No,' Rose said emphatically. 'I am not. I have too much work on hand at Harlequin to consider having a child at the moment. There's plenty of time for that.'

'You'll be thirty-two this year,' her elder sister Helen reminded her. Helen was approaching her fortieth birthday in February and not looking forward to the event.

'Not until September, which means that I am barely thirty-one at the moment,' Rose pointed out sweetly.

Her mother, used to getting her own way, pursed her rouged lips in a girlish pout. 'It isn't often that I get my three daughters and their families under my roof at the same time. Your room's all ready for you—' she was beginning when her husband, glancing at his youngest and most determined daughter, intervened.

'My dear, I believe that Rose has made up her mind, so we might as well accept her decision graciously.' He crossed to the bell pull by the fireplace. 'I shall ring for Gordon and ask him to put their overnight luggage into the car.'

Since Alex had shown no interest in learning to drive, Rose had taken lessons and bought herself a small motorcar, which she loved dearly. The overnight cases were soon installed, and she heaved a sigh of relief as she started down the driveway, leaving her family grouped on the steps, waving goodbye.

The kitchen table had been carried into the parlour with some difficulty earlier in the day and covered with Kirsty Paget's best tablecloth. Now the snowy lace was almost hidden by plates of shortbread, sandwiches, scones, cakes and black bun – a very rich fruity cake traditionally eaten at New Year.

'Anyone would think,' Todd Paget said as he and his wife surveyed the table, 'that you're expectin' tae feed the whole of Paisley.'

'While *you* keep them merry.' Kirsty nodded at the sideboard, which held every glass in the house, along with bottles of whisky, sherry and ginger wine.

'It's Hogmanay, lass, ye've got tae be welcomin' when folk arrive.' Todd picked up his newspaper and settled by the fire while Kirsty seated herself at the table, her hands lying idly in her lap for once.

She hated the New Year season, for try as she might to look forward towards a better future, her mind always insisted on turning the clock back to the past. Every life had its ups and downs, but there were times when Kirsty felt that she had had more downs than most. She had been raised by her widowed father, a dour man who, on discovering that she was pregnant by Sandy MacDowall, his young apprentice, had beaten her sweetheart savagely and then thrown sixteen-year-old Kirsty out.

After five years of struggling to support herself

and Alex, her son, she had married Matt Lennox, another dour widower in need of a woman to care for his own son, Ewan. When her father, to her astonishment, left the house and the small cabinet-making workshop to her, Matt insisted on moving to Paisley, where her father's journeyman, Todd Paget, was looking after the business. A few years later Matt died, and eventually Todd and Kirsty married.

'Ye're a million miles away, woman,' Todd said just then, and she jumped, but then smiled at him.

'Just remembering how I never wanted to come back to Paisley after the way my father treated me and poor Sandy, when he found out I was carrying Alex. It was Matt who wanted a new life for all of us. And if he hadnae been so determined I might never have met you. I'd be a lonely widow.'

'No' you. You'd have found another husband no bother. I'm just glad that I was here.'

'So am I. But you'd a price to pay. If we hadnae come to Paisley, Ewan would never have met Beth Laidlaw and run off with her just before your wedding.'

'I think I got the better part o' the bargain. Beth left him soon enough, didn't she? There's no doubt in my mind that she'd have done the same tae me.'

'I wonder where she is now?'

12

'Far from here, I hope. If she ever does turn up she'll only bring trouble with her.'

'Here they are, home at last,' Todd ended as they heard voices just outside the window.

'Are you sure you're not expecting a baby?' Alex asked as Rose drove down the long driveway from her parents' large house.

'Of course not. If I was, you'd be the first to know.' She slowed the car as it emerged between the stone pillars on either side of the gateway so that she could scan the roadway to either side. 'There'll be plenty of time for babies later, but not now, especially with Caitlin getting married soon.'

'It's not like you to be tired.'

'I'm not, that was just an excuse.' She turned the car on to the road and picked up speed. Alex hated being fussed over and so it would not be wise to tell him that she had changed their plans for his sake. 'I suddenly realised as we got to the dessert that I was totally and absolutely and dreadfully bored,' she said lightly. 'I've never enjoyed the company of my mamma and my sisters, and I enjoy it even less now that we're all older. They can't talk about anything other than the problems of getting good servants nowadays, or raising children. I love my nephews and nieces dearly, more than I love their parents in fact, but I'm not a bit interested in domestic discussions about their upbringing.'

'You might feel differently when we have children of our own.'

'I doubt it – I'll enjoy them, of course, but I hope that I never let them become my sole topic of conversation. Would you like me to drive to Espedair Street? Your family aren't boring, like mine.'

'Let's just go home. We'll see them all tomorrow.'

So she was right, Rose thought. He was feeling worn out. Aloud, she said, 'So we will. Home, then.'

The rest of the journey passed in silence and when Rose gave Alex a swift sidelong glance she saw that he had fallen asleep. He had had a bad time recently, and he had not yet recovered fully. He had been invalided out of the army after being caught in a bomb blast in France, where he had been serving in the front lines, then not long after their marriage he had fallen victim to the influenza epidemic. He had survived, unlike thousands of others, and although he insisted that he had got over it completely he still tired easily. Sometimes, when they were alone at home in the evenings, he could fall into a sudden doze and waken between ten and forty minutes later without even being aware that he had been asleep.

'Isn't it lovely to be home again?' she said with genuine pleasure as she drew the car to a halt by the side of the road. Her voice roused him, and as he sat upright she went on in order to give him a moment in which to collect his wits, 'You didn't mind me dragging you away from the others, did you?'

'Of course not. To tell the truth, I wasn't looking forward to the rest of our visit. I never feel comfortable with your parents. They're very civil, but I'm always aware that they think you married beneath you.'

She leaned over to kiss his cheek. 'Pay no heed to them. You're the one who got the worst of the bargain, and I'm a very fortunate woman.'

Alex was silent for a moment, but then he said suddenly into the darkness within the car, 'There's times I worry in case I can't make you as happy as you deserve.'

'Don't be daft!'

'I'm not being daft, just sensible.'

'It's that blasted influenza – it's left you feeling morbid. Come on,' Rose ordered, opening her door, 'let's get upstairs.'

# 2

Rose and Alex were still living in the bachelor flat in Paisley Road West that Alex had rented a few years earlier, when he had moved from Paisley to Glasgow and started working for his father. They planned to find something larger, but had not yet got around to it.

'I think I'll go to bed,' Alex said as soon as they went in.

'Do you want anything to eat first?'

'Good Lord, no. Your mother fed us like kings.'

Rose stretched her arms above her head, then ran her fingers through her hair. As always happened, hairpins cascaded to the floor.

'Oh, drat.' She knelt to pick them up. 'A cup of tea? I'm having one.'

'No thanks. You don't want to stay up for the bells, do you?'

'Not really. We've got a busy day ahead of us tomorrow.'

'Do you mind having to do all that visiting? New Year can be a bit of a nuisance sometimes.'

'Absolutely not. We must be fair, and in any case, tomorrow belongs to your family, and I much prefer them to mine. You go along now and I'll follow you in a little while.'

Coming upstairs to the flat they had met some neighbours on their way out to see in the New Year with friends or family, but nobody was likely to call on them. They were both out all day: Rose at Harlequin, the thriving dressmaking business she and Caitlin had set up between them, and Alex at the furniture workshop he managed for his father, so apart from exchanging greetings should they happen to meet on the stairs or in the close, they were strangers to their neighbours.

When Rose had made and poured her tea she added a little cold water so that she could drink it quickly, but even so, she went into the bedroom to find that Alex was already sound asleep. He had left the light on, and as he was lying on his back she took the opportunity to study him, careful not to let her shadow cover him. He had always been wiry and thin-faced, but the war years had stripped what flesh there was from his bones and he had not yet regained all the weight lost. His body scarcely mounded the blankets and his straight nose stood out in sharp relief, while his closed eyes were almost sunken, as was his mouth.

Asleep and vulnerable, he looked, Rose suddenly thought, just as he would when he was a very old man.

She stepped back swiftly from the bed, her body gripped by an involuntary shiver – the sort of tremor that folk normally referred to lightly as someone walking over their graves. It took a moment for her natural strong character to reassert itself and dismiss the morbid thought.

In the few weeks between Alex's last letter from France and the arrival of official word that he had been wounded in a direct hit that had taken the lives of several members of his battalion, she had thought that she would never see him again. When he finally arrived home she had insisted on their marrying as soon as possible, superstitiously convinced that once he belonged to her she would be able to protect him. But within a month of their marriage he was fighting the influenza that had found him, in his weakened state, an easy victim. Rose had scarcely left his side throughout the course of the illness, and had wept with relief when he began the long slow climb towards recovery.

Life could be vexing, she thought as she prepared for bed. She had always resisted her mother's efforts to turn her into a copy of her elder sisters, who had both married suitable men and settled down to raising families in the comfortable homes their husbands provided for them. From the cradle, her life had been one long fight against her parents' wealthy background until the day she had met up with the Lennox family and finally found a purpose to her existence. At first she and Alex, two strong characters, had sparred and argued every time they met, and it had taken some time for them both to accept the fact that their antagonism was not down to a mutual dislike, but a strong mutual attraction. Marrying him had been the best thing that had ever happened to her, and she was determined to devote the rest of her life to making him happy, since that was clearly the only way of ensuring her own happiness.

While Rose drank her tea and Alex fell into a deep sleep, his half-sister Caitlin was asking, 'You've still got the black bun and the coal, haven't you?'

'Aye, and the whisky, all safe in my pockets,' Murdo assured her. Tradition insisted that a household could only have a good year if the first person to step across the threshold was a dark-haired man

19

bringing with him whisky, coal and food to ensure that the residents could be sure of a year without want. Murdo, with his black hair, was the obvious choice.

'I want to wait with you,' Rowena said at once. The big Highlander was her hero, and she loved being in his company.

'You will not,' Mary told her niece. 'Murdo can manage fine by himself.'

'But he'll be lonely!'

'No I'll not, for Lachie's going to wait with me, aren't you, Lachie?'

'I don't know – mebbe I should just go home,' Lachie muttered.

'No, please stay!' Mary said at once.

'Of course he's staying – he'll come in with me and I'll make sure that I'm the first to step over the door,' Murdo assured her. 'Go on now, before you all catch a chill.'

'Is Murdo outside?' Kirsty asked as soon as her daughters came in.

'Ready and waiting, and Lachie with him,' Caitlin assured her.

'D'you think there'll be enough to eat?'

'Mam, you could feed an army with this lot!' Mary protested.

'You never know – it's a sharp night, and cold

20

weather makes folk hungry. Was the town busy?'

'Packed like sardines in a tin,' Mary said. 'I was glad to turn for home, to be honest. I can't be doing with crowds.'

'I was glad too,' Rowena confided, dropping to the rug between her grandparents' chairs. 'There was a nasty man who wouldn't leave Mary alone, and Lachie had to—'

'Och, it was just a poor old drunk,' Mary said swiftly. 'He didn't mean any harm. Lachie and Murdo saw him off no bother. Now then, d'you think Murdo remembered to bring his mouth organ, Rowena?'

The ruse worked, for Rowena immediately forgot about the scene at the Cross. 'I'll run out and ask him if it's in his pocket,' she said, making for the door.

Caitlin hauled her back. 'You're not going out there without a coat. And I'm sure he has the mouth organ, since he's never without it.'

'Anyway, it's near time for the bells.' Todd laid his pipe down carefully and went to open the window. 'Quiet now, and listen . . .'

Kirsty got to her feet and they all stood silent, straining their ears, while the clock on the mantelshelf ticked out the final minutes of 1919. At first, all they could hear was the sound of footsteps hurrying along the pavement and the occasional voice, but then the town hall clock began to chime in the distance.

As Rose put the light out and slipped into bed beside Alex her sharp ears caught the sound of bells chiming. 'Happy New Year!' she heard someone shout in the street below, and the cry was taken up by several other voices.

She leaned over her slumbering husband and kissed him lightly on the lips. 'Happy New Year,' she whispered, and he stirred, murmured something, and fell back into a deep sleep.

She curled her body around his and closed her eyes. It would be the best year they had ever known, she promised herself, and him. She would not allow anything to spoil it for them.

In Paisley, the final, twelfth chime died away to be replaced by the sound of windows being thrown up along the length of Espedair Street and voices shouting, 'Happy New Year!'

Todd put his arms around his wife and kissed her soundly. The doorknocker banged against its polished brass plate and Rowena rushed into the hall and returned with Lachie and Murdo; Murdo's hands filled with the blessings intended to bring good cheer to the household. As soon as the bottle, coal and piece of black bun had been laid on the table Rowena hurled herself at Murdo, who lifted her off her feet and kissed her on the cheek.

'Happy New Year to you, pet,' he said, and then set her down and turned to Caitlin. Although his ring was on her finger and 1920 would see their marriage, he gave her a chaste kiss on the cheek, for Murdo did not like to display his feelings in public.

Almost at once the doorknocker went again, not for the last time that night. The first to arrive were Todd's sister and her family, who lived not far from Espedair Street, then neighbours came calling, every group with a bottle to share round. Murdo was persuaded to play his mouth organ and Rowena, an accomplished country dancer, was the first to do her party piece, spinning and leaping neatly on the very small area of flooring left available. Songs were sung and poetry recited before the entire company settled down to a general sing-song.

By two o'clock the children who had been allowed to stay up for the occasion were being taken home and Rowena was beginning to flag. Kirsty coaxed her upstairs and into bed, ignoring the girl's protests that she could not possibly sleep yet.

'I'll stay with you and we can have a nice quiet talk, then we'll go back down if you can't settle,'

23

Kirsty offered, and five minutes later, leaving Rowena in a sound sleep, she went back downstairs on her own. They were still singing lustily in the parlour, but instead of joining them she went through the kitchen and out of the back door to the yard, taking a coat from the peg behind the door as she went. The night air was cold, but not cold enough to prevent her from sitting on the wooden bench by the house wall.

She stared out into the darkness, seeing in her mind's eye the yard in daylight, covered with fresh, pristine snow marked only by tiny footprints – just as it had been on the day that Fergus, her last-born, had died after toddling into the covered passageway known as a pend at the side of the house, and into the path of a horse bringing in a cart loaded with timber for the workshop. Kirsty had never forgiven herself, and never would, for the moment's inattention that had allowed the adventurous little boy to slip from the house unnoticed.

The back door opened, then closed again. 'I thought ye'd be out here on yer lone,' Todd said, coming to sit by her. 'Are ye all right?'

'I'm fine. I just needed a wee while to myself.' She leaned against him, enjoying the solid feel of his arm against hers. She had married Matt for security, but her marriage to Todd, four years her junior, had been a love match.

'Thinkin' about the past, were ye?' He always seemed to know what was going on in her mind.

'I cannae help it at this time of year.'

'We need tae look ahead,' Todd said into the darkness. 'We've just walked intae a new decade, and a new beginning. And an end to wars – at last. Mebbe now men'll have the sense tae talk through their differences instead of turnin' tae violence.'

'Amen to that,' Kirsty said, with all her heart. Alex had come home from the war, but his step-brother, Matt's son Ewan, had not been so fortunate. A ladies' man, Ewan had eloped with Beth Laidlaw only weeks before she was due to marry Todd. Nothing more had been heard of the runaways until five years later when Rowena, dirty, cold and bewildered, had been delivered to Espedair Street by a carter, together with a note from Ewan. Beth had left him for another man and, unable to look after their daughter, he had sent her to his family while he himself went off to Australia. He had joined the Australian Army during the war and Alex had met him in France. A few days later Ewan had been killed.

Closing her eyes, Kirsty offered up a short prayer for her stepson's soul, then as a sudden shiver passed through her, she said, 'We'd best go inside before our visitors start wonderin' what we're up to.'

Todd was on his feet first, turning to take her hands and pull her up beside him. Then he took her into his arms and kissed her – a more passionate kiss than was usual among middle-aged couples.

'Todd Paget!' she protested when he finally released her. 'What d'you think you're doing?'

'Kissin' my wife. And I cannae think of any better way tae start the new year,' he said, and she blushed in the darkness like a young girl.

As they returned to the warmth of the house she found time to wish briefly that her first-born, her Alex, could have been with them. But now that he was married he had other folk to think of. And she would see him and his wife later on in the day, for their Ne'erday dinner.

At the very moment he came into his mother's mind, Alex struggled upright in bed, shouting unintelligible words and fighting against the entangling bedclothes. Before Rose was properly awake she was sitting up beside him, pulling him into her arms, holding him when he tried to break away.

'It's all right,' she said over and over again close to his ear, her voice deliberately even and calm. 'You're safe; you're at home with me, nothing bad can happen now. It's all right, Alex.'

Gradually his struggles eased and his desperate, terrified voice sank to a low wailing, which in its turn faded away. He stopped struggling and clutched at her, holding on to her as though afraid that if he let go he would never find her again. She rocked him in her arms, murmuring to him soothingly and feeling the tremors that racked him calming down.

'I-I must have been dreaming,' he said at last, his grip slackening.

She reached out for the small towel that she kept on her bedside table and wiped the perspiration from his face and neck. 'Would you like some tea?'

'No, I'll be all right now that you're here.'

They lay still and silent in each other's arms and she listened as his breathing slowed and then began to take on a rhythm that indicated that he had fallen asleep again.

When they were first married the nightmares had been frequent and on more than one occasion he had struggled against her so fiercely that he'd left bruises on her shoulders. He had never knowingly spoken to her of his time in the trenches, but during the influenza's delirium it had all poured out. She had listened, shocked and appalled by what he and the other soldiers had seen and experienced.

But strangely, the delirium seemed to have helped, for now the nightmares were less frequent. She had never told him, and never would, what he had revealed to her while raving in the grip of the fever; nor would she ever tell another living soul.

But now that she knew something of what it had been like for him in the mud and blood and incessant mind-numbing din of the trenches, she was amazed that he had emerged from it without losing his mind entirely.

# 3

Motherless from early childhood, Fiona Chalmers, born Fiona MacDowall, was the apple of her father's eye. Thanks to the tough determination that had taken him from an orphanage to a job as apprentice for Kirsty's father, Murray Galbraith, then on to set up his own business and, finally, his own large Glasgow furniture emporium, Sandy MacDowall had become a wealthy man and his only child had wanted for nothing.

Fiona's marriage to George Chalmers, a man several years older than her, had been dull and unexciting, and when George was called up to serve in the navy shortly after war broke out Fiona wasted no time in moving from the marital home in Fort William to her father's comfortable flat in

Glasgow. When George died of influenza on his way home at the end of the war she remained in Glasgow, gradually taking over the running of the flat. Her father, happy to have her close by him as before, made no objection. His only protest came when she had her long fair hair cropped in the latest style.

'But you had such lovely hair – why let them cut it all off?'

'Not all of it.' Fiona ran a hand over the smooth shining helmet moulded snugly to her head. 'It's all the rage now, Father, and it's much easier to look after. You'll soon get used to it.'

On the first day of the New Year she sat at the dressing table in her pretty bedroom and again ran a hand over her head, enjoying the feel of soft, short hair against her palm. In her own view the new, formal style emphasised her classic features and large brown eyes. And, she thought, clipping on the diamond earrings George had given her on their wedding day, her small neat ears were now seen to their best advantage.

She wet a finger and smoothed it over each eyebrow carefully before selecting a pale pink lipstick, the colour just enough to make a subtle difference to her cupid's bow mouth, but not quite enough to make her father frown at her.

Blotting her mouth carefully, she inspected

herself in the mirror and nodded approval. She had recently emerged from her obligatory year of mourning and today she wore a charcoal-grey cotton dress with three-quarter-length sleeves beneath a knee-length overdress in deep-lilac voile printed with violet flowers. A snowy white shawl collar was caught and held at the soft curve of her bosom by a bunch of artificial violets.

She got up, bent to smooth her silk stockings over slender, well-shaped legs and went out of the room and into the dining room, where she cast an eye over the table.

'Everything's ready, Mrs Chalmers.' The house-keeper came in, carrying a tall white vase. 'Where do you want this, ma'am?'

'I'll take it, Mrs Dove. You've put the sherry out?'

'It's on the sideboard.'

'Good. That's all for now, thank you.' At least Fiona had learned one thing from her marriage – how to deal with servants. Mrs Dove had been Sandy MacDowall's housekeeper for many years, and as Fiona grew up the woman had seemed more like one of the family than a paid servant. But George had been a firm believer in keeping servants in their proper place, and since returning to Glasgow Fiona had adopted a polite but remote attitude towards Mrs Dove and the maid who assisted her.

On occasion, when she found reason to reprimand, she had seen a swiftly subdued gleam of anger in the older woman's eyes, but that was of no matter. Servants were paid to do as they were told, George had said, and if they didn't like being servants then it was up to them to find some other kind of work. It was probably the most intelligent thing that he had ever said, Fiona thought as she placed the white vase on a small side table and stepped back to study it. The tall evergreen branches it held looked perfect, and so did the two dark-blue vases, one on each window sill, containing several sprays of branches bearing bright red berries. She was admiring them when her father came in.

'What do you think, Father?'

'It looks very nice. You have an artistic touch, my dear.'

With a faint upward movement Fiona's shoulders fielded the compliment and tossed it aside. 'You look tired. Perhaps it was a mistake to invite Alex and Rose to lunch today.'

'Nonsense, it's Ne'erday and I want my family about me.'

'They might not stay long.'

'They can stay as long as they like.' Sandy crossed to the window to look down on to the street. 'I always enjoy Rose's company. Alex has chosen his life partner well, do you not think so?'

'Of course,' Fiona agreed smoothly, her voice easy but her face suddenly blank. Sandy, scanning the street for the first sight of his daughter-in-law's car, didn't notice. He was on the verge of his fifties, and his hair and moustache were silver, with no trace of the redhead he had once been. He had always held himself well, but now his shoulders were faintly bowed.

'I wonder if I should take driving lessons?' Fiona said.

'There's no need. Fletcher can drive you anywhere you want to go, and if I'm using him then you can easily get one of the other men from the store to drive you. There are two cars in the garage there that you can use.'

'Rose doesn't use a driver.'

'That's because she's an independent woman with a business of her own. Driving her own car's part of her nature.' He continued to watch the street below while Fiona, nibbling at her lower lip, studied his back.

'Have you ever thought of retiring, Father?' she asked, and he swung round and looked at her in astonishment.

'Why should I do that?'

'You've earned some time off. Wouldn't you like to go on a cruise, or take up a relaxing hobby?'

'Not particularly. In any case, Alex needs to get

settled in again, after being away at the war, then being so ill. It wouldn't be fair to land him with the responsibility of running the business until he's fully recovered.'

'Alex isn't your only child.' Fiona's voice was sharp. 'I'm here now.'

'But you've got your own life to lead. You're young – you'll meet someone else.'

'Even if I do it needn't stop me from helping in the business. Wasn't I of use to you when Alex was away?'

Sandy's sharp blue eyes softened as he looked at his lovely daughter. 'Indeed you were, my dear. I don't know how I could have managed without you.'

'Well then,' Fiona was beginning when the blare of a horn in the street below captured her father's attention.

'It's them – Alex and Rose are here.' He made for the door, ignoring Fiona's, 'Father, let Mrs Dove open the door, it's her job!'

The MacDowalls lived on the first floor of a handsome tenement building. By the time Fiona had reached the spacious entrance hall of their flat, the door had been thrown open and her father was halfway down the stairs. Frowning, she went on to the landing in time to see him greet Rose, who came running up to give him a warm hug.

'Happy New Year to you, Sandy, and my goodness, how well you look!' she said warmly, and then, glancing up the staircase, 'Fiona, you look wonderful too! Happy New Year! I really like your hair.'

She came leaping up the ten or so steps with all the style, Fiona thought spitefully, of a clumsy young colt attacking its first hill. It did not help to know that if she spoke the thought aloud Rose would probably laugh and agree with her.

Alex, taking the stairs more slowly than his wife, arrived to shake hands with his father while Rose was hugging her sister-in-law, who stood stiffly within the circle of her arms.

When they all reached the hall Mrs Dove was waiting to greet the guests and take their coats. Rose insisted on hugging her and wishing her a good New Year, while Alex did the same, but with a handshake instead of a hug. It wasn't until the housekeeper had gone off with the coats that he turned to his half-sister.

'Happy New Year, Fiona.'

'And to you, Alex.' As he bent to kiss her on the cheek she turned her head slightly at the last moment so that his lips met hers, putting her arms around him and holding him close when he tried to pull away.

'You look tired,' she said when she finally released him.

'I feel fine – stronger every day.'

'She said the same thing to me,' his father told him. 'Pay no heed, it's just woman talk. They like to think that we men need coddling. Come and have a sherry before we eat.'

He was about to lead the party into the drawing room when Fiona stopped them. 'I told Mrs Dove to put the sherry decanter and the glasses in the dining room. Lunch is almost ready and we might as well go in now.'

She led the way to the room and insisted on pouring and handing out glasses of sherry, which they drank by the long windows until Mrs Dove came in with the first course.

'I thought that you and Rose should sit across from each other, Alex,' Fiona said swiftly as he moved to his usual place at the foot of the rectangular table. 'I'll sit opposite Father.' She took her seat while Alex, after a moment's puzzled hesitation, drew out a chair for his wife and then went round the table to sit opposite her.

'Your clothes are very pretty, Rose,' Fiona said in her clear, cool voice as the door closed behind the housekeeper. 'Are you wearing Caitlin's designs?'

'Yes, I am.' Rose wore a wrap-around blouse in ivory silk, trimmed with black silk and caught at the waistline with a large black button. A

36

matching, trimmed bodice filled in the deep V of the blouse, and her three-tiered pleated skirt was also ivory silk trimmed with black.

'She's very talented. You must be delighted to have her working for you.'

'Caitlin,' Alex pointed out to his half-sister, 'is a partner in Harlequin, not an employee.'

Fiona's carefully plucked eyebrows lifted slightly. 'Of course – I'd forgotten. How I admire the way she has risen from such humble beginnings.'

'It's because she has a great deal of natural talent, and a willingness to work hard,' Rose put in swiftly, seeing Alex open his mouth to make some crushing retort. 'Women like you and me, Fiona, should be grateful that we've had such comfortable lives, with family money behind us to make up for our lack of talent.'

For a moment Fiona's lovely face went blank with astonishment, then the gold lights in her eyes blazed at Rose as she realised that she had been subtly reprimanded for her sly belittling of Caitlin. 'So you feel that you have no talent?' she said at last, unable to think of any better jibe in reply.

'Certainly not compared to Caitlin. But fortunately for both of us, I did have the money to buy the old mill and turn it into a business where her talent could be recognised and enjoyed – and rightly rewarded.'

'You demean yourself, Rose. You have a great deal of determination,' Sandy smiled down the table at his daughter-in-law, 'as well as a capacity for hard work that many men would be proud to possess.'

'But now that you're a married woman, are you not planning to give up your business, Rose?' Fiona threw herself back into the fray.

'Not at all. We're busier than ever and I would die of boredom if I were to stay at home all day with little to do.'

'You have a lot to do! Surely you don't expect Alex to go on living in that tiny little flat – you could fill in your days looking for a more suitable home and furnishing it.'

'We'll move eventually, probably this year, but I doubt if Rose would need a lot of time to set it to rights,' Alex said easily.

Rose smiled across the table at him. 'That's true, and in any case, I've no wish to stay at home. I enjoy meeting people and I love being involved in something that fills every minute of my day,' she was saying when Mrs Dove returned to collect their empty dishes.

'I agree with Rose when she says that being at home all day would be too boring,' Fiona remarked casually, when the housekeeper had left the room. 'So, since George has gone I shall sell the house in Fort William and stay here in

Glasgow to look after Father. And since I learned quite a lot about the business over the past few years, I'm going to take part in that as well. I hope to be of use to Father – and to you, Alex. You still look pale and we mustn't forget that you've been through a great deal.' She reached out a slender hand and laid it on her half-brother's arm. 'Perhaps you should take more time off, and return to work gradually, over a period of months.'

'I wouldn't dream of it.' Slowly but firmly he removed himself from her touch. 'Getting back to my everyday life will be of more benefit to me than anything else.'

'I get the distinct impression,' Rose remarked three hours later as she drove west towards Paisley, 'that your dear sister is getting her feet well and truly under Sandy's table in more ways than one. I don't suppose you noticed, but the place is full of feminine touches that weren't there before.'

'Father seems to be pleased that she's staying on in Glasgow. And Fort William was George's home, never hers.'

'I suppose not. It's such a pity that George died.' Rose honked the horn at a group of small boys playing football in the road. They scattered, making faces and catcalling, and she smiled at them as she drove by.

Once she was in the Espedair Street house Rose began to relax for the first time in almost twenty-four hours. It was such a pleasure to be with the people she considered to be Alex's real family. She loved the safe, cosy feeling of the small house; it was so unlike her own childhood home, which was so large that the residents could, and usually did, spend most of their time in separate rooms.

She and Kirsty had first met when Kirsty was her mother's sewing woman – a post she lost through a piece of thoughtlessness on Rose's part. Horrified by the result of her stupidity, Rose had sought Kirsty out in an attempt to make amends, a move that turned out to be the most sensible thing she had ever done, for it introduced her to Caitlin and Alex.

Recently home from finishing school, bored and restless, Rose had been entranced by the small second-hand clothes shop where Kirsty worked with Jean Chisholm. She had been drawn to the place again and again, and was instrumental in the purchase of the shop next door, which enabled Jean to expand her business. And eventually, using an inheritance from her grandmother, and taking advantage of Caitlin's natural gift for colours and design, she had opened Harlequin.

As usually happened when they went to Espedair Street, Alex scarcely had time to greet his mother and sisters before Todd whisked him off to the workshop, where they could smoke and talk business in peace, without having to raise their voices against a background of female chatter. Jean Chisholm was spending Ne'erday with the Pagets as she usually did, having no family of her own, and even without the men in it the parlour was quite crowded. Jean and Kirsty were discussing the clothes shop, while Mary helped ten-year-old Rowena to dress the new doll she had received for Ne'erday. 'I thought Murdo would be here,' Rose said to Caitlin.

'Och, you know what he's like. He first-footed us last night, but he's not one for socialising. Highlanders are happier with their own folk.'

'You'll be getting married this year.'

'Once Murdo's got the gatehouse to his satisfaction.' Murdo had formerly woven materials for MacDowall and Son, but while Alex was in the army Fiona had dismissed him, claiming that the emporium couldn't afford its own weaver. Rose had then asked him to work for Harlequin and offered him accommodation in the mill gatehouse. A ground-floor room of the gatehouse had been

41

converted to take the loom and now Murdo was renovating the rest of the building in his spare time, and turning it into a home for himself and Caitlin.

'It shouldn't take long,' Rose said cheerfully. 'Are you going to design your own dress, or is that unlucky? I can find someone else to do it if you want, mebbe in one of the Glasgow houses.'

'There's time enough to decide that.'

'Speaking of designers, d'you not think that we're just about ready to bring someone in to work with you?'

'Can we afford it?'

'I think we could, this year. There have been a lot of orders since the war ended and you've had to work hard. It's not fair.'

'I enjoy it.'

'Even so, you can't be expected to keep it up once you've got a husband and a home to look after.'

When Caitlin and Mary went into the kitchen to get the food ready, it seemed only natural for Rose to follow them and pick up an apron — something else, she thought contentedly, that she could never do in her own mother's house, or in her father-in-law's.

'Geordie Marshall's gettin' tae be awfy troubled with the rheumatics,' Todd was telling Alex in the workshop. 'And his eyes arenae what they used tae be, either. His wife's no' keepin' well an' I think she'd like for him tae be at home more. I could dae with someone tae replace him.'

The small cabinetmaking business had originally belonged to Kirsty's father, but after being reunited with his birth father Alex had bought the workshop from Kirsty so that it, together with a workshop Alex supervised in Glasgow, could supply handmade furniture for Sandy MacDowall's big Glasgow store. Todd, a man who prized contentment above ambition, was happy to run the place for his wife's first-born.

Alex leaned back against a bench, breathing in the familiar smell of glue and the mixed aromas of the different timbers used in the workshop. It was at times like these that he felt a moment of nostalgia for the old days, when he had worked here himself.

'How's the apprentice coming along?' he asked, returning almost reluctantly to the present.

'Young Kenny? He's a willin' enough lad, but he's still got a lot tae learn. Ye'll mind that Geordie only came in tae help out while poor Bryce was away at the fightin'. If he'd come back like we all thought he would . . .'

Todd let the words trail into silence and both men stood in silent tribute to Bryce Caldwell and the other young men who had been cruelly denied the opportunity to return home to pick up the reins of their ordinary lives. After a respectable time had elapsed and he judged it decent to return to the matter in hand, Todd lifted a hand to the bowl of his pipe, which immediately nestled into his cupped palm like a small child settling into familiar adult arms. Removing the stem from his mouth he allowed a cloud of soft blue-grey smoke to escape from between his lips, before replacing the pipe and saying round it, 'Geordie tells me that there's an Irish family moved intae the top floor of his tenement. The man seems tae have worked as a cabinetmaker back in Ireland.'

'Would you be willing to take him on?'

'If he's up tae the job.'

'Then get Geordie to fetch him here so that you can have a look at him. If you're happy with him, it's fine by me.'

Todd shuffled his feet slightly. He was a worker by nature, not an employer. 'I'd as soon you were here too, when he comes.'

Alex knew that there was little point in arguing, and in any case, why should his stepfather be made to do something that he didn't want to do? His mind ran ahead, checking through his duties in Glasgow.

'I can be here around four o'clock on Monday

afternoon. Tell the man to come here then and we'll see him together,' he said as Rowena came scampering down the length of the backyard to summon them to their Ne'erday dinner.

# 4

At first sight, Joseph McCart was not impressive. He was slightly smaller than the average height, thickset and dressed in a shabby jacket and trousers that did little to protect him against the January chill. A large tweed cap with a few holes in it was pulled so far down over his face that little could be seen but the tip of his nose, red with the cold, and a mouth held tightly shut, as though its owner feared that it might forget itself and start to babble secrets to all and sundry.

Alex first saw his prospective employee loitering about on the pavement when he himself arrived at Espedair Street. Pausing at the house door, he glanced over his shoulder at the man, who hurriedly began to walk away, head down, shoulders hunched and his fists pushed into his jacket pockets.

There was nobody in the house when Alex let himself in; his mother must be busy in Jean Chisholm's shop in Causeyside Street, and Rowena had probably gone to visit Murdo after leaving school. When she had first arrived in Paisley, rejected by her mother and then sent by her father to live with relatives she had never seen before, Rowena had been so difficult that the family was almost driven demented by her tantrums. It was Murdo, the silent Highlander who at that time worked at the loom in a small room accessed from the pend, who had calmed her. For some strange reason, only he had the ability to help Rowena overcome her mistrust and settle down to life with her new family, and whenever possible she spent time with him.

Alex went into the kitchen, where he helped himself to a piece of his mother's home-made shortbread before letting himself out of the back door into the yard. He walked down the yard, past the small drying green with some washing hung on the line and then past the stack of weathered timber to the workshop. As he reached the door he glanced over his shoulder and glimpsed the stranger again. This time the man seemed to be peering into the open mouth of the pend.

47

Even as Alex saw him, the figure moved swiftly back and out of sight. Frowning, Alex went into the warmth of the workshop. Todd, Geordie and the apprentice, Kenny, were all at work.

'Is he not here yet?'

'No' yet,' Todd said placidly. Young Kenny was tending to the glue pot sitting on the fire and Alex went over to spread his hands to the welcome heat.

'I telt him four o'clock, sir,' Geordie said. 'He should be here any time now.'

'There's a rough-looking man hanging about in the street. That wouldn't be him, would it?'

'Shabby like, wi' a cap that looks tae be too big for his heid?' Geordie asked, and when Alex nodded, 'That sounds like Joe. They've no' got much money, ye understand, Mr MacDowall, so he cannae dress well. That's why he needs the work.' He made for the door. 'I'll away out tae see if it's him.'

'It's not a good start for someone wanting work,' Alex commented when the old man had limped out. 'I thought he was hanging about with a mind to robbery.'

'From what I've heard from Geordie, the family havenae long come over from Ireland. It must be hard for them, settlin' intae a place where they don't ken anyone,' Todd said.

'I suppose so.' Alex himself had had experience of coping with changes in his life, the most traumatic being his meeting with Sandy MacDowall, the man who turned out to be his real father. After a bitter quarrel with his stepfather, Alex had changed his name from Lennox to MacDowall and moved to Glasgow, where he had had to get to know Sandy MacDowall.

Geordie was back in minutes, the man Alex had thought to be a potential robber with him. 'Here he is, Mr MacDowall. This is Joseph McCart, come tae see ye about a job. This is Mr MacDowall that owns the workshop, Joe, and this is Mr Paget that runs it. And that's Kenny, the 'prentice lad. Take yer cap off, man.'

Joseph McCart snatched the cap from his head, revealing a mop of black curly hair. It was still difficult to see his face, for he kept his chin tucked into his chest and his eyes on the ground.

'Stand over by the fire,' Todd invited. 'It's a cold day out, is it no'?'

'It is that, sor,' McCart said gruffly in a strong Irish accent. He shuffled over to the stove – his shoes, Alex noticed, were thin and badly in need of patching – and after rolling the cap up and pushing it into one pocket he held out his hands to the warmth. They were the hands of a workman, stubby-fingered, strong and calloused.

'You're not long in Paisley, Geordie says.'

'No, sor. A few weeks, just.'

'And what brought you here?'

The man's head jerked up suddenly and Alex found himself looking into dark eyes narrowed with suspicion. He blinked, surprised — it was surely a fair question and he saw no reason for the man's reaction. It was a few seconds before McCart looked down again and muttered, 'I thought there might be more work here.'

'You lost your job in Ireland?'

'The place I worked in was destroyed in a fire.'

'An accident, was it?' Todd asked. Fire was necessary to a cabinetmaker, not only to heat the glue pots, but also to create the steam that softened timber and allowed it to be bent into shape. With all that wood around, it did not do to have any careless workers.

'Aye — but not of my doin', sor.'

'Nobody thought it was,' Todd intervened. Getting information from the man was like pulling teeth, but between them Todd and Alex got enough to discover that Joseph McCart was indeed a time-served cabinetmaker, and when Todd suggested that he finish off the task that he himself had been doing, McCart quickly proved his worth. When Todd started to talk about the current jobs on order the man seemed to relax and for the first

50

time since coming into the workshop he began to talk comfortably and freely.

After a while Alex glanced at his stepfather and saw that Todd was warming to the man. Their eyes met and Alex tried to indicate caution with a slight lift of his eyebrows. Todd responded with a quick, imperceptible nod of his head and then told the Irishman, 'We'll give you a month's trial. When can you start?'

'Tomorrow?'

'That would suit me,' Todd said, while Geordie beamed in the background.

'We've not talked about wages,' Alex pointed out.

'Ah now, Mr MacDowall, I'm sure ye'll be a fair employer an' not cheat on yer workers.' McCart grasped his hand and shook it warmly, then turned to shake Todd's hand. 'I'm grateful tae the both of yez, and I'll not let yez down.'

'Are you sure you've done the right thing?' Alex asked when the man had gone. 'I was trying to tell you that we should have a think and a talk before offering him the job.'

'Why's that? He knew what he was talkin' about – he's a cabinetmaker, there's no doubt about that.'

'Yes, but even so . . .' The man did seem to know the work well, but at the same time there was something about him that made Alex feel he was holding back information that would not have pleased them had they known it. 'We know nothing about him,' he said.

'You're surely not turnin' against the man just because he's from Ireland?' Todd asked, puzzled.

'It's nothing to do with where he comes from. He must need the work badly, to agree to start without even asking about the wages.'

'He does,' Geordie chipped in. 'He's got a wife and lassie tae feed, and his old mother lives with them an' all. Ye've done him a good Christian service by givin' him work, Mr MacDowall.'

'He's a dour sort, is he no'?' Kenny piped up.

'I'm no' bothered about that, son. Better a dour man who gets on with it than one who'd as soon use his tongue than his hands – eh, Kenny?' Todd said with heavy meaning, and the apprentice blushed and bent his head over his work.

Rather than catch the train back to Glasgow from nearby Canal Street station, Alex decided to walk to the Hunterhill area of the town, where his wife and younger sister had turned an old empty mill into their fashion house, Harlequin.

Two large cars, each with its uniformed attendant, stood before the door, so Alex, with no wish to meet up with any of Harlequin's wealthy clients, went first to the gatehouse. The door was on the latch and as he let himself in he heard the steady clack of a loom from the room to his right.

Murdo Guthrie worked at the loom, while Rowena sat at a small table in the corner with her schoolbooks spread out before her. A fire burned in the large fireplace, making the room pleasantly warm on this chilly winter's day. Rowena beamed up at Alex when he went in, while Murdo nodded a greeting.

'What are you working on?'

'Och, it's some material Mrs MacDowall needs to make up a costume for one of her ladies.'

'You've got quite a lot of cloth there,' Alex pointed out. He knew that all the clothes that came from Harlequin were originals, and that their clients were safe in the knowledge that they would never meet another woman wearing the same style made in the same material to the same pattern.

'I understand that the lady in question's of a generous size,' Murdo said in his slow, courteous Highland speech. 'And there's to be a matching coat.'

'Mmm.' Alex studied the cloth on the loom. It was a pleasing pattern of gold, brown and russet, and his inner eye could see it looking splendid on the seats of a set of dining-room chairs.

'I wish you'd come back to work for me, Murdo.'

'I'm not so sure that would be a good idea.'

'Why not?'

'What's seven times nine?' Rowena broke in.

'Find out for yourself,' Murdo told her, and she pouted.

'I can't. I hate the seven times table!'

'You'll only learn to like it when you can say it. So on you go,' Murdo said firmly, while she stuck the end of her pencil in her mouth and glared at him, stretching her large blue eyes to their widest extent in an attempt to convey her annoyance.

'They'll fall out and then how will you be able to see?' Alex pointed out, and a scowl drew her brows together over the glare.

'Pay no heed,' Murdo advised, then slid back into their own conversation. 'Mrs Chalmers wouldn't like to see me working for you again, since she was the one who turned me off.'

'That was when I was away in the army and knew nothing of what was going on here. I'm back now, and I decide who we employ.'

'Aye, but . . .' the Highlandman took his eyes from the cloth he was weaving long enough to flick a quick look at Alex '. . . she's still there, is she not?'

'Yes, but I'm in charge. Would you be willing to work for MacDowall's again?'

'Mrs MacDowall's been very good to me, letting

me stay here when I had no other place to go. I'd not want her to think that I'm ungrateful.'

'You could work for us both,' Alex suggested. 'Would you be willing to do that if my wife agreed to it?'

'Mebbe, if it was all right with your father. But Mrs Chalmers—'

'Never you mind Mrs Chalmers, Murdo. How are you getting on with doing this place up?'

'It's coming along but there's still a fair bit of work to be done.'

'I think that my wife is hoping that Caitlin will have a spring wedding.'

'I doubt if the house will be ready by then,' Murdo said, almost sharply.

'Sixty-three!'

'What?' Alex asked, confused by the sudden interruption.

'Seven times nine is sixty-three.' Now Rowena was all smiles. 'Murdo,' she raised her voice, 'seven times nine is—'

'Aye, I heard you. Did I not say that you could do it? Write it down seven times. That'll make you remember it.'

'Then will you play a tune so that I can dance before I have to go home?' Rowena loved dancing, especially to the music Murdo played on his mouth organ.

'Aye, I will. In just another minute.'

Just then one of the cars that had been parked outside the mill swept past the window. One client gone, one to go, Alex thought. Time to go and see Rose.

Finding her small cluttered office empty, he went into the next room, where Mary, Harlequin's bookkeeper, worked at her neat desk. It was true, Alex thought wryly as his younger half-sister smiled a welcome, that you could tell something of people's natures by looking at their workplace. Not a hair was out of place on Mary's sleek brown head, and her white blouse and black skirt looked as though an expert laundress had ironed them only moments before.

'Rose is still with a client, but she won't be long.'

'I'll wait in her room,' Alex said. He felt more at home in the midst of clutter than in Mary's pristine surroundings.

Rose swept in a few minutes later, almost throwing herself across the room to wrap her arms around him. 'How wonderful to see a real man after a whole day devoted to dressing women!' she said when she had kissed him. 'Especially when the man is you.' And then, as he released her, 'Let's have a glass of brandy before we go.'

'Just a small one.' He eased some sketches aside

so that he could perch on the corner of the desk, watching her as she fetched two glasses and a decanter from the corner cupboard. A selection of drinks was kept there, together with some fine crystal glasses, for the benefit of the clients and any male companions who might escort them. There was also tea and coffee available, but according to Rose, a surprising number of the ladies opted for something stronger.

He was pleased to see that today she was wearing the long-sleeved, silk harlequin top that he loved. Caitlin, who seemed to know instinctively how to make her friend's long, angular and somewhat gawky figure look graceful, had designed it. The material was a mass of diamonds in vivid colours; Rose had been wearing it on the day that Alex had suggested that her new fashion house be called Harlequin. Today it was worn over a long black skirt, slightly flared to cope with Rose's tendency to stride about like a man. When she and Caitlin first met Rose had claimed that with her difficult build, clothes never looked right on her and were only worn in order to avoid startling horses. Caitlin's ability to transform Rose Hamilton, as she had been called then, into someone who could look stylish and smart had brought all the Hamilton family's well-to-do friends flocking to Harlequin when it first opened.

'How did you get on with the interview at the workshop?' Rose asked her husband as she handed him a small brandy.

'All right, I suppose.'

'You only suppose?'

'I'm not sure about the man. There was something secretive about him.' He frowned, trying to put his instinct into words. 'I don't know what it was — he's a cabinetmaker, there's no doubt about that. Perhaps he needs to get to know folk before he can be comfortable with them. Anyway, Todd seemed to take to him. I'd have liked to talk things over first, but he offered the job to the man before I knew what was happening. He said there would be a month's trial though, so that's something.'

'I'm sure that Todd's a good judge — and he's the one who has to work with this new person.'

'Mmm.' Alex took a sip of brandy; as was to be expected, it was excellent. Rose's upbringing had taught her to have impeccable taste and she always bought the best, even though their combined income was not generous. 'I stopped in at the gatehouse for a word with Murdo. That's a nice cloth he's got on the loom.'

'I'm pleased with it myself, and so's Caitlin. It's for Mrs Hepburn. She's a good client, and worth the extra work.'

'I'd like to get Murdo to do some work for us,

58

if you're willing. In fact, I'd like him to work for us on a regular basis, if you don't mind sharing him.'

Rose's eyebrows lifted slightly. 'What will your father say to that?'

'I'm quite sure he'd agree with me.'

'And what about Fiona? She dismissed him – I doubt if she'll be pleased to see him reinstated. She said that MacDowall couldn't afford him.'

'That's nonsense.'

'I thought so at the time.'

'I was away in the army then, but now I'm in charge again and I want Murdo to do work for us.'

'Mmm,' Rose said, then, 'We'd need to be careful, Alex. For instance, that cloth on the loom just now – you couldn't have that pattern.'

'It would look good on a set of dining-room furniture we're making in the Glasgow workshop at the moment.'

'Oh no!' Her voice was suddenly sharp. She had been leaning against the wall but now she straightened and glared at him. 'If I – if Caitlin and I agree to share Murdo with MacDowall and Son, you'll not use any Harlequin patterns. You'll have to have your own. Imagine what would happen if Mrs Hepburn were to go out visiting dressed in the cloth that Murdo's weaving for her at the moment, and what if the friend she visited had bought her dining-room furniture from you, with the same material on it. When she sat down to have her lunch the poor woman would merge into the furniture! She'd be humiliated and I would lose a good client.'

'From the amount of cloth that Murdo's making, I would say that it's more likely that the chair would merge into your Mrs Hepburn,' Alex said in a spurt of laughter. 'In any case, your clients live in Paisley and most of mine live in Glasgow. Chair and client may never meet.'

'We're not going to take that chance. *If* we agree to sharing Murdo, and if he wants to be shared—'

'He does, as long as you're willing.'

'I'll have to talk to Caitlin and Mary first,' Rose was saying when Caitlin came in.

'Talk about what? Hello, Alex.'

'I was just telling Murdo that I could use some of his work. He's willing to work for both of us, if you three are happy about it.'

'He's said he'd like to do it?'

Caitlin's eyes were her best features; neither blue nor green, they could be best described as turquoise. Now they widened in surprise.

'Yes. Is that a problem?'

'No,' Caitlin said swiftly. It seemed selfish to

protest that if Murdo had to spend more time at his loom he would have less time to work on the gatehouse.

'*If* we all agree,' Rose repeated, leaning on the first word, 'I'm going to ask John to draw up a contract specifying that we do not share patterns.'

John Brodie, a childhood friend and one-time suitor, was a member of his father's law firm. He had helped Rose to set up Harlequin and had some shares in it himself. He also assisted Mary with the firm's financial accounts, purely as a friend.

'Of course,' her husband assured her. 'Now come on, it's time to go home.'

'Before you go, Rose, we could do with another seamstress in the sewing room. There's so much work to do that the women we have can scarcely keep up with demand.'

'D'you want to advertise for someone?' Alex had taken Rose's coat from the stand in the corner and she was slipping her arms into the sleeves as she spoke, as eager as he was to get home.

'If we do that we'd have to interview applicants to make sure that they're going to be good enough. I was thinking of asking Mother and Jean if we could borrow Teenie for a month or two.'

'Teenie?' Rose and Alex both stared at her, grins breaking over their faces. Teenie Stapleton was a hard worker who could operate her sewing machine with remarkable speed. She was also very short-sighted, which meant that her head, covered at all times with a turbaned hat, was bent low over her machine, the needle pounding up and down only inches away from her nose. Although she had finally become the owner of a pair of glasses that magnified her eyes quite frighteningly, Teenie had never been able to overcome her habit of looking as though she had collapsed onto her sewing machine.

'Are you sure?' Rose asked, while Alex chimed in with, 'I can't see Teenie Stapleton as a Harlequin employee.'

'I can see her in our sewing room, though – there's nobody better. We know that she's efficient, and fast.'

'Would she be willing to come here? And would your mother and Jean be willing to do without her?'

'I think I could persuade them, and as for Teenie, we have more modern sewing machines than they have in the shop. I'm sure that she would love to work on one.'

Rose picked up her bag and gloves. 'I'll leave it to you them, Caitlin. It would certainly make our lives a bit easier,' she said as Alex ushered her out of the door.

★

'I liked working for Alex,' Murdo said when Caitlin raised the subject that evening. 'I've no objection tae weavin' for him again, as long as you and Mrs MacDowall have nothin' against it.'

'We haven't. It's just,' she hesitated, then plunged in, 'if you've got more weaving to do you'll have less time to work on the house.'

'I can manage the two well enough.'

'Rose was asking me today if we'd set a date for the wedding.'

'There's plenty time for that,' Murdo said, and when she looked up at him she saw that his mouth was set in a firm line — a clear indication that he had no interest in saying any more on the subject. So there was no use in asking him why he seemed in no hurry to marry her, when it was all that she herself wanted and longed for.

# 5

Mary Lennox was never seen with her hair untidy or a mark on her blouse or a smudge on her neat little face, not even when she had cleaned out the fire or blackleaded the range. Kirsty sometimes wondered aloud if her younger daughter slept standing up in a corner of the bedroom, for when Mary woke in the morning, instead of being tousled or puffy-eyed like normal folk, she was neat, tidy and ready to welcome the new day with a calm serenity.

So it came as a shock when she burst in through the back door one evening, her face red and wet, her hair raked out of place by frantic fingers and her hat hanging on to the back of her head by one hatpin.

'God save us!' Kirsty yelped, while Todd's favourite pipe almost dropped from his open mouth. The table had been pushed to one side so that Rowena could show off a new dance she had learned at school, and now she stopped in mid-step, poised on one foot with her arms spread out, while the reel Murdo, her accompanist, had been playing on his mouth organ trailed away into silence.

'Mary?' Caitlin jumped up. When she touched Mary's arm she discovered that the girl was trembling. 'Mary, what is it? Where's Lachie?' she went on, suddenly realising that her sister, who had gone out with her boyfriend, was on her own. Mary's mouth, a red, wet square, emitted a high-pitched whimper. 'Has someone – were the two of you attacked in the street?'

Murdo tossed the mouth organ down and surged to his feet. 'I'm goin' tae see what's happened tae Lachie!'

'And I'll go with ye!' Todd said, and both men were gone in an instant.

'Gran . . .' Rowena whimpered, rushing to the safety of Kirsty's lap, while Caitlin tried to guide her sister to the chair that Todd had vacated. 'Sit down and I'll get you a drink of water,' she was saying when Mary pulled herself clear, glared at the three of them through streaming eyes, screamed, 'Leave me alone!' and then fled through the inner door, slamming it hard behind her. They could hear her sobbing noisily as she ran upstairs.

'Go after her, Caitlin, and try to find out what's amiss,' Kirsty begged. 'Rowena, there's no need tae fret, darlin'. I'm here, and Granddad and Murdo'll be back in a minute.'

'Go away!' Mary shouted when Caitlin tapped on the door. 'Don't come in – I don't want to see anyone!'

'You're going to see me, for I'm already in.' Caitlin closed the door behind her. 'Mary, what happened to you? Where's Lachie? Did he get hurt?'

'I wish he *had* got hurt!' Mary had been lying face down on her bed; now she sat up, pulled her hat off and threw it across the room. 'I wish he'd never been born! I wish *I'd* never been born.' Then, glaring at Caitlin, 'He's jilted me!'

'Lachie? Surely not!'

'Why not? What did he ever see in me in the first place?' Mary bounced up from her bed and went to the small table that, with the addition of a mirror, served as a dressing table. Throwing herself down on the chair in front of it, she stared into the mirror. 'Look at me – what man would want to marry someone who looks like this?'

'You don't usually look like that,' Caitlin said reasonably. 'You usually look very nice.'

'Very nice isn't good enough though, is it?' Mary swung round from the mirror and glared at her sister. 'Very nice isn't pretty, like you, or striking like Rose. Women who look very nice just get j-jilted!' She turned back to the table, laid her arms over it, put her head down and wept as though her heart would break.

Caitlin started to move towards her, hand outstretched, but then hesitated before finally leaving the room, deciding that it was best to let Mary have some time on her own. When she got downstairs Todd and Murdo were in the kitchen.

'. . . not a sign of him,' Todd was saying, while Murdo added, 'Mebbe I should go round to his house to see if he's there. He might be lying somewhere, hurt.'

'He's not,' Caitlin suddenly felt rage against Lachie building up within her. 'He's not hurt at all,' she said to the surprised faces turned to her. 'It's Mary who's hurting, for Lachie's jilted her. Rowena, pet, how would you like to sleep in my room tonight?'

'Does Mary not want me near her?' Rowena and Mary shared a room, while Caitlin had the room over the pend to herself.

'It's not that – I just thought we'd leave her on

her own for tonight. She's a bit upset and I'm going to make fresh tea and take a cup upstairs to her.'

Mary was sitting up in bed when Caitlin returned to her room. The weeping was over and she was staring into space, her arms hugging her knees.

'What am I to do, Caitlin?'

'Forget about Lachie, for a start. Here, drink this.' Caitlin handed the cup over and sat down on the bed. 'What did he say?'

'He said,' Mary hiccuped, then took a sip of tea before she went on, 'that he thinks I'm too grand for him now.'

'Too grand?'

'B-because I'm working at Harlequin. He finished work early today and came to the mill to walk me home from work, and he s-saw me in the costume I wear when I'm working. He said . . .' her face crumpled again '. . . that he's an ordinary labourer and I'm too grand for the likes of him and I could do better for myself.'

'That's daft! I mean,' Caitlin said hurriedly, 'daft for him to say a thing like that.'

'I said that, but he'd not listen. It's my own fault!'

'How could it be your fault?'

'M-mind that drunk man we met at Hogmanay? The one that bumped into me and tried to get me to have a drink with him? Lachie tried to defend me and I lost my temper with him for making a fuss in front of folk,' wept Mary, who even as a child had hated drawing attention to herself. 'I wish I'd held my tongue, Caitlin, instead of scolding him when he was only trying to defend me! Mebbe he's used it as an excuse – mebbe he never wanted to marry me, and this is his chance to get away!'

'Did you want to marry him?' Lachie MacInnes and Mary had been walking out for years, but marriage between them had never been mentioned.

'We'd talked about it happening one day, and I liked the idea well enough. I thought he did too, but he's changed since he's been away at the war, Caitlin. He's not the person he used to be.'

'That's happened to a lot of the men who went to fight. They've seen things and had to do things that you and me know nothing about.'

'What am I going to do?'

'Mebbe Lachie was never the right man for you, Mary. Mebbe there's someone else waiting to meet you, someone more special, who'd never hurt you.'

Mary shook her head vigorously. 'No, there isn't. I'm not pretty like you. Who'd look at me twice?'

There was a soft scratching sound on the door

69

panels and Rowena put her head into the room. 'Is it all right if I get my things?' she asked in a whisper. 'I'm sleeping with Auntie Caitlin tonight.'

'Come in, pet.' Mary rubbed her hands over her swollen tear-streaked face in an effort to hide some of the signs of her weeping, then smiled at her niece. Rowena returned the smile nervously and left the room as soon as she could. When she had gone, Mary repeated, almost viciously, 'Who'd look at me twice? I'm the plain one of the family.'

'You're not plain, and lots of men would think themselves lucky to have a wife like you.'

'Only because I'd be good at looking after the housekeeping money,' said Mary, pushing her cup back at Caitlin. 'I'm never ever going to trust another man again. I'm going to be a spinster all my life!' Then she turned her face to the wall and closed her eyes.

Caitlin crept into her own room and got ready for bed in the dark so that Rowena would not be disturbed. But she had no sooner climbed into bed when a voice only inches away said, 'Auntie Caitlin, do you think I'm pretty?'

'You should be sleeping.'

'I was, but I woke up again.' Rowena moved closer so that her lips tickled Caitlin's ear as she asked again, 'Do you think I'm pretty?' Clearly she had heard Mary's 'I'm not pretty like you. Who'd look at me twice?'

'I think you're very pretty.'

'I think you are too. Was my mummy pretty?'

Although it had been years since Caitlin had set eyes on Beth Laidlaw, she could still recall her glossy black hair and clear green eyes. Cold eyes, but at the same time, eyes a man would happily drown in.

'She was very beautiful.'

'Do I look like her?'

'A bit, but you're more like your daddy.' Caitlin was grateful for that; Beth had always reminded her of the cold-hearted Ice Queen in a fairy story, whereas Ewan had been full of life. 'Your daddy was a handsome man.'

'Oh, I know that already.' Mary had given a portrait photograph of Ewan to Rowena when she had first arrived in Espedair Street, and Rowena still slept with it beneath her pillow. Over the years it had become cracked and faded, and his eternally young, handsome face had almost been kissed out of existence. 'My daddy's the best-looking man in the world – except for Murdo,' she said, and then, her mouth soft and warm against Caitlin's neck, she whispered, 'Auntie Caitlin, can I live with you and Murdo when you get married?'

'Don't you want to stay here with Granny and Granddad and Mary?'

'I can still visit them every single day, but what I really want is to live with you and Murdo. Can I – *please*?'

'We'll see. We're not getting married for a while yet because Murdo still has a lot of work to do on the gatehouse. Now go to sleep or you'll be snoring in the classroom tomorrow.'

'I want one of the upstairs rooms at the front,' Rowena murmured before falling into a deep sleep almost at once.

Mary was her usual neat self in the morning, though slightly red-eyed. Everyone carefully avoided mentioning the events of the night before, but at the same time they all treated her with great consideration. Kirsty put cream on her porridge instead of milk, Rowena sat by her at the table and kept passing sugar and butter and bread in an attempt to anticipate her every wish, and even Todd asked her how she felt and if she had had a good night's sleep.

'For goodness' sake,' she finally burst out, 'will you all stop behaving as if I've just recovered from a serious illness? I've been jilted, that's all!'

'What's jilted?' Rowena promptly asked.

'Left on the shelf.'

'But why would anyone leave you on a shelf? What shelf?' Rowena, confused, stared at the dresser with its array of Kirsty's best china on the upper shelves.

'It's just a thing that folk say,' Caitlin hurried to explain to her niece before things got worse.

'It means,' Mary said, buttering a slice of toast so vigorously that crumbs sprang in every direction, 'that Lachie MacInnes doesn't want to walk out with me any more. And before you ask why, Rowena, I don't know why he's changed his mind. And don't you go asking him about it either, for we're not speaking to him. None of us!' she emphasised, glaring round the table.

'Oh well, there are plenty more fish in the sea,' Rowena said, picking up her porridge spoon.

They all stared at each other over her bent head before Todd asked, 'Where in the world did you hear that one?'

'Miss McLardie said it in class last week when Maggie Walker was crying because Sadie O'Donnell wouldn't be her friend any more. She said it meant that Maggie would find another friend. Mebbe you'll find another Lachie, Auntie Mary.'

'I'm sure there are as many of them around as there are herring in the sea,' Mary said with a sniff, 'but I'm not going to be bothered by any of them. From now on I'm going to concentrate on my work.'

'I tried tae find out what's going on in Lachie's head,' Murdo told Caitlin, 'but I didnae get much sense out of him. He just kept saying that Mary's too good for the likes of him.'

'That's just daft! She's still the same Mary that she ever was – you must know that. And so should Lachie!'

'I can't force him tae change his mind. Nobody can.'

'I suppose not. Mebbe he never was the right man for her. Mebbe she'll meet someone else. I hope so, for I've never seen her so miserable.'

They were strolling along Causeyside Street, stopping now and again to look in shop windows. Murdo fell silent, and when Caitlin looked up at him, she saw that his face had the closed-in look she remembered from the time when he'd first come to Paisley. Caitlin suddenly began to wonder if those dark days when she'd been drawn to the silent Highlander, yet unable to break through the defences he had thrown up between himself and the rest of the world, were still uncomfortably close.

'Murdo,' she said at last, 'you wouldn't do that, would you?'

'Do what?'

'Think that I was – well – think the same about me as Lachie's thinking about Mary.'

'No, of course not. We're promised to each other, are we no'?'

'Yes, but . . . Let's get married soon, Murdo!'

'We will, once the house is ready.'

'We don't need to wait until then. We can manage with the place as it is, and once I'm living there I can help you with the work that has to be done.'

'I want it to be just right for you.'

'I don't care about that. I could have lost you to the war, Murdo, and now that you're back home safe and sound I don't want to wait any longer than we have to.'

'We won't,' he said, and she had to be content with that.

Joseph McCart proved to be a willing worker and a good timekeeper. He arrived early every morning, early enough to be in the workshop by the time Todd got there. In the middle of the day, when Todd went to the kitchen for something to eat and Kenny stayed in the workshop to eat his sandwiches, Joseph sat out in the yard no matter what the weather might be, sheltering in the lea of stacked timbers from rain, sleet or snow if necessary.

He was hunkered down on the ground with his back against the yard wall, chewing his way through the two thick slices of stale bread and the wedge of hard cheese he had brought with him for his midday meal, when Rowena came out of the house and made for the large flagstone set in the middle of the patch of grass known as the back green.

At first sight of the girl Joseph pressed himself closer to the wall and reached up to pull the peak of his cap further down over his eyes, as though hoping the action would make him invisible. But Rowena didn't notice the slight movement further down the yard. Skipping on to the stone, she paused, spread her arms out to either side, and then began to dance to the music she could hear inside her head.

Joseph watched as she spun and leaped, pointing her toes and arching her arms over her head. She began to dance faster, then faltered as large heavy drops of rain began to fall. She looked up at the sky, scowling her disapproval at the interruption, then blinked and rubbed her face as one of the drops landed in one blue eye. She looked back at the house before, hit by inspiration, she scurried into the roofed pend and began to dance again, moving so confidently that the watcher almost began to believe that he, too, could hear the music.

When the dance ended, Rowena picked up the hem of her skirt delicately between the forefinger and thumb of each hand, put one leg to the side, swept the other behind her, and curtsied low. It was as she straightened again that she glanced down the length of the yard and saw her audience.

Joseph had no time to escape back into the workshop. Even as he began to scramble to his feet she was standing before him. 'Hello, you must be my granddad's new man. I'm Rowena Lennox.'

He fumbled at his cap, tugging at it in salute. 'Joseph McCart, miss.'

'Do you like working here?'

'Aye, miss. I'd best get back . . .'

'It's all right, you don't have to go back to work until Granddad comes out of the house. He's not really my granddad,' Rowena prattled on, 'because *he* died a long time ago. I never met him. My gran married this granddad later. Though she's not my real gran either, because she wasn't my daddy's real mother. She married his father after he was born.'

She smiled up at him, and seemed to be waiting for him to say something. Since Joseph could not make any sense from the sudden rush of family information, he cleared his throat and said haltingly, 'You're a good dancer.'

'Did you see me?'

'I was sittin' here eatin' my dinner,' he began to explain hurriedly, but she was already off. 'I like dancing more than anything else in the whole world. That big stone there's my dancing stone – it's very good for practising on. But when it's wet, the pend and the wash house come in handy.'

'My wee girl likes dancin' too.'

Rowena's face lit up. 'You've a wee girl like me? What's her name? How old is she?'

'Cavan – she's just turned eleven, miss.'

'I'm ten. I don't think there's a girl called Cavan in my school.'

'She goes to St Catherine's school.'

'Oh, you're Catholics. Can I meet her? P'raps I could come to your house, or you could bring Cavan here.'

Joseph began to panic at the thought of what the ould yin would say if he let this talkative child with her passion for asking questions near their home. 'I don't know about that, miss.'

'Is she shy? Could you not bring her to one of the ceilidhs at the Gaelic Chapel hall up School Wynd? That's where I learned to dance. Murdo plays the mouth organ there. Murdo comes from the Highlands and he's going to marry my Auntie Caitlin. The next ceilidh's next Wednesday night. *Please* let Cavan come to it – please?'

'I–I don't know . . .' Joseph was stammering when Todd Paget came down the yard from the house.

'Rowena, your gran's wondering where you've got to,' he said easily when he spotted the man and girl. 'Off you go now, and stop botherin' poor Joseph.'

'I wasn't bothering him, I was talking to him. He's got a daughter called Cavan and she dances, like me. She's coming to the next ceilidh – isn't she?' Rowena said to Joseph's back as he and Todd disappeared into the workshop.

# 6

Alex was late for the usual monthly meeting with his father. The offices were situated on the top floor of MacDowall and Son's emporium, a three-floored building in Hope Street, but instead of taking the lift, which was slow and somewhat noisy, he headed for the stairs, deciding that he could do with the exercise.

Opting for the long route through the store meant that he had to run the gauntlet of a steady chorus of 'Good morning, Mr Alex' as he reached each department. He smiled and nodded to right and left, wishing each of them a good morning, and was beginning to feel quite breathless when he arrived at the accounts department. Passing through one final flurry of greetings, he finally gained his father's office, saying as he went in, 'I'm sorry I'm late, I was held up at the factory . . .' He closed the door and turned to face the room, then stopped short as he realised that there were four people in the room instead of the usual three.

Sandy MacDowall sat at his big desk, his back to the window, facing the empty chair that awaited Alex. Myra Webster, Sandy's middle-aged, efficient secretary, sat by his side, notebook and pencil at the ready, while Martin Sloan, the store manager, sat at one side of the desk. On the other, looking very businesslike in a crisp white blouse and navy-blue skirt and jacket, sat Fiona.

'Good morning, Alex, how lovely to see you – at last,' she said, and then, as he took his seat, 'Perhaps we can begin the meeting now?'

'I didn't expect to see you here, Fiona.'

'Hasn't Father told you?'

'I haven't had time,' Sandy said, and then, looking over the top of the spectacles he now had to wear all the time, 'Fiona's going to take over from John Kilbride, Alex.'

'The floorwalker in charge of the second floor? But I thought that we were going to discuss his retirement and replacement this morning.'

'Unfortunately, John took a heart attack late on Friday night,' Martin Sloan's voice was sombre.

'His wife contacted me on Saturday and I passed the news on to Mr MacDowall.'

'Poor old John!' The man had come back from retirement to replace the floorwalker who had enlisted in the navy and had not survived the war. John had been eager to retire permanently, and was only waiting for someone to be appointed in his place. 'He's not . . . ?' Alex said, his voice hushed.

'No, no, he's in Glasgow Royal Infirmary, and his wife hopes that he'll make a good recovery. But he'll not be back here, that's for sure. When she heard about our problem, Mrs Chalmers kindly offered to step into the breach, so to speak.' Sloan smiled at Fiona, who gave him a warm smile in return.

'Do you know anything about the work involved, Fiona?' Alex, dismayed by bad news of a man he had always liked, and by his half-sister's unexpected appearance at this business meeting, was trying to gather his wits together.

'You forget that I helped Father with this place when you were winning the war, Alex. I'm sure that I'll manage very well, with some assistance from Martin and the staff.'

'I'm sure you will,' Sandy put in. 'And I'll be here to guide her, Alex.'

'Of course. Well, we must advertise the post as soon as possible, and get interviews under way.

Fiona won't want to be tied down to this place for too long.'

'You misunderstand, Alex,' Fiona said sweetly. 'I'm not filling a gap; I intend to remain in the post. Though if you feel that an interview is necessary,' her brown eyes met and held his, 'I would of course be happy to oblige.'

'Don't be silly, my dear, of course we don't need an interview. I'm sure you will carry out the work very well,' Sandy assured his daughter.

'But if Alex isn't happy . . .'

'I'm sure that Alex is as pleased with the news as I am.' Sandy MacDowall raised his eyebrows at his son, who shrugged.

'I merely thought that Fiona might find the work tedious, but if she wants to continue with it, I have no objection.'

'Thank you, Alex.' Fiona made it sound as though he had just given her a very special gift. 'After all,' she added, 'the workshop is your special responsibility, so my being here surely won't bother you.'

'Of course not. As a matter of fact . . .' Alex turned to his father . . . 'talking of the workshop reminds me – I've asked Murdo Guthrie, the weaver to work for us again.'

'What? But I dismissed him!' Fiona blurted out.

'Yes, you did, and now I've reinstated him,

though we're going to have to share him with Harlequin, as Rose refuses to let him go entirely. He did some excellent work for us in the past, as you know, Father.'

'Yes he did,' Sandy agreed, and if you want him to weave for us, I'm happy to approve your decision, my boy. Now then,' he went on without noticing his daughter's tight mouth and angry eyes, 'shall we proceed with the meeting?'

'Martin Sloane was gazing at her with all the awe of a little boy staring in the window of a sweet shop,' Alex told Rose that evening. 'She's got him wound round her little finger – and my father as well.'

'As long as she hasn't got you under her spell, I'm content.'

'Good God, no! I learned the truth about my dear half-sister several years ago. And once learned, that lesson is never forgotten.'

'I'm pleased to hear that. I'm sure that Martin Sloan will soon find out for himself that Fiona's more of a nippy sweetie than the luxury chocolate she makes herself out to be,' Rose said briskly, 'and Sandy might well begin to regret letting her have her way. While Fiona's spinning a rope to hang herself, you've got plenty to do. I spoke to Caitlin and Murdo this afternoon, and we've all

84

agreed that Murdo can weave material for MacDowall and Son as well as Harlequin – but not the same patterns, and not at our expense. Our orders come first. John looked in too, and he's going to prepare an official agreement between the two businesses.'

Alex grinned across the dinner table at her. 'That is good news! We've got a special order in from one of our best customers, and I think that she would like some special cloth woven for the seats and backs of the chairs. I'll be sure to go to Paisley this week some time, so that I can have a word with Murdo about it.'

'I think he's concerned about what Fiona might do when she hears that he's going to be working for you again. He's no wish to be turned off by her a second time. He's a very proud man, Alex. I'd not want him upset, nor would Caitlin.'

'I'll reassure him about that too. Fiona said this morning that the workshop is my kingdom, and getting Murdo back gives me the chance to show her that she has no control over my decisions. This customer I mentioned has ordered a cabinet too, and she wants it decorated. I think I might do that myself.'

'Will you have the time?' While he was still working for his stepfather in the Espedair Street workshop he now owned, Alex had developed an interest in hand painting furniture. Matt Lennox had done his best to belittle the talent, but it had brought in extra orders and resulted in a meeting between Fiona and Alex and, ultimately, between Alex and his real father. MacDowall's still did some decorated furniture, but the work was mainly carried out by a man specially hired for the purpose.

'I'm going to make the time,' Alex said with growing enthusiasm. 'I'd like to do some designing again, and the painting itself is soothing.'

'If it gives you pleasure then I certainly think that you should do it.' Rose tried to sound casual, though she was secretly delighted. At last, Alex was beginning to look and sound like his old self. He hadn't had a nightmare for some three weeks. 'Perhaps you could design some special painted furniture as a wedding gift for Caitlin and Murdo.'

'I think that's a very good idea.' He reached across the table to take his wife's hand. 'You're a clever woman.'

'Isn't that why you married me?' Rose countered, and as they grinned affectionately at each other she began to feel that at last the terrible war years were behind them and her Alex had come home.

*

As always when a ceilidh was being held, the Gaelic Chapel hall was filled with folk. As soon as Caitlin, Rowena and Murdo arrived, Murdo took his mouth organ from his pocket and went off to join the other musicians while Rowena, completely at home and among friends, scurried across the hall and plunged into the midst of a group of young people. Caitlin, as always, searched for Mhairi, the elderly woman who had befriended her when she began to attend the ceilidhs. Mhairi spotted her first, and it was the woman's skirling shriek of welcome that caught Caitlin's attention. Craning her neck in the direction of the sound, she saw an arm waving wildly, and then as she went nearer, she saw Mhairi's snowy white head and beaming smile.

'I thought you'd be here tonight.' The woman slid along the bench to make room for Caitlin. 'Rowena would never let you miss a ceilidh, would she? Where's Mary? And young Lachie? Too busy courtin' to join us?'

When Caitlin told her what had happened, she drew her breath in with a hiss and shook her head. 'Och, the poor lass, that's a terrible thing to happen to her. What possessed Lachie, when he had such a nice wee sweetheart there?'

'Nobody knows but him. Murdo tried to talk to him, but it was no use.'

'We can't force folk to do what we think they

should do,' Mhairi agreed, then, with sudden interest, she went on her lovely soft Highland voice, 'Would you look there, now — we've got strangers visiting us tonight.'

A small group hesitated at the door, half in and half out and looking as though they might at any moment take fright and disappear back into the dark late-January night. The group was made up of a man, dark and swarthy, with his cap pulled down over his eyes, a woman in a shabby dark coat and a shapeless wide-brimmed felt hat and a girl around Rowena's age, wearing a beret pulled down over dark hair, with a cloak wrapped round her body. The girl seemed to be urging the adults forward into the hall, while they held back.

'Someone needs to welcome them,' Mhairi said, and began to struggle up, wincing as her rheumaticky joints protested.

'I'll go.' Caitlin well remembered her own shyness when she attended her first ceilidh. If Mhairi had not taken her under her wing she might well have fled that night from the crowd of strangers, many of whom were speaking a language she didn't understand.

She was halfway across the room when Rowena arrived by her side. 'It's Joseph, and his wee girl.'

'Who?'

'Joseph. He works for Granddad and he has a wee girl like me who likes dancing. I told him to bring her here.' They had reached the door, and Rowena rattled on, 'Hello, Joseph. You came, then. Is this Cavan?'

'Aye. And my wife, Shelagh.'

Caitlin had not yet met the new cabinetmaker. Now she held out her hand. 'How do you do? I'm Caitlin Lennox.'

He hesitated for so long that she felt embarrassed and rejected. She was about to let her hand drop to her side when he summoned the courage to take it in his calloused grip for a moment. 'This is my wife, Shelagh,' he said again, and the woman ducked her head and murmured something.

'And I'm Cavan.' The girl tilted her chin up and spoke out clearly, her beautiful dark eyes fixed on Rowena. 'I'm eleven years old – just.' Long black hair spilled from beneath her beret to fall on her shoulders. Her round face was creamy-skinned, with a full mouth and neat nose, and large, very dark eyes sparkled from below a sweep of dark lashes. The beautiful woman she would become one day was already to be seen hovering below the surface of the child's face.

'I'm ten,' Rowena informed her. 'Joseph says that you like dancing. So do I.'

'I do Irish dancing,' Cavan said. 'I come from Ireland.'

'Come and meet the others.'

'Mammy?' The girl glanced up, waiting for permission. Her mother's hand lay on her shoulders and for a moment Caitlin saw the slim, work-roughened fingers tighten as though the woman was going to try to keep her child close by her side. Then the man said something to her in a low voice and her hand fell away from Cavan who, as though released from a tether, immediately followed Rowena across the hall.

'Come and sit with me and Mhairi,' Caitlin suggested, but Joseph McCart shook his head.

'I have to get back. The ould yin – my mother – doesn't keep well. She shouldn't be left on her own for too long. You stay,' he added to his wife when she put a hand on his arm. She cast a nervous glance over her shoulder at her daughter's departing back, then looked up at him.

'You'll come to fetch us later?'

'Of course I will. In an hour,' he said, then slipped out of the door so quickly that Shelagh McCart was left gripping empty space with the hand that had been on his arm.

'There's a seat over here. I was nervous the first time I came to a ceilidh,' Caitlin reassured her companion as she steered her across the floor. 'But

Mhairi soon put me at my ease. Mhairi, this is Shelagh McCart, from Ireland.'

'Welcome to ye, my lass. Are ye new to Paisley? Och, you'll soon settle down,' Mhairi said comfortably as the young woman's head gave an almost imperceptible nod. 'That bonny wee girl that came in with you – your sister, is she?'

'My daughter.' Shelagh's voice was as light as a feather.

'Your daughter? Och, my dearie, you don't look old enough to be a mother. Take your things off an' be comfortable; it gets warm in this hall once the hoochin' and stampin' starts.'

Slowly, reluctantly, Shelagh removed her coat and then her hat. Hair as dark and glossy as her daughter's swung over the left side of her face, almost covering her eye and cheekbone. As she squeezed in between Caitlin and Mhairi the musicians struck up a lively reel and at once people who had been sitting on benches lining the walls or standing in groups, chattering, flocked on to the floor to form sets of eight.

A middle-aged man offered his hand to Caitlin, who jumped to her feet. As she took her place in one of the circles she saw that Rowena and Cavan were in the next set. The Irish girl had shed her cloak to reveal a green dress with a bodice cut straight across the top, short loose sleeves and a flared skirt. Caitlin's gaze moved to Shelagh in time to see someone approach the young woman, hand outstretched in an invitation to join the dance. Shelagh's dark hair shimmered about her face as she shook her head. She put her hand up swiftly to still it and hold it in place. Then the people on either side of Caitlin linked hands with her as the dance began.

It was one of Caitlin's favourite Scottish dances, and one of Rowena's too. Fast and furious, it called for speed and stamina. As she swung past Mhairi, Caitlin saw with amusement that although the old woman was no longer able to keep up with such energetic dances, she could still use her voice. While her hands crashed together in great hearty claps timed to match the music's beat, her head was tipped back and her mouth open to emit yells of encouragement to spur the dancers on.

When the dance finally ended Caitlin collapsed on the bench, breathless, shaking her head when another tune began, just as fast as the last one, and someone else tried to coax her on to the floor. 'Too much for me,' she said breathlessly.

This new dance was for couples instead of sets of eight, and Rowena and Cavan, both bright-eyed and rosy-cheeked with exertion, were already on the floor, partnering each other.

The dance was halfway through when folk

began to falter and then come to a stop, moving away from the centre of the floor. As a space cleared before her, Caitlin saw that Cavan McCart had broken away from Rowena and was dancing on her own – a form of dance she had never seen before. The girl was straight-backed, her head held high and her arms down by her sides instead of being held up in the Scottish way. Amazingly, the upper half of her body remained almost motionless while her feet followed a quick and intricate pattern of steps that set her long black hair bouncing on her shoulders and the short flared skirt swinging about her thin legs.

Rowena, too, had stopped dancing and stood by, watching open-mouthed as Cavan leaped and twirled. She spun round, her hands moving to her hips, then they returned to her sides as she swiftly kicked one leg out in front then swung it back behind her. As she danced, her feet thudding on the floor to the rhythm of the music, she seemed unaware that she was the centre of attention. Someone began to clap to the beat and the others joined in. And still the young Irish girl danced on, in a world of her own.

'My, would you look at that!' Mhairi said, thrilled. 'Is that the way the Irish dance, Shelagh? It's bonny,' she went on as the young woman nodded, a smile trembling on her lips as she watched

93

her daughter. 'Faster,' Mhairi mouthed to the musicians, swooshing her hands at them in a shooing motion, and the fiddler, drummer, accordionist and Murdo on the mouth organ obligingly stepped up their tempo. Cavan's feet became little more than a blur of movement as she kept time effortlessly with the new beat, while Rowena's blue eyes widened until they seemed to fill half her face.

For Caitlin's part, her attention was fixed on the girl's green satin dress; it was clearly too small for her but as she moved it shimmered beneath the overhead lights and gold and silver threads stitched into narrow horizontal bands of braid glittered as the skirt swung and flared.

Faster and faster went the music, and faster and faster danced Cavan McCart, until the tune came to an abrupt end and the dancer to a sudden stop, blinking in confusion as the place erupted into applause around her. She looked at the smiling faces, and then, her own face flooding with embarrassed colour, ran to her mother.

Rowena was close behind her. 'What sort of dance was that?'

'It's Irish,' Shelagh told her, adding, almost apologetically to Caitlin and Mhairi, 'She should really have proper jig shoes so that she can tap out the beat, but she grew out of them, so she's just got the soft shoes.'

The music started up again and dancers flocked on to the floor. Now that she was no longer the centre of attention, Cavan visibly relaxed. When Rowena pleaded, 'Cavan – would you teach me how to do your Irish dancing?' the girl said, 'If you'll teach me how to do your kind of dancing.'

They beamed at each other and Caitlin realised that at last Rowena had found a friend.

Someone took her up for the next dance, and the next, and it was a while before she got the chance to speak to Shelagh again. 'Cavan's dress is very pretty. Did you buy it in Ireland?'

'I made it – a lady I clean for gave me some clothes she's finished with, and there was a green satin dress among them. I bought the braid in a draper's.'

'My mother's friend Jean Chisholm has some good materials in her wee second-hand clothes shop in Causeyside Street. My mother works there sometimes. You're a seamstress, then?'

'I used to be, before—' Shelagh stopped suddenly, and then went on, 'Before Cavan was born.' Then she jumped to her feet before Caitlin could say anything else. 'Here's Joseph, come back to walk us home. I'd best go.'

'You'll come to the next ceilidh? I think Cavan will want to.'

'I don't know. I'll see what Joseph thinks,'

Shelagh was already scooping up hats and coats. Arms full, she hurried over to where Joseph stood just inside the door, and as soon as the dance was finished and Cavan had joined them, the little family disappeared into the night.

# 7

Rowena couldn't wait for the next ceilidh.

'I wish Cavan was in my school, then we could see each other every day. Mebbe,' she suggested, brightening, 'I could start going to her school.'

'You can't do that. Only Catholics can go to that school.'

'I could become one, couldn't I? Tell me how to do it.'

'It's not as easy as all that,' Caitlin said. 'You'll just have to wait until the next ceilidh.' Secretly, she felt that even although Cavan had had a good time, Shelagh McCart was so shy that she would not want to face another ceilidh.

But she was wrong. The Irish family appeared halfway through the evening, huddling in the doorway to watch the dancers whirl by. Rowena, who had been watching the door anxiously, made a beeline for the group as soon as the dance was over, and she and Cavan darted off towards the group of young folk. Caitlin waved to Shelagh who, after a word to Joseph, made her way to where Mhairi and Caitlin sat, while her husband melted back into the darkness outside the door.

He didn't reappear until the end of the evening, and Caitlin noticed that for the final half-hour Shelagh grew increasingly agitated and was scarcely able to take her gaze from the door. She and Cavan were the first to put their coats on when the evening ended, but still Joseph McCart had not arrived.

'If your husband doesn't come for you, we'll walk you home,' Caitlin offered.

'I'm sure he'll be here. It's the ould yin – his mother,' Shelagh explained. 'She's doesn't keep well. He might not be able to leave her.'

Murdo came over and was introduced to Shelagh.

'And this is my friend, Cavan,' Rowena said proudly. 'She's going to teach me Irish dancing and I'm going to teach her Scottish dancing. Murdo plays the mouth organ for me, so that I can prac- tise,' she explained to Cavan, who, suddenly shy in Murdo's presence, was standing close to her mother.

'You'll play for the two of us, won't you, Murdo?'

'Aye, surely.' He smiled down at the dark-haired girl. 'I know some Irish tunes that might do for you.'

'Can Cavan come to the gatehouse after school with me tomorrow?'

'If you want.'

'I don't know . . .' Shelagh began, the one eyebrow not hidden by her sweep of hair tucking into a worried frown. 'We'd have to see what your da says, Cavan, and your grandma.'

Cavan's eyes narrowed in a rebellious look that Caitlin, trained by years of living with Rowena, recognised. 'I want to see Rowena after school, Ma. Please? Just for one hour?'

'Cavan, I don't know,' Shelagh said again, and then, her voice lightening, 'Oh, here he is.'

As the little group moved towards him Joseph looked apprehensive. For a moment Caitlin thought that he might take to his heels with his wife and daughter fleeing after him through the dark streets. But he held his ground, even giving Murdo's proffered hand a swift shake.

'Please, Mr McCart,' Rowena said in her sweetest voice, and with her most winning smile, 'can Cavan and me meet each other after school tomorrow to play?'

'Please, Da!' Cavan coaxed. 'Just for a little while?'

'I suppose it would be all right, as long as you're home by five o'clock,' he said grudgingly, and the girls both gave an excited skip.

'He seems to be scared to let Cavan have any fun,' Caitlin said as she and Murdo walked back to Espedair Street. Rowena, as always happened on ceilidh nights, was dancing along the pavement ahead of them. 'It's as if he believes that Paisley folk are all bad people.'

'He's just being careful. I don't think they've been here long, and it takes time for some folk to get to know their neighbours.'

Perhaps, Caitlin thought as they walked along arm in arm, the McCart family had been badly hurt in the past, like Murdo, and had learned not to trust strangers. Rowena had been the first person to break through the defences that Murdo had built around himself when he came to Paisley, and when Caitlin herself had begun to fall in love with him she had despaired of ever finding a way to let him know how she felt. The despair deepened when she learned from Mhairi that Murdo had begun to build his protective wall after his small son had drowned and his wife, weakened in spirit and body by grief, had succumbed to a chill not long after.

It was only when Murdo was conscripted into

the army and he and Caitlin, at her instigation, started writing to each other that they began to know each other, even though they were at that time hundreds of miles apart. When Murdo came back to Paisley at the end of the war, Caitlin, now certain that he was the only man she would ever want to share her life with, threw all her inhibitions off and pursued him with such determination that she finally forced him to recognise and admit his growing feelings for her.

'You'll come in for a wee while?' she suggested as the three of them halted outside the Lennox door.

'I'd as soon get back.'

'Night night, Murdo.' Rowena threw her arms round his waist and burrowed her head into his chest. 'See you tomorrow, after school,' she said, her voice muffled by his jacket. 'And I'll have Cavan with me.'

'Aye, I'll see the two of you tomorrow.' He watched her lift the latch and slip into the house, then turned to Caitlin.

'I'll see you tomorrow, too,' he said, and kissed her swiftly before turning and striding into the night without looking back.

As she followed Rowena slowly into the warmth of the house Caitlin wondered if she had really managed to break through his defences, or if they

101

were rebuilding themselves quietly but steadily, brick by brick, without anyone noticing.

The ould yin, Bernadette McCart, slept in the bed recess in the kitchen, while Cavan had a small room, little more than a cupboard. The front room had been turned into a bedroom for Joseph and his wife.

Waiting for Joseph to come to bed, Shelagh shivered beneath two blankets that were so old and had been washed so frequently they had lost their warmth. Every now and again she lifted her head from the flat, hard pillow and strained her ears, but she could hear no sound through the wall that divided their room from the kitchen. They must be speaking quietly, so as not to waken Cavan.

'They' was the wrong word, since she knew that Joseph would be silent, his head and shoulders bowed beneath the lash of the ould yin's tongue. Shelagh was aware from bitter experience that her mother-in-law's whisper could cut far better than her normal speaking voice.

She had blown the candle out, but a street lamp shining through the uncurtained window lit up the room. She stared up at the yellowed ceiling, making out some of the cracks and stains and seeing, in her mind's eye, those hidden in the

102

shadows; for once she allowed herself the luxury of thinking of the little cottage she and Joseph had lived in previously – the cottage he had carried her into after their wedding. The cottage where she had been happier than ever before in her entire life, and where Cavan had been born.

A tear slid from the corner of each eye to trickle down over her temples and into her hair. Then, as she heard a soft step in the little square hall, she hurriedly scrubbed the dampness away with both hands.

Not a word was said while Joseph stripped his clothes off, for the ould yin had ears as sharp as a cat's fangs, though there were times when it suited her to pretend that her hearing was dull. Shelagh waited until her husband had scrambled in beside her and found a comfortable way to lie on the thin, lumpy mattress before she whispered, 'Is she settled down now?'

'As settled as she'll ever be outside of her coffin. Though God knows when she'll ever agree to get into that.'

'Joseph, don't speak like that of your own mother!'

'I'm near to the end of my tether, Shelagh. Sometimes I think we should have stayed where we were. Things might have been better . . .'

'Ah, don't!' Shelagh clutched at him as though

trying to reassure herself that he was really there with her, safe in her arms. 'You know it could never have been good there – not for us.'

'I don't know what to think any more.'

'You were right to say that Cavan could spend time with that wee girl, Joseph,' she said against the hard line of his jaw. 'It's not her fault we had to come here. She needs a friend and they're nice folk. Did that wee girl's own grandda not give you work?'

'Aye, he's a decent enough man.'

'I like the folk I've met at the dancing,' Shelagh said wistfully. 'Most of them were driven out of their homes in the north and they've had to make new lives for themselves here, just like us. They're contented enough. Old Mhairi's kind, and Caitlin Lennox, too. Cavan wants to keep going to their ceilidhs. She misses her friends, Joseph.' And so do I, she thought, a lump forming in her throat. She missed the neighbourliness of the village at home, and she missed her own family and the friends she had grown up with. Loneliness ate deeper into her soul day by day.

'She can go to the ceilidhs, I've told you that.'

'But your mother—'

'Pay no heed tae her. Leave her tae me. She shouldn't be your worry.'

Shelagh could have said that it was easy for him

to tell her to pay no heed to the ould yin. He escaped every day to work among other folk, but apart from getting out to do the occasional cleaning job she had to stay in with his mother. She had to put up with more than he realised.

'Leave her to me,' he said again, reaching out to touch her face. She put her hand over his and for a moment it was as though they were still back in Eire, in the comfort and safety of their own little cottage, just the two of them, and Cavan.

As though he sensed her thoughts, Joseph put a strong, warm arm around her. Comforted, Shelagh turned to face him, her body nestling close to his. The chill left her, and she slept.

The decision, one day, to send his car home and walk the two miles back instead of travelling in comfort, together with an unexpected heavy shower of rain that had drenched him during the second mile, resulted in a heavy cold for Sandy MacDowall. At first he shrugged off Fiona's suggestions that he should stay at home until the worst of it was over.

'Better to work it off. I'll have a hot toddy every night before I go to my bed and it'll be gone by Saturday.'

But on Saturday night his cold was so bad that Sandy cancelled a visit to Alex's flat for dinner, and on Sunday he was so ill that Fiona, despite his breathless protestations, sent for the doctor.

It was not until Monday morning, when he arrived at the office for the monthly meeting, that Alex discovered that his father had pneumonia.

'Why didn't you send for me?'

'You and Rose have little enough time together,' Fiona protested. 'I didn't want to break into your only free day.'

'You know that we would both have come at once. How bad is it?'

'Bad enough. I tried to get him to stay home last week, to get rid of that cold, but he paid no heed. Isn't that right, Martin?' his half-sister appealed to the store manager, who nodded his head vigorously.

'You did that, Mrs Chalmers, but he was determined to work the cold off.'

'And now look where it's got him,' Fiona sighed.

'Where is he? In hospital?'

'Dr Blackie agreed with me that he's best in his own home.'

'You've left him there, with only Mrs Dove to look after him? You should have stayed with him yourself.'

'For goodness' sake, Alex!' Fiona gave the tinkling laugh that had once captivated him – as clearly, he realised now, as it captivated Martin Sloan, who laughed along with her. 'Don't be so old-fashioned. This is the twentieth century – women don't have to be tied to the kitchen sink any more. I've hired a trained nurse and she'll stay in the spare bedroom until Father's well again. And whether he likes it or not, I'm going to have a telephone installed so that I can keep in contact with her when I'm here.'

'Would it not be easier for us to appoint another floorwalker to take your place until Father's back on his feet?'

'As I said,' Fiona's voice was suddenly crisp, 'we women are emancipated now. Some of us have even got the vote – or hadn't you heard? I like working here and I don't intend to give it up now that I've settled in. If you're so concerned about him why don't you take time off from your own work, or ask Rose to give up the fashion house?'

Alex telephoned Rose as soon as he returned to the factory. 'She's as hard as nails,' he fretted. 'She seems to care more about working in the store than her own father's well-being. After all he's done for her!'

'At least she's brought in a trained nurse, and Mrs Dove's a capable woman. I'm glad your father's

107

able to stay at home; I don't think he would take kindly to lying in a ward in one of the Glasgow hospitals, being bossed about by a matron.'

'We don't even know what the nurse is like. I'd go to the house now but there's so much work on here. I'll have to wait until this evening.'

In her office at Harlequin, Rose put a hand over the mouthpiece of her telephone and gave a very faint sigh, her mind running over the work programme for the day. Then she removed her hand and said, 'I could spare an hour or so this morning, but I have to be back for early afternoon. We have a rather difficult client coming in for a fitting at two o'clock. I'll drive over to visit your father now, if you like.'

'Would you? You're a wonderful woman and I love you very much!'

'I love you too,' she said, adding, after she had ended the call, 'Why else would I be dashing off to Glasgow to see your father at a moment's notice? It's certainly not for his sake, or Fiona's.'

Then she went to ask Caitlin, hard at work in the sewing room upstairs, and Mary, frowning over invoices in her small office, if they would cover for her for the rest of the morning.

Muriel Dove's face brightened when she opened the door and saw Rose standing in the foyer.

'Mrs MacDowall, it's good to see you!'

'My husband telephoned to tell me what's happened. He won't be free until this evening, so I said that I'd look in to put his mind at rest. How is Mr MacDowall?'

'Poorly — but the doctor says that he's going to come through it, and the nurse seems very capable. She's taken over the whole house,' Mrs Dove confided in a whisper as she took Rose's coat, 'and she's taken over Mr MacDowall too. I'll let her know that you're here.'

She tapped gently on her employer's bedroom door. After a long moment it opened and a tall, uniformed woman came out into the hall, closing the door quietly but firmly behind her.

'This is Mr MacDowall's daughter-in-law, come to see him,' Mrs Dove's voice was surprisingly meek. 'This is Nurse Gemmell, Mrs MacDowall.'

'How do you do?' The nurse inclined her head slightly. 'My patient is resting at the moment.'

'I would like to see him,' Rose said firmly, and a slight frown wrinkled Nurse Gemmell's smooth brow.

'I'm not sure—'

'I only have a few minutes, and my husband is very anxious to find out how his father is. I assured him that I would see the patient for myself.' Rose moved towards the door, bearing down on the woman and giving her no option but to open the door and lead the way, her snowy starched headdress flapping like the wings of a large white bird.

'Mr MacDowall, are you asleep?'

'Of course I'm not asleep – how can I sleep with you fussing over me all the time?' Sandy's voice, though very weak, still had a snap to it.

'Your daughter-in-law has come to see you. You can only stay a minute,' the nurse added to Rose before she moved away from the bed.

'She'll stay as long as she wants to stay! Rose, it's good of you to come.' The sick man held out both his hands, and Rose took them in hers. They were burning hot and his face flamed against the white pillows.

'Alex can't come himself because he's needed at the factory, so he asked me to represent him. He'll be in this evening, though.' She sat down on a chair by the bed. 'How do you feel?'

He still held her hands in his, as though believing that somehow he could draw health and strength from her body to nourish his. 'Ach, I've been better. That damned cold wouldn't go away and now look what it's done to me.'

'You'll get over it quickly.'

'I have to. I've got every reason to get better quickly.' He glanced at the starched white figure by the window and then looked back at Rose, closing one eye in a meaningful wink. Taken by surprise, for he was not normally over-endowed with a sense of humour, she almost laughed out loud.

'You're being well cared for,' she said instead, adding, 'It's a pity Fiona couldn't have stayed at home to look after you, though.'

'She knows nothing of the sick room, and in any case, she's doing a grand job at the store. Did Alex tell you she's become a floorwalker there?'

'He did.'

'Very popular with the staff, and with the customers too, young Sloan tells me. And she's enjoying herself. She needs to get her life sorted out, poor lass. It's cruel to be widowed at such a young age. It's a whole new world now, Rose – young folk know how to forge ahead these days. There's you with your own business, and Alex and Fiona running MacDowall and Son between them . . .' He started to cough, and the nurse immediately appeared by his side and held a glass of water to his lips. He drank a little before pushing the glass away.

'I think you need to rest now, Mr MacDowall.' Nurse Gemmell flashed an accusing look at Rose. 'Talking's not good for my patient. He needs to rest his lungs.'

'I must go in any case. We'll be back tonight –

Alex and I. Get a good sleep just now,' Rose said gently to her father-in-law, then allowed herself to be eased from the room.

# 8

Rose had found a capable local woman to act as housekeeper when she and Alex married and moved into his small flat. The woman had her own key and let herself in after her employers had left in the morning. When they arrived home at night she had gone, leaving the flat clean and neat, the laundry done and the evening meal cooking in the gas oven.

The housekeeper was a good cook, but that evening Alex scarcely ate any of the food she had prepared for them, and barely gave Rose time to enjoy her dinner. She had had a busy and tiring day, and although she was as thin as a rake and, as she pointed out herself, shaped like one as well, she had always had an excellent appetite.

'I want to finish this,' she protested when her husband, who had jumped up from the table and disappeared into the hall, came back with their coats over his arm.

'How can you sit there eating when my father's ill?'

'Starving ourselves isn't going to get him better any faster.' Rose, breaking the rules instilled in her from babyhood by her mother, spoke with her mouth full, realising that the only way she could eat and argue was to do both at the same time. 'In any case, he's in good hands.'

'What? I can't hear a word you're saying, woman!' He had thrown her coat over the back of a chair and was shrugging his arms into his own sleeves.

Rose swallowed hard, risking indigestion. 'I said, he's in good hands.'

'I'd like to make sure of that myself.'

'I made sure for you this morning.' She scooped up another forkful of the delicious beef stew that had been simmering in the oven all afternoon and put it into her mouth, then, as he picked her coat up and held it out for her, she got to her feet, realising that further protest would not get her anywhere. She buttoned the coat and, throwing a silent promise that she would eat them later to the plate of jam sponge and the jug of custard

114

languishing in the kitchen, jammed a hat on top of her mass of brown hair and followed Alex out of the flat.

Nurse Gemmell flatly refused to allow more than one visitor in the bedroom, claiming that her patient was not strong enough to cope with two, let alone three people crowding around him, so Rose and Fiona withdrew to the sitting room, leaving Alex with his father.

'I think,' Fiona said as she poured tea, 'that it's time he retired.'

'Sandy? But he's worked all his life. He would hate to retire.'

'He doesn't need to work now. Alex and I can look after the business between us.'

'Fiona, your father may have made a lot of money, but he's still a son of the working class. Working is what he does.'

'Working–class people work because they have no choice. Sugar?'

'I never touch the stuff.'

'Father doesn't have to work any more. He can retire without any worries about money.'

'That doesn't matter. He's still working class. It's in his blood and his bones. What would he do with himself all day?'

'He could take up fishing.'

'In Glasgow? I don't think there are any fish in the Clyde.'

'He can fish out in the countryside. Or go for nice healthy walks. Or he could take up art — some people do.'

'I can't really see Sandy MacDowall painting a picture of cows grazing in a field.' As Rose had expected, her hurried meal had brought on indigestion, but even so, she was still hungry. She helped herself to a piece of Mrs Dove's shortbread, telling herself that the niggling pain in her stomach was caused by hunger rather than having had to bolt her dinner.

'There are other things that he could do,' Fiona said testily. 'I'm sure he'll think of something.'

'I don't believe that he would agree with you,' Rose was saying when Alex came into the room.

'Who would agree about what?'

'Fiona wants your father to retire.'

'He'd never do that!'

'You've just seen him, Alex. How does he look to you?' Fiona asked, and his shoulders slumped.

'Old. Ill. I've never seen him look so — vulnerable.'

'Exactly. He's not fit to go on running the company.'

'He will be, when he's better. Not for a while, perhaps,' Rose admitted as her sister-in-law threw

116

her a scathing glance, 'but once he's had the chance to convalesce I think he'll be more than ready to get back to his usual life.'

'And I think that we would be wrong to encourage it. If his health collapsed again it would be our fault, and I for one,' Fiona said with a sudden catch in her throat, 'would never forgive myself if that happened. I'd always feel responsible. Wouldn't you, Alex?'

'I doubt if it would happen,' Rose said decisively before her husband got the chance to answer. 'This is the first time he's ever been ill as far as I know. Why should we be so quick to assume that it will happen again?'

'Because he's getting older. He's not as strong or as fit as he used to be.'

'For goodness' sake, Fiona, he's only forty-nine. He has years left yet! My father's five years older than that and he's still going to the office every day.'

'Your father,' Fiona was beginning to sound irritable, 'has had a comfortable life. Mine has had a very hard life. You must remember that he was raised in an orphanage and thrown out of it to make his own living when he was little more than a child. He had a terrible struggle in his early life and it's taking its toll now. Alex, you agree with me, don't you?'

117

'I don't know what to think. He looks so ill,' Alex said again.

'He does, doesn't he? Sit down, Alex, and have some tea.'

He shook his head. 'If you don't mind, I think we should get back home. We both have an early start in the morning,' he said, and Rose, who had been about to take another piece of shortbread, drew her hand back from the plate.

'I don't think that your father should retire,' she said as she drove home. 'He's used to working – he wouldn't know what to do with himself. Retiring would be far worse for him than getting back to work.'

'Fiona might have a point.'

'She doesn't!' Rose said fiercely, tooting the horn at a drunk man who was weaving his way across the road in front of them. He stopped, almost falling over as he turned, his feet tripping over each other, to investigate the source of the sudden noise. Then, seeing the car and the two faces peering at him through the windscreen, he raised his right hand high in the air before sweeping it down again in an elaborate bow.

Rose gurgled with laughter as she gave him a royal wave in return. She waited until he had finally reached the safety of the pavement before

118

driving on, giving him another wave as she passed. 'I love the West of Scotland folk,' she said. 'There are such wonderful characters among them!' Then, returning to the matter in hand, 'Alex, you mustn't let Fiona bully your father into retiring. He's got years of work in him yet. I think that giving up now would kill him faster than keeping on.'

'You weren't quite truthful about your own father back there. He only goes into the office three times a week, if that.'

'I know, and then only to get away from Mamma. And who can blame the poor soul for that? I married you to get away from her,' Rose said blithely, her spirits still lifted by her encounter with the gallant drunk. 'In any case, Fiona was right when she said that my father's had a comfortable life. Men in his position are more than happy to let others earn their money for them while they lead easy lives. But Sandy MacDowall isn't like that and you mustn't let Fiona try to change him, because it won't work.'

'But he looked so frail tonight – seeing him like that frightened me.'

'He looks frail because he's ill. He'll look much better next week, I promise you. But if he's talked into giving up control of the business against his will, he's going to look frail all the time. It will only harm him – and you.'

119

'How can it harm me? Look,' he said as she drew the car in to the kerb outside their flat then turned in her seat, ready to reply, 'let's leave it for now. The only thing I care about at the moment is getting him better. After that . . . we'll wait and see.'

Once in the flat he opted to go to bed. Left on her own, Rose, her indigestion suddenly replaced by hunger, fried the potatoes she and Alex had left on their plates earlier and had them with the cold remains of the stew. Then she ate the jam sponge and custard before stacking the plates on the draining board.

'I'm a human dustbin,' she told the kitchen contentedly as she did so. 'But at least, thank God, I'm not Fiona Chalmers!'

When Rose woke the next morning it was to find herself wondering just what Fiona was up to. The woman stuck in her mind for all the world like an irritating fly buzzing around a lamp, as she drove into Glasgow to order material, then headed for Paisley. She arrived at Harlequin to find Mary and one of the seamstresses hovering in the foyer. They pounced on her as soon as she appeared.

'Miss Lowdon's come in unexpectedly to have some of her wedding trousseau fitted,' Mary announced.

'What do you mean, unexpectedly? Did she not have an appointment?'

'No, it's for tomorrow. But she says that something important has come up for tomorrow, so she decided to come here today instead.'

'That's very inconvenient,' Rose said irritably. It had taken a lot of time and a lot of Caitlin's and Mary's patience, but now most of their clients had learned to keep to arranged appointments. But obviously, not all.

'I know, but the thing is – her mother is with her.'

'Oh.' Mrs Lowdon was married to a very wealthy man, and she seemed to think that money could forgive every trespass there was. 'Can't Caitlin deal with them?'

'She's gone out to do a home fitting.'

'What about Grace? She's in charge of the sewing room – surely she can deal with the Lowdons.'

The seamstress wrung her hands. 'She's gone to the dentist with a terrible toothache. The next appointment is for eleven o'clock and she and Caitlin both said that they would be back by then. None of us bargained for the Lowdons' sudden appearance.'

'The thing is,' Mary broke in, 'Teenie's in there with them, doing the fitting.'

'Teenie?' Rose's voice shot up an octave. 'But Teenie doesn't attend fittings. She's never been trained to do them!'

'I know, but she was coming in to work when they arrived, and apparently she said she'd do it.'

'We couldn't stop her, Mrs MacDowall,' the seamstress said nervously.

'For goodness' sake – make some tea and bring it into the fitting room. The best china, mind!' Rose ordered as she pushed past the two of them.

Elizabeth Lowdon, the bride-to-be, stood in the middle of the floor, draped in a cream silk evening dress. Teenie Stapleton was on her knees, shuffling around the young woman like an attentive worshipper adoring a sacred idol – or a worker bee attending to its queen, Rose thought as she took in the scene. Teenie's head was covered, as always, in a tight woollen turban. Today's model was in dull green wool, and she still had her coat on. Her mouth bristled with pins and she muttered unintelligibly to herself as she worked, her nose almost touching the material.

Elizabeth's mother sat by the window, and the two Lowdons, used to Caitlin and Grace, both always dressed smartly but simply in black skirts and snowy white blouses, stared at Teenie as though they had come across a species of animal that they had never seen before.

'Mrs Lowdon, Miss Lowdon. We expected you tomorrow morning.'

'It . . .' Mrs Lowdon wrenched her eyes away from Teenie, cleared her throat and tried again, her voice a shadow of its usual strong tone, 'Tomorrow wasn't convenient.'

'I see. If you had telephoned, we could have made another appointment. However,' Rose said, some imp of mischief suddenly seizing hold of her, 'I see that our Miss Stapleton is looking after you.'

Just then Teenie spat the pins out into the palm of her hand and twisted her head so that she was peering up at the future bride. Elizabeth Lowdon, suddenly confronted with two hugely magnified grey eyes staring up at her from a small face, shied like a horse at a jump.

'Right ye are, hen,' said Teenie, 'that'll do for this frock.' And then, clambering breathlessly to her feet, 'D'ye want tae get out of it an' we'll have a look at the next yin?'

The door opened and Mary came in bearing a tray.

'I ordered tea,' Rose told Mrs Lowdon, who was watching her daughter being removed from the evening dress by Teenie as though she were a row of peas being shelled from a pod.

'Thanks, pet,' said Teenie. 'Make mine strong, will ye? I'm parched!'

*

'I'm so sorry, Mrs MacDowall,' Grace agonised a few hours later, when she, Mary, Caitlin and Rose met in Rose's office. A widow with three children, she had been in charge of the sewing room from the start. She was pleasant but efficient, and able to get the best out of her staff. She was also very good at coping with clients, no matter how difficult they may be.

'I could mebbe have waited until after work to see the dentist, but I was up all night with the toothache. If I'd realised that Teenie was going to—'

'It's not your fault, Grace,' Mary interceded. 'If those daft women hadn't come breenging in here without an appointment it would never have happened. I'll have to find a way of telling all the clients that they can only be seen at the appointed time.'

'Teenie meant no disrespect,' Caitlin added. 'She was just treating the Lowdons the way she would have treated a customer in Jean's shop. It's a pity they chose to arrive just when you and I were both out, Grace – you could say that it was brave of her to take over when she's never been in our fitting room before.'

'You don't think we're going to lose the Lowdons, do you?' Grace asked anxiously.

'Of course not – we've almost finished

Elizabeth's trousseau and they can't leave us until it's done,' Caitlin assured her.

'They both know, too, that if they leave us now they'll have to pay for the work we've done on it so far,' Mary added, while Rose said, 'Without us, they'd either have to buy their clothes ready-made or go to Glasgow. And they would have to go far in any case to find a designer as good as Caitlin.' She smiled at her sister-in-law, then her smile broadened to a grin. 'Mind you, of all our clients, I'm glad that it was the Lowdons who met up with her. They're such terrible snobs, the two of them, and it was a pleasure to see the look on their faces. It's the first time I've ever seen Mrs Lowdon keep her mouth shut!' Then, returning to the business in hand, 'Talking of Teenie, she's a grand worker, but she's only on loan and I'm sure that Kirsty and Jean are missing her. We're going to have to start looking for a new seam-stress to take her place.'

# 9

Mary, intent on adding up the list of figures on the page before her, didn't even realise that someone had come into her office until a small bundle carefully wrapped in white tissue paper was placed on her desk, a few inches from the ledger before her, but just close enough to be seen from the corner of her eye.

Startled, she looked up. 'Mr Brodie? I didn't expect to see you today. Did I miss something out when I gave you last month's figures?'

'You never miss out so much as a full stop or a pound sign. They're immaculate, as always. I just came in to give these to you.' John Brodie indicated the small object that he had placed on her desk.

She opened it to reveal a bunch of violets, their delicate heads drooping slightly from stems that seemed too slender to support them. Here and there a single drop of water shimmered against the deep purple of a petal. When she bent her head over them she was suddenly aware of their scent, fresh and delicate.

'They're beautiful. But isn't it too early for them?' She glanced up at the window, spattered with rain. Arriving that morning she had had to fight her way against a cold wind, and her umbrella had almost been blown outside in as she'd struggled out of the shelter of the gatehouse and begun to cross the open courtyard.

'My mother likes fresh flowers in the house whatever the season, so we have greenhouses for the purpose. But I grew these myself, in a sheltered corner of the garden.'

'But . . .' Mary was still confused '. . . why are you giving them to me?'

'Because you've been looking sad lately, and I wanted to see you smile again.'

Mary, a self-contained person even in childhood, had never been good at receiving sympathy. Looking up at his kind face she thought for a dreadful moment or two that the tears that had been hovering just behind her eyes ever since Lachie had rejected her were going to overflow.

She stared down at the ledger on her desk and blinked hard until the figures covering the lined pages stopped shimmering and returned to their former pristine condition. Then she said primly, 'Thank you, that's very kind of you.'

'It's my pleasure.' He laid a pin on the desk. 'I brought this so that you could pin them on. Perhaps I could—'

'I can manage, thank you.' Mary went to the mirror, the pin in one hand and the violets in the other. As she pinned the flowers to the lapel of her neat black jacket she could see the two of them reflected in the glass – her, small and neat, plain of face and with her ordinary brown hair swept up into a knot at the top of her head, and John Brodie beyond her left shoulder, standing by the desk, about a head taller than herself. Like Mary, he had the sort of looks that allowed him to merge into a crowd without being noticed, but his clothes, although plain, were clearly of the best material and perfectly tailored, and the watch chain across the front of his waistcoat looked to be of pure gold.

When the flowers were in place Mary allowed the tips of her fingers to caress their soft, cool faces for a moment before turning to smile at him.

'They're very beautiful and you are very kind, Mr Brodie.'

'John,' he said, as he had often said before.

'I'll put them in water when I get home. Are you sure that it's all right to pin them on for now? They look so fragile.'

'Flowers are sturdier than you think. Would you like to see where they were grown – and the greenhouses?'

The question was so unexpected that 'Yes, I would, very much' came out before she had time to replace it with a polite refusal.

John Brodie beamed. 'Next Sunday afternoon? I could collect you at two o'clock,' he said when she nodded, suddenly tongue-tied.

'No – I'll meet you at the gates of Brodie Park. You live by the park, don't you?'

'Yes, my father's house is close to the entrance. Two o'clock on Sunday, then,' he said. 'Well, I had better leave you to your work.'

When he had gone, Mary returned to the ledger, reaching up a hand every now and again to touch the violets.

Only the very rich lived by Brodie Park, at the west end of Paisley. Folk like the Coats, who owned the town's two large thread mills, the Craigs, who ran an engineering business, the Galbraiths, well known for their successful grocery stores and the Robertsons. Mary had worked in Robertson's jam and marmalade factory before joining Harlequin. A thought struck her as she walked up the driveway by John's side on Sunday afternoon.

'Brodie Park isn't named after someone in your family, is it?'

He laughed. 'No, it is not. We're not important enough.'

Mary found that hard to believe. The Brodie family home was as large as a tenement building, but much more beautiful. All these rooms, she thought, for only one family. What a terrible waste!

'When I invited you I thought that my parents would be home, but they're lunching with friends,' John said as they approached the front door. 'So we're on our own, I'm afraid. I hope you don't mind.'

He looked so concerned that Mary had to suppress a smile at the very idea that spending time alone with such a gentleman could sully her reputation.

'Not at all,' she said, and he beamed as he ushered her up the steps into a huge entrance hall.

'I've ordered tea in an hour – I thought you would like to see the garden and the greenhouses first. We'll go out by the flower room,' he added as they crossed the hall and went down a wide carpeted corridor. 'The greenhouses are close by that side of the house.'

At the end of the corridor they went down another three steps on to linoleum, leaving the carpeting behind as they went through a door leading to a small room lined with cupboards and shelves, most of them holding empty vases. The floor was flagged and a large sink sat below the window.

'This is where my mother arranges flowers for the house.' John opened a door leading to a small courtyard. 'The greenhouses are just around the corner.'

Mary was fascinated by the long glassed areas with a central corridor running between slatted shelving filled with plants. The moist, warm air smelled of damp earth and greenery, and as she and John walked together, stopping now and again so that he could introduce her to a particular plant, she found herself speaking in hushed tones, as though trying not to disturb the flowers and vegetables.

John knew the names of every one of them. When they had explored the two long greenhouses he took her outside and showed her the rose garden and the kitchen garden before taking her to a small copse where crocuses, snowdrops and daffodils grew beneath the trees.

'This,' he said, leading her to a small grassy tree-enclosed area, 'is where I grow the violets.' He bent

131

and parted the grass so that she could have a better view of the clusters of delicate purple flowers nestling amid their green leaves. 'I discovered them when I was a boy, and I've been looking after them ever since. You should come here in the spring, when the bluebells are out. But right now,' he added as a light pattering sound was heard on the green canopy above them, 'I do believe that the rain's arrived. Come on, let's go back to the house for some tea.'

John had had the foresight to take an umbrella from the flower room, and he held it carefully over his guest's head as they returned to the house, approaching it across a stretch of smooth green lawn instead of going back the way they had come.

Stone steps led to a crazy-paving terrace and from there they went through french windows to a pleasant sitting room where a uniformed maid was setting tea on a table before a blazing fire.

'Thank you, Eileen,' John said cheerfully, and the girl bobbed a curtsey and shot a swift, all-seeing glance at Mary before leaving the room. John waved his guest to one of two sofas facing each other across the table and then settled himself on the other. 'Would you like to pour the tea?'

The teapot and hot water pot were silver and the cups so delicate that Mary's heart was in her mouth lest she hit the pot against one of them and broke it. It was a relief when the tea was poured and she was able to sit back and enjoy it.

'It must have been wonderful to have a garden like that to play in when you were small.'

'It was. My father instilled a love of gardening in me at an early age when he gave me my own flower and vegetable beds. I still do a lot of work in this garden, though I don't live here any more.'

'You don't? But surely there's plenty of room,' said Mary, raised in a society where grown children tended to leave the family home for one of two reasons: to make more room for the rest of the family or to marry.

'Indeed there is, but I'm a little too old to be living under the parental roof. I have a flat in Neilston Road – not far from the office. I still spend most of my weekends here though, pottering about in the garden or the greenhouse. What do you do in your spare time?'

'Nothing, really. I help my mother around the house, then there's Rowena, my niece – I help her with her homework, or we go for walks. I don't have any special talents – I can't sew nearly as well as Caitlin or my mother.'

'I think you're extremely talented,' John said firmly. 'Auditing the books has been so easy since you took over as Harlequin's bookkeeper, and I

133

know that Rose is impressed by the way you've managed to get some of the more difficult clients to pay their bills. She said that it was like getting blood from stones.'

'It was probably more difficult for her, since so many of them were her mother's friends, or had been her own playmates when she was growing up,' Mary was saying when the door opened and a woman's voice said, 'Here you are!'

'Hello, Mother.' John got to his feet. 'Come in and meet my guest. This is Mary Lennox,' he went on as Mary hurriedly but carefully put down her cup and saucer and struggled out of the depths of the soft couch. 'Mary, I would like to introduce you to my parents.'

Mrs Lennox was not a large lady, but the long plume trailing in her wake from the top of her hat, together with the flying ends of a long lacy scarf looped several times round her throat, gave her the look of a ship in full sail as she bore down on Mary, an extended kid-gloved hand cleaving the air before her as a figurehead would part the waves.

'How do you do, my dear?' Her booming, confident voice filled the room. 'I'm sorry I wasn't here to greet you when you arrived. I do hope that my son has been looking after you.'

'Adequately, Mother,' John said calmly. 'We've

toured the garden and now we're enjoying a very nice tea. I'll ring for a fresh pot and more cups.'

'I've already seen to it.' Mrs Brodie sat on the sofa her son had just left, while her husband, a quiet, grey-haired man who bore a strong resemblance to his son, shook hands with Mary. The maid brought in a second tea tray and when they had settled themselves down again, John now sitting beside Mary with his parents opposite, Mrs Brodie began to find out all she could about her son's guest.

When she discovered that Mary lived in Espedair Street the woman raised her carefully plucked eyebrows. 'And where would that be?' she asked.

'Not far from here, Mother,' John told her. 'Mary is the bookkeeper at Harlequin, Rose MacDowall's fashion house.'

'Oh, I see.' Mrs Brodie raised her eyebrows again, and Mary reminded herself that since John's mother was a client, Caitlin had almost certainly seen her in her underwear, while nobody, apart from her mother and sister, had ever seen Mary unclothed.

'Rose has done very well, hasn't she? I have some very nice gowns made by Harlequin.'

'And it was Mary's sister Caitlin who designed them,' John said proudly. 'Mary's interested in flowers, so I invited her here today to see the gardens.'

'Ah!' Now that she knew that her unexpected visitor wasn't harbouring hopes of marrying her precious son, Mrs Brodie relaxed, and the rest of the visit passed in light conversation.

In an attempt to keep the violets alive as long as possible Mary had put them in a small sugar bowl in her room, but when she went upstairs that night she saw that their heads were drooping even lower on their slender stems, and the petals had begun to soften and wrinkle with age.

She lifted them from the water and dried the wet stems carefully with blotting paper, then she put two fresh sheets of blotting paper into a book and lifted the tiny flowers to her nose to inhale their faint scent one more time before carefully arranging each blossom on one sheet and covering them with the second sheet. Then she closed the book carefully and put it away.

Rowena and Cavan McCart had got into the habit of meeting each other after school. On most days they went to the Harlequin gatehouse where, if Murdo had time, he would play the mouth organ so that Cavan could teach Rowena the intricacies of Irish dancing and Rowena could reciprocate by teaching the Irish girl some Scottish dances.

If Murdo was too busy to play for them the girls practised their dance steps outside or, if the weather was inclement, they sat in a corner of the weaving room doing their homework together to the steady clack of the loom. When the fashion house closed for the day Caitlin and Mary came to the gatehouse to collect them, walking back to Espedair Street by a longer route so that they could drop Cavan off at her own home.

Caitlin and Mary soon noticed that once they reached the street where she lived, Cavan showed signs of being anxious to get away on her own. With a swift 'Bye, see you tomorrow' she would dart ahead and disappear up one of the closes like a rabbit fleeing into its burrow ahead of a predator.

On one occasion, when Caitlin opted to stay behind with Murdo and the girls were with Mary, Rowena peered into the dark maw of the close that had just swallowed Cavan up. 'It's very dark, isn't it? And . . .' she drew in her breath in a long sniff '. . . it doesn't smell very nice.'

'It's a slu— It's a very old building,' Mary said. 'A hundred years old at least, and hundreds of folk have lived in it.'

'I wouldn't want to live there.'

'Mebbe Cavan's folk can't afford anything better.

Mebbe they weren't able to bring much money over from Ireland when they came here.'

'She said that they lived in a cottage before they came here. It had a garden where her mother grew potatoes and carrots and onions for them to eat. It can't be nice to live in a place like this after being in a cottage with a garden. I hope,' Rowena said, 'that Granddad pays her father a lot of money. Then he can save it up and use it to move into somewhere nicer.'

'They probably need a lot of money, poor souls,' Mary agreed.

Sometimes Cavan came to Espedair Street after school, and the girls, breathlessly humming a tune or clapping a rhythm for each other, danced on Rowena's dancing stone in the middle of the drying green in the backyard. If the wind was cold or if it was raining, they played in the wash house with Rowena's dolls, but whenever they could, they practised on the dancing stone.

'It's a right bonny way of dancing, that Irish way,' Kirsty said to Todd one evening. 'I watch from the kitchen window when they're too busy to notice me. They make a bonny pair, spinnin' round like a wheel, each with a hand on the other one's shoulder, or with both hands joined, and Rowena's chestnut hair and Cavan's black hair swingin' out as they go.'

'Aye, it's nice that the lassie's got a proper friend

at last. But just wait until they fall out — it'll be floods of tears. I've seen it happen with my sister when we were weans. Lassies are aye fallin' out wi' each other an' makin' up again.'

'Not these two,' his wife said firmly. 'They're mebbe from different countries, but they're like two peas in a pod. They'll never fall out.'

When she was at Espedair Street Cavan was allowed to wait until her father finished work so that they could go home together. Although she loved the sound of Murdo's loom, and found it easier to dance to the Highlander's music, Cavan liked going to Espedair Street best, because Rowena's gran was so kind and welcoming. The two girls were greeted with mugs of milk and a home-made scone or pancake, still warm from the oven and waiting to be eaten with a good spread of melting butter. Sometimes they had a rock cake, crunchy on the outside but soft on the inside, studded with juicy currants. And later, before Cavan's father arrived to fetch her, there would be bowls of home-made soup with a large floury boiled potato set in the middle like an island in a delicious thick sea.

Rowena's gran was so unlike the grumpy, difficult ould yin at home that Cavan found herself thinking of them as the good fairy and the bad fairy, like a story from one of her precious books.

139

For her part, Kirsty found herself growing fond of the pretty Irish girl who had such good manners, and who kept thanking her for even the smallest kindness in her lovely soft Irish voice and with her sparkling smile.

Although she found her husband's new cabinet-maker quiet to the point of surliness, any thoughts she may have had as to the man's real character were dismissed when she saw him with Cavan. On her first visit to Espedair Street she and Rowena were in the backyard when Joseph McCart emerged from the workshop, his shoulders hunched against the world and his peaked cap pulled as low over his eyes as it would go.

As soon as she saw him Cavan shouted 'Dadda!' and ran to throw her arms around his waist and nuzzle her face into a coat so threadbare that it must have done little to keep out the bitter March winds blowing from snow-topped hills. The man tousled her dark hair, his mouth, which was all that Kirsty, at the kitchen window, could see of his face, breaking into a wide smile. Releasing him, Cavan seized his hand and pulled him over to where Rowena stood on her dancing stone. The two girls seemed to be speaking at the same time, jiggling about with excitement, before Rowena stepped aside and Cavan took her place on the flagstone. While Rowena clapped a rhythm,

Cavan executed a few steps, toes pointing perfectly, one hand at her waist while the other arched above her head. When she stopped her father beamed again, then shook Rowena solemnly by the hand before putting an arm around his daughter's shoulders and leading her to the pend.

'Mr McCart says that I'm a grand wee teacher,' Rowena said proudly when she came into the kitchen. 'He's a nice man!'

'I'm glad of that,' Kirsty said, and meant it.

When she told Todd about the scene later he said, 'Why should you be surprised at the man havin' a fondness for his own wee lassie?'

'He's such a dark-looking creature, with never a word to say for himself, and Rowena's never been invited to their house, so I just wondered if mebbe he wasn't a nice person.'

'Away with ye, woman,' her husband said affectionately. 'He's quiet, that's all, and he cannae help his looks. Speakin' for myself, I'm pleased that he's a quiet worker, and a good one. I couldnae be bothered with someone that worked his tongue harder than his hands.'

'That coat of his is awful thin, is it not? And Caitlin says that the mother seems to wear hand-me-downs. They must be awful poor.'

'Mebbe they had to spend all the silver they had on the fare to Scotland. That's happened to a lot of the Irish, poor souls. But some of them end up doin' very well for themselves, and I see no reason why Joseph McCart shouldnae be one of them, given time.'

'There's an old grandmother too, from what Cavan says. Caitlin told the mother about Jean's shop, but as far as I know, she's not come in yet. We've got some good things – there's a coat I know of that's definitely warmer than the one Mr McCart was wearing today. Mind you, Cavan always seems to be dressed warmly. Mebbe they're doing without so that she'll be all right. D'you think they'd take it amiss if I went to the house to ask the woman to come to the shop?'

'I'd tell ye tae leave it tae her tae come tae you, but I know ye'd not pay a bit of heed,' Todd said easily, reaching for his newspaper. 'So you do what ye think best, lass.'

# 10

March, which had come in like a lamb, bringing with it the promise of spring, went out like a lion. A late snowfall blanketed Paisley, causing problems for the elderly as they inched their way along the pavements, but delighting the children who rushed to the nearest slopes with sledges, trays, planks of wood and anything else that they could lay their hands on.

The temperature lifted slightly the next day, turning the snow to a grey slush churned up by horses' hoofs and cart and van wheels. Washing dishes at the sink that morning Kirsty happened to see Joseph McCart arriving for work, splashing his way through the thick slush, the collar of his shabby coat turned up to shelter the back of his neck. As she watched, he took his bare hands from his pockets and blew into them in an attempt to warm them.

When her housework was done she put some home-made girdle scones into a bag and set off for the old tenement building where, she knew from Mary, the McCarts lived. Once, many years ago, it had been a sturdy, handsome building, looked after by the folk that lived in it, but the passing years, coupled with uninterested factors, had gradually reduced it to a slum inhabited by folk too poor to pay more than a few pence in rent every week.

Kirsty's nose wrinkled as she ventured into the miasma of smells that had soaked into the damp stone walls over time, and she had to screw up her eyes as she went from grey daylight into the cellar-like close. She was still trying to get used to the dim light filtering down from the grimy window at the top of the first flight of stairs when she stubbed her toe on the first step.

The treads were worn in the middle and the single banister moved slightly beneath her fingers as she climbed cautiously. As was usual in Scottish tenements, the window and the shared water closet were on a half-landing, with another flight of stairs to climb before she reached the next floor. She peered at the three doors, but none of them boasted a nameplate, or even a scrap of paper nailed to the doorframe with the occupants' surname scrawled on it in pencil, so she had to knock on the first door.

It opened so swiftly that she took an involuntary step back, certain that the tall thin man facing her had been crouched behind the door, listening to her fumbling steps coming up the stairs.

'Aye?'

'I'm . . . I'm looking for Mrs McCart.'

He leaned forwards, his top half approaching her while the rest of him stayed firmly inside. She took another step back, wishing she had tried another door. For a long moment he stared suspiciously at her, then he snapped 'The Irish lot – ower there.'

'Thank you.' Kirsty went to the opposite door and lifted her hand to knock on the wooden panels. Then she hesitated, realising that she had not heard the first door closing. She turned to see the man still watching her, the whites of his eyes gleaming and his mouth half open. Since he showed no sign of retreating, she turned away from him and knocked.

Several minutes passed before a soft, uncertain voice asked from behind the door, 'Who is it?'

Kirsty put her lips as close as she dared to the stained wood. 'Kirsty Paget – your Cavan plays with my granddaughter, Rowena.'

In the pause that followed, she glanced round and saw that the door across the landing was closed, though not quite shut. She could sense the man pressed to the gap, his ears and eyes alert. Then she turned back to the McCarts' door as it began to open.

'Mrs Paget, did you say?'

'Caitlin's mother. You've met her at the ceilidhs. You're Mrs McCart?'

'Aye.' The girl at the door didn't look much older than Cavan. She had the same striking looks, and a fall of dark hair swept across one eye.

'I came to speak to you about the wee clothes shop I work in. Caitlin says that she mentioned it to you. You're a seamstress, she says.'

'Aye, a bit.'

'Can I come in?' Kirsty asked, made bold by the knowledge of the man listening and spying across the landing.

'I-I suppose so.' The door opened just wide enough to allow her into a tiny dark hall that scarcely had room for the two of them.

'Shelagh, who is it?' a harsh voice wanted to know.

'A visitor.'

'What are ye talkin' about, ye silly girl. A visitor, indeed! Who is it that's come to our door?'

'You'd best come through.' Shelagh McCart led the way into a kitchen, small, and furnished with little more than a wooden table, four wooden chairs and a dresser. An armchair stood by the range, filled, Kirsty thought at first sight, by a pile of discarded clothing. Then the mass stirred and a white head that looked for all the world like a badly knitted cover for a teapot lifted to reveal a pear-shaped face. The eyes, sunk into fat, were heavy-lidded, and the nose must once have been imperious. Now it was more of a beak than a nose. The lower half of the woman's face seemed to balloon into round cheeks that almost overhung a small down-turned mouth and the chins beneath it.

'And who might you be?'

'This is—'

'I asked her, not you!'

'I'm Mrs Paget. Joseph McCart works for my husband, and Cavan's friendly with my grand-daughter Rowena. You'll be Mr McCart's mother?' Kirsty said pleasantly.

'What d'ye want?'

'I was just saying to your daughter-in-law that I work in a wee second-hand clothes shop in Causeyside Street. We often get good clothes in from folk with plenty of money and we've got some very nice warm garments in at the moment. If you would like to come and have a look round,' Kirsty added to the younger Mrs McCart, who was looking as though she would like to sink through the linoleum-covered floor, 'you might find something that would suit yourself and your husband. We don't charge much and—'

'Get out of here and take yer impertinence with ye!' the older woman ordered.

'Mrs Paget's just tryin' to help—'

'Interfere, more like. Nosyin'! The McCarts don't need help from the likes of youse. Out of here, I tell ye, before I drive ye out!' The woman's voice rose to a shriek and a red swollen hand clutching a stick suddenly appeared from her many wrappings. 'Out!' she repeated, struggling to get to her feet.

'Wheesht now!' the younger woman pleaded, wringing her hands.

'I'm going,' Kirsty said and dropping the bag of scones on the table, she fled. As she gained the top of the stairs Shelagh said from the doorway, 'I'm sorry, Mrs Paget, I know ye mean well, but the ould yin's not used to strangers.'

'It's all right. But come to the shop some time. You'd be welcome,' Kirsty said. Then as a screech came from the room behind the girl's back, she went down the stairs as quickly as she could.

Too embarrassed to admit that she had gone against his advice and been soundly punished for it, Kirsty decided not to tell Todd about her visit to the McCarts' flat. Every time she thought of it she cringed inwardly over the humiliation she felt.

She was just beginning to push it out of her mind when, a few days later, Shelagh McCart crept into the second-hand clothes shop, hiding behind the fall of thick black hair that covered part of her face and peering nervously at the racks of clothing with her one visible dark eye. When Kirsty spoke to her the young woman spun round nervously, putting a quick hand up to her face.

'I'm Kirsty Paget – I came to your house the other day.'

'Yes. I'm sorry, Mrs Paget,' the girl said in her soft Irish accent. 'The ould yin – my husband's mother – wasn't feeling well. She didn't mean to be so discourteous to you.'

'It was my fault. I should mebbe have asked your husband about the best time to call instead of just—'

'No!' the young woman said sharply, and then, as Kirsty blinked at her, 'I mean – Joseph worries about us being a nuisance to folk and he's not very good with strangers. I-I didn't tell him you'd come to the house.'

Her visible eye met Kirsty's and held it, pleading silently for understanding. When Kirsty said, 'I know what you mean. Scotsmen are terrible for dealing with visitors too, so I never said a word to your husband or mine about my visit.' Shelagh gave a faint sigh of relief and her solemn face broke into a smile that suddenly banished the shyness and gave her features such radiant beauty that Kirsty was taken aback for the second time.

'So you decided to come in to see our wee shop? It's Jean's really – Jean Chisholm. We were at school together and when I came back to Paisley I started helping her. We run it between us now. Jean's out at the moment, but you'll have met our Aggie?'

'Aggie?' Shelagh cast an alarmed glance around the crowded interior as though expecting someone else to jump up from behind the counter, or peek round the side of a clothes rack.

'The tailor's dummy chained to the wall outside. We have to keep her chained because the local laddies would like fine to whisk her away for devilment, wee scamps that they are.'

'Oh.' A faint smile crossed the younger woman's face. Then she said, 'You mentioned warm clothes – my husband could do with a jacket.'

'Or a coat, mebbe? We've got a nice coat in that might fit him.' Kirsty hurried to the rack to find it. 'It's scarce been worn.'

Shelagh felt the thick cloth and then asked

150

doubtfully, 'How much would ye be askin' for it?'

'A shilling.'

'It's worth more, surely?'

'The folks that come in here can't afford much, so we keep our prices low.'

'I'll take it.' Shelagh brought out a shabby purse and paid swiftly, as though anxious to get the coat before anyone else claimed it. As she stuffed it into her large shopping bag, Kirsty saw the girl glance around the shop.

'No need to hurry away – I'll leave you to have a look at what we've got,' she offered, and Shelagh rewarded her with another smile. 'Just let me know if you need any help or want to buy anything else.'

Kirsty retreated to the back room, where she was taking in a skirt for a customer and started pinning the new seam, listening for the bell that would signal the arrival of another customer – or Shelagh McCart's departure. For a good ten minutes all she could hear was Shelagh's light footsteps as she moved around, or the occasional rustle of clothes being examined. Then a tentative cough took her back through to the main shop.

'I was looking for something in a good strong material,' Shelagh said when Kirsty appeared. 'It's for my daughter Cavan – the dress she wears for

151

dancing's getting too small for her. I need a material that'll hang well for the dancing.'

'We've just got in a bag of clothing from one of the big houses – the ladies there never wear the same dress twice and we depend on them for quite a lot of our stock. There's a ball gown that might do you. Come on through,' Kirsty invited, and the young woman came round the counter to follow her into the back shop.

'Here it is – I was just looking at it this morning.' Kirsty pulled out the ball gown and shook it out. 'It's got a lace overdress, but if I pull that aside you'll see that the main dress is in a good silk-satin. Strong, but not too heavy. The colour would be just right for your Cavan, too.' She lifted out both arms so that the dress spread over them, its peacock-blue colour shimmering in the light from the window.

Shelagh's eye widened and a soft gasp escaped her parted lips. 'It's perfect, so it is!' A slim, work-reddened hand stroked the material reverently before plucking at it to open out the skirt. 'There's easily enough material to do a dress and mebbe a nice wee waistcoat and skirt to go with her white blouse.'

'There is. You can just see her in a dress made of this material. She's a bonny wee dancer, Cavan, and a nice lassie too. Our Rowena's delighted to have her as a friend.'

152

Shelagh ducked her head in shy acknowledge-
ment of the praise, then chewed at her full lower
lip before asking, 'How much would you be
wanting for this dress?'

Kirsty had already taken in the younger woman's
shabby, expertly darned clothing and the bag,
clearly with its best days having been given to
many previous owners, over the girl's thin wrist.
'A shilling.'

'It's never just a shilling! It must have cost
pounds and pounds when it was new!'

'It would indeed, but it's been worn since then,
and most of our customers are like you – they're
looking for something they can cut down and turn
into something else. Who but the very rich would
have need of a dress like this? A shilling's a fair
price, especially if you come back here to buy any
braid or ribbon or buttons you might want to go
with Cavan's new dress – or even something for
yourself, or your man, or his mother,' Kirsty coaxed.

Shelagh gazed hungrily at the beautiful
material. Already, Kirsty knew, she was seeing her
daughter dancing in her new frock, spinning and
leaping in a shimmer of peacock blue. 'Well, if
you're sure,' she said at last, and dug into the depths
of her bag to produce the thin purse, as well worn
as the bag itself.

'D'you want me to make it for you?'

'No, no – I used to be a seamstress back in – back home.'

'Do you have a sewing machine?'

'I can manage fine with my needle.'

'Come in here for a minute.' Kirsty led the way into the next room, which held two sewing machines and a kitchen table used for cutting and measuring. 'When I first started working with Jean we only had the one wee shop, but then she bought over the shop next door so that we could have more room to store the stock, and have this wee sewing room as well. You can have the use of one of the machines if you like – and this is a fine big table for measuring and pinning.'

'I couldn't!'

'Aye, ye could. The woman that uses that machine's helping out at Harlequin, down by the river. Jean wouldnae mind you using the machine – they're best kept busy to stop them seizing up,' Kirsty told her.

She could see the young woman's mind working as she gazed first at the sewing machine and then at the table. It would be much more pleasant to work here, and she would be away from the lash of the old woman's tongue as well.

'If you're sure,' Shelagh said at last, and it was decided.

When the Irishwoman had gone, Kirsty dipped

into her own purse and added a shilling to the coin already in the till. She could afford the price Jean would expect better than Shelagh McCart, with her darned clothes and shabby bag. Cavan deserved the best – and while she was using the sewing machine Shelagh could always earn any extra trimmings she might need by doing a bit of sewing for the shop. Kirsty had heard from Caitlin about the superb job the woman had done on the dress Cavan wore to the ceilidhs.

Alex, working on the suite of bedroom furniture he had designed for Caitlin and Murdo, was astonished when his father arrived in the workshop, accompanied by Fiona.

'I thought you were still at home.'

'That's where she would like me to be,' Sandy grumbled, though he was smiling, and the look he threw his daughter was affectionate. 'She's like a mother hen with her fuss fuss fuss.'

'Someone needs to worry about you,' Fiona protested. 'I tried to tell him that we're looking after his business very well between us, Alex, but he just wouldn't listen to me.'

'I believe you – and haven't I already said that you and young Sloan are making a grand job of the store between you? But I like to see things for myself.' Sandy, thinner than before, and still pale after his illness, was making use of a silver-topped cane today, Alex noticed. He leaned his weight on it as he walked slowly round the pieces of furniture, studying the craftsmanship and also the design Alex was painting on one of the dressing-table drawers.

'That's bonny. I didnae know that you were decorating furniture again.'

'I was asked to do it a month or so back when a customer ordered a cabinet, and then Rose suggested we should order some bedroom furniture from MacDowall's and I should paint it as my sister Caitlin's wedding gift.'

'Oh yes, Caitlin's marrying that weaver, isn't she?' Fiona wrinkled her forehead to indicate that she was thinking hard. 'The one from the Highlands.'

'His name's Murdo Guthrie.'

'When's the wedding? We must send them a gift, too.'

'They've not set a date yet, but it'll be as soon as Murdo's got the Harlequin gatehouse ready for them to live in,' Alex said shortly.

This time, Fiona's carefully plucked eyebrows shot up. 'But how is the poor man going to manage that now that you've insisted in contracting him to weave for us as well as for Rose and Caitlin?'

'He'll manage fine.'

'Perhaps this wasn't the best time to take him on after all, Alex.'

Help arrived from Sandy, who broke in with, 'I'm glad you did persuade him to come back to us, Alex. We've got customers who like to know that everything they buy is original, including the upholstery, and they're usually the ones with the most money to spend. I like this work, Alex — you should do more of it.'

'Perhaps you should concentrate on it,' Fiona suggested. 'I can — we can easily find a supervisor to run this factory, then you'd be free to concentrate on your painting.'

'I can manage both easily enough, Fiona.'

'There was a notice in the post today,' Sandy said thoughtfully, 'about a furniture exhibition in Edinburgh in the middle of May. Mebbe you should go there, Alex, to advertise our furniture department. Take some samples of your decorations as well.'

'If you think it would be of use.'

'I'm sure it would. It's time we were reaching out to folk further than the Glasgow area. You'll agree to it?' Sandy asked, and went on when his son nodded, 'Then I'll send a reply when I get back to the office. Now I'm off to have a look at the factory itself. No, no, you stay here. I want to see what's going on without giving them any warning that I'm here.'

157

'I can promise you that they'll all be working, the same as always,' Alex called after him as he stumped off through the door leading to the large furniture workshop. He was about to follow his father when Fiona said quietly, 'I was just thinking . . .'

'Thinking what?' Alex asked suspiciously.

She ran her finger across the back of a chair, tracing the outline of the nosegay of flowers and leaves painted on it. 'That first time we met. Do you remember, Alex?'

'I remember.'

'That was at a furniture exhibition, here in Glasgow. I quite fell in love with your work and I ordered some painted furniture from you. I can still see the pleasure in your eyes at getting such a good order. And I can still remember how pleased I was to be able to make you look so happy. We were both younger – too young to have more sense. And of course, we didn't know then that we were—'

'Fortunately, it all worked out for the best,' Alex said abruptly, gathering his brushes together and putting them into a jar of turpentine.

'Did it? I sometimes wish that we had never found out that we shared the same father. Do you ever wish that, Alex?'

'No.'

Fiona came to him, putting a slender, gloved hand on his arm and looking into his face with wide, gold-flecked brown eyes. 'Are you sure?'

Once, being so close to her had made his knees go weak and his heart start to hammer in his chest. Now, it just made him feel deeply uncomfortable.

'I'm quite sure,' he said and, pulling away from her, he followed their father into the factory proper.

## 11

'What damned cheek!' Rose stormed when Alex told her about his conversation with Fiona. 'First she tries to push your father into retirement, then she has the impertinence to suggest that you should concentrate on decorating furniture and let someone else run the factory. And you can be sure that she'd lose no time in charming the factory manager just as she's done with Martin Sloan in the store. How dare she?'

'You know Fiona – she likes to meddle, but it doesn't mean much. How could it? Father's back in his office and I have every intention of remaining in charge of the factory.'

'Why do you have to be so tolerant? I know that the two of you were quite close before you discovered that you shared the same father – have you still got a soft spot for her?'

'Of course not! All that business was over long ago.'

'Alex, what would have happened if you hadn't discovered that Fiona was your half-sister?' Rose's voice was suddenly subdued.

He looked over at her, startled. 'What's the sense in asking me that? I'm very happily married, and grateful that it's to you and not to anyone else. And that's an end of it.'

'I just wondered if that was an end of it as far as Fiona's concerned.'

'Of course it is. She married George Chalmers before I married you. If he was still alive she would be living quite happily in Fort William now.'

'I wish he was alive.'

'So do I, every day. Surely that answers your question?' Alex said, and put an end to the discussion by opening his newspaper. Rose, who had learned at an early age from her mother that one should never try to come between a man and his daily newspaper, opened a book and looked at it without actually seeing a word on the pages before her.

She had a strong feeling that even although Alex and his father had formed a firm bond in the five years since they'd found each other, Fiona still saw her half-brother as an interloper, and was determined to force him out of Sandy MacDowall's life if it was at all possible. Rose, on the other hand, was equally determined that she would not succeed.

Fiona, she thought idly, turning a page in order to seem to be intent on her book, resented the words 'MacDowall and Son' over the handsome three-storey store in Glasgow, and over the furniture factory as well. Not that 'MacDowall and Daughter' would look right. In a way, Rose could sympathise with Fiona, for she too felt that it was unfair that male children were looked upon as natural heirs, even though they might be dullards compared to their less privileged sisters. Marie Stopes' book *Married Love* had pride of place in the bookcase standing against the living-room wall, and Rose agreed whole-heartedly with Stopes' view that 'Far too often marriage puts an end to women's intellectual life', and 'Marriage can never reach its full stature until women possess as much intellectual freedom and freedom of opportunity within it as do their partners'.

The first time Rose's parents had spotted the book on a visit to their youngest daughter and her new husband they had been struck dumb with embarrassment – even more so when Alex assured them that he had read the book himself and fully

162

agreed with its theme. Rose thanked the fates that she had managed to find such a sensible, intelligent husband, rather than the mindless idiots that her equally mindless sisters had found for themselves.

It was then that the idea came to her. Latecomer though he might be, there was one way in which Alex could cement his claim as his father's heir – a way that Fiona, at the moment, could not use. But it would involve Rose, and it would also require her to make a considerable sacrifice.

She turned another page and glanced up at her husband. He was intent on his newspaper and all she could see of him was his red hair and red-gold eyebrows. As though aware of her gaze, he lowered the paper slightly and looked up, smiling at her. 'This is my favourite time,' he said, 'just the two of us alone together.'

'Mine too,' Rose said, knowing that she would do anything, no matter what it was, for Alex.

In bed that night she waited until she could tell by his slow, deep breathing that he was asleep before turning to him and sliding an arm around his chest. He roused enough to turn to her, as she knew he would, and she kissed him slowly and deeply, drawing him close.

'All right?' he mumbled drowsily.

'Yes,' she said against his shoulder, crossing her

163

fingers. When at last they parted he slid back into sleep at once, while Rose lay awake by his side for a while, hoping that her plan had succeeded.

The dress that Shelagh McCart made for her daughter was exquisite – there was no other word for it. She had come to the shop every day and worked hard at the spare sewing machine, scarcely saying a word to anyone other than a shy 'Good morning' when she arrived, 'Goodbye, and thank you for your kindness' as she left, and accepting the offered cups of tea with pink-cheeked gratitude.

'It's the bonniest thing I ever saw.' Jean reached out a hand to the dress, drawing it back at the last moment as though the material was too precious to touch. 'Bonnier than the dress it came from.'

'I'd not say that.' Shelagh blushed with pleasure and stared down at her feet.

'I would,' Kirsty said firmly. 'You did it so quickly, too.'

'I'm used to it. Cavan's been dancing almost as long as she's been walking, and I've been making dresses for her competitions for years now.'

'She's a competition dancer?'

'Not just now, but she did well back home in – in Ireland. This dress wouldn't do for the competitions, though. A competition dress would have to be made of very fine wool in emerald green. And the collar,' Shelagh said, her voice soft with memories, 'would be crocheted in fine cotton, with a pattern showing the stage the dancer has reached.' She was silent for a moment, a silence that Jean and Kirsty shared reverently without knowing why. Then coming out of her reverie the young Irishwoman finished briskly, 'But this frock's just grand for the ceilidhs. I'm grateful to both of you.'

'And we're grateful to you for the bits of work you did for us,' Kirsty told her.

'It was a pleasure to use such a good sewing machine.' The young woman began to fold the dress up, but Jean stopped her.

'D'ye think . . . Could your wee lass not come here to try the frock on? I'd like fine tae see her wearin' it.'

Shelagh blushed again. 'I could get her to come here from school tomorrow,' she suggested, then hung the dress up carefully before going home.

'D'you think that she'd consider doing more work for us, even if it was just until we get Teenie back?' Jean said when the two friends were alone.

'We could always ask. We'd pay her, of course.'

'Of course,' Jean agreed. 'I'm missin' Teenie, and that sewin' machine looks lonely without her. When d'ye think we'll get her back?'

Kirsty was good at keeping her own counsel, and not for the world would she have told Jean about the occasion, told to her by Caitlin in confidence, when Teenie had taken over the fitting room and reduced two of Harlequin's most important clients to stunned silence.

'Caitlin says that they're looking for someone for their sewing room but they've not found the right person yet. Mebbe I should ask her to look in tomorrow to see wee Cavan trying on her new dress,' she said, struck by a sudden thought. 'Mebbe she'd think of taking Shelagh on at Harlequin, so that Teenie could come back here.'

Cavan's shining black hair swung around her flushed face and the peacock-blue silk-satin flared about her long slim legs as she pirouetted before her admiring audience on the following afternoon. She danced a few steps, then spun round again before dropping into a curtsey. She rose gracefully and then, suddenly made shy by the spontaneous burst of applause, ran to her mother's side.

'Is that no' bonny dancin'?' Jean enthused. 'Is that the way they do it in Ireland?'

Shelagh, as flushed with excitement and as shy as her daughter, nodded, while Rowena said proudly, 'Cavan's good at it. She's won cups, but she couldn't bring them over here when she came because there wasn't room for them in her bag.'

'Can I see the frock?' Caitlin reached out a tentative hand, and Cavan, urged forward by her mother, moved within reach.

'Grandma, can I have a pretty dress like that?' Rowena whispered so loudly into Kirsty's ear that she winced.

'That's a special one for Cavan, pet, so that she can do her Irish dancing. You've got your tartan skirt for your Scottish dancing.'

'I'll be making a waistcoat and skirt from the same material for Cavan – there's enough material to do the same for Rowena as well – if you'd like one,' Shelagh added almost timidly.

'Oh yes! Then we'd be dressed like sisters!' Rowena clapped her hands, then asked, 'When can you start? Will I come to your house to have it made?'

'It can be done right here,' Kirsty said swiftly as Shelagh hesitated, biting her lip. 'We've got sewing machines, and room for Mrs McCart to work.'

'Are you sure?' Shelagh asked, and when Jean nodded vigorously, she told the two girls, 'Come here after school tomorrow and I'll measure you both.'

Caitlin had said very little, but her mother could tell by the look on her face that she was thinking hard. She watched as Cavan changed back into her usual day clothes and Shelagh carefully folded the new dress and put it into her shopping bag, then said, 'I'll walk a bit of the way with you.'

'Me too,' Rowena added, and the four of them set off, the girls skipping ahead while Caitlin and Shelagh followed.

At first Caitlin, terrified that if she tried to land her catch too soon she might lose it, asked about the making of the dress, and Shelagh, comfortable with a subject she knew well, began to relax and answer her questions, explaining that the dress should have been made from fine wool, with a collar of white needle-point lace in a design that told of the standard the wearer had reached.

'And rich folk have special handmade shoes that can click out the beat, but folk like us have to make do with what we can get. Cavan has pumps for the light dances, but her hard shoes are too wee for her now. She never complains, though. I sometimes think,' Shelagh said, her eyes bright with pride in her daughter, 'that if she had to wear red-hot shoes like that wicked stepmother in the fairy story she'd do it with never a complaint, for she's so desperate about the dancing that nothing else matters.'

'Is she in for any competitions just now?'

A shadow crossed Shelagh's face. 'No, no – we'd probably have to take her to a big city like Glasgow to find Irish dance competitions, and she'd have to have the right dresses and shoes for them anyway. For now, she's just enjoying the wee ceilidhs and I'm trying to teach her what I can. I won some competitions in my own girlhood, so I know something about it, though not much.'

'We've got a whole room full of materials at Harlequin,' Caitlin said carefully. 'There might be something there to make the right sort of dress for Cavan.'

When there was no reply she dared a sidelong glance at her companion, peering round the barrier of black hair, and noticed with a sinking sensation that Shelagh's mouth had tightened.

'I couldn't afford that. Your mother's been very kind and Cavan's got all she needs now, thanks to her.'

'I wasn't thinking about you buying from us. I was going to suggest that you could earn it, and mebbe make enough money to buy proper dancing shoes for Cavan. I was wondering,' said Caitlin, taking the plunge, 'if you would be willing to come and work for us, in our sewing room.'

'Oh no, I couldn't do that.' Shelagh quickened her step, catching up with the girls and almost tramping on her daughter's heels in her agitation. Cavan and Rowena looked round at her, surprised, then began to move faster.

'Your work on that dress was perfect. We badly need another seamstress. You would be helping us out.'

'I've got the ould yin – his mother – to care for. I can't be away from the house for too long.'

'Even half a day at first, to see how you feel about it, would help. It would make such a difference to us,' Caitlin urged. They had almost reached her mother's house, and the girls stopped, then came trotting back.

'Ma, can I not go and play with Rowena for a wee while?' Cavan beseeched, gazing up into her mother's face. 'We'll do our homework together first, won't we?'

Rowena nodded vigorously. 'Please?'

'If you've got five minutes to spare you could come in for a cup of tea, then we can make sure they get settled at the table with their school books,' Caitlin suggested, and after a long, indecisive moment Shelagh allowed herself to be led into the house and be seated by the kitchen stove.

'No!' Bernadette McCart thumped her cane vigorously on the floor and almost at once a shout of protest could be heard from below.

'Mother, how often do we have tae tell ye not tae do that?' Joseph said in despair. 'Ye'll be gettin' the four of us thrown out of this place wid yer

170

bangin' on other folk's ceilin's. If ye don't stop it I'll have tae take yer stick away.'

'Ye'll feel it round yer ear first,' his mother snapped back, and then, leaning forward in her chair and glaring at Shelagh, 'Did ye hear me, girl? I said no and that's an end of it.'

'I've already said yes.' Shelagh's throat was so dry that the words rasped out, but even so her own daring amazed her. Never, in all the time she had been married to Joseph, had she dared to defy his mother, the matriarch and head of their family group.

'What did ye want tae go and do that for?' Joseph was as shocked as his mother. 'Without even talkin' it over with me first?'

'Because I want to work. I'm good with a needle, and a sewing machine — mebbe it's the only thing I am good at, but all the more reason to make it work for me and for the rest of us,' she rushed on, ignoring the hand her husband put on her arm and his soft, 'Ah, now, girl, that's not true at all.'

'Your place is here, lookin' out for me!'

'I said I'd only work in the mornings. I'll settle you first and be back before you know it.

'It's for Cavan,' Shelagh told her husband, turning away from the old woman in the armchair. 'She needs better clothes, and better

171

feeding too. I know you do your best, Joseph, and I'm proud of you for it – for everything you've gone through without a word of complaint – but where's the sense in you taking all of the burden of looking out for us and feeding and housing us when I can help you? Is that not what marriage is all about – helping each other, and our family too?'

'Joseph McCart, are you goin' tae stand there and let her talk such nonsense? You should make sure she knows her place and keeps tae it. If I'd said such things tae your daddy he'd have taken his fist tae me, so he would!'

'He did take his fist tae ye, Mammy, often. But that was a long time ago, and I'm not my daddy.' Joseph looked down at the wife he loved with every beat of his heart.

'No, you're not your daddy, right enough,' his mother sneered. 'Ah, the poor man that he is, he must be turnin' in his grave at this very moment, hearin' the way you're lettin' her be so impertinent tae the both of us.'

'That's enough!' Shelagh turned on the old woman. 'My Joseph's as good a man as any other. Have you forgotten what he did to keep us safe? What he did for you, when it meant risking his own life? If you can't respect him you've no right to be here at all!'

172

There was a shocked silence. Bernadette McCart sagged back in her chair, her large face frozen with disbelief, one hand creeping up her sagging bosom to snatch with agitated fingers at her throat.

Shelagh was almost as shocked as the ould yin by her own outburst, but she knew that if she didn't make use of the sudden surge of courage, it would all go to naught. She and Joseph would lose the battle that constantly raged between them and his mother. She looked back at her husband. 'I've already told Caitlin Lennox that I'll start tomorrow, and I'll work in the mornings so that I can keep the house going and look after your mother and be here when Cavan comes home from the school. I'm doing it, Joseph, and I'm doing it for Cavan – and for you – and for me.'

Summoning up the final dregs of her strength she walked past him and out of the door. Two steps took her across the small square hall and into the poky room she and Joseph shared. Once there, she closed the door quietly, then collapsed on to the bed where she buried her head in the pillow that smelled of her husband.

Only then did she allow her body to start shaking.

## 12

'Come with me,' Alex said. He was leaning against the window sill, watching his wife pack for his visit to the Edinburgh furniture exhibition.

'You've already asked me that and I've already explained that I'm needed at Harlequin. Now that the war's over and life's got back to normal it's as though every single girl in Paisley has decided to be a June bride.' Rose folded a shirt deftly, wrapped it in tissue paper and laid it carefully into the case. 'Promise me that you'll remember to unpack as soon as you arrive at the hotel, and hang everything up very carefully.'

'Don't worry, I won't let MacDowall and Son down.'

'Be damned to MacDowall and Son,' Rose said

briskly, 'I'm the one who doesn't like to be let down.'

'So come with me and then you can make sure that everything's unpacked and hung up properly.' He lunged forward suddenly and she only just managed to elude the hands that reached out for her.

'Behave yourself! You'll only be gone for four days – even if I had the time to spare it would hardly be worthwhile the two of us going for such a short time. In any case, you'll be too busy with the exhibition to do any sightseeing.'

'Is Caitlin to be one of your June brides?'

Rose straightened up and massaged the small of her back with both hands. She had noticed that her back ached more frequently these days, and she had no appetite at all in the mornings. But it was too early to say anything to Alex. 'I wish she was, but Murdo's still working on the gatehouse. Caitlin doesn't say much, but I think she's beginning to wonder when it will ever be ready. Which ties do you want?'

'You choose. You're better with colour schemes than I am.'

'I leave that sort of thing to your clever sister. That one, that one and . . . that one,' Rose decided, then folded them deftly. 'I think that's the lot.'

'Good.' Alex snapped the case shut, moved it

to the floor and then scooped his wife up into his arms and deposited her on the bed. 'Since you refuse to accompany your lord and master to Edinburgh as a respectful wife should, you can at least give me something to remember you by while I'm away.'

Without quite meaning it to happen, Mary had fallen into the habit of going for a walk with John Brodie every Sunday afternoon. For some reason – never discussed – they always met at a prearranged spot some distance away from both their homes, and they always walked out into the countryside, never round the town. There were plenty of good walks to choose from – following the River Cart, or going up to the braes, or taking the road leading to the nearby town of Barrhead. Nobody else knew about their growing friendship, which suited Mary as she had no wish to be teased by her family, or have them misunderstand what was simply a casual friendship.

John was of the same opinion. 'My parents would like to see me settled down with a wife and children and, to tell you the truth, there was a time when I thought it might happen. But she married someone else.' Mary had asked no questions, but after a moment he added, with a swift sidelong glance at her, 'As a matter of fact, she

176

married your brother. It surprised me, because they could never meet without quarrelling; I suppose that for them, quarrelling was a peculiar form of courtship. I expect that I was too quiet a fellow for a firebrand like Rose. But I did love her.'

'Describe love to me.'

'What?' He was startled by the question, and so was Mary. She felt her face colour, but stuck to her guns.

'I used to walk out with a young man – Lachie, his name is – and when he jilted me I was quite heartbroken because I thought I must be in love with him. But I don't know if I was, really. What's it like?'

They walked along in silence for several minutes before John said, 'It's like the curate's egg – good and bad in places.' He swished at the grass by the hedgerow with his stick. 'I remember feeling happy whenever I saw Rose, and missing her when we weren't together. She made me feel very . . . alive all the time. And it hurt when I discovered that I'd lost her. But it soon stopped hurting.'

'I don't think I was in love with Lachie,' Mary said thoughtfully, 'unless different people feel love in different ways. I liked him, and I was upset when he decided to stop seeing me, but that might just have been hurt pride.'

'Why did he want to stop seeing you?'

'He's a carter, and when I moved out of Robertson's marmalade factory and started working at Harlequin he felt that I was too grand for him.'

'Stupid man,' John said vigorously. 'You're still the same person you were when you worked at Robertson's, aren't you?'

'That's what I thought. He used to go to the ceilidhs we – my sister Caitlin and me and our niece Rowena, and Murdo, of course – attend. That's where I first met him. But he hasn't been there since we stopped walking out together. I think he may have a new sweetheart now, but that doesn't bother me at all.'

'Look there.' John suddenly drew her over to the bank at the side of the road, gently easing a clump of long grass aside with his walking stick. 'A clump of wild violets.'

He bent and carefully picked one of the tiny flowers, handing it to Mary with a courtly bow. 'For you, my lady.' Even though it was small, the blossom was generous with its scent. She breathed it in deeply, then tucked the flower carefully into the envelope she carried in her pocket. John knew so much about the countryside that she had begun to build up quite a collection of pressed flowers gathered on their walks.

178

They went on for a while in a comfortable silence, eventually broken by John remarking, 'Birds in the spring.'

'What about them?'

'Listen.' He took her hand in his, bringing her to a standstill. 'Stand quietly and listen.'

She did, and suddenly realised that the warm air was filled with the sound of birds, some twittering busily, others sending out clear, pure calls of two or three notes repeated over and over again.

'We take our wild birds for granted,' John said. 'We don't stop and listen to them often enough. The sound of them made me think of lines from a poem we had to learn at school, by William Blake, "Then the Parson might preach, and drink, and sing, And we'd be as happy as birds in the spring." I loved that couplet. It seemed to me at the time, and ever since, that birds are happy because they live for the moment and accept whatever may come into their lives.' He smiled at her, slightly embarrassed. 'I expect that that sounds foolish.'

'Not at all. I like it. Would you write it down for me?'

'Of course. I knew that you would understand,' John said, and they walked on again, comfortably silent together.

*

On the very next day Mary was crossing the paved courtyard on her way home after work when Lachie came through the open door of the gatehouse. He was carrying a bag of tools and balancing a plank of wood over one shoulder. He started to walk down the three steps to the courtyard, then stopped short as he caught sight of her.

Mary, too, hesitated, then changed direction and headed directly for him. 'Hello, Lachie.'

'Mary.' He nodded at her, dropping the bag to the ground and lowering the plank.

'How are you?'

'I'm grand. Yourself?'

'Never better,' she said cheerfully. 'Are you giving Murdo a hand with the place?'

'Aye,' he said as Caitlin came to the door.

'Lachie, Murdo says can you fetch some more of these long nails?'

'Aye,' Lachie said again. As he scurried off to the gates leading to the street, Caitlin came out to join her sister.

'Are you all right?'

'I'm fine. In fact,' Mary said, 'I'm better than fine. I'm downright grand, now that I know I've got over him.'

'Good. D'you want to come in and see what Murdo's done to the place? I'm hoping,' Caitlin said as she led the way into the gatehouse, 'now that Shelagh McCart's doing such a grand job in the sewing room I might be able to spend a bit more time here, helping Murdo and Lachie.'

The gatehouse was a square building, solid enough to have withstood years of neglect without giving way to wind and weather. The room that had been altered to take the loom lay to the right of a hall running from the front entrance to the back of the house. Murdo's narrow cot and a small cupboard for his clothes were in the room to the left, with a table, kitchen chair and old armchair as the only other furniture. The kitchen was behind his room and the rest of the area at the rear of the house was taken up by a pantry, coal cellar and water closet.

'The man's been living like a monk,' Mary said after peering into Murdo's living quarters, 'but it's such a nice house, Caitlin. Look at those ceilings, and the size of the windows. You'll be able to turn it into a right nice place — once the work's been finished,' she added, raising her voice as a hammer started banging above their heads.

After looking round the rest of the ground floor they went upstairs. A small square landing lit by a glass window set into the roof opened on to two fair-sized bedrooms at the front, and a smaller room and bathroom at the back.

Murdo was on his knees in one of the front rooms, pounding new planks into place. A third of the floor had been relaid and before him stretched a yawning hole, while a pile of new planks lay against one wall. When the door opened he stopped work and sat back on his heels, running an arm across his hot forehead.

'It's comin' on.'

'Slowly,' Caitlin said while Mary went to examine the patches of faded wallpaper clinging to the walls.

'This'll take some time to get off. I'll help you if you like. What sort of paper are you going to put on?'

'None. I'm going to paint all the walls,' Caitlin said, and when they both looked at her in surprise, 'I want it to look fresh and clean. We can think about wallpaper after we've been in for a while.'

'All the flooring up here has to be replaced,' Murdo remarked, and she looked at him in dismay.

'Are you sure? The planks are sound enough, are they not?'

'Some are warped, and they're all badly scuffed. Best to do the job properly while we're at it.'

'How long will that take?'

He shrugged. 'Hard to say.'

'Then we'd better go and let you get on with it,' Mary offered, and when the sisters were down in the hall and the banging had resumed upstairs, she said, 'He's determined to get everything right for you, isn't he?'

'I wouldn't mind scuffed floorboards, or even creaking floorboards. We can put linoleum over them, and mats. I just want to get started on the painting, and I want to buy furniture, and measure the windows for curtains. Oh, Mary!' Caitlin burst out in sudden anguish, throwing out an arm to indicate the room that held Murdo's bed. 'I want to be his wife and to live here with him. I'd happily move into that one room with him until the rest of the place is finished, but he won't hear of it.'

'Surely that shows how much he cares for you. He wants everything to be perfect for you – and it will be. All it takes is time and patience.' Mary tried to calm her sister, and when Caitlin managed a weak smile, she went on, 'Are you coming home?'

'I'm going to stay here for a while and make some dinner for Murdo and Lachie. Tell Mother I'll be back later.'

When Mary had gone, Caitlin wandered into the room where Murdo slept and smoothed the covering over his bed, then on an impulse she knelt beside it and laid her cheek on the pillow, breathing in the masculine smell of him. She closed her eyes for a moment, imagining that when she opened them she would see his face on the pillow beside hers, then jumped hurriedly to her feet as she heard Lachie come into the house.

She waited until his boots had clattered noisily up the wooden staircase before going into the kitchen to start work on the food she had brought with her that morning. As she peeled the potatoes, Mary's words came back to her. 'He wants everything to be perfect for you – and it will be. All it takes is time and patience.'

Did Murdo really want everything to be perfect for her? Sometimes Caitlin wondered. On many occasions since the end of the war she had designed wedding dresses for women of her own age, or younger, who had been able to welcome their menfolk back from the war. She had watched them in the fitting room, eyes bright and faces flushed with excitement as they tried on their gowns. Their men had been impatient to marry them as soon as possible, but Murdo seemed to be in no hurry. He was perfectly content to take a long time to get the house ready for her.

Sometimes she wondered if he really wanted to marry her, or if, instead, he secretly wished that he had never committed himself to taking her as his wife.

# 13

Alex travelled through to Edinburgh on the afternoon before the exhibition was due to start. On arrival at his lodgings, a three-storey house in one of the old narrow wynds off the Royal Mile, the landlady, a small woman with bad-tempered eyes and thin lips so close to her pointed nose that they almost seemed to be a moustache, escorted him to his room on the top floor.

'I don't mind providing porridge and bread and tea in the morning, but no other meals. Hot water's taken to every gentleman's room for washing in the evening and for shaving in the morning. I don't let rooms to ladies. They expect to be waited on hand and foot.'

With that, she stumped back downstairs and Alex surveyed the small shabby room with wry amusement, recalling Rose's instructions to unpack as soon as he arrived and hang everything up carefully. A curtain in one corner hid a rickety rail, so he hung his suit on it, hoping that it wouldn't collapse and throw it on the dusty floor.

The painted furniture had been despatched by carrier the day before and he spent the rest of the day at the exhibition hall, unpacking each item and checking it carefully to make sure that it had not been damaged in transit. Once that was done he went about the task of setting up his wares in the area assigned to him. As he had done years ago at his first exhibition in Glasgow – the exhibition where he had met Fiona – he had packed a few items to enhance the furniture; a book or two to leave on a table, a fan and one of Rose's wide-brimmed summer hats to be laid on the top of a small cupboard, as though left by someone who had just stepped into the next room, and a shawl to be draped across the back of a chair.

Standing back to study the effect, he looked thoughtfully at the shawl, then rearranged it, picturing Rose as she had looked that morning when they'd said goodbye. She had looked so –

she had been glowing, he realised. There was a new bloom to her skin and a sparkle in her eyes; there had been a difference about her that he couldn't quite identify.

Recalling her only made him all the more eager to get the exhibition over so that he could return home as soon as possible. Right now, he thought, as he had another try at draping the shawl, he didn't give a damn whether he sold any furniture or not. He just wanted to be with Rose.

When everything had been set out to his satisfaction he had a look at the other exhibits and met his fellow exhibitors, then went with some of them to a nearby inn, where they talked business over a meal. The promised hot water had been left in his room by the time he got back to his lodgings, and had lain long enough to turn cold. He washed quickly and got into bed where, tired though he was, he tossed and turned for a while, unused now to being on his own, before sleep finally arrived.

He woke early to the sound of footsteps on the stairs and knuckles rapping at doors on the floor below his. Getting up at once, he was dressed in shirt and trousers by the time his turn came. Someone banged on the door and a woman's voice bawled, 'Here's yer hot water.'

'Bring it in, will you?' Glancing at the fob watch Rose had given him as a wedding gift, Alex saw that he only just had time to shave and go downstairs for some breakfast if he wanted to get to the hall before the doors opened to the public.

The woman who brought in the ewer dumped it down on the table by the basin and scrubbed her hands against the sides of her drab skirt. 'There you are.'

'Thank you.'

She had turned away from him, towards the door. Now she looked back at him. 'Oh, we've got a gent stayin', have we? Most o' them don't ken how tae say thanks.'

He hadn't bothered to look at her, but the comment attracted his attention and he saw that what little light there was from the window had fallen on her face. Her greying hair was pulled back tightly and the lines on her forehead and at the corners of her eyes and mouth hinted at a hard, thankless life. Her once flawless skin was grey with ingrained dirt and marked with smallpox scars, while her once slender neck was thickened but, even so, Alex knew her by the green eyes, dulled now but still with a distinctive, slightly eastern slant at their outer edges that he had not forgotten.

'Beth? Beth Laidlaw?'

'Ye recognised me, Alex?' She shot him a sarcastic grin that revealed a gap where two or possibly three teeth had once been, and put a shiny red hand on one hip in a youthful, coquettish gesture that only managed to make her look foolish. 'I thought I knew ye, but I wasnae sure till ye spoke there. And it's Beth Lennox – yer brother married me. Made a respectable woman of me, he did – or tried to.'

'What are you doing here?'

'Earnin' my livin'. I could ask you the same thing – you've not come lookin' for me, have ye?'

'I'm showing furniture at an exhibition here.'

'Lizzie!' a voice corkscrewed up the narrow staircase. 'Where are ye? There's folk down here wantin' fed!'

'I have tae go,' Beth said.

'I need to talk to you. Can I meet you this evening, about nine o'clock?'

She hesitated, eyeing him, then said, 'I'll come tae yer room then. Bring somethin' tae drink.' And then she hurried away.

Shelagh McCart was trying with all her might to run from the man who wanted to catch her and hurt her, but it was hard to move swiftly, burdened as she was by the heavy bag she clutched in one

189

hand, and by Cavan, who kept trying to pull free of her other hand. To make things worse, for some reason she had left the road and was running across a bog; her feet sinking into soft ground with every step, making it more and more difficult to drag them free in order to move forward.

If only Joseph were there to help her – but he had disappeared into the mist ahead. She called his name and thought she heard him answer; his voice gave her hope and added energy, but the bag was becoming heavier, and now Cavan was a dead weight on her other arm and the man chasing them was closing in. She could feel his breath on her neck and sense his hands reaching out to snatch at her skirt.

She stumbled and almost fell, then all at once Joseph was coming towards her, his face chalk-white apart from the trickle of blood running down his forehead and dripping on to his work shirt.

'Joseph!'

Her own voice woke her. She was sitting upright in bed, staring into the darkness, the blanket clutched tightly in both hands.

'Mmm?' He stirred beside her, then mumbled, 'What is it?'

'Nothing.' She lay down again. 'Just a bad dream. I'm all right.'

He put his arm around her and was asleep again within seconds, while Shelagh lay awake, recalling the sight of Joseph coming towards her, with blood running down his face, just as he had looked on the night he had gone out, ignoring her pleas not to, and returned late to their cottage in Ireland. The night she had taken one look at him and known that the life she loved was over for ever.

The two of them had packed the few possessions they could manage to carry, listening all the while for the sound of heavy feet on the road outside, the crash of fists against the door of their small cottage. Waiting for the retribution that would surely come if they didn't manage to flee first.

When they roused the ould yin she grumbled and argued until Joseph, out of his mind with fear for his family, shouted at her to be silent and do as she was told for once, or she'd be left behind to starve in a ditch. Cavan, bewildered and still half asleep, kept saying, 'But why, Mammy? Why, Da?' She had started to cry when she discovered that her pet canary couldn't go with them; Shelagh's eyes filled with tears as she recalled her daughter's heartbroken sobs as Joseph carried the cage outside and left it with the door jammed open so that the confused bird, hopping from perch to perch, could fly free.

'He doesn't want to go, Da, he doesn't want to

leave me and I don't want to leave him,' Cavan had wept while Shelagh whispered to him when he came back indoors, 'It'll die, Joseph. It doesn't know how to fend for itself.'

'It'll have to take its chance, the same as us,' he had growled at her.

They had travelled for days and nights, and when Joseph finally decided that they could be safe in Paisley, Shelagh surveyed the small, dreary flat he found for them and thought that she would never be happy again. Her heart broke for the cottage Joseph had carried her into after their wedding – the perfect ending to a day filled with laughter and song and dancing and friendship. All gone now, for ever.

Sometimes their new life, a constant struggle in a country alien to her, made her wonder if she was still in the cottage, locked in a nightmare and unable to rouse herself. At times like these she prayed to the Virgin Mary and all the saints that she would wake up to find herself back home, and safe again. But then she began to wonder if it were the other way round – if the good things she had known before had been nothing more than a lovely dream, and Paisley the only reality.

But in the three weeks since Caitlin had offered her work as a seamstress, Shelagh's life had begun to hold promise again. She looked forward to spending her mornings in Harlequin's large, airy sewing room, her sewing machine whirring busily while beautiful material slid along beneath her fingers. She liked Grace Watson, the supervisor, and the other seamstresses. They had welcomed and accepted her, and didn't ask any awkward questions about her former life in Ireland, or why she and Joseph had decided to move to Scotland. Rose MacDowall and Caitlin and Mary Lennox were kind folk, and above all, it was good to have some time away from the ould yin. Cavan liked her new school and although there were no competitions for her to enter, she loved being able to dance at the ceilidhs. She had made a good friend in Rowena Lennox, and Joseph seemed content with his job in the cabinetmaker's workshop in Espedair Street.

His mother still complained endlessly about being left on her own in the mornings, but the wee bit of extra money Shelagh now earned helped to buy the occasional treat for the old woman – and for Cavan.

Having finally put the fear and the bad memories behind her and reached a happy thought, Shelagh made herself concentrate on a mind picture of her daughter in her new dance dress, her small face lit up with the pleasure of wearing it, until at last she drifted into a dreamless sleep.

★

Rose wished that she had gone to Edinburgh with Alex. The thought of being alone in the flat on Monday evening had driven her to invite herself to dinner with her parents, but by the time the meal was over she was utterly bored by her mother's chatter about social events and the way the war had ruined good servants and given them ambitions above their natural station in life.

She spent a restless night and woke early on Tuesday morning, leaving the flat as soon as she was washed and dressed. The cleaners hired to come in early each morning to prepare the old mill for the day were just leaving as she brought her little motorcar to a standstill in the paved courtyard. Before going inside she drew off one glove and checked the earth in both of the large pots gracing the entrance. It was damp, and drops of water sparkled on the petals of the bright flowers. Murdo had already watered them, as he did every morning.

Once inside the building Rose left her bag, coat, hat and gloves in her office and enjoyed a rare solitary tour of the entire place, starting with the top floor. Blinds were drawn against the sun, for here, on shelving all round the walls, they kept bolts of materials, stored first by type and then by colour. The middle of the room was taken up with tables holding every colour of thread there was, as well as

194

scissors, pins and needles, ribbons, braids, artificial flowers, cards of hooks and eyes, studs and any other trimmings and fastenings that might be necessary.

The middle floor of the small mill had been divided into two rooms. The larger was the sewing room, with two big cutting tables and two other tables holding four sewing machines between them. Grace Watson's desk in one corner held a large ledger in which was noted details of every client's measurements, together with a description of every item made for that particular client. Rose flipped through it and smiled as she saw that with her usual efficiency Grace had also devoted a page or two to the client's likes and dislikes and any other personal foibles that those who attended to her should know about.

She crossed over to one of the long windows, her shoes clicking over the wooden floor, and looked down at the River Cart making its way along between green banks to Paisley Cross, and eventually to the River Clyde. It was a pleasant place for the women to work – a far cry from some of the dreadful sweatshops she had heard about. The other smaller room on that floor held material needed for current work, together with drawers holding the necessary accessories.

On the ground floor, the magazines put out for clients awaiting their turn in one of the fitting rooms had been fanned out carefully. The fitting rooms themselves were spotless, and ready for the day's callers. Rose was about to go into her office when Mary, Grace and Caitlin bustled in together, laughing over something.

'Goodness,' Mary said when she saw Rose, 'are we late?'

'No, I'm early.'

'I collected the post from the gatehouse,' Mary held up the bundle of envelopes as Grace went upstairs to her own domain. 'I'll bring it in when I've sorted through it.'

'Did you know, Rose, that Fiona Chalmers has booked a fitting for this morning?' Caitlin asked as her sister disappeared into her own small office.

'Fiona? No, I didn't.'

'She telephoned yesterday. An informal evening dress. Grace and I will talk to her first about colours and materials before we check her measurements. Do you want to be there? She'll probably expect it.'

Rose pulled a face. 'I'd rather not, but you'd better show her into my office when she's done. I'll give her a drink, then speed her on her way as soon as I can.'

'Not one of your favourite people?'

'You know me well enough to realise that I don't suffer fools gladly, Caitlin.'

'I wouldn't describe Fiona Chalmers as a fool. In fact, I think she's extremely sharp.'

Rose was swept by an involuntary shiver. 'Yes, she is – too sharp. I think she's trying to take over MacDowall and Son and ease Alex out altogether.'

'But she can't do that – Mr MacDowall's already named Alex as his heir, hasn't he?'

The sewing women came hurrying in, so Rose drew Caitlin into her office, closing the door against any listeners. 'When Sandy made Alex his heir Fiona was married and living in Fort William. Now that she's widowed and living in her father's house, things have changed.'

'Are you telling me that her father's disowning Alex?'

'Not at all – as far as he's concerned everything's as it was before. Even Alex thinks that everything is as it was before, but I don't agree. I think that Fiona looks on herself as her father's true heir. She was born in wedlock, and Alex wasn't.'

'You must talk to Alex about this.'

'I've tried, but he still tends to think of Fiona as a vulnerable young woman who would never do anything underhand. I don't believe that Alex, or Sandy for that matter, will realise the truth until it's too late.'

'But we can't let Alex be done out of his inheritance!'

'I don't intend to,' Rose said grimly, and then, as someone knocked at the door, 'Bring Fiona in here before she leaves and I'll try hard not to put hemlock in her sherry. It would be so bad for Harlequin's image if one of our clients expired on the premises. Come in?'

Fiona settled herself comfortably in the armchair and crossed slim, silk-stockinged legs.

'Have you settled on the dress you want Caitlin to design for you?' Rose poured a glass of sherry for her guest and put it on a small table by Fiona's side.

'It's black silk georgette with large white dots. Full sleeves and a square neck, and I'm going to have the skirt calf-length with a front slit. Caitlin suggested an over-tunic in white silk, belted with a pleated black sash. I believe that it's going to look very dramatic.' Fiona sipped at her sherry then asked, 'Aren't you having one?'

'Not at the moment.'

'I've ordered the dress because it's Father's fiftieth birthday at the end of June . . .'

'I know. Alex and I were talking about it just before he went off to Edinburgh.'

'. . . and I've decided,' Fiona went on as though Rose hadn't spoken, 'that he should have a party to mark the occasion.'

'Do you think he'll want a party?'

Fiona shrugged. 'You know what men are like – they hate fuss, but we have to mark his half-century, don't we? I've booked a firm of caterers and ordered the invitations. Once Father knows that it's all arranged he'll be happy to go along with it, I'm sure.'

'Did you speak to Alex before you made all those arrangements?'

Fiona raised an arched, carefully plucked eyebrow. 'Why on earth would I do that?'

'Sandy's his father too.'

'Men aren't interested in that sort of thing, and in any case, it's my responsibility as my father's daughter.'

'So his son has no say in the matter?'

'You forget that I was born a MacDowall,' Fiona said sweetly. 'Alex took the name only a few years a—'

She broke off as John Brodie hurried in, a sheaf of papers in his hand.

'Rose, I— Oh, I'm sorry,' he said as his eyes fell on Fiona. 'I didn't realise that you had company. I'll come back later.'

'Please don't leave because of me,' Fiona gave him her sweetest smile. 'I'm not a client – well, I am, but I'm family as well, so won't you join us? Rose has some excellent sherry.'

'Well . . .' he hesitated '. . . if you're sure that I'm not intruding.'

'Of course you aren't intruding, John. Sit down. Fiona, John Brodie is a dear friend of mine who helped me to start up Harlequin and still deals very patiently with any legal business we incur. John, this is Mrs Chalmers, Alex's sister.'

'Fiona.' She held out a hand to John. 'And I'm Alex's half-sister. As a friend of Rose, you probably know that Alex's mother and my father were never legally married.'

The decanter in Rose's hand twitched and a few drops of sherry trickled down the side of John's glass. She reached for a napkin and wiped them off. Given the choice, she would have liked to throw the sherry over Fiona, and it was a relief when John removed temptation by taking the glass from her. She sat down behind her desk, watching his eyes devouring Fiona, who looked very becoming in a pale-gold fine wool suit almost exactly the colour of her smooth, expertly bobbed hair.

'Caitlin's going to design a dress for me to wear at the party I'm holding for my father's fiftieth birthday,' Fiona was explaining. 'It's at the end of June.' Then, widening her brown eyes at him, 'You must come to it.'

'But I don't know your father – I w-wouldn't want to intrude on a family occasion.'

'Nonsense!' Fiona held up a slim hand and he stopped floundering and stammering at once, for all the world, Rose thought, like a well-trained dog. 'It's not just for family, we'll have lots of friends there as well. In any case, since you and Rose are old friends you must know Alex as well. And now you've met me, which makes you a friend of the family. So that's decided. I've asked Caitlin to extend an invitation to her mother and stepfather, Rose, and I've invited Mary. And I suppose the weaver will have to be invited too.'

'Murdo? I would expect so, since he and Caitlin are engaged to be married,' Rose said drily.

Fiona gave an irritated twitch of the shoulders, then said, 'Well, I must be off. There are so many things to arrange. Goodbye, John.' She uncurled herself from the armchair and John immediately shot to his feet and shook her proffered hand. 'I'm so glad we've met at last.'

'Can I drive you anywhere?' John asked, and her hair shimmered as she shook her head.

'I came in my father's car. The driver's waiting outside for me.'

'I'll see you out,' Rose and John said at the same time.

'I'm on my way out in any case,' John swept on. 'Rose . . .' he looked about vaguely and then noticed the papers he had put down on a corner

201

of the desk '. . . you and Caitlin need to sign these. I've marked the places. I'll collect them tomorrow.' He hurried to open the door as Fiona moved towards it.

## 14

The furniture Alex had painted as a wedding gift for Caitlin and Murdo attracted a fair amount of interest, and by the end of the first day of the exhibition his order book was beginning to fill up. All the credit went to the furniture, he knew, for he was more involved in coping with the shock of seeing Beth again than in representing MacDowall and Son.

As previously, he went with some of the other exhibitors for a meal before returning to the lodging house. He had almost reached the door when he remembered Beth's request for a drink. A good idea, he thought as he went back to the corner of the street, where he recalled passing a public house. During the day he had begun to think of the trouble the woman could cause if she decided to come back to Paisley. Whatever happened, he must prevent that from occurring.

The house was silent, but he hadn't been in his room for ten minutes before she tapped at his door and entered. 'Did ye get a bottle?'

'Will port do?' he asked, and she shrugged.

'It's as good as anythin', I suppose,' she said and, dipping a hand into the pocket of her blue serge skirt she produced a cup and handed it to him before sitting down on the only chair. She had discarded her apron, and teamed the skirt with a blouse that looked as though it might once have been cream-coloured, but was now a dingy grey, as though it had been washed too often in well-used water. She had tried to smarten it up with a bunch of wilting cloth roses pinned to the collar. There was something about that feminine touch that stirred sympathy in Alex.

'How are you, Beth?' He filled her cup almost to the brim and handed it to her, before pouring a drink for himself.

'Doin' very well, as ye can see for yersel',' she said with heavy sarcasm before drinking deeply. Then, wiping the back of her hand across her mouth, 'But I'm no' doin' as well as you are, by the looks of ye.'

'What brought you to Edinburgh?'

'A man, of course.' She drank again, then handed over the cup to be filled.

'The man you left Ewan for?' He poured more drink and she took the cup and put it to her lips.

'Where did ye hear that?' she asked when she finally lowered it.

'He told me.'

'It wasnae that man. It was the next one – or mebbe the next.' She drained the cup and again held it out to be refilled. 'Are ye no' drinkin' wi' me?'

He took a drink. 'It's the final day of the exhibition tomorrow. I have to keep my wits about me.'

'In that case . . .' she held out a hand and when he passed the bottle over she wedged it securely between her knees. 'So Ewan went snivellin' back tae Paisley, did he? Back tae his daddy and his mammy?'

'He never returned to Paisley. I met him in France, during the war. He went to Australia after you disappeared, and he was serving with the Australian Army. He told me that you'd left him to look after Rowena. He was killed just a few days after I spoke to him.' Alex watched Beth closely, but the news had no impact on her at all.

'Are ye still livin' in Paisley yersel'?'

'I'm in Glasgow now. Your father died, and your sister and her husband run the shop.'

'Her!' Beth had refilled her cup; now she greedily gulped down a mouthful of port. 'I never liked her. I wouldnae want tae set eyes on her again — and I doubt if she'd want tae set eyes on me.' She stared down into the half-empty cup and then looked back up at him, her green eyes narrowing. 'Is Ewan's dad still livin'?'

'He died before Ewan did.'

She looked at him with sudden interest. 'The business, the one Todd worked in — is it yours? He should have left that tae Ewan, and I'm still his wife . . . I never married any of the other men.'

'The business belonged to my mother, not Ewan's father. She sold it to a Glasgow man.'

'Oh.' She thought for a moment, then she asked, 'What about the wean?'

'Your daughter?'

'Aye. Where's she now?'

'Living in Australia, I suppose,' Alex said casually. It had taken long enough to get Rowena settled in Paisley after being abandoned by her parents; the last thing she needed now was to be confronted with this greedy slattern of a mother.

Beth emptied the bottle into the cup and then dropped it to the floor. It landed with a clatter and Alex picked it up and stood it in a corner.

'Sometimes I wonder if I should go back tae Paisley,' she said. 'Back home.'

The very idea filled him with horror. 'It's not home any more, Beth. You said yourself that you don't get on with your sister, and I doubt if she'd welcome you.'

'Bitch that she is!' She sniffled and drained the cup, tipping her head back to make sure that she got every last drop of port. Then she glanced around, as though wondering if there might be more drink available.

'I have to be up early tomorrow,' Alex said.

'Ready for yer bed?' She got up, swaying towards him. 'Want some company?'

'I'll be fine on my own.'

'You never liked me, did ye?' she snapped at him, and then caught by another sudden change of mood, her eyes filled with tears. 'Nob'dy wants me any more!'

'Look, Beth, I just want to get some sleep. Here,' he took a note from his pocket and thrust it into her hand, 'take this. Buy yourself something nice.' More drink, probably.

Her eyes widened as she looked down at the money. She pushed it down the front of her blouse and said, leering, 'I don't mind earnin' it.'

'There's no need.' He began to sweat.

'Mebbe I should just go back tae Paisley with

207

ye tomorrow. It's miserable here, Alex. They don't pay me enough tae keep a flea alive.'

'Would it help if I sent you some money every month?'

'Why would ye do that?'

'You were married to my stepbrother – I'm willing to help you since he can't. I could manage five pounds a month, posted to you here at the lodgings?'

She paused, head on one side, peering at him, and then said sulkily, 'Ye'd forget about it as soon as ye got away from here.'

'I give you my word I wouldn't. Wait a minute . . .' The ledger holding details of orders received at the exhibition lay on the rickety dressing table; he turned to the back page and scribbled a few words, then signed it and tore out the page. 'There you are, a promissory note. Five pounds every month, sent to you at this address. I've included the address of the place where I work so that you can contact me there if I let you down. But only if I let you down, mind.'

She took the paper and read it slowly and carefully, her lips shaping every word. 'All right then,' she said at last, folding it and pushing it down the front of her blouse to join the note he had already given her. And then, at last, he managed to ease her out of the door.

★

On Tuesday evening Rose had to force herself to return to her normally cosy little home, which without Alex in it had suddenly become too large and not deserving of the word 'home'.

After making herself eat the solitary meal that the housekeeper had prepared for her, she picked up a book but soon put it down again and began to wander restlessly from room to room.

'What have you done to yourself, you daft woman?' she said, exasperated, when she happened to see herself in a mirror. 'You used to pride yourself on your independence, and now look at you, moping like a child abandoned by its mother. How *could* you let a man get you into a state like this?'

As Alex left his room the next morning a fellow lodger was coming from his own room across the landing. 'Sleep well?' the man asked, grinning.

'Well enough.'

'She tires a man out, doesn't she?'

'Who does?'

'Lizzie, who else?'

Alex felt his face begin to burn. 'Are you implying . . . ?'

'I saw her go intae your room, man. I come here every year – I know Lizzie of old, and so do most of the other regulars.' The man slapped Alex on the shoulder and stood back to let him go down the rough wooden stairway first. 'She's an active filly, given her age. You can do worse than use our Lizzie tae lull ye tae sleep.'

Alex bit back the angry retort that longed to escape his lips and hurried down the stairs, determined to sit as far from his companion as he could. But as soon as he went into the room where some of the other lodgers were already eating, he could tell by their leers and winks that they, too, thought that he'd shared his bed with Beth the previous night.

To his relief she didn't appear; presumably she was busy in the kitchen. He ate swiftly and left the room, waiting in the corridor until the landlady appeared with a loaded tray.

'I won't be here tonight – I have to get back to Glasgow as soon as the exhibition ends this afternoon. How much do I owe you?'

'Ye'll have tae pay for tonight – I'll no' be able tae let the room out now.'

'I know that. Just tell me what I owe and let me be on my way.' He dug into his wallet and paid the ridiculously high sum she claimed, then hurried upstairs and packed his bag before fleeing the house, relieved that he didn't encounter Beth again.


'Can you both manage without me for an hour or two?' Rose asked Caitlin and Mary in the morning. 'I told Fiona that I'd go to Glasgow to discuss this birthday party she's holding for Alex's father.'

'Of course, you go ahead,' Caitlin said. 'We'll be fine, won't we, Mary?'

'Of course we will. If anyone asks for you specially, Rose, I'll get them to arrange an appointment for tomorrow.'

It had been some time since Rose had visited her father-in-law's large emporium. In recent years Sandy MacDowall had bought up stores on either side of his, and MacDowall and Son occupied almost an entire three-storey block on Hope Street. The original shop had sold only furniture, but now MacDowall and Son had several departments, including fashion, millinery and glassware. When Rose made enquiries she was told that Mrs Chalmers could be found on the second floor.

She travelled up in a lift operated by a young lad in uniform and stepped from it to see Fiona in deep conversation with a saleswoman, both wearing smart black skirts and jackets over crisp white blouses. She waited, wandering around the stands of dresses on display, until Fiona turned away, her conversation finished, and saw her.

'Rose, this is a very pleasant surprise. Have you

211

come to buy a frock for the birthday party? Don't tell me that Harlequin can't come up with something suitable!'

'I wondered if you had time for a talk. A *private* talk,' Rose added, suddenly realising that Sandy MacDowall was probably in his office.

'Of course. Just a moment . . .' Fiona bustled off to another counter to speak to the woman in charge of it, then returned to Rose. 'I'll take a twenty-minute break. Let's go up in the lift. We have a tearoom now, on the top floor. It's proving very popular with our clientele,' she went on as she pressed the button to summon the lift.

The tearoom was furnished like a large drawing room, with heavy draperies at the windows and plenty of space between the tables to ensure privacy. Fiona led her visitor to a window table and a uniformed waitress scurried over at once to take their order.

'Do you have time to see round the store before you go?' Fiona asked. 'I've made quite a few changes, including this place.' She waved an arm to indicate the tearoom. 'Father's delighted with the way—'

'I haven't come to be shown around,' Rose interrupted. 'I'm here to finish the conversation we had yesterday.'

'Oh? What were we talking about?'

'You seem to think that Alex has no rights as far as his father is concerned. MacDowall and *Son*, Fiona, not MacDowall and Daughter.'

'Oh dear.' Fiona shot a sweet but malicious smile across the table. 'I seem to have ruffled some feathers.'

'You've done more than that. Don't waste your "innocent little miss" performance on me, Fiona. It might work very well with your father and with most of the men you know – including Alex at times – but I find it empty and feeble.'

The waitress returned with fresh-made tea in a silver teapot and a selection of cakes and scones. 'You know, I can't imagine why Alex wanted to marry you,' Fiona said when the girl had gone.

'Surely you do – apart from the fact that we love each other, we're very alike. We're both ambitious and hard-working, not to mention outspoken.' Rose picked up the teapot and began to pour tea, adding with slight emphasis, 'And neither of us suffers fools gladly.'

'It's such a pity that you and I can't get on better, Rose. I think we may well have more in common than you realise . . .'

'I don't believe that we have anything in common.'

'We're both businesswomen. Our fashion department's doing very well now,' Fiona said. 'I'd like to see some Harlequin clothes here.'

'Harlequin only does originals.'

'There's no reason why you couldn't bring out some copies. We could both do well out of them. You should think about it. Do you take sugar?'

'Lemon, thank you.'

'And then there's Alex,' Fiona said thoughtfully as Rose eased a slice of lemon into a cup, resisting the inclination to drop it in from a height and splash her companion. 'He's an important part of both our lives.'

'Of mine, certainly. You seem to be set on removing him from yours – and your father's.'

'Ah, but that's mainly for his own good, and for mine. You do know about . . .' Fiona took a sip of tea, the wide brown eyes that had captivated John Brodie only the day before openly challenging Rose over the cup's rim '. . . about Alex and me, don't you?'

'I know that when you first met you liked each other very much, but you didn't realise then that you shared the same father. Fortunately, you found out the truth before liking developed into anything further. If, that is,' Rose said, 'it would ever have done so.'

'Alex wanted it to develop, I'm sure of that.'

'Alex was younger then, a callow youth with no real understanding of life. A lot has happened since then. He's a mature man now.'

214

'He was devastated when we discovered that we could never be anything other than brother and sister to each other.'

'And what about you, Fiona – were you devastated?'

'Of course. Alex was my first love, and a woman never gets over her first love, does she?'

'Alex was, still is and always will be my first love.'

'Really? Why am I surprised to hear that?' Fiona sneered, then as Rose sipped her tea, refusing to rise to the jibe, 'Do you know, Rose, I sometimes wonder what would have happened if we hadn't found out when we did. Think how dreadful it would have been if we had married!'

'You didn't, so there's no point in dwelling on it.'

'You speak as though our feelings for each other were little more than childish infatuation. We may have been young, but there's no doubt in my mind that Alex loved me deeply. That's why I believe that it would be best for him to break away from the family business, and from me, so that he can stand on his own feet.'

'He's already doing that. He's developed the furniture-making side of the business and made his father all the richer through his work. I doubt if Sandy would be willing to let him go.'

'He would, if it was what Alex wanted. If it was what *you* wanted.'

'But it's not what Alex and I want. He's found his real father and I'm happy for him, and for Sandy. As for whatever there once was between the two of you when you first met, I can assure you that Alex got over it long ago.'

'You think so? I know that it was difficult for him when I came back to Glasgow after George went off to war.' Fiona's face softened and she gazed beyond Rose's shoulder as though looking back into the past. 'I remember once when I visited him in his flat, and our true feelings for each other almost got the better of us. I doubt if Alex told you about that.'

Really, Rose thought, Fiona should seriously consider a career on the stage. The woman was a natural actress. Aloud, she said, 'As a matter of fact, he did. He told me that you were waiting at the flat when he got home one evening, having coaxed his housekeeper to let you in. You made embarrassing advances towards him and he had to show you the door.'

Fiona's creamy skin flushed brick red and her eyes sparked fire. 'Well of course he would say that,' she snapped. 'He wouldn't want to admit to anything else, would he? Not to his wife!'

'Alex and I don't lie to each other. I believe

his version. Since you feel so concerned about seeing my husband regularly, I have an alternative suggestion: why don't you go back to Fort William and leave the rest of us to get on with our lives?'

'My father needs me here.'

'Sandy is one of the most independent men I have ever met. He has a very capable housekeeper, and Alex and I are close by if he should need us.'

Fiona glared, then said, 'There's nothing for me in Fort William now that George is dead.'

'Oh, I'm sure George Chalmers wasn't the only wealthy bachelor in the town.'

'I have no intention of marrying again. In any case, I'd far rather stay in Glasgow where I belong, with my father.'

'And eventually take over MacDowall and Son.'

'I like to keep busy. Father's pleased to see me taking an interest in the business.'

'Alex is his father's heir.'

'Alex is *my* father's bastard,' Fiona said levelly, 'whereas I am his legal heir.'

'Men favour their sons over their daughters.'

'Only when the daughters stand by and let them.'

'I told Alex that you wanted to force him out of the business, and I was right.'

'Of course you're right, but that's not going to

217

help you. I have my father's interests at heart and he knows it.'

'Why are you doing this, Fiona? You're a rich widow and you'll inherit more wealth from Sandy one day. We both know that Alex would never deprive you of what's rightfully yours.'

'I'm surprised to hear you ask me that, Rose. You run your own business, don't you? You were born into comfort, like me, but you didn't settle for looking after the home and ordering servants about. Why should you expect me to?'

'Because we're so very different. Do you know what I think, Fiona?' Rose said slowly, 'You've been trying to tell me that Alex still loves you, but you know that isn't true. You're saying it because you think it will hurt me. I think the shoe may be on the other foot — I think that you still love Alex, even though he's your half-brother, and you want to punish him for marrying me.'

The flush drained suddenly from Fiona's face, apart from a crimson spot over each cheekbone. 'That's nonsense!'

'Is it?'

The adjacent tables were empty, but even so, both women had remembered to keep their voices low. Now Fiona leaned across the small table and hissed, 'You jealous cat!' with such vehemence that Rose felt warm spittle land on her cheek. 'What Alex sees in you I can't imagine!'

'Neither can I, my dear, but I'm the one with his ring on my finger,' Rose's voice was sweetened by triumph. She dabbed at her face with a napkin before rising and picking up her gloves and bag. 'I believe that we really do understand each other now. Thank you for the tea.'

As she made to leave, Fiona caught hold of her wrist. 'If you take my advice, you'll make Alex see sense.'

'I never take advice,' Rose assured her. 'I usually find that it doesn't work. But let *me* give *you* a word of advice. Don't try to push Alex out of your father's life. You won't succeed.'

'You think not? You underestimate me.' Fiona's eyes were cold, her voice hard. 'All my life I've got what I wanted, and I always will.'

'You didn't get Alex, did you? And you never will. I'll see to that,' Rose said, and walked out of the tearoom.

# 15

Back at Harlequin, Rose found that all had gone smoothly in her absence and there was nothing for her to do. She wished that some urgent problem had cropped up, for adrenalin surged through her rangy body and she badly needed something to keep her occupied. As she looked round the small office the rush of euphoria she had experienced towards the end of her quarrel with Fiona began to evaporate. She laid both hands gently on her belly. It was still flat and firm but she knew now that it wouldn't stay that way for much longer. She would have to tell Alex soon.

Fiona's fury at the end of their meeting, the way she had literally spat her hatred across the tea table, was still fresh in her mind. The pretence was over – they had said things to each other that could never be unsaid or forgotten. Battle had commenced, and it might become a bloody business. A fight that, for the sake of her husband and his unborn child, she had to win.

But in the meantime there were other things to think of. For one thing, she would have to take time off from work for the birth, though she had no intention of leaving until she had to. She went looking for Caitlin and found her in one of the fitting rooms with Grace and Shelagh McCart. Shelagh, to Rose's surprise, was wearing a cream silk afternoon dress banded with coffee-brown silk on the simple neckline, three-quarter-length sleeves and hem. Grace was on her knees pinning the hem, while Caitlin looked on thoughtfully.

'Florence Peacock has let us down again,' she said when Rose appeared. 'She wants this dress to be ready for next Monday, but instead of coming in this afternoon for a fitting as she promised, she's gone off to Edinburgh for the day. Luckily for us, Shelagh has exactly the same measurements.'

'And more style,' Grace grunted through a mouthful of pins. 'She looks better in it than that Miss Peacock will.'

Rose had to admit that the dress looked perfect on Shelagh. 'It's a pity,' she said, when the alterations were done to Caitlin's satisfaction and Shelagh and Grace had gone upstairs, 'that it's only the rich who can afford the finest clothes when folk like Shelagh look better in them, but can't afford them. That reminds me – have you designed your wedding dress yet?'

'There's no hurry. By the time Murdo's got the house to his satisfaction anything I design now will probably be out of fashion.'

'So you don't have any idea when the two of you are getting married?' Rose asked and then went on, when Caitlin shook her head, 'He shouldn't be doing it all on his own.'

'Lachie's giving him a hand when he can. You know Murdo, he isn't fond of company, especially when it's folk he doesn't know. I'd better go up and see Grace about that dress,' Caitlin said, and hurried out.

Rose returned to her office, frowning. While she was having the baby she needed to know that Caitlin would keep Harlequin running smoothly. Caitlin was her best friend as well as her partner and sister-in-law and Rose dearly wanted her to be happily married and settled in the gatehouse with Murdo, for her own sake as much as for Harlequin's. She counted on her fingers and estimated that Murdo had some seven months to complete the house and marry Caitlin before Rose had to give up work.

Suddenly, at the rate he was going, seven months didn't seem to be long enough.

Rose drove back home after work, thinking longingly about a glass of wine and an hour or so lounging around the flat, perhaps listening to the gramophone. To her surprise, she smelled food cooking when she let herself in. The woman who kept the place clean and left evening meals to be heated, or eaten cold, had been expressly told that while Alex was away, Rose didn't want cooked meals.

She threw her hat at the hook on the hallstand, missing it as usual, and marched into the small kitchen to find Alex stirring something on the stove.

'What are you doing here?'

'I live here, or hadn't you noticed?'

'But you're in Edinburgh until tomorrow.'

'Oh dammit, I forgot,' he said. 'I shouldn't be here, should I? D'you want me to go back there until tomorrow?'

'Put that ladle down,' she ordered, and when he did as he was told she flew into his arms. 'Oh Alex, I'm so glad to see you! I've missed you – you were right, I should have gone with you. Was it terrible?'

'Missing you was pretty terrible,' he said in a

muffled voice. 'But the business bit was — Rose, do you think you can loosen your grip? I'm beginning to see double.'

As soon as she stepped away he took the chance to fold her back into his arms and kiss her — a long, hard kiss. 'That's better,' he said when he finally released her.

'What's wrong?'

'Nothing at all. In fact, I got a lot of orders.'

'There's something else . . .' Her vivid blue eyes, her best feature, looked deep into his. 'Why did you come home early?'

He had already made up his mind that he was not going to tell her about the meeting with Beth. The woman belonged to the life he had had before Rose, and he would not let her intrude into his marriage. 'The exhibition ended and I decided that I'd had enough of Edinburgh. I wanted to be here with you,' he said, and then it was his turn to look closely at her. 'You've had a bad day. What happened?'

Rose wasn't going to spoil his homecoming by telling him about her quarrel with Fiona. 'Just busy.'

'It's more than that. Tell me.'

She shrugged as well as she could, given that she was still in his arms. 'I had a bad day yesterday — your dear half-sister came in for a fitting and she's decided to hold a birthday party for your father.'

'That sounds like a good idea,' Alex said. Then, as she remained silent, 'What else did she say?'

'Not a thing out of place. You know me, I just feel all out of sorts when Fiona's around.'

'Don't let her bother you.' He kissed the end of her nose. 'Though that's one thing we have to think about now – a special birthday gift for my father. Do you have any ideas?'

The right time had arrived. Rose took a deep breath. 'Well . . . there's his first grandchild,' she said thoughtfully. 'D'you think that would do?'

Alex's jaw dropped. 'What? You mean that you're . . . ?'

'I mean that *we*'re pregnant. You're just as much to blame as I am.'

'Are you sure?'

'You're my husband – who else can I blame?'

'I mean, are you sure that you're expecting a child?'

'Quite sure. I got a book. I haven't been to the doctor yet because I'm supposed to wait until the first three months have passed.'

'When? The birth, I mean.'

'Not until the end of the year. Ages yet.'

'You must stop work at once.'

'I must *not*! I'm as well as I ever was and I

intend to go on working until the very last possible minute. What would I do with myself for all those months without Harlequin? Do you want your son to be born to a mother who's gone mad with boredom?'

'It could be a daughter. Couldn't it?' Alex rubbed his forehead, dazed by the unexpected news.

'No, it's going to be a son.' It had to be a boy, to keep MacDowall and Son going. Rose had already started to concentrate her mind firmly on that thought.

'How do you feel about this? I thought you didn't want children just now.'

'I thought I didn't, but I was wrong. This is the right time. What are you cooking?'

'A sort of stew thing. I put in lots of vegetables — and sliced potatoes too. Do you think it smells all right?'

'Perfect,' Rose said. 'Let's have a glass of wine before we eat.'

'Are you sure that you should?'

'Alex MacDowall, I am not letting you or anyone else turn me into a baby factory. While I am carrying your son,' Rose said, patting her stomach, 'he is going to have to learn to live my way.'

'A half-glass for you. Wait till my father hears about this!'

'And my parents – and your mother and Todd.'

'They've already got grandchildren, but it's different for my father – he grew up without knowing anything about his blood kin. Fiona and I are all he's got, but now he's going to have a grandchild. The next generation of the MacDowall family.'

'Oh yes,' Rose said, 'I never thought of that. Another generation to inherit the business. He'll be delighted.'

'Let's go and tell him after we've eaten.'

'I thought we would tell him at the birthday party.'

'I can't wait until then.' Alex took both her hands in his. 'I can't possibly wait until then!'

She smiled at him, delighted by the pleasure she had given to him. 'All right, you win. We'll tell him tonight.'

Abandoned at the door of an orphanage within hours of his birth and raised in the institution's harsh, unloving environment, Sandy MacDowall had never learned to express affection. Now, learning that he was to become a grandfather, he had to fight hard to keep his emotions in check. It was such a struggle that he had to turn away suddenly from Alex and Rose and pretend to be rearranging the drawn curtains at the window.

They looked at each other in dismay, both convinced that the news had come as a blow rather than a pleasure.

'Father?' Alex ventured at last. 'Are you displeased?'

'Displeased? How could I be—' Sandy's voice broke on the last word. He choked, harrumphed into his handkerchief, then gave up the struggle and swung back to face them, his eyes bright with tears.

'Dammit, man, can you not see that I've gone soft in the head with the pleasure you've just given me? A grandfather – me! It's the best thing that could happen to any man!'

'Rose wanted to keep it quiet until your birthday party and make it our present to you, but I couldn't wait to tell you.'

'Quite right.' Sandy blew his nose and dabbed his eyes. 'For pity's sake, lassie, you'd have had me greetin' like a wean in front of my guests if you'd had your way. Does this mean that I'm the first to be told?'

'I only heard the news myself two hours ago, when I got back from Edinburgh. It went well, by the way.'

'Ach, never mind about Edinburgh, I'll hear all about that in the morning. See here, now,' Sandy said, lumbering forward to give his daughter-in-law a hug and deposit a kiss on her cheek. When they drew apart he shook Alex's hand vigorously. 'Wait till Fiona hears that she's to be an auntie!'

'If you don't mind,' Rose said swiftly, 'we'd prefer to keep this a secret between the three of us until your party, even from Fiona and my parents and Alex's mother. It's still early days and we shouldn't be telling anyone for a few weeks yet, just in case.'

'Of course, of course. Just as well Fiona's staying the night with one of her friends,' Sandy said, mopping at his eyes again. 'It'll give me time to pull myself together before I face her in the morning.'

Fiona's decision to have a family dinner before the other guests arrived for Sandy's birthday party suited Rose admirably. For the occasion, she chose to wear a pale-green linen suit already in her wardrobe. The jacket was long and smartly tailored, worn over a square-necked silk blouse in a darker green, and the skirt had a slight flare.

'Are you sure?' Caitlin asked doubtfully. 'It's a bit ordinary for a party. Wouldn't you rather have an evening dress, or even a blouse and skirt? I could organise something in time.'

'No-need. You've designed such a lovely outfit for Fiona, and I don't want to outdo her. After all, she is our hostess,' Rose said sweetly, and Caitlin's doubt deepened to suspicion.

'You're not planning something, are you?'

'Of course not. I hope Murdo's coming?'

Caitlin's face clouded, as it tended to do these days when Murdo's name was dropped into the conversation. 'I'm not sure. You know how he hates to be with a lot of folk he doesn't know, and Fiona's not exactly his favourite person. I'm going to wait until the day of the party and have one last try at coaxing him. You're sure about the costume, then?'

'Quite sure,' Rose said cheerfully.

When she had a minute, she slipped quietly out and crossed the courtyard to the gatehouse. As she pushed the door open the muffled beat of the loom was suddenly louder, and when she went into the big front room it was to find the Highlander working industriously, his body moving rhythmically as he kept the shuttle flying to and fro, carrying the weft thread across the growing pattern. It was almost as though he were part of the great wooden structure that took up most of the room.

He was so preoccupied with the pattern blooming on the rollers that he didn't see her until she moved round to stand by his side. Then he stopped the loom hurriedly and started to scramble up.

'Stay where you are, Murdo, I'm just in for a minute. Is this for us, or for MacDowall and Son?' she went on as he subsided back on to the bench.

'For Alex.'

'It's nice – but then, all your work's good. How do you feel about working for Alex as well as for me? It's not too much for you, is it?'

'Not at all.'

'I just wondered,' Rose said. 'I know that you're trying to get this place put to rights before you and Caitlin marry, and I'd not want the wedding to be delayed because you had too much work to attend to.'

'I can easily enough do both. I work on the house in the evenings, and on Sundays.' He kept his eyes on the loom as he spoke.

'Are you coming to my father-in-law's birthday party?'

'I-I'm not one for parties,' Murdo said awkwardly, his fingers fidgeting together.

'Neither am I. When I lived at home my parents and my sisters always seemed to be inviting people to the house, and I hated it. I hid away in the summer house, where they couldn't find me. But it would be nice to see you there, Murdo,' Rose went on, 'for Caitlin's sake. I think she's as shy about it as you are, and it would help her to have you there. Will you think about it?'

231

For a moment his dark eyes stared straight into hers and to her surprise, Rose found herself watching a man locked in a struggle that was tearing him apart. Then he said, 'Aye, I'll think on it.'

'Is anything troubling you, Murdo?'

He ducked his head down so that she saw nothing but his unruly black hair.

'What would be wrong?'

'I don't know, but if anything ever worries you, I hope that you know that you can speak to me about it. I can promise you that I'm good at keeping secrets.'

Again, the Highlander looked up at her, but this time his gaze was clear and untroubled. 'So am I,' he said.

'Well now . . .' For some strange reason, Rose felt flustered. 'Can I have a look around the place?' she asked, for want of anything better to say. 'I'd like to see what you've done to it.'

'Of course.'

As she went upstairs she heard the loom start its steady clacking rhythm again.

From the upper floor, Rose glanced out of one of the front windows. The paved courtyard below was pleasing to the eye, and so was the old mill, with its double doors and window frames painted a strong blue and the big pots of bright flowers.

Murdo Guthrie puzzled her. She respected the

taciturn Highlander not only for his talent as a weaver, but for his strong independence, but now she wondered if Caitlin had chosen to spend the rest of her life with the wrong man. Rose could fully understand why Caitlin had fallen in love with Murdo; he wasn't handsome in the classical sense, but there was something very attractive about this man from the wild northern bens and moors and deep silent lochs, with his strong body, tumble of black hair and those amazing dark eyes of his.

But would Murdo make Caitlin as happy as she deserved to be? *Could* he make her happy? That unexpected glimpse she had had of some turmoil within the man had disturbed her; she had no idea what was wrong, but she knew for certain that if he could not put it right, then Caitlin would suffer. The girl adored Murdo, and all she wanted was to be his wife. If he were to reject her now . . .

# 16

'I don't know about this,' Kirsty fretted, holding the official invitation gingerly, as though it might suddenly bite her fingers. 'It's one thing going to Sandy's birthday party for a wee while, but I never thought we'd be expected to go there for our dinner first. It says it's to be a family dinner and we're not family.'

'Of course you're family – you're Alex's mother and he's Alex's father,' Caitlin pointed out.

'But that was years ago – we're both different people now.'

'You're still parents to your son. Mr MacDowall will be hurt if you don't go – you too, Todd.'

'We'll have tae get dressed up.' Todd looked as uncomfortable as his wife did at the prospect.

234

'We're not used tae socialising. We like our own fireside of a night, don't we, Kirsty?'

'Well, now's your chance to be a bit adventurous. It's only for the one evening,' Mary coaxed. 'And we'll all be there with you – me and Caitlin and Murdo and Alex and Rose.'

'And me?' Rowena asked hopefully.

'You'd not be able to stay up late.'

'I would!' Rowena scowled at Mary. 'I stayed up late last Ne'erday. And I like parties.'

'This is a party for grown up folk; you'd not like it. Anyway, you're not going and that's that.'

'But I can't stay here all by my own self. If I'm too wee to go to this daft party, I'm too wee to be left alone. I might cry, and there'd not be anyone here to hear me!'

'Of course I'd not let you stay here all on your own.' Kirsty hugged her precious grandchild. 'Mebbe it would be best for me and Todd to—'

'You're going to Sandy MacDowall's party,' Mary said firmly. 'We'll ask Jean here for the evening.'

'Or I could ask Cavan if I could go to her house,' Rowena suggested hopefully, but Kirsty, who had never forgotten the fearsome old woman who lived with Cavan and her parents, shook her head.

'We're not going to trouble them. You can have a party here one day soon, and invite Cavan,' she added, and the mutinous scowl that had begun to draw Rowena's brows together vanished, to be replaced by a delighted smile.

'Really? With cake and games?'

'With everything,' Caitlin promised.

'And can I get a wee bit of a party when Jean comes to look after me? Can I put on my best frock and get juice to drink?'

'Ye drive a hard bargain, lassie,' Todd grunted from behind his pipe.

'Let her have her parties, Todd. It's not much to ask,' his wife said. 'I'll need to get your good suit out and give it an airing. It's not been worn for a while.'

'What about yourself, Mam? Come to Harlequin,' Caitlin urged, 'and we'll find something nice for you to wear.'

'And me working in Jean's shop with all the lovely clothes the rich women hand in? Let them go to Harlequin – it's not for the likes of me.'

'Of course it is!'

'No, no. I'll find something in Jean's shop, and if it needs altering Teenie can see to it for me. I'd not feel right in a fancy frock,' Kirsty insisted.

On the evening of Sandy MacDowall's party, Rowena was allowed to stay up a little later than usual, so that she and Jean could have the party she had been promised.

'She's upstairs, putting on her best frock,' Kirsty said when Jean arrived. 'But make sure she's in her bed by nine at the latest. I've got some juice for her to drink, and I've bought some fancy wee cakes, and some sweeties.'

'We'll manage fine.' Jean took off her coat and gloves, but as always, she kept on her hat. 'You look smart, Kirsty. Teenie's made a grand job of that dress.'

'Aye, she has that.' Kirsty smoothed the dark blue dress over her ample hips. It was plain but well cut, and as luck would have it, the woman who handed it in at the shop had had much the same build as Kirsty. Teenie had only had to let it out a little, and had improved the square neck by adding a bunch of white silk roses. 'Between you and me, Jean . . .' Kirsty lowered her voice, glancing at the door to make sure that neither of her daughters was close enough to hear her '. . . I doubt if Harlequin could have done better.'

'I think you're—' her friend began, and then as her gaze moved beyond Kirsty to the doorway she let out a short scream.

Kirsty, spinning round, gave another scream as she saw the apparition in the doorway. 'In the name of God, lassie, what's happened to ye?'

'D'you like it?' Rowena came into the room, beaming. She had on a yellow silk dress with frills

237

round the bottom of the skirt and a bunch of gold ribbons at the neck. Her long hair had been brushed until the red highlights in the rich brown tresses made it gleam like chestnuts in the sun, then tied back with a yellow ribbon. But it was her face, with its huge black eyes seemingly sunk into her head that had startled the two women.

'Do you like my eyes?' She beamed at her grand-mother and Jean, unaware that the smile only made her look more grotesque.

'Like them? You look like a – I don't know what. What have ye done?' Kirsty choked.

'I've made my eyelashes look all thick and black like Cavan's. Aren't they nice?'

'How did ye do that?' Jean asked faintly, one hand clasped to her heart.

'I put soot on them. I've seen Auntie Mary doing it with her eyes. I borrowed her wee brush.'

'Mary doesnae put soot on her eyelashes!'

'Auntie Caitlin says that Cavan has lovely sooty Irish eyes, so it made sense for me to use soot, didn't it?' Rowena's wide blue eyes peered out at the women from within their black sooty caves, then, as Todd said from behind her, 'What's all the stramash about?' she swung round on him. He glanced down and took an involuntary step back.

'Look, Granddad, I've got sooty eyes, like Cavan. Aren't they pretty?'

Rowena put a hand up to her face and Jean and Kirsty both jumped forward, shrieking, 'Don't touch!'

Kirsty reached her first and captured the girl's hands in her own. 'Don't touch – you'll get soot all over your nice frock. Come on now, upstairs with you. You're going to get your face washed!'

As she and Rowena, protesting all the way that she had already washed her face, disappeared up the stairs, Todd came into the parlour, shaking his head.

'What does the wean think she's doin'?'

'Givin' hersel' nice sooty Irish eyes like her wee friend has.' The words were no sooner out of Jean's mouth than a faint shriek was heard from upstairs.

'Now what?' Todd said.

'I think that your Mary's just tried to use her wee mascara brush.'


Sandy MacDowall, at the head of the table, looked distinguished in the dinner jacket Fiona had insisted on buying for his special birthday. Despite his original reticence he was enjoying himself. Fiona, as hostess, was seated at the opposite end of the long table, while Alex sat at his father's right hand, with Rose opposite him. Kirsty, Todd and Mary made up the rest of the party. Caitlin should have been there, but Murdo had been unable to face the prospect of being a dinner guest as well as having to attend the party, so Caitlin had opted to wait behind so that she could travel to Glasgow with him. It was the only way she could make sure that he put in an appearance.

Fiona, beautiful in her new black and white georgette dress from Harlequin, kept the conversation moving easily, even going out of her way to make certain that Kirsty and Todd were involved.

'You look very pretty, Rose,' she said sweetly.

'Thank you, Fiona.' Rose, too, could be sweet when she wanted to, and this evening she could afford to be magnanimous. 'So do you.'

'You're positively glowing, Rose,' her father-in-law added, beaming at her.

She beamed back at him. 'I feel quite glowing, as a matter of fact.'

'It's because Alex is back from Edinburgh. Poor Rose was quite desolate while he was away, weren't you?' Fiona said. 'Perhaps you should go with him next time.'

'Perhaps I should.' Rose waved away the offer of more wine.

When the meal was over Fiona got to her feet. 'We still have the best part of an hour before the rest of our guests arrive. Why don't we women

240

have our coffee in the sitting room and leave the men to enjoy a glass or two of port?'

'Before you go, Fiona,' Sandy said as chairs were shuffled back, 'I believe that Alex has an announcement to make.'

All eyes were suddenly on Alex, who cleared his throat. 'Rose and I have a special birthday gift for Father. Rose, would you like to do the honours?'

Rose smiled across the table at her husband. 'I think that you should do it.'

'Very well.' Alex took a deep breath and glanced all around the table to make sure that he had everyone's attention before he said, 'Rose is expecting our first child. The next generation of the MacDowall family is on its way.'

As the table erupted with cries of surprised pleasure Rose took time to glance at Fiona and saw, to her delight, that the other woman's eyes were wide with shock. But more was to come. When the excitement began to fade Sandy MacDowall rang the bell by his hand.

'I already knew about the wee bairn,' he said as Mrs Dove came in, bearing a tray filled with glasses, 'and I'd like you to join me in a toast to Rose and Alex, and to my first grandchild. Mrs Dove, there's a glass of champagne there for you as well. You'll join us, I hope?' He got to his feet, smiling at his son and daughter-in-law. 'To Rose and Alex, and to their firstborn – my grandchild. And yours, Kirsty.'

When the toast had been drunk, he went on, 'And I have some news of my own. When I heard that the MacDowall family's going into its third generation, I decided to have another look at my business affairs. A new will was drawn up and signed yesterday, leaving the emporium equally between Alex and Fiona, and the furniture workshop to Alex, since he's done such a grand job of building it up, while this flat will be Fiona's. As to any moneys I might leave – half will be divided between the two of you, and half will be put into a trust fund for any grandchildren there may be in the future. Ladies and gentlemen, please join me in drinking to the future success of the MacDowall family.'

'Did you see Fiona's face when you told them about the baby?' Rose said gleefully to Alex as she drove them both home.

'I was too busy watching my father. The man's over the moon about the prospect of becoming a grandfather. It was good of him to let us know about the new will.'

'It's certainly put a stop to any thoughts Fiona might have had about taking everything and leaving you with nothing.'

'I still don't believe that she ever had plans like that.'

'Of course she did. She's already admitted—' Rose stopped suddenly, but it was too late.

'What do you mean by that?'

'Nothing.'

'Come on, Rose, it didn't sound like nothing. What's been going on?'

'Can't this wait until we get home? I'm trying to concentrate on my driving.'

He said no more, but when they arrived at their tenement he jumped out of the car and strode ahead of her up the stairs and into the flat. When she arrived he was standing in the small living room, still wearing his hat and coat.

'Well?'

'Can we talk about this in the morning?'

'We never have time to talk in the morning. Have you been trying to fight imaginary battles for me, Rose? Have you been upsetting Fiona?'

'*Me* – upsetting *her*?' The sheer injustice of the accusation took her breath away. She wrenched her hat off and threw it across the room. 'That . . . that *woman* had the audacity to tell me that she didn't need to involve you in her plans for Sandy's birthday party because she's his legal daughter, whereas you only took his name a few years ago.'

'When was this?'

'While you were in Edinburgh. She came to Harlequin for a fitting for the dress she wore tonight, and I offered her a glass of sherry, as I always do with special clients. I look on my husband's half-sister as a special client, even though she herself doesn't seem to see you as blood kin.'

'Surely you've got more sense than to let her needle you with a silly remark like that. Haven't you?' Alex asked, and then, as his wife chewed her lower lip and kept silent, 'There's more, isn't there?'

'I couldn't let her away with it, so I went to the shop the next day and asked her to tell me just what's going on in that head of hers.'

'For God's sake, Rose, will you never learn to mind your own business?'

'This *is* my business! You might be willing to let her strip you of your rightful inheritance, but I'm not going to allow it. And now there's my son's inheritance to think of too!'

'*Our* son – or daughter.'

'Our son. It will be a boy.'

Alex brushed the diversion away with an impatient gesture of one hand. 'Tell me about your meeting with Fiona.'

'If you must know, she implied – so clearly that I couldn't possibly have imagined it – that you're still in love with her.'

He stared at her, colour rushing into his face

244

and then ebbing away just as swiftly. 'That's ridiculous! We share the same father – how could I look on her as anything other than my sister?'

'That what I told her, but she refused to accept it. She tried to shock me with her version of the night you came back here and found her waiting for you. Thank heavens,' Rose said fervently, 'you were honest enough to tell me about it. If you had kept quiet about that, Alex, I might have fallen right into her trap. As it was, when she discovered that I already knew, she did her best to persuade me that you'd lied to me about the real outcome.'

'You know I told you the truth! You know that I sent her home – that I would never have . . . All I could think of at the time was that it would have been like making love to Caitlin or Mary.' He almost choked over the words.

'I know. And I know you don't have any feelings of that sort for her, but you did have, before you discovered that you're Sandy's son – there's no shame to that. But, Alex, it's my belief that she still has feelings for you.'

'Don't be absurd! She'd be mad to think anything like that.'

'I think she may be just a little bit – unbalanced. If you ask me, she married George Chalmers because she couldn't marry you, and she can't stand to see you happy with me. Nor can she bear to see Sandy making a fuss of you. He was delighted with our news, wasn't he? I've never seen the man so happy. But I was watching Fiona tonight, and she was so angry. Even if she finds a new husband and starts a family of her own, our child will be your father's first grandchild, and she'll never be able to better that!' Rose said with bitter satisfaction. 'It was the best birthday gift anyone could give him – and she had no idea that it was going to happen.' She smiled at him and then, as he merely stared back at her, his face expressionless, she said, 'What is it?'

'I was just thinking that it was the last thing *I* had expected to happen. Especially considering the way you snapped at your mother when we had dinner with them on Hogmanay and she wondered if you were carrying a child. You've always been so determined to concentrate on Harlequin – you told me that just before we married, and I agreed to wait until you were ready to start our family.'

'And I'm ready now. I'm looking forward to having this baby, Alex, really I am.'

'Are you sure? Six months isn't a very long time. I can't help wondering why you changed your mind so suddenly.'

'I'm a woman. We're famed for our ability to

change our minds faster than we change our clothes, and that's often enough, surely.'

'Don't be flippant. You've always been so careful to use that gadget — what's it called? That diaphragm. I don't remember you being without it. I don't remember us talking about having a baby.'

'These things happen. Half the people alive today were unplanned. You, for one, and probably me as well, though it's not something that I could talk to my mamma about. Which reminds me, we must tell my parents soon. Tomorrow evening, perhaps?'

'You're a businesswoman, Rose, and more efficient than most folk think you are. How else could you have set up Harlequin? I can't imagine you having an unplanned child.'

'Alex, the baby's on his way and we're happy about it. Sandy's happy about it, and so is your mother. My mother will also be thrilled because for once I'm doing something she'll approve of.'

'You've been obsessed with Fiona recently, convinced that she's going to deny me my inheritance. Then suddenly we're going to have an unplanned baby, you and I. A child that, to quote your own words, will ensure my inheritance. Ten minutes ago you were crowing over the fact that Fiona couldn't possibly manage to get the better of us. Are you sure this child wasn't planned?'

'For goodness' sake, you're imagining things!' Rose ran her hands through her hair, showering pins all over the place. 'Leave them,' she went on when Alex knelt to gather them up. 'The housekeeper will pick them up in the morning.'

'Why should she? We're so different, Rose.' He continued to collect the pins, one by one. 'We come from such different backgrounds. You're used to being waited on by paid servants and having your own way, whereas I respect other people and try to believe the best of them – even Fiona.'

He located the last pin and got up, putting them carefully into a small glass bowl on the mantelpiece. 'I'm going to bed.'

'Alex, don't leave things like this. Listen to me—'

'Sometimes,' Alex said, 'I think that I hear you more clearly when you're not talking. And that's because sometimes you don't tell me the truth. Goodnight.'

# 17

'You sly creature, you!' Caitlin said as soon as Rose walked into the sewing room. She was working at one of the cutting tables and when Rose arrived she put down the large scissors and went over to hug her sister-in-law. 'What a wonderful surprise! Rowena couldn't wait to get to school this morning to tell everyone that she's going to have a new little cousin. Mary and I have told everyone here,' she added, but there was no need, for Rose had known as soon as she saw the huge grins on the seamstresses' faces that her news had been well broadcast.

'I knew already,' Grace Watson said smugly. 'I've known for weeks. Congratulations, Mrs MacDowall.'

'How did you know, and why didn't you tell me?'

'It wasn't my news to tell, Caitlin. And when you've had weans of your own, you'll know when another woman's expectin'. It's somethin' to do with the way they walk – there's just a look about them. When's it due, Mrs MacDowall?'

'Not until the end of the year, so I've got a long time to go yet. Time enough for you to get married, Caitlin, and moved into the gatehouse so that you and Mary and Grace here can look after Harlequin while I'm away.'

'You're planning to come back afterwards?' Caitlin asked.

'Of course. I'd not want to give Harlequin up when we're doing so well.'

'You might change your mind when the wean arrives,' Grace said.

'I won't. I'm not the sort to go all soft over a baby. I'll get a good nurse for him – it,' Rose said hurriedly as Grace opened her mouth to correct her. She felt that by referring to the unborn child as 'he' as often as possible she would be more likely to have the male heir that Alex needed, but apparently that sort of thing didn't go down well with other folk. As she went downstairs to her own office, she realised that she would have to use the word 'it' out loud when mentioning the baby, and keep calling it 'him' in her own mind. It was irritating.

'You were radiant last night, but today you don't look as happy as you were,' Caitlin said when she went into the office later. 'Did the party tire you out? Perhaps you should go home early and have a rest.'

'For goodness' sake, don't start mollycoddling me! It's only a baby – women have them all the time and think nothing of it. Childbirth is a natural thing. I've been told that peasant women working in fields in some countries go behind walls and have their babies before getting straight back to work. I think that's a much better idea than making a fuss the way we do in this country!' Rose flared, and then, when she saw the hurt surprise in the girl's eyes, 'Oh, I'm sorry, Caitlin, I shouldn't take it out on you.'

'Take what out on me? What's happened?'

Rose sagged back in her chair. Caitlin was her best friend as well as her sister-in-law. She was the only person Rose could speak to without fear of being misunderstood, judged or repeated.

'It's Alex. He thinks that I'm having this child purely to spite Fiona.'

'But that's ridiculous. He was as thrilled as you were last night. And Mr MacDowall was even

251

more excited than either of you. It was the best birthday present you could have given him.'

'That was the idea. But we had a row when we got home last night. Alex has got it into his head that I deliberately became pregnant in order to spite Fiona.'

'What?' Caitlin's voice rose up the scale. 'That's the daftest thing I've ever heard!'

'Daft, mebbe, but it's true.' Rose's voice broke on the final word and she sniffed hard, fishing in the pocket of her jacket for a handkerchief. 'Oh, dammit, Caitlin, I never cry! Is this part of what happens to women when they're carrying a child?'

'What d'you mean, "it's true"?'

'I did want to spite Fiona. She's jealous of Alex, and she's as good as told me that she's determined that he'll not inherit anything from Sandy. She thinks that it should all go to her. That's why she's staying on in Glasgow, and why she's working in the emporium now. Alex is aware of the way she is, but you know what men can be like – he keeps thinking that everything will be all right. But I don't think it will, unless he makes sure of it. Then I realised that having a child – giving Sandy an heir to carry on the MacDowall name – would make Alex's inheritance safe. So I . . . arranged it,' Rose said almost primly. 'And it worked. You saw the way Sandy was last night. And Fiona was

252

furious. Even if she finds a man within the next week and marries him and gets pregnant quickly, our child will be Sandy's first grandchild. I was so pleased with Sandy's reaction, and Fiona's, that I couldn't help having a wee gloat on the way home, and Alex realised that the baby hadn't been an accident after all. He's so angry with me, Caitlin!' She scrubbed at her eyes with the handkerchief.

Caitlin watched helplessly, longing to comfort her friend but not knowing how best to do it. 'Mebbe it wasn't the right way to go about it,' she finally ventured, 'but he's pleased about the baby, I could see that last night. It'll work out, Rose, I'm sure it will. You do want this wee one yourself, don't you?'

'Yes, of course I do! I've always wanted to have Alex's children – perhaps not as soon as this, but one day. I *do* want it,' Rose repeated firmly, 'but I wish now that I had talked to Alex first. I don't want the wee scrap to be born to parents who aren't speaking to each other.'

'Och, you'll be speaking to each other long before then. You know Alex – his pride's hurt. You'll just have to wait for him to get over it. Wasn't that the way of it before the two of you got married? As I remember it, you quarrelled all the time. I knew that you loved each other long before either of you did.'

Rose nodded ruefully. 'You're right, but I had hoped that the quarrelling was over for good.'

'I doubt that – not with his red head and your outspokenness.'

'I suppose you're right there too. Now then . . .' Rose gave her eyes one last dab and reached for her bag. She took out her powder compact and began to cover all traces of her tears. 'I'm going to stay on here for as long as I can because I couldn't do with sitting around at home twiddling my thumbs and waiting for the birth. You have to marry Murdo before then, Caitlin. If you were living in the gatehouse you'd be able to concentrate on this place.'

'I'll pass your instructions on to Murdo,' Caitlin said cheerfully. Despite her worries on the previous evening, he had arrived to escort her to Sandy MacDowall's party, looking quite handsome in his best suit and the white shirt she had bought for the occasion. She had been proud to be seen out with him, even though he had been his usual quiet self, and had insisted on them being the first to leave as the evening wore on.

'I went to have a look at the gatehouse the other day. The work seems to be taking longer than we'd all expected.'

'I know.' Caitlin's smile faded. 'He's being so pernickety about it. Sometimes I wonder if he's using the work as an excuse to keep putting the marriage off.'

'He'd never do that!' Rose had the sense to realise that at that moment Caitlin needed comfort, not to hear that Rose, too, was beginning to have doubts as to Murdo's true intentions. 'What is it about men that makes them such thrawn creatures? Why can't they just accept that we women know what's best for them, instead of trying to work against us all the time?'

'Talking about houses, your flat isn't large enough for the two of you, let alone a baby and a nurse. You'll need to think about moving.'

'Lord, yes. I hadn't thought of that. I hadn't thought of anything, really. I suppose I'll have to get clothes for it, and a pram – and something for it to sleep in.'

'I wouldn't worry about any of that. Leave it to Mam and your own mother. Do your parents know about it yet?'

'We're going there tonight – if Alex agrees. If not, I'll have to go on my own,' Rose said gloomily. 'What on earth will they think if I turn up without him to give them news like that?'

'You won't,' Caitlin assured her. 'Alex might be angry about the way you went about things, but he's still pleased about the baby. And he'd not let you down in front of your parents.'

255

'I hope you're right. But enough of allowing our menfolk to fill us with gloom and doom,' Rose said briskly. 'Let's do something interesting. Let's stage a fashion display. We haven't had one since the day we opened, and that went down very well.'

'Do we have time?'

'Mary has the diary in her office. Come on . . .' Rose bounced up from her chair and led the way across the foyer.

'You certainly took centre stage last night,' Mary greeted her sister-in-law. 'Mam hasn't been able to talk about anything else since. She's going to start knitting for you today.'

'Bless her. I don't know one end of a knitting needle from the other. Did you see Fiona's face?' Rose couldn't help crowing. 'Poor John – she monopolised him from the moment he arrived, and used him as an excuse not to have anything to do with me or Alex.'

'He seemed to be enjoying it,' Caitlin said. 'It was a lovely party, wasn't it, Mary?'

'Yes, it was.' Mary glanced at the open ledger on her desk. 'Were you looking for something, Rose?'

'The diary. Caitlin and I have decided that it's time we had another fashion display.'

An hour later they had decided on the end of

July. 'Four weeks' time,' Caitlin said a trifle nervously. 'Do you think we can manage it?'

'Of course we can. It'll be hard work, and perhaps we all need a bit of a challenge. Why don't we ask some of our clients to be our models, same as last time?' Rose suggested. 'Older women as well as the younger ones – they all enjoyed taking part at the opening. And we could include your Rowena and that pretty little Irish friend of hers.'

'Aren't they too young?'

'Not necessarily, Mary. We could make a dress for each of them to model, and as payment. That might bring in some orders for younger clients. They could also take the guests' wraps when they arrive, and help to serve canapés and petits fours afterwards. They'd love that, I'm sure. They might even be willing to demonstrate some of their dances for our guests.'

'Rowena would, at the drop of a hat, and Cavan was accustomed to dancing in competitions when she lived in Ireland,' Mary said. 'You'd need to ask Shelagh about her though.'

'We'll persuade her. I'm looking forward to it already.' Rose beamed at the sisters and then ran her hand through her hair without stopping to think. 'Oh, bother!' she said as the inevitable hairpins showered to the ground. 'I keep forgetting about them, and they're such a nuisance!'

'Why not have your hair bobbed?' Mary suggested from the floor where she was picking up hairpins.

'D'you think I should?'

'I'm sure your hair would look good in a bob, and you wouldn't need to use hairpins then.' And, Mary thought to herself, she and the others would be saved the bother of having to pick up the pins every time Rose ran her fingers through her hair and dislodged them. 'I've heard that hair can become difficult to manage when a woman's carrying a child,' she added.

'Oh Lord – my hair's always been difficult. I don't think I could bear it if it got worse! I'll do it – as soon as possible.'

'What will Alex say?' Caitlin wondered.

'Never mind what he thinks, it's my hair, and I can do what I want with it.'


To Rose's relief, Caitlin had been right when she said that Alex would not let her go alone to break the news to her parents. When they met in the flat that evening Alex was quieter than normal, but when she suggested going to Paisley to break the news to her parents, he agreed at once. During the visit he was his usual self, and on the way home she dared to suggest that they would have to start house-hunting.

'We'll need a room for the baby, and another room for the nurse.'

'What nurse?'

'I don't want to give up Harlequin. I'm going back to it once the child's safely delivered, so that means bringing a nurse in to look after it. She'll expect to have her own room.'

'I'll leave it to you to find somewhere suitable. You have a better idea than I have of what's required.'

'I thought we'd try for one of those nice houses further west, halfway between Harlequin and your place of work.'

'Good idea,' Alex said, and then a silence fell between them again – not the comfortable silence they usually shared, but the silence of two people who had suddenly become estranged.

And may never become close again, Rose thought, fear gripping her heart at the very idea.


When Mrs MacDowall arrived in the sewing room in search of her, Shelagh McCart's first thought was that she had done something wrong. She stared up at Rose, one hand going as usual to the thick black hair that always covered the upper left part of her face. Her lips were parted and her one visible dark eye filled with dread.

'Is there something wrong with my work, Mrs

MacDowall?' she asked tremulously in her lovely Irish accent.

'Goodness no, your work's perfect, and if you could manage to let us have some afternoons as well as mornings, we'd be very pleased. I'm actually after a favour – we're going to have a fashion display at the end of July, and we were thinking that it would be nice to have Rowena and your Cavan there to help to look after our guests.'

'Cavan?'

'They're bonny girls, and Caitlin's going to make frocks for both of them to wear. They'll keep the frocks afterwards, of course. They might even give a short dancing display during the evening. What d'you think?'

'I'd have to ask himself and—' Shelagh was about to add, 'the ould yin,' but stopped herself, realising that a grand lady like Mrs MacDowall wouldn't understand why the ould yin was allowed to rule the McCart household with a rod of iron. It was the way things were in Shelagh's part of Ireland. 'I'd have to see what he thinks,' she ended lamely.

'Try to persuade him. I'm sure that Cavan would love it.' Rose gave her a warm smile and turned away, but then turned back suddenly. 'Shelagh, do you think that I should get my hair bobbed?'

'I-I think it would look very nice. You have lovely hair, Mrs MacDowall.'

'So do you. Thank you – I think I will,' Rose said, and was gone in a swirl of skirts and a waft of light scent.

When she went home at midday Mary told Rowena, also home for her lunch, about the plan to have the two girls at the fashion display. Rowena lost no time in telling Cavan when they met up as usual after school that afternoon.

'And we're going to get frocks specially made for us – and they won't cost any money!' The two of them jigged about in their excitement and a group of schoolboys on the opposite pavement stopped to laugh and jeer. Rowena immediately advanced to the kerb and began to make the ugliest faces she could at them. The boys retaliated, but when she stuck her tongue out and then progressed to yelling insults, they began to move across the road.

'Run!' Rowena grabbed Cavan's hand and the two of them fled along the pavement, dodging round adults, skipping out on to the road when necessary and then back to the pavement to avoid being run down by horses, carts and vans. The boys began to gain on them and the girls redoubled their efforts, their skirts flaring round long thin legs and their shoes – sturdier in Rowena's case than in Cavan's – thudding on the paving stones. They rounded the corner into Espedair Street, satchels swinging out dangerously from their long straps, and shot into the pend just as the fastest of the boys was about to catch hold of Cavan's long black hair.

Through the pend the girls raced, past the door that led to the small room where Murdo had once plied his loom, then round the corner and into the backyard, where they flattened themselves against the wall and tried to get their breath back.

'D'you think they'll come in after us?' Cavan whispered.

'Just let them try. My gran'll take the floor brush to them if they do, and my grandda and your daddy'll leather their backsides for them,' Rowena boasted. 'Let's see if they're still there.' She would have peered round the corner and into the pend, but Cavan caught hold of her arm.

'Don't! Let's go into the house, Rowena,' she begged.

'You're surely not scared of a bunch of daft laddies, are you? They couldnae even catch us,' Rowena said scornfully.

'I just want to go into the house.' Cavan was more terrified than Rowena could guess. She knew what it was like to be menaced, not by boys but by grown men and women; ugly, filthy words pouring from their open red mouths and hate in their hearts for a little girl who had done no harm other than being born into a different religion from them. She had seen at first hand what human beings could do to each other, and the jeering, running boys had brought back all the terror she and her family had fled when they came to Scotland.

'But they can't come in here,' Rowena was beginning to argue when to Cavan's relief Mrs Paget, sturdy and comforting and safe, appeared at the back door, an empty basket in her hands.

'There you are – what have the two of you been up to this time?'

'We got chased by lads on the way home. We're hiding,' Rowena informed her grandmother cheerfully. 'They might come in after us.'

'They'll have more sense than to do that. And they'll be long gone by now, off looking for more mischief. You two can just give me a hand to take in the washing, for it'll be dry, then you can have some milk and two of the rock cakes I took out of the oven half an hour ago,' Kirsty said, and Cavan's new, safe world began to settle comfortably around her again, like a magic cloak that made her invisible to bad people.

She made sure, though, to stay with Rowena

until her da came walking up from the workshop at the end of the yard. The two of them were practising an Irish dance for the fashion display when he arrived but Cavan broke away from Rowena as soon as he arrived and ran to throw her arms around his waist. He patted her on the head and smiled at Rowena before he and Cavan, hand in hand, began to walk home.

As they emerged from the pend she glanced swiftly from side to side, but there was no sign of the boys. As Rowena's gran had said, they would have gone off elsewhere as soon as their quarry escaped. Cavan began to skip along the pavement, keeping her hand in her da's and swinging their two arms together. 'Da, you'll never guess what me and Rowena are going to do.'

'What's that?' It had been a long, busy day and Joseph was anxious to get back to the flat for a bite to eat and a mug of hot strong tea, then a seat by the fire with his newspaper.

'Next month Mrs MacDowall and Rowena's Auntie Caitlin are going to have a grand showing of the frocks they make. They're going to have ladies wearing the clothes so that everyone can admire them, and they want Rowena and me to dance for them.'

'They want what? Why would they want ye to do that? Ye're making it up!'

'I'm not,' Cavan protested, cut to the quick. 'It's all true. Rowena's Auntie Mary told her and Rowena told me. We were practising one of the dances when you came to get me just there. One Scottish one, and one Irish one.'

'Ye're not doing it.'

'But Da, they're going to make frocks for us, and we can keep them!'

'It's not a good thing, Cavan. Ye'd have all the fine folk that go to that fashion house lookin' at ye.'

'I had folk looking at me when I danced in Ireland. I liked it. Please, Da, *please* let me do it!'

'What will yer ma say? And the ould yin?'

'Ma'll say yes, I'm sure she will. And my gran . . .' Cavan shivered suddenly. The ould yin never wanted her to have any pleasure in her life. She didn't want any of them to have pleasure. Cavan had been glad when her mammy defied the ould yin and went to work for Mrs MacDowall. Mammy was happy there, Cavan could see it in her face and hear it in the confident lilt of her voice when she talked about Harlequin, though she never mentioned her work in front of the ould yin because it always made her angry.

'We don't have to tell her,' Cavan ventured.

265

'Please, Da? I'll be good for ever and ever if you'll just let me do this!'

'We'll see. Just say nothin' at all about it until yer mammy and me have had a talk.'

# 18

'She loves dancing in front of folk,' Shelagh whispered into Joseph's ear. They were in the privacy of their bedroom, but even so, the ould yin always seemed to know everything that was going on. Sometimes Shelagh wondered if the woman had the ability to turn herself into a fly on the wall, or an earwig crawling through a crack in the bare floorboards. She felt that if she got up in the night and crept through to the kitchen, she would find the ould yin's body lying in the inset bed, eyes open and empty because her soul was off somewhere else, spying. 'You should see her at the ceilidhs, Joseph – she looks so happy, the way she used to be, before . . . before.'

'I don't want any trouble – God knows we've

had enough of it! You know that we can't draw attention to ourselves,' Joseph went on as his wife stayed silent.

'Cavan wouldn't be drawing attention to herself.'

'She'll be dancin' in front of folk.'

'Rich folk that buy their clothes from Harlequin. Why would any of them be interested in the likes of us, or what happened back in Ireland?'

'Ye never know,' he muttered uneasily.

'Mrs MacDowall says that Cavan can have a frock made especially for her to keep, without it costing us a penny piece. She'd like that.' Shelagh raised herself on one elbow so that she could look down at her husband. 'Joseph, with all that's going on over in Ireland, why would the folk that chased us out of the place even want to find us again? They got their way – they ruined our lives and it's thanks to them that we're living in this cold damp house and scarce earning enough to keep body and soul together. Have they not done enough to us?'

'I'm still alive, and that's reason enough for them not to forget us. I know what they're like – they'll not forget; not until I'm lyin' in my grave.'

'Don't say that!' Shelagh wound her arms around him, holding him tightly. 'You'll die an old man,' she said into his throat, 'in your own bed and in your own time, with Cavan's children and grand-children there to mourn you!'

'Dear God, I hope you're right.' He stroked the silky black hair lying across his chest, then put a finger beneath her chin and tilted her face to his. When he kissed her, her lips were wet, and tasted salty. 'Ah, don't cry, Shelagh. You're right – we're safe enough here.'

'If you mean that, you can let Cavan dance at the fashion display. She's had to give up so much, Joseph, and she's never once complained. I'll be there myself, and I promise you that I'll watch out for her.'

'Promise me that ye'll watch out for both of yez.'

'So we can both go?'

'Aye, ye can. But not a word of it to the ould yin, for she'd never allow such a thing. The less she knows, the better for all of us.'

Shelagh fell asleep in his arms, but he lay awake for a long time, cherishing the softness and warmth of her against his body and listening to her every breath. He wished with all his heart that he could find the money to give her and Cavan – and the ould yin too – a better life. They didn't need much, for they had never had much. Just a cottage with a wee bit of garden where he could grow vegetables and Shelagh could have the flowers she loved, and Cavan could run and dance beneath the sun's warmth. They had had all that before it all went wrong, in little more than the blink of an eye.

Sometimes, now, he thought that it might be better for Shelagh if he had never set eyes on her, and never lost his heart to her. It might have been better if Cavan had never been born. If things had been different, Shelagh could well have married someone her family approved of, and be living happily in her own country. He himself would only have the ould yin to watch out for instead of carrying fear in his heart and mind, his blood and bones, every minute of the day, and especially during the long dark hours of the night.

But without Shelagh and Cavan, his own life would be worthless. If anyone ever hurt either of them he knew that he would kill without compunction. He had heard somewhere that when a man had killed once, the second time was always easier. And he believed it.

Rose and Caitlin had no idea how much their amusement over the way Fiona had monopolised John Brodie at her father's party wounded Mary. Beneath her usual air of calm competence she had felt quite out of her depth at the party, and had been eagerly awaiting John's arrival. After greeting his host and hostess he had made his way over to her, looking as relieved as she was to find what her mother would describe as a 'weel-kent' face.

But they had only talked for five minutes before Fiona arrived and swept John off to see some painting she had bought for her father's birthday. Mary, not included in the invitation, watched him go, glancing back at her and looking for all the world like an anxious five-year-old leaving his mother on his first day at school. She had expected him to return, but instead Fiona kept him by her side, introducing him to one person after another. Watching, Mary saw him gradually begin to relax and enjoy himself. And why not? John had been brought up in a grand house, by wealthy parents. This was his world, not Mary's.

She had been glad when the evening was over, and she and her parents returned home. When Kirsty, falling into her fireside chair and easing sore feet out of smart, uncomfortable shoes, said, 'My, there's nowhere like your own place, is there?' Mary agreed with all her heart.

She and John had arranged to meet at the entrance to the Royal Alexandra Infirmary for their usual Sunday walk; when the day turned out to be cloudy and cool and more like an autumn day than the beginning of July, she donned warm clothing and sturdy shoes and took an umbrella from the stand in the narrow hall as she went out. If he didn't turn up – and she was beginning to wonder if he would, since she hadn't seen him since the party – then she'd go walking on her own. She needed to get away from everyone and everything for an hour or two.

But John was waiting outside the infirmary, his face breaking into a smile as he saw her approach with her usual swift, firm step. 'I thought the weather might put you off,' he said as they shook hands.

'Oh no, I enjoy our Sunday afternoons.'

'So do I.' He took her arm. 'I thought we might go out along the road to Barrhead today.'

They hadn't gone more than a hundred yards when the clouds that had been menacing Paisley all morning suddenly began to deluge the town. Mary put up her umbrella and John took it from her so that he could hold it over her. Within minutes he was soaked.

'Can't you hold it over your head as well as mine?'

Raindrops flew from his face as he shook his head. 'It's not big enough – and this downpour seems set for the afternoon. I wonder . . .' he hesitated and then said diffidently, 'My flat's only a bit further on. I could offer you tea, if you don't mind the two of us being there on our own.'

'Of course I don't mind,' Mary said at once, and five minutes later he was unlocking the door and ushering her into his second-floor flat, saying apologetically, 'It's quite basic, I'm afraid. A housekeeper comes in during the week to keep it clean, but it lacks a woman's touch. This is the living room.'

'I think it's very pleasant.' Mary approved of the neatness and the space; the room was large and adequately furnished, with a folding table against one wall, a desk, a couch, two chairs grouped around the fireplace and a small occasional table beneath the window. The only other furnishing was a large and well-filled bookcase.

'Take your coat off and I'll hang it up to dry in the kitchen. It's warmer there.' John took it from her, together with her gloves, hat and umbrella, and hurried out. The room was pleasantly warm because the fire was lit and had been banked up, ready for his return. Mary crossed to the bay window, flanked by long thick curtains, and looked down on Neilston Road, interested in seeing it from another angle.

'I've put the kettle on.' John came back into the room and removed the fireguard so that he could poke the fire into life. 'I have coffee, if you would prefer it.'

'Tea would be lovely, thank you.'

He went out again and she studied the bookshelves. Many of the books were legal tomes, but

273

there were others on birds, wild flowers, gardening, trees and art, as well as novels by Dickens, Galsworthy and Arthur Conan Doyle – all names she recognised, but had never read.

The wealth of titles made Mary feel so ill-read that she retired to a comfortable fireside chair, making a mental note to make time to read proper books rather than magazines and newspapers.

The coals in the grate had begun to blaze and the rain now lashing against the windows made the room feel cosy and welcoming. She was almost asleep when John arrived with a loaded tray and brought over a small table so that they could take their tea in comfort.

'I'll pour, shall I?' he suggested, and Mary snuggled deeper into her chair and smiled at him.

'Yes please. I feel very cosseted – I'm not used to being looked after.'

'You're the sort of person who should be looked after – you're such a hard worker.'

'Working at Harlequin isn't nearly as hard as working in Robertson's jam factory. It was horrible in the summer, with the place so warm and the wasps being lured in by the smell of the marmalade and the jam. I'm grateful to Rose for giving me the job I have now.'

'She's very pleased to have you there – and your sister too.' He put her teacup within easy reach and laid a triangle of sponge cake on a plate for her before settling down in the chair opposite. 'Did you enjoy the party the other night?'

'It was very nice.' Mary took a bite of jam sponge.

'I'm sorry that I didn't manage to spend more time with you, Mary, but Fiona – Mrs Chalmers – wanted me to have a look at the painting she had bought for her father. A very handsome landscape.'

'I saw the books on art in your bookcase. I didn't realise that you were interested in it. Do you paint?'

'Oh no, I don't have that talent. But my godfather was a collector, and he taught me to appreciate fine paintings when I was a lad. I have a few pieces of my own now.' He nodded at the paintings on the wall. 'Nothing very valuable, but work by artists I like. Mrs Chalmers is apparently interested in art as well. She's a charming young woman, isn't she? An excellent hostess.'

'Yes indeed,' Mary agreed, and took another bite of cake. She had enjoyed her first bite, but for some reason the second wasn't nearly as good.

Fortunately, most of the afternoon was spent talking about various subjects, though Fiona's name cropped up more than once. Even so, Mary enjoyed her visit, and when the time came to leave she was reluctant to tear herself away from the fireside, and from her companion.

'I'll walk home with you,' he suggested as he helped her on with her coat.

'I wouldn't dream of it. I don't have far to go and I have my umbrella. In any case, I think the rain's beginning to ease off now.' Mary fastened the last button on her coat, pinned her hat on and smiled up at him. 'Perhaps the weather will be kinder next Sunday, and we can take that walk along the road to Barrhead.'

'Ah – I'm afraid I won't manage to meet you next Sunday.' He looked a little embarrassed. 'Fiona – Mrs Chalmers – is taking her father to Kelvingrove Art Gallery on Sunday afternoon and she's invited me to accompany them.'

'Oh. I see.'

'Why don't you come with us? Have you ever been to Kelvingrove? It's well worth the visit,' he urged when she shook her head.

'I'm sure it is, but I'd better not. Now that Rose and Caitlin have decided on another fashion display I'll be busy making out lists of guests and planning refreshments. We don't have much time and I'd rather start work on it early, just in case something unexpected crops up at the last minute.'

'That's what I admire about you, Mary. You're so efficient. Well, you and I must make a point of visiting the art gallery one Sunday soon,' John said as he opened the flat door.

276

'I shall look forward to it.' Mary smiled up at him, but as she stepped out into the rain, which had begun to fall fast again, her heart felt as heavy and as grey as the sky above.

To all involved with Harlequin, July seemed to rush by. As had happened at the opening several years earlier, some of the regular clients agreed to model clothes that had been designed for them.

'Such fun!' said one, while another remarked, 'It's like being in a play, isn't it?'

Rose and Mary had to take on the arduous task of planning the order of events and holding rehearsals, which proved to be difficult, since the models all knew each other socially and tended to spend more time chatting to each other than learning how to move and turn in order to show the clothes off to their best advantage.

'Perhaps we should think of hiring proper models,' Rose suggested after one particularly difficult afternoon.

Mary shook her head. 'It would cost a fortune, and in any case, they're all wearing clothes made to fit them. They wouldn't necessarily fit professional models.'

'But did you see the way Mary Hastie trudged down the middle of the floor like a middle-aged housewife? And she's only twenty-two. Oh God, I wish we'd never thought of this dratted display!' Rose ran her hands through her hair without thinking and then groaned as the hairpins began to tumble down. 'I must, must, *must* get my hair cut. Those pins spend so little time on my head that I might as well throw them on the floor when I get up in the mornings and be done with it!'

Mary crouched down, glancing up at Rose while her hands moved about, finding hairpins by touch. 'When Miss Hastie turned to trudge back, did you not see the way her skirt lifted and flared? It gave her a sudden grace and elegance that she doesn't really have. That's because the gown was designed for her, and the material and pattern carefully chosen. We don't make clothes for models, Rose, we do them for real people. And real people come in all shapes and sizes, and in all age groups too. I think we should ask more of our older ladies to take part as well,' she suggested.

'That's a good idea. I wonder if my mamma would agree to model that nice little costume Caitlin designed for her?'

'And what about finishing off with a bridal theme? There's that pretty young woman from Brookfield, the one who got married in Paisley Abbey last month to the son of an Honourable. Why don't we invite her and her bridesmaids to model their wedding finery for us? The audience would love that.' She held out a handful of pins.

'Mary, what would we do without you? What a perfect finish!' Rose began to pin up swatches of brown curly hair, without much success. 'Let's do it.'

'I'll telephone her mother right away. I think she should be back from her honeymoon by now. But first,' Mary said, moving to stand behind Rose, 'why don't you let me pin your hair up for you?'

# 19

Alex and Rose were still behaving like polite strangers sharing the same flat. The estrangement made Rose feel wretched, and there were times when she thought that Alex must be as miserable as she was. Then there were times when she thought that perhaps he preferred it that way. She was also worried about the way his nightmares, which had started to ease off, were becoming frequent again.

There was only one thing that kept her going – Harlequin and the coming fashion show. At least when she was at work she was too preoccupied to fret over her failing marriage.

Rowena and Cavan, thrilled to be taking part in such a grown-up occasion, came in to be measured for their dresses and were enthusiastic over Caitlin's choice of buttercup-yellow for Rowena and emerald-green for Cavan. Caitlin also insisted on making a new two-piece outfit for Rose, who gasped, as did everyone else, when she saw the long loose jacket in deep rose-red silk, designed along the lines of an artist's smock with a floppy white silk bow at the throat. The jacket was worn over a slightly flared purple skirt, both disguising Rose's pregnancy, which had recently begun to reveal itself.

'I can't wear that!' she said, aghast. 'It's too stylish for me!'

'It's perfect for you,' Caitlin corrected her. 'Nobody else has the colouring or the carriage to carry it off.' She scooped up the clothes and draped them over her arm. 'Come down to the fitting room and try them on.'

Ten minutes later Rose peered cautiously at herself in the long mirrors skilfully arranged so that she could see a back view as well as a front view. 'I look so . . . so . . .' Unable to think of the right word, she shrugged helplessly, and the silk rippled with the movement, its colours shimmering back at her.

'You look like the woman who owns Harlequin,' Caitlin said, trying to hide her own delight with her design. 'It's dramatic, but it's you.'

'I can't believe it. I grew up looking like a clothes horse — the wooden kind that you put in front of the kitchen fire with wet clothes draped over them,' Rose explained. 'My poor mamma despaired of me because nothing looked right on me. But since you came along, I look so different.'

'Anybody can wear ordinary clothes, but you weren't made for them. Not many folk can wear clothes like that.' Caitlin gestured towards the mirror. 'But you can. As for your hair — we'll draw it back and put combs in it.'

During the two weeks before the fashion show the women in the sewing room had to work past their usual stopping time in order to get everything ready. As well as the new clothes for Rose and the two girls, some of the clients who had agreed to model their own clothes needed last-minute adjustments, while others were modelling clothes that had not yet been completed.

Shelagh was asked to work in the afternoons as well as the mornings, and agreed, even though the ould yin punished her for it by making her life as difficult as possible when she was at home.

Mary, too, welcomed the rush and excitement of organising the display. She rarely saw John now, other than when he called in at Harlequin. Following on the visit to Kelvingrove Art Gallery with Fiona and her father — an outing that, by all accounts, he had greatly enjoyed — he was invited to tea with the MacDowalls on the following Sunday, and to a private showing at a small art gallery on the Sunday after that. And there had been an evening when Fiona, finding herself with two tickets to the theatre and nobody to go with, had turned to John for assistance. He had enjoyed the play very much, he told Mary the next day.

Mary made lists and wrote out invitations in her neat, careful hand. She noted every reply, worked out the amount of food and wine needed, made sure that there was sufficient china, glasses and cutlery, ordered napkins with 'Harlequin' printed on them in rainbow-coloured letters, had programmes printed out, listed the models and the clothes they would wear and, after careful consultation with Rose, Caitlin and Grace, worked out the order of the show in precise detail.

When the day arrived she made sure that the place was spotless, the chairs in place for the audience, the food and drink laid out and the armfuls of flowers she had ordered carefully arranged in large vases especially borrowed from Rose's mother for the occasion.

Just when everything seemed to be ready, a note arrived for Rose. Mary opened and read it, then took it up to the sewing room where Caitlin and Grace were checking that the designs to be used that evening had been hung up carefully and in the correct order.

'Florence Peacock's just sent a message to say that she can't take part tonight.'

'What? Of course she'll have to take part,' Caitlin said firmly. 'She can't change her mind now – she promised!'

'I doubt if you can tell her that, since she's on her way to the South of France. Apparently some dear friends have just invited her to join them, and she simply couldn't resist.' Mary waved the note at her sister.

'That woman's the limit,' Grace snapped. 'She never arrives for a fitting on time – if she bothers to arrive at all.'

'So what are we going to do now?' Mary asked Caitlin.

'That's up to Rose – I'm far too busy to worry about it.'

'Rose isn't here. She left an hour ago, saying that she had some business to attend to and she'll be back in this afternoon. That's why I opened the note that came for her; I had a feeling that it might not be able to wait until then.'

'For goodness' sake! We'll just have to forget about Miss Peacock's appearance.'

'But hers are among the nicest outfits in the whole display,' Grace protested.

'I can't help that.'

'There's one way out . . .' Mary drew the other two aside so that they couldn't be overheard, though it was unlikely that any of the machinists could hear anything above the busy whirr of their machines. 'You used Shelagh McCart once when Florence Peacock missed a fitting, didn't you, Grace?'

'Aye, that's right. Their measurements are almost identical,' agreed Grace, who had a photographic memory when it came to measurements. 'Shelagh's a wee bittie thinner, probably because she doesn't eat enough, but a pin here and a pin there would take care of that.'

'And she's beautiful, too. I think she could do it, Caitlin.'

'If she'd agree to it.' Caitlin looked doubtfully at Shelagh, bent over her sewing machine. 'She's such a shy lassie.'

'Grace, give me five minutes, then ask Shelagh if I can have a word with her. I'll do my best,' Mary said, and hurried downstairs to her tiny office.

Shelagh arrived five minutes later, her one visible dark eye wide with alarm.

'You wanted to see me, Miss Lennox?'

285

'Sit down, Shelagh. I've got a favour to ask,' Mary said when the other young woman had settled herself gingerly on the edge of the chair by the desk. 'You're coming to the fashion show tonight with Cavan, aren't you?'

'Oh yes, she's looking forward to it – and Miss Caitlin's made her such a beautiful dress!' Shelagh's concern vanished, to be replaced by a radiant smile. 'I'll be helping the ladies in and out of their dresses for the show, too.'

'I wondered if you would do something else for us.'

'Of course, if I can.'

'One of the ladies – Miss Peacock – can't be here tonight, and Grace says that you're the same height and size as she is. We have her outfits here and I want you to model them in her place.'

'Me? Oh, I couldn't do that!'

'Of course you could. You know who I mean – you modelled one of her dresses before, when she went off gallivanting instead of coming in for a fitting. All you have to do is walk along before the audience and then back again, then turn round to show the clothes off, then leave. It's easy.'

'No, I couldn't . . . I . . . please don't ask me!' Shelagh McCart's left hand swept up to cover the fall of hair across the left side of her face as she blundered to her feet. She turned to flee the room and as she did so her right hand brushed against a corner of the desk, sending a pile of neatly folded programmes crashing to the floor. She immediately dropped to her knees and began to gather them up.

'I'm so sorry, Miss Lennox!' Crouched on the floor, she could not be seen, but her voice, now thickening with panicky tears, drifted up from the other side of the desk. 'I'm a clumsy eejit, so I am – all your nice papers – I'll have them tidy in no time.'

'Don't worry about it, Shelagh.' Mary, horrified by the way her simple request had upset the young woman, hurried round the desk. 'They're only papers, I can easily gather them up mys—'

She rounded the desk and then stopped abruptly as Shelagh's head jerked up to reveal a mass of purple scar tissue covering the left upper side of her otherwise lovely face, overlying part of her forehead and upper cheek and dragging her eyelid down to droop over the left eye.

Mary only had one swift glimpse of the damage before Shelagh dropped the papers she had begun to gather up and clapped both hands over her face, tucking her chin into her neck and crouching at Mary's feet like a wounded animal.

'Shelagh . . .' Mary reached down and touched the soft black hair, but the young woman jerked

287

away from her hand with a whimper of protest. Mary straightened, wondering if she should seek help from Grace or Caitlin, then decided that she had done enough damage.

'Shelagh,' she said to the downbent head, 'I'm going to make a pot of tea for the two of us. You gather up the programmes, if you will, then sit down and wait for me. Nobody else will come in, I promise you.'

She wondered, as she made the tea in the small kitchenette at the back of the building, if Shelagh would take the opportunity to rush back to the safety of her own home, but when she returned to the office the programmes had been piled neatly on the desk and the Irishwoman was sitting quietly, her hands locked in her lap and her head down.

Mary poured tea and waited until Shelagh had taken her first sip before asking quietly, 'What happened, Shelagh?'

There was a pause before the other woman gave a long, low sigh then half-whispered, 'An iron – fresh from the brazier.'

'An accident?'

Shelagh's hair shone like ebony as she shook her head. 'My da – he's a blacksmith, and he always was a hot-tempered man. When Joseph and me decided to get wed Joseph wanted us to tell my parents together, but I decided to speak to my da

288

first, on my own. I knew my da would be angry and I didn't want Joseph hurt. I went to the forge and told my da that I'd made my mind up and there was no changing it, even if it meant that I'd never be allowed to see my own folk again.'

Her hand shook slightly as she put it up to cover the scar protectively and Mary, absorbed as she was in the other woman's story, made a mental note to find nice gloves to hide Shelagh's work-roughened fingers.

'I was ready to be knocked to the ground, for that had happened often enough before. I never thought of the brazier and the irons heating in it. He . . .' She picked up her cup, then put it down again when tea slopped over the rim. 'He threw one of the irons at me and I didn't manage to get out of the way in time.'

'He did that just because you wanted to get married?'

Shelagh picked the cup up again, this time with both hands. She looked fully at Mary, realising that there was no sense now in trying to cover her face. Even so, her thick hair hid all but an edge of the puckered scar. 'You don't know what it's like in Ireland, Miss Lennox. You see, Joseph's Catholic, and so am I, now. But I was a Protestant then. We're not supposed to marry with the other kind.'

'What did your husband do when he found out what had happened to you?'

'He went to face my da and from what I heard, they each gave as good as they got. My ma had sent me off to my aunt's since she knew that I couldn't stay at home any more. Joseph and me got married, him with his face and hands swollen and bruised, me with my bandages still on.'

'Shelagh, I'm so sorry!'

'Och, it was years ago, and I've never regretted marrying Joseph, even though I've not seen my family since. But I don't need them – I've got all the family I need.' Shelagh's voice suddenly strengthened and she lifted her head proudly on her long slender neck, smiling. 'All the family I'll ever want. D'you see now why I can't do as you ask tonight?'

'I don't see why not. We could soak your hair with sugared water to make it stay in place and I'd stay with you when you're changing, to make sure that you're all right. Nobody else needs to know,' Mary hurried on, 'for they'll never hear it from me, I promise you. Say you'll do it. You'd enjoy it!'

'But the ladies the clothes are made for are to wear them,' Shelagh protested frantically. 'They won't want to share a changing room with the likes of me!'

'How would they know who you are? If you ask me, you look more of a lady than most of them do. But I tell you what – you can change here, in my office. Cavan and Rowena too – I think there's room for the three of you.' Mary glanced around the small space. 'We'll move the desk into the corner. And Grace will find some nice underwear for you, and pretty gloves to match Miss Peacock's outfits. Please say that you'll do it, Shelagh!'

'If you really think that I could do it, I'd like to. You make such lovely clothes here, it would be a pleasure to wear them, even if it's only for a wee while. I love working with the beautiful materials and the ribbons and all,' Shelagh said shyly.

'Good for you! The small fitting room's empty – why don't we go in there now and try on the clothes you'll be wearing? We can try the sugared water, too, and you can practise walking and turning. And I'll see that there's a wee bit extra in your wages for this.'

Rose swept in an hour later, nodding cheerfully when Caitlin told her about Florence Peacock, and Mary's solution.

'We can always trust Mary to solve our problems, and Florence Peacock's no loss. I expect

Shelagh will carry the clothes off better than Florence ever could. That young woman has a natural grace that has nothing to do with being born with a silver spoon in one's mouth.'

'Are you well? I just wondered when you disappeared this morning if you had to see your doctor,' Caitlin added as Rose's eyebrows rose.

'My goodness no, I'm as fit as a fiddle. I was on other business altogether. What do you think?' Rose swept her hat off to reveal a short, casual hairstyle with a light fringe over her forehead. She whirled around to show how the hair had been shaped to the nape of her neck.

'It's perfect!'

'D'you really think so?' Rose demanded, and when Caitlin nodded she gave a sigh of relief. 'I've been so worried! The hairdresser seemed to be cutting for hours, and when I finally opened my eyes my poor rejected hair lay all over the floor. I suddenly wanted to ask her to gather it all up and put it back the way it was, but it was too late.' She ran her hands through her hair, then beamed at her sister-in-law. 'No hairpins falling all over the place! It feels so . . . light and free! Do you think Alex will approve?'

'I'm sure he will. Didn't you tell him you were having it done?'

Rose shook her head and then, charmed by

the novelty of it, shook it again. 'That feels so different. I haven't mentioned it to him. For some reason men seem to like women to have long hair – my sister Eleanor has such a tiresome time with her hair, but her husband's forbidden her to have it cut by one inch. If Alex had been against me having mine shortened it would only have made me all the more determined to do it. In any case, I felt that this was something that I had to decide for myself. Now then, let's go and see if Mary needs any help – though I've no doubt that she has everything under control, as always.'

By the time the first car swept in through the gates and the first uniformed chauffeur assisted his passengers to alight, all was ready. Rose and Caitlin welcomed each guest at the door, while Grace and the seamstresses, all but Shelagh, tucked away in Mary's office, were upstairs with the clients who were to model the clothes designed and made for them by Harlequin.

Rowena, dressed in yellow, and Cavan, in emerald-green, greeted each guest with a stylish curtsey before taking their coats to be hung up in Rose's office. Once the audience was seated in the larger fitting room John Brodie, who had been pressed into service, offered something to drink while the two girls brought in silver trays filled with an assortment of sandwiches and biscuits.

Fiona and her father were among the earliest arrivals. Her brown eyes widened when she caught sight of Rose.

'My dear, you look positively – dramatic. When did you get your hair cut?'

'This afternoon.' Rose summoned up a sweet smile, which Fiona returned with equal insincerity.

'You're quite stunning, Rose,' Sandy MacDowall said warmly, then, with relief, 'Ah, you're here, Brodie!'

'Yes, sir, Mary summoned me.' John shook the older man's hand and was reaching out to shake Fiona's when she stepped forward, lifting her face to his. After a moment of embarrassed hesitation he stooped to kiss her proffered cheek. 'Hello, Fiona, you look lovely.'

'Thank you, John.' She smoothed the fur collar of her pony skin coat before unfastening it and allowing him to slip it from her shoulders. Rowena pounced on it and bore it away.

'Mary said that there would probably be some male companions here tonight, Mr MacDowall, so I've been detailed to offer them refreshment in Rose's office,' John said. 'Unless, that is, you would prefer to watch the fashion show, sir?'

'Oh no, not at all,' Sandy assured him. 'Where's this office, then?'

'Isn't Alex here to support your venture?' Fiona asked as John ushered her father away.

'He's busy, but he said he would try to get here. Through there,' Rose said, and turned with relief to some newcomers.

The fashion display worked out just as Mary had planned. She watched anxiously as Shelagh made her first entrance, but if the young Irishwoman felt nervous she managed to hide it. The fine wool costume that had been made for Florence Peacock fitted her slender figure perfectly, thanks to Grace's clever pinning and tucking, and although Shelagh, as ever, kept her head slightly averted from the audience's gaze so that they saw little more of her face other than the usual fall of black silky hair, she held herself well as she entered. As rehearsed carefully that afternoon with Mary, she walked unhurriedly and easily across the room in her borrowed shoes, then turned with a natural grace. Once the right, unblemished side of her face was presented in profile to the watchers, she lifted her chin proudly, still looking neither to left nor right as she walked back to the entrance. There, she paused and turned gracefully to show the back of the costume, then she was gone. On her second entrance, wearing a cream silk afternoon dress, she moved with even more natural grace, drawing murmurs of admiration from the audience.

'That dress will never look as lovely on its owner as it does today,' Caitlin whispered to Mary.

There was a warm round of applause for the finale – a young bride in a simple but beautifully draped gown in white duchesse satin, and her four bridesmaids in pale-blue silk with love knots embroidered in deep blue around boat-shaped necklines.

It had been decided that Rowena and Cavan would give a brief dancing display once the fashion show had ended, to music provided by the accordionist who played at the ceilidhs. The girls finished to enthusiastic applause, but when the man from the *Paisley Daily Express* tried to take their photograph, Cavan shook her head and fled to Mary's office, and the safety of her mother.

'That's a pity,' the photographer said. 'Bonny wee lassie, too.'

'I'll fetch her back.' Rowena headed for the door, but Mary stopped her.

'Leave her be, she's just shy.'

'But I wanted us to get our picture taken together!' Rowena protested, then subsided as she saw by her aunt's face that Mary wasn't going to put up with any nonsense.

'So what's your name, pet?' the photographer wanted to know when the picture had been taken. 'And your pretty wee friend's name?'

Rowena opened her mouth to reply, then closed it again as Mary started to answer for her. Just then, Caitlin called Mary away, and Rowena found herself free to say importantly, 'I'm Miss Rowena Lennox, and my friend is Miss Cavan McCart.'

'What did ye say her name was? I've never heard a name like that.'

'Cavan.' Rowena spelled it out clearly. 'It's Irish. Cavan comes from Ireland, and she's a very good dancer. She's won competitions in Ireland. I'm a very good dancer too, of course. She taught me some Irish dancing and I taught her some Scottish dancing.' She would have said more, but after writing both names down carefully in his notebook, the photographer hurried off.

# 20

When the invited guests and amateur models finally disappeared into the night, Mary announced triumphantly that she had collected the names of several women who wanted to order outfits from Harlequin. 'And some of them asked about dresses for their little girls too, after seeing Rowena and Cavan looking so pretty. I wonder if we've made a mistake there,' she added. 'Not with the girls, of course, but do we have time to do children's clothes as well?'

'We might have, if we bring in a new designer.' Rose was glowing with the success of the venture. 'We keep talking about that, Caitlin, but we've never done anything yet. Mebbe the time's come.'

'Mebbe, but not tonight, for it's been a long day. Let's go home.'

'Yes, let's.' Rose stretched to ease her aching back and ran her hands through her hair. The gesture was made without any thought, but the sensation as her fingers suddenly emerged into thin air instead of continuing through long locks reminded her sharply that Alex still didn't know what she had done. It also reminded her that he had not kept his promise to come to Paisley when he finished his own day's work. She had been so busy, and so elated by the success of the evening, that she hadn't even realised until now that he wasn't here.

'You go on,' she urged the others. 'I'll lock up.' Tired though she was, she needed some time on her own before returning to the flat.

When they had gone she went upstairs to make sure that all the clothes displayed that evening had been hung up properly, then returned to the ground floor and went into her office, realising all at once that she was bone weary and in need of something to strengthen her before she faced the drive home.

She was pouring some sherry into a glass when she heard the outer door open and Alex call her name.

'I'm in here.' She turned from the corner cabinet

299

in time to see him stop short in the doorway, his eyes widening as he saw her. Suddenly as tongue-tied as a shy young girl, Rose waited until finally he said, 'You look – magnificent.'

'You like the outfit? Your sister designed it.'

'But I doubt if any other woman could carry it off as well as you do. You look so . . . different.'

'I've had my hair cut.' She revolved slowly.

'So you have.'

'Do you like it?'

'I don't know. I'll have to get used to it – but it looks good on you,' he added swiftly.

'Thank you.' They were still speaking to each other as though they were strangers, but then again, Rose thought with regret, they had become strangers over the past few weeks. 'Would you like a drink?'

'Whisky, please. I'm sorry to have missed your special evening,' he said as she turned back to the corner cupboard. 'A new client came in and kept me talking longer than I realised. Was it a success?'

'Very successful.' She gave him his drink and then sat behind the desk while Alex stayed on his feet. 'We got some new clients, and several orders.'

'I'm glad.'

'Both our mothers were here, and Jean, and my sisters. My mamma modelled a costume we had made for her. She tried to pretend that it was all very boring, but I think she secretly enjoyed the novelty of it. And Fiona and your father came as well.'

'I hope that Fiona behaved herself.'

'She did. And so did I,' Rose added, and saw a smile tug at his lips. He tipped a generous amount of whisky into his mouth and swilled it around, taking time to enjoy its bouquet before swallowing it down.

'This old building has seen some memorable meetings between you and me, hasn't it? Remember how angry I was when you bought it from under my nose?'

'I remember, but I still don't regret doing it.'

'Then Caitlin asked me to make the furniture for you. You and I still weren't speaking to each other when I came to see about that.'

'I was going to leave all the talking to Caitlin, but she couldn't be here. It was difficult for both of us, wasn't it?'

'We managed.'

'We had to,' Rose said drily. 'Then there was the night before the first fashion show, when you said that the sign was crooked and you insisted on re-hanging it, and you almost fell off the ladder.'

'And you lost your temper with me when there was no need at all.'

'You might have been killed!' She could still

recall the cold terror that had gripped her as she saw the ladder, with Alex perched on the topmost rung, begin to sway. 'And then you enlisted and went off to the army without saying goodbye to me.' Her voice shook on the final few words as she remembered the pain of knowing that he was gone and might never come back; the realisation that she might spend the rest of her life regretting that she had not had a chance to say goodbye, or tell him how much she cared for him.

Alex, recognising the tremor in her voice, retreated into dry humour. 'If I'd told you I had enlisted you would probably have lost your temper with me yet again. I didn't want us to part on bad terms.'

'Of course I'd have been angry with you for being daft enough to volunteer when you didn't have to. What else could you expect?'

'Would you have preferred me to hide safely at home until they came to drag me to the front?'

'Yes – no – I don't know!'

There was a sudden silence, during which he finished his whisky while Rose angrily pushed papers about her desk. Then he said, 'But when I came back on leave I came here to see you – remember that day? This is where you agreed to be my wife and this is where I promised to love

302

you for the rest of my life – no matter what. Have we made a mess of things so soon, Rose?'

'Yes, we have,' she said. And then, rising to her feet, 'but it's not too late to put things right, if that's what you want.'

'Of course I want it!' He moved to meet her and when she went into his arms they closed tightly around her. 'I still want to spend the rest of my life with you,' he murmured into her ear, 'more than ever, the way you look tonight, shorn head and all.'

'It's not shorn!' a muffled, indignant voice said. 'It's very stylish.'

'It is,' Alex agreed, and kissed her. Then, when he finally released her, he said, 'Let's go home.'

'Yes,' Rose said contentedly. 'Let's.'

For once, they took their time over breakfast the next morning, reluctant to go their different ways. Happiness, and possibly approaching mother-hood, had given Rose a glow that she had never had before, Alex thought as he smiled across the table at her. And he liked the way her short hair tousled becomingly about her face.

'I'm glad you got your hair cut – it looks very pretty.'

'It feels much better, but I should have told you that I was going to do it. We shouldn't keep

303

secrets from each other, not even little secrets like that.'

'No,' Alex agreed, then remembered his meeting with Beth in Edinburgh. 'Rose—'

The housekeeper's key turned in the front door lock and Rose jumped to her feet. 'Good heavens, is that the time? I must rush; we've got so much to do after last night.'

She hurried round the table to drop a kiss on his cheek, and then he was alone, listening to her voice in the hall, then the sound of the front door closing.

Tonight, he promised himself, he would tell her about Beth. As she had said: no more secrets.

He made a point of getting home at a reasonable hour that evening, but it wasn't easy to find the right moment to speak about his meeting with Beth in Edinburgh. Rose had found time to gather details of two bungalows for sale and as soon as they had eaten she spread the papers out on the table.

'They both look quite hopeful, but I think that I like this one best. It has a nice garden and a living room and a small dining room with french windows leading out on to the garden, and three bedrooms – one for us, one for the nanny and one as the nursery. You do understand how important it is for me to keep working, don't you?'

'Yes, I do.' He took her hand and kissed it. 'I promised before we married that I wouldn't expect you to be the sort of wife who stays at home and warms her husband's slippers, and I meant it.'

'Even though it means coming home to cold slippers?'

'Even so. And it applies to both of us – you have to put your feet into cold slippers too.' Alex could not imagine her settling down to be a housewife, even after the birth of their child.

'You're sure?'

'Rose, I fell in love with you because of the person you are. I don't want to change you in any way.'

She gave him a loving smile. 'You're the only man in the world that I could live with! Can we have a look at both houses at the weekend? We need to make a decision soon – I want to move in before I get so fat that I have to be rolled up the garden path.'

'You won't. Rose, while I was in Edinburgh—'

'I meant to tell you that I had tea with my parents yesterday, before the fashion display. They want to provide the perambulator and the crib. I said that I would ask you about it.'

'Not the crib, I've already started working on that.'

'You have?'

'Of course. I wanted it to be a surprise for you, but since you've mentioned it – what's the matter?'

'Botheration and bedknobs!' Rose stormed as unwanted tears suddenly flooded her eyes. 'I never cry!'

'Come here.' Alex dabbed gently at the tears with his handkerchief. 'What's wrong with crying? Women do it often.'

'I don't. Apparently it's the baby, but if I'm going to keep bursting into tears for the next five months or whatever, I'll be wishing I hadn't bothered.'

'No sense in wishing that now. We're both stuck with it,' Alex teased, and to his consternation, the tears threatened to return.

'Is that what you think? That it's something we're stuck with?'

'I only meant . . . That's something else we're going to have over the next five months; you getting tetchy over nothing.'

'I always get tetchy over nothing. It's one of my endearing features.'

'True. I should have said tetchier.' He grinned at her, a grin that gave her the courage to say, 'Alex, you were right. I should have spoken to you about having a baby, but I thought you would have said not yet.'

'I would have, if you'd told me why you had decided to have it now instead of later. It's the wrong reason to bring another person into the world, Rose – to spite Fiona and to ensure that I'll inherit my share of the business.'

'I know, but it seemed like a good idea.'

'Tell me one thing,' Alex said, suddenly serious. 'Do you really want it?'

'Of course I want it! It's our baby, yours and mine, and I can't wait to see it!'

'Then that's fine,' he said, and kissed her. 'Because I want it too.' And then, grasping the nettle, 'Rose, you said this morning that we shouldn't keep secrets from each other. Sit down – I have something to tell you.'

Her blue eyes immediately darkened. 'Something bad?'

'Not for us, but perhaps for other people. While I was in Edinburgh I met Beth Laidlaw,' he said, then, as she looked puzzled, 'Beth Lennox, I should say. She and Ewan were legally married.'

'She and— You mean Rowena's mother? Good heavens!' Rose said as he nodded. 'Where did you meet her?'

He told her the whole story, leaving nothing out, and ended with, 'I thought it easier to send her money in order to keep her away from my mother and Todd – and from Rowena. Perhaps it was wrong of me to let her assume that Rowena's living in Australia, but I couldn't bear the thought of the trouble she could cause for the kid if she came back to Paisley. Beth carries trouble with her everywhere she goes. She broke Todd's heart when she eloped with Ewan. He's happier now than he could ever have been with her, and perhaps that's another reason why I don't want to see them upset by Beth.'

'I think you did the right thing. From what I've heard of her, this woman could only bring grief to Rowena, and to Kirsty and Todd.'

'I should have told you as soon as I came home, especially about the money I agreed to send every month, but—'

'Oh, that doesn't matter,' Rose dismissed the words with a wave of her hand. 'It's just lucky that we can afford to pay her.'

'Even though we're buying a house and having a baby?'

'We'll manage. I know that she's caused a lot of heartache,' Rose said after a moment, 'but at the same time I can't help feeling sorry for poor Beth. She's made a terrible mess of her own life as well as other people's.'

'Don't feel sorry for her,' Alex said grimly. 'She hurt Todd, and walked out on her own daughter, and Ewan too. She didn't turn a hair when I told her that he had been killed in the war. He might be alive today if he hadn't gone to Australia and been conscripted into their army. His battalion was almost completely wiped out that day.'

'If he had stayed here he would still have gone into the army and might have been killed. And he let Rowena down too, don't forget. She's the one we should be thinking about. Ewan's gone, and from what you say about her Beth's beyond redemption. But Rowena has her whole life ahead of her. We must make sure that it's a good life, Alex.'

'We will – all of us. I think she's set her heart on living with Caitlin and Murdo when they marry. She adores Murdo.'

'*If* they marry.'

'What do you mean? Caitlin's not changing her mind, is she?'

'Oh, Caitlin has no doubts – she wants to marry the man as soon as possible, and I want to see her happily settled before this child of ours arrives,' Rose patted her belly, 'but Murdo seems to be dragging his heels. Caitlin's beginning to wonder if he still wants to marry her. Perhaps you should speak to him?'

Alex shook his red head. 'Leave it to Caitlin. If she wants him so much she might have to fight for him. We've done enough tampering, keeping Beth's whereabouts a secret and paying her to stay away from Paisley. From now on we should both be concentrating on our own lives and leaving the others to run theirs.'

From the kitchen window Kirsty watched Rowena and Cavan kneeling together on the big flagstone that Rowena had christened her 'dancing stone'. The current edition of the *Paisley Daily Express* lay before them, open at the picture of Rowena at the Harlequin fashion show. Both sets of elbows rested on it, both backsides stuck up in the air, and their two heads were close together, the early August sunlight catching chestnut glints from Rowena's curls and blue highlights from Cavan's straight black hair.

'Miss Rowena Lennox was partnered by Miss Cavan McCart, a talented young Irish dancer who now lives in Paisley,' Rowena read out, and the two girls beamed at each other. 'Doesn't it sound grand? I wish you hadn't run away, Cavan, then we could have had a picture of the two of us.'

'My da wouldn't have wanted it.'

'Why not? Is he ashamed of the way you look?'

'Of course not. It's just that he doesn't want any of us to draw attention to ourselves because of what happened back home,' Cavan said absently, her eyes on the picture. Then she sat back suddenly on the grass. 'I don't think I should have said that.'

'Why not? What happened?'

'Nothing happened,' Cavan said swiftly.

'But you just said – I thought we were best friends!'

'We are.'

'Friends don't keep secrets from each other. I've told you all about me,' Rowena said, hurt. 'I told you about my mother going away and leaving me and my daddy, and him having to send me here on a cart because he had to go far away to find work and he couldn't take me with him. And about Uncle Alex meeting him in the war and my daddy promising to come and get me as soon as the war was finished. Only . . .' her blue eyes, with their distinctive tilt at the corners, darkened '. . . he got killed. I've even shown you his picture, and hardly anyone's seen that!'

Cavan stared at her best friend, her only friend, her own face screwed up in distress. 'But I don't know why my da and my ma don't want folk to know anything about us, and I don't know why we had to come here from Ireland. I just know that that's the way it is.'

'They might tell you when you're older,'

311

Rowena suggested. 'They think we're too young to know about the interesting things. When they do tell you, you must promise to tell me.'

'I will!'

'Give me your solemn oath,' Rowena insisted, and Cavan drew a cross with one finger in the area she believed her heart to be.

'Cross my heart and hope to die if I should lie,' she intoned gravely.

'And I'll keep your secret locked away here,' Rowena doubled her hand into a fist and thumped it on the left side of her rib cage, 'for ever. I won't tell anyone even if they torture me.'

'I don't think anyone would do that.'

'You never know,' Rowena said darkly. And then, the serious discussion over, 'Gran bought two newspapers today so that you can have one. Let's go and get it.'

They were scrambling to their feet and brushing grass from their skirts when Kirsty came out and handed each of them a boiled potato, fresh from the pot and wrapped in newspaper to make them easier to hold. The girls sat on the bench that Todd had set up against the house wall, legs swinging as they ate.

'This,' Rowena said happily, 'is the best way to eat a potato.'

Cavan nodded, then closed her eyes and wished

hard for everything to go well for her and her family, and for them to stay here for ever, safe from whatever fretted her mammy and her da.

# 21

Caitlin pushed the door open and went into the gatehouse. The place, usually filled with the loom's clacking or the sound of hammering or sawing, was silent for once. She stood in the hallway for a moment, looking up the sweep of the stairs and trying to imagine the place as it would be when it had finally become a home. She pictured Murdo at the door after his day's work, smoking his pipe and enjoying the evening air while she put the children to bed upstairs. She could almost smell their supper cooking in the kitchen and saw herself, pink-cheeked and happy, coming down the stairs to join her husband . . .

She desperately wanted to open her eyes and find herself in the scene that she had imagined so many times, but when they did finally open, reluctantly, it was to the bare floorboards instead of well-tended linoleum and plastered walls where she had imagined paint and well-chosen pictures. There was no smell of cooking, just the faint mingled scent of tobacco, and damp earth from the pit that had been opened in the former drawing room to accommodate movement of the loom's treadles.

She called Murdo's name, and when he answered she went in to find him in his shabby armchair, his beloved pipe in his mouth and a book in his hands. He set both aside and scrambled to his feet.

'Caitlin, I didn't think ye'd be coming tonight.' His voice, soft and deep, every word spoken with the careful precision of a man whose natural tongue was Gaelic, made her tingle from the tips of her toes to the roots of her hair. She loved him so much, and yet at the moment it was a love that made her unhappy because she was no longer sure that it was reciprocated.

'I felt restless, so I thought I'd walk along here and spend some time with you.' She went to him and to her relief he opened his arms and drew her in against his chest. She nestled there for a long, delicious moment, then lifted her face to his. He bent his head and kissed her.

'Have you eaten?' she asked when they drew apart.

315

'Aye, I had something when I stopped work for the day.'

'My mother sent some scones.' She handed over the bag and as he opened it the smell of fresh baking wafted out.

'Will you have one yourself?' Murdo held the bag out, but she shook her head.

'I've already had my share,' she said, then watched with affectionate amusement as he scooped out a buttered scone and crammed it into his mouth. 'Is Lachie not coming over to help you tonight?'

Murdo shook his head and swiped the back of his hand across his mouth to dislodge stray crumbs. Then he swallowed before saying, 'He's busy tonight. He's courting again – a lassie from Sneddon Street.'

'Is he indeed?'

'You'd mebbe better not be saying anything to your sister,' he suggested.

'Best not, though I think she's well over him by now. Can I help you with whatever work you're doing?'

'No, no, I'd not want you getting yourself hurt.'

'I'm not daft, Murdo – I know how to be careful, and sensible. Too sensible, sometimes.'

'I can manage fine on my own. Would you like to sit down?' He indicated the armchair.

'No, I'm fine. We've decided to bring in another designer,' Caitlin told him. 'Rose was saying the other day that it would help to free me so that I could get ready for our wedding. And I'll be running the place while she's away, so I won't have as much time to spend on designing.'

'The business must be doing well, then.' Murdo looked into the bag and then carefully folded over the top and set it aside, clearly deciding that he would eat the other scones when he was free to concentrate on savouring them.

'It is.' Caitlin hesitated, eyeing him warily, then went on, 'Murdo, she's anxious for us to set the date. She wants to see me living here in the gatehouse before she takes time off to have her baby.' Then, when he said nothing, she added, 'I'm eager to be here myself. D'you think we could set a wedding date for the beginning of September?'

He fiddled with his pipe, avoiding her eye. 'I don't think the place'll be ready by then.'

'How much more d'you have to do?'

'Och – quite a lot.'

'Then take up Rose's offer to bring workmen in. If you did that we could surely be married by the middle of September.'

'I've told you before, Caitlin, I don't want strangers tramping about the place and mebbe getting things wrong. Me and Lachie can see to it ourselves.'

'But how long will that take?'

'As long as it needs to take – I can't just give you a date! It's a house, not a frock for one of your fancy ladies.'

'Sometimes,' Caitlin said, putting her fears into words for the first time, though they had been in her mind for many long months, 'I wonder if you want to marry me.'

'I do, but—' He stopped. 'Och, Caitlin, I can't be doing with all this fuss. Can you not just be content to leave things as they are?'

'No, I can't. I want to be with you all the time, not just now and again. What were you going to say just there?'

'Nothing.'

'Tell me, Murdo. There's something wrong and I need to know what it is. So tell me and let's put an end to all this – this nonsense. Tell me here and now whether or not you really intend to marry me.'

There was a long silence, then finally he said, 'I-I have my doubts.'

She had suspected it, perhaps even known it, but even so, hearing him say it felt as though he had suddenly turned and struck her with all his might. Caitlin felt the breath swoosh out of her,

318

as though her heart had suddenly swelled up and crushed her lungs. She reached out blindly and her fingers caught and held the back of the ordinary wooden chair by the table.

'So now we know,' she said when her breath finally returned and she was able to speak. 'We're not going to get married, are we?'

'I never said that. I just want us to wait until we're sure.'

'I'm sure, Murdo. I've always been sure. But I'll not marry a man who doesn't want me,' she said, and turned towards the door. To her relief, her legs still had the strength to carry her through it and along the hall to the front door. She heard him call her name but she continued on her way, though she did pause briefly with her hand on the door latch, hoping against hope that he would come after her to tell her that it had all been a silly mistake and he wanted her still.

But he didn't, so Caitlin lifted the latch and went out into the pleasant summer's evening and walked home, unaware of the people she passed and the streets she traversed. When she got to Espedair Street, she entered by the pend leading to the backyard and the workshop. There, she leaned against the door of the small room where Murdo had once lived and worked the loom, and finally let the tears flow.

★

Back in the gatehouse, Murdo Guthrie stayed where he was, staring down at the floor, until he heard the outer door open then close behind Caitlin. He muttered a curse in his native tongue and slammed a fist down on the table. It landed on the paper bag she had brought, smashing the buttered scones within to greasy crumbs.

Unfortunately, Cavan was so excited about her best friend's photograph appearing in the *Paisley Daily Express* that she could not resist showing the newspaper to her grandmother.

'That's Rowena Lennox, Grandma. She's my best friend and she's a dancer, like me. Isn't she pretty?' she enthused, while Shelagh and Joseph, unable to stop her in time, looked on, horrified.

Bernadette McCart smoothed the newspaper out across her large lap and peered down at it, her lips mouthing the words of the caption silently. She read to the end, then looked up at her son and daughter-in-law.

'Her name's in the newspaper now.'

'That's because me and Rowena were dancing . . .' Cavan started to explain, then her voice faltered and died as she took in her grandmother's stony expression.

'In the newspaper – and us supposed to be quiet about ourselves.'

'Cavan, would you run down to the backyard and see if the washing's dry yet?'

'We only put it out a wee while ago, Mammy. It'll still be wet.'

'Go on down now and see.' Shelagh caught up the tin basin used to transport the washing to and from the lines in the backyard and thrust it at her daughter. 'Go on, now – and take your time in case you trip on the stairs and hurt yourself,' she called after Cavan as the girl went out.

'Ma, it wasn't her fault,' Joseph said as soon as the door closed. 'She wouldn't think—'

'Aye, like her da. You never think, do ye, Joseph McCart? Draggin' me here to this place instead of lettin' me die with dignity in me own country!'

'You'll not die here, Mother. We'll go back to Ireland soon.'

The old woman's malevolent glare swept from Joseph to Shelagh. 'You're as stupid as he is if ye think that. We'd be in Ireland still if that man of yours – that son of mine,' she added with such contempt that Joseph winced, 'had the spirit to stand up to those Doyles instead of running away and forcing the rest of us to go with him.'

'I couldn't leave you on your own, Ma!'

'I'd be better there on my own than here with the two of you. Your da must be turnin' in his grave at the way his only son's let him down. Any man worth spittin' on would have avenged his da's murder, but not you!'

'What could Joseph do against that lot?' Shelagh burst out. 'They'd have killed him, the way they killed his father. D'you want me to be a widow like yourself?'

'Better the widow of a brave man than the wife of a coward!'

Shelagh had always been afraid of her mother-in-law, even though the woman was crippled and totally dependent on her and Joseph. But now she moved forward, her fists clenched. 'Don't you call my Joseph a coward. Don't you dare do that—' she started, but Joseph caught at her arm.

'That's enough out of the two of you, now. Ma, Cavan meant no harm. She's just a child and she doesn't understand. Shelagh, come away.' He led her to their bedroom, for once ignoring his mother's ranting.

'Don't let her fret you like this,' he urged, closing the door. 'It's not worth it.'

'I can't bear it when she calls you a coward.' Shelagh was shaking with anger; she wrapped her arms tightly around her thin body in an effort to contain it.

'Och, she's just an old woman, dragged away from the only place she's ever known in her life.'

'That doesn't give her the right! You're the only

child she's got left since your da drove the rest of them away. She's got nobody else to look out for her but you and it's wrong of her to speak to you like that. You're not a coward!'

'I'm not my da, and that's all that matters to her.'

'Your da was a bully. How can she be so proud of him when he beat her all their married life — and you and the others as well. When he killed your sister!'

Pat McCart's violent life had ended in bloodshed not long before Shelagh met Joseph, when he was set upon late one night on his way home, too drunk to defend himself. Her own father had a quick temper — he had, after all, marked her for life with that hot iron when she insisted on marrying Joseph — but on the whole he had been able to keep it under control, while Pat McCart's wife and children had known little more than blows from him. The older children had left home as soon as they were able, leaving Joseph, the last-born, to take the worst of the punishment. One sister hadn't left home in time. She had died when she was ten years of age; of a bad fall in the house, the story went, but Joseph, a toddler at the time, had witnessed the girl's final beating, and had wept as he told Shelagh about it.

'Mebbe she thinks that the way my da was is the way a man's supposed to be,' he said now.

'Mebbe she's right.' Although nobody knew who had beaten her husband to death, Bernadette put the blame on the Doyles, a large, lawless family who had always been mortal enemies of Pat's. She had never forgiven Joseph for leaving Ireland instead of staying and avenging his father.

'You're more of a man than your father ever was. You took on Liam Doyle even though you knew he could have killed you.'

'I had good enough reason for that, after what he did to you!' Joseph's voice and face were suddenly savage, and he fisted one hand and slammed it into the palm of his other hand.

'Ah now, you know you don't mean that. You've been angry with yourself every single day since for what you did to the man, I know you have. You might have your da's blood in your veins but you've not got a violent nature. Would I have married you if you had?'

Then, as he shook his head but stayed silent, her tone changed. 'Joseph, you don't think there's any harm done in the newspaper? It's not as if Cavan's in the picture, though it's a shame in a way, for she was so pretty in her new frock.'

'If there has been harm done we'll find out soon enough.'

'How would anyone from home ever see that story?'

'There's plenty of other Irish folk in Scotland – in Paisley.'

'Nobody who knew us before. And there's always been Irish folk in Scotland, ever since the famine – why would they be bothered about us?'

'You don't know the Doyles – they've got long memories, and a long reach. If anyone ever laid a finger on Cavan I'd—'

'Don't!' Shelagh clung to him, trembling at the very thought.

'I'd kill him and never feel a moment's guilt. Mebbe we should have stayed at home and sorted this business out once and for all. That would have made the ould yin proud of me.'

'D'you think I want to be a widow, or Cavan wants to be without a father? We did the right thing, Joseph,' she pleaded, and to her relief he nodded.

'I suppose you're right. I just want something better than this for you and the wee one. I want us to be safe, to have a decent life.' He ran a hand through his dark hair. 'Sometimes I wonder if it'll ever happen, Shelagh.'

'It will; we're both working for good honest folk and we're beginning to put a bit of money by. Give it another year and we'll be out of here and into a better house. It'll be all right – you'll see.'

The door opened and Cavan's head appeared in the opening. 'Mammy, the washing's still wet, so I left it on the line. And now my gran wants to use the chamber pot.'

'I'll see to her. You get to your bed, now,' Shelagh said, and hurried out.

'Why's Grandma so unhappy here?' Cavan asked her father. 'The people are nice, and Rowena's a good friend.'

'She's old, Cavan. Old folk find it hard to settle away from the homes they've known all their lives.'

'But we'll take her back home one day, won't we?'

'Aye,' Joseph said, stroking his daughter's hair. 'Aye, one day we will.'

'Are we both very unlucky, or very unattractive?' Mary wondered.

'Perhaps we were never meant to marry.' Caitlin dabbed at her red eyes with a damp, balled-up handkerchief. When she had finally ventured into the house it was to discover to her relief that Kirsty and Todd had gone to their beds and Mary was alone in the kitchen, reading a book. She had taken one look at her distraught sister and prescribed hot milk with honey in it. Now they sat at either side of the range, mugs in hand, sipping at the comforting drink.

'You're definitely marriage material,' Mary told her sister firmly. 'You're pretty and you'll make a wonderful wife and mother one day – when you find the right man.'

'I thought I had.'

'I thought that too – about you and Murdo, I mean. You were made for each other, Caitlin. What on earth is wrong with the man?' Mary demanded angrily. 'He adores you!'

'Not any more. I've known for a while that there was something wrong. If he'd really wanted to marry me he would have had the gatehouse ready long before this.'

'Should you not try to find out just what's bothering him?'

'I did try, but he'll not tell me. I'm dreading having to tell everyone,' Caitlin confessed.

'It's hard, but you just have to keep your chin up, look them in the eye and get it over with. And remember that it's nobody's business but yours when all's said and done.'

'How will I ever be able to face Murdo again?'

'In the same way – chin up, look him straight in the eye and lock your knees tight so that they don't give way and send you crashing to the floor. If you want my advice, you'll go back to see him and have it out with him.'

'I can't!'

'Of course you can, and you should.'

'Stop fussing me, Mary. What about you? You should be taking your own advice, not leaving it all to me.'

'I never ever saw myself as a wife because I always knew that I was plain compared to you. I resigned myself to spinsterhood while I was still at school. I think that I would make a very good spinster aunt. And that means that you must have children I can be a spinster aunt to.'

'Alex and Rose are having a baby – won't that do?'

'Not really. They don't live nearby, and much as I like Rose the baby might take after her side of the family and be too grand for me. So I must depend on you.'

'Have you never seen yourself as someone's wife? What about Lachie?'

'Mebbe I did think of us marrying one day, but I wasn't entirely surprised when he jilted me.'

'Murdo . . .' Caitlin's voice wobbled slightly on the name, then rallied '. . . says that Lachie's courting again. A lassie from Sneddon Street.'

'Good luck to them both. He wasn't for me, and I wasn't for him.'

'Was there never anyone else?'

Mary buried her nose in her mug, inhaling the smell of hot milk and honey. Pictures ran through her mind: John Brodie putting a tiny bunch of violets on her desk, showing her through the greenhouses in his parents' magnificent garden, plucking a flower from beneath the hedgerow on one of their Sunday walks and telling her all about it, or pausing to draw her attention to the bird-song . . . Then she saw him smiling with flattered surprise at Fiona, explaining to Mary, embarrassment in his voice and his kind face, that he was seeing Fiona next Sunday, and the next Sunday again . . .

'No, never anyone else,' she said. 'I am definitely cut out to be a spinster aunt.' She finished off her milk and got to her feet. 'Let's go to bed. Things won't look better in the morning, but they will, eventually – I promise you.'

329

## 22

The next few days were indeed hard for Caitlin, but with Mary's advice ringing in her ears, she managed it. The hardest part was telling everyone, and listening to their astonishment and then their commiserations. Rowena's first reaction was one of disbelief, and then there were tears when she realised that her two favourite people were not, after all, going to get married, and her dream of being one of Caitlin's bridesmaids was not going to come true.

Alex, who had almost finished painting the set of bedroom furniture that was to have been a wedding gift, asked Rose, 'Should I just send it to the emporium's furniture department?'

'Absolutely not! Finish it, then put it away. They'll surely make up their quarrel.'

'And if they don't?'

'Then we'll have it for our new house,' Rose said promptly.

Meanwhile Caitlin was burying herself in her work in an effort to push Murdo from her mind. When the inevitable happened and she came face to face with him while hurrying through Harlequin's foyer, it came as a shock. Her face, seemingly unaware of what had happened between them, began to melt into its usual warm, welcoming smile, and had almost made it when her brain took over and managed to order the muscles to shape themselves into a blank expression.

'Good morning, Murdo. If you're looking for Rose, she and Alex are looking at a house they want to buy. She'll be back by dinnertime.'

She managed to do as Mary suggested – lock her knees against their sudden trembling, lift her chin and look him straight in the eye. That would have been the most difficult part, for one glance from his dark eyes, as deep and mysterious as the darkest loch, always made her heart turn over. But he was looking everywhere but at her, twisting the cap he had snatched from his head between his hands.

'I was wondering,' his soft voice said, 'if she would come and have a look at the cloth on the loom. I've started it but I want to know if the pattern's right for her.'

'I'll ask her to go over as soon as she arrives.'

He started to speak, then stopped to clear his throat before trying again. 'I need to get on with it now, for there's an order in from Alex waiting to be done after this.'

'In that case, I'd better go over,' she said reluctantly. 'Give me five minutes.' Once he had left she hurried upstairs to ask Grace to go with her.

'Can you not manage on your own?'

'Grace, you know fine why I don't want to be alone with him. Come on – it'll only take a few minutes!'

'It reminds me of my weans when they were wee,' Grace grumbled as they walked across to the gatehouse, 'and the way they carried on when they fell out with their pals.'

'This is more serious than that. You can surely see why I don't want to be alone with him.'

'Caitlin, you were born for each other, anyone can see that. Mebbe this could be the chance for you to sort out your differences. Mebbe I should leave you on your own.' Grace half turned, ready to walk back to the mill, but Caitlin caught at her arm and forced her towards the gatehouse.

'There's a lot to do today and there's no time for me and Murdo to sort out anything, even if we wanted to. But he doesn't – and neither do I. I've got my pride, Grace!'

'Just like the weans when they fell out,' Grace sniffed as they went into the gatehouse.

Rose and Alex's new home was still in Paisley Road, but about a mile further along the broad thoroughfare linking Paisley and Glasgow. Rose, flushed with excitement, insisted on driving Caitlin, Mary and Kirsty to see it.

'This,' she said, leading them into a large room at the rear of the house, 'will be the nursery. As it looks out over the garden it will be nice and quiet. The nurse will have the room next to it, while we have the front bedroom. Our housekeeper's agreed to come in every day as she does now, and we'll have to find a gardener – and a designer for Harlequin – as well as a nurse for the child. Fortunately this place is all ready for us to move in to almost at once, but even so, there's so much to think of!'

'Can we afford to pay a second designer?' Caitlin's voice was doubtful.

'I believe we can. Orders are coming in as a result of the fashion show, and it's time we made a decision,' Rose said briskly. 'Mary, would you help me draft an advertisement for the Glasgow newspapers?'

'Of course. And you should ask your mother

333

to help you find the nurse, and your father to help with the gardener.'

'Mary, what would I do without you?' Rose hugged her sister-in-law. 'You make it all sound so possible!'

'Everything's possible, if you just take it a step at a time,' Mary told her calmly, while Kirsty added, 'And as for the wean's clothes – me and Jean and your own mother can see to all that, Rose.'

'I'm beginning to see the future already.' Rose beamed at them. 'Alex and me and the baby in our beautifully furnished new home, as happy as birds in their nest. Isn't it exciting?'

'It's amazing,' Kirsty said that evening in her own kitchen, 'how well Rose is looking. You'd have thought that someone as . . .' she fumbled for the right word, then said '. . . as *different* as she is might not take kindly to carrying a wean. But she's neither up nor down about it.'

'She's too busy to be up or down,' Caitlin said. 'And she's happier than she's ever been before.'

'I wish . . .' Kirsty stopped, then said, 'Och, I'm tired of pussy-footing about, Caitlin, so I'll just come out plump and plain and say that I wish you could be as happy as she is.'

'I will be. Just give me time.'

'But I hate tae see ye hurtin', lassie.'

334

'Everyone has to have some hurting in their lives. I'm sure you've had your share.'

'More than her share,' Todd said unexpectedly from behind his newspaper. 'But Kirsty's always been strong enough to cope – and you're like her, Caitlin. You'll be all right.'

'I know I will. And I'm too busy with Harlequin to fret about myself. There's so much going on there!'

By mid-August furniture was being moved into Rose's new house and Harlequin had a new designer. Ella Morrison was a pleasant young woman who had worked in one of Glasgow's best fashion houses, and was eager to become involved in a small but thriving business like Harlequin. She and Caitlin got on from the moment they first met and Rose more or less hired her on the spot.

'If you like her, Caitlin, then that's all that matters, since you've to work with each other. And since Grace approves of her too, there it is – we have a new designer. Now all we have to do is to make enough money to pay her wages as well as our own!'

A week later she and Alex moved house. Rose decided against inviting everyone to a house-warming party, opting instead to give small separate dinner parties for her parents and sisters, Sandy MacDowall and Fiona, and Alex's family.

To her surprise, Fiona suggested that John Brodie be invited with her and her father. When Rose said, 'I was going to ask John if he would like to come on Alex's family's evening, since he knows them well.' Fiona raised her eyebrows.

'But John knows us well – he's been to the art galleries with us on more than one occasion, and to tea. Surely we're his kind of people, rather than the Lennox family.'

Rose repeated the conversation to Caitlin and Mary. 'She's such a snob,' she complained. 'How dare she suggest that John's uncomfortable with people who aren't as wealthy as his family? He enjoys your company and always has. I've a good mind to ignore her.'

'I think you should do as she asks,' Mary said quietly. 'After all, there are quite a few of us and only two of them. John may well prefer to be with them.'

'I doubt it. Perhaps I should give him the choice.'

'I wouldn't do that,' Mary said, and then, as the other two looked at her in surprise, 'I just think that it would be awkward for him, having to choose. Best to do as Fiona asks.'

'I suppose so, but I hate to please her since she never tries to please anyone else,' Rose grumbled.

Then, her face lighting up, 'But at least we're keeping the best to the last — my own family are so formal, and so are the MacDowalls, but I'm looking forward to the Lennox clan's visit!'

As she had anticipated, it was a happy, noisy evening. Rose and Alex, worn out from the move and from two bouts of formal entertaining, were able to relax and enjoy themselves. Jean, considered to be one of the family, had been included in the invitation, and as soon as the obligatory tour of the house was over she and Kirsty went to the kitchen, where they helped the housekeeper, who had agreed to stay on after her usual hours, to prepare the dinner and serve it.

The Lennox family arrived back in Espedair Street in high spirits. Because it was an event for adults Rose had taken Rowena and Cavan to see the house after school on the previous day, and Shelagh McCart had agreed to take Cavan to Espedair Street to spend the evening with Rowena.

Shelagh, too, had enjoyed herself. Ensconced in a comfortable armchair by the range, and with a pile of darning on her lap, she soon stopped work and gave herself over to the pleasure of being in such a pleasant kitchen. The girls were upstairs in Rowena's bedroom and now and again she could hear the murmur of voices and an occasional peal of laughter. Then came the steady but faint thump of feet as they worked on one of their dances. A small piece of coal rustled its way down through the larger pieces in the grate, but apart from that there was no other sound. No complaints from the ould yin, she thought contentedly. No big body blocking the heat from what, at home, was never more than a meagre fire. She closed her eyes and imagined that this was her house, and that she was waiting for Joseph to come in from work. One day, it would all happen . . .

When the girls came downstairs she made tea and put out the plates of home-made scones, pancakes and dumpling that Kirsty had left for them. The two girls sat on the rug at her feet, enjoying their own private party, and Shelagh could happily have stayed there all night – perhaps for ever – but good things never lasted long enough. All too soon the front door opened and the Lennoxes came trooping in, flushed and bright-eyed from their own evening's enjoyment and apologising for taking so long to get back.

'We were fine,' Shelagh assured them, 'but we'd best be getting home now. Come on, Cavan.'

'I'll walk with ye, lassie,' Todd said.

'No, we'll manage, Mr Paget.'

'Ye've done us a kindness and the least I can dae is tae see ye safe home.'

'I'll come too,' Mary offered, seeing Shelagh's consternation. 'Just to the corner of your street, for it's getting late.'

'I want to go too!' Rowena clamoured.

'Well, seein' that there's no school tomorrow,' Kirsty conceded. 'But don't be long.'

The streets were quiet as they made their way to the McCarts' building, the two girls running ahead. Shelagh was her usual shy self, but Mary kept up a conversation with Todd, bringing Shelagh in now and again.

The girls reached the final corner first and disappeared round it. 'Cavan . . .' Shelagh began to walk faster, anxious now that her daughter was out of sight.

'They'll no' be far ahead, lassie,' Todd assured her placidly.

Rowena and Cavan, hand in hand, were halfway between the corner and the dark close leading to the McCarts' flat when they met the man. As often happened in that street, not all the gas lamps were working and since he was leaning against the wall he was no more than a dark shadow blending in with the stone. They didn't see him until he straightened and stepped forward into their path. The two girls stopped, their grip on each other tightening.

'A grand night, lassies,' he said. 'My, you're bonny

wee things, are ye no'? And what would yer names be, then?'

Cavan tugged at Rowena's hand, trying to pull her back to the corner, but Rowena stood her ground, giving him her first name in a clear voice.

'And you, wee miss?'

Cavan shook her head, but Rowena was already saying, 'This is my friend, Cavan.'

'Cavan, is it? Would that be an Irish name?'

'Yes, she does Irish dancing and I do Scottish dancing,' Rowena was saying when Shelagh rounded the corner, a step ahead of Todd and Mary.

'Girls, come back here!' Her voice was sharp with worry. They turned to look at her.

'We were just talking . . .' Rowena began, then turned to the man for confirmation, only to find that he had gone.

'Who was that?' As soon as Shelagh reached them she put an arm round Cavan's shoulders and drew her close, as if for protection.

'Just a man.' Rowena was puzzled. Men sometimes spoke to her in the street, usually to tell her that she had pretty hair, or a bonny wee face. Most of them were drunk at the time, but friendly drunk, as her granddad put it; she knew they didn't mean any harm.

'Was he Irish?'

The two girls looked at each other and Cavan

moved even closer to her mother, affected by the fear she could sense, but not understand. 'I don't know,' Rowena said as the others arrived.

'We'll be fine from here,' Shelagh said swiftly. 'It's only a few steps to the close now.'

'We'll see ye tae yer door,' Todd offered.

'No, we're fine!'

'I'll go with Shelagh and Cavan,' Mary decided. 'You and Rowena wait here, Todd,' and before he could object she swept the other two along the pavement and into the close which, as she had expected, was as black as night.

They fumbled their way along, Mary ready to scream for Todd if her hands, patting their way along the damp walls, happened to touch a sleeve, or, even worse, another hand. But to her relief they reached the bottom of the stairs without encountering anyone.

'We'll be all right from here.' Shelagh set a foot on the first step. 'Thank you for coming in with us.'

'I'll wait here until I hear your door closing.' Like Cavan, Mary sensed the other woman's fear and, like Cavan, she was puzzled by it.

'Goodnight to you.' Shelagh took her daughter's hand and went up into the darkness, knowing the hollowed steps so well by now that she was sure-footed even in the gloom.

341

'We'll say nothing to your da about that man,' she said quietly to her daughter as they reached the first landing.

'What man? The one in the street? Does my da know him?'

'No, of course not. He was just a man on his own way home, so no reason to talk about him. It was a grand night, wasn't it?'

'Yes,' Cavan said happily, the man immediately forgotten. 'It was the best time I've ever had. I wish we had a house like Rowena's.'

They had climbed the second flight and reached their own door. 'We will,' Shelagh said as she lifted the latch. 'We will, one day.'

Standing at the bottom of the stairs, Mary heard a door open and then close overhead. With relief, she turned and hurried as fast as she could to the safe familiarity of the street, and Todd.

Rose poured a second cup of tea, leaned back in her chair and looked round the small dining room with pride. She had never in her life given much thought to her surroundings; from the day of her birth to the day of her marriage she had lived in her parents' large house, paid for by her father and furnished to her mother's taste, and after that she had been perfectly happy in Alex's small flat, heedless of the fact that the entire kitchen, bathroom, living room and bedroom could have fitted easily into her parents' drawing room. All that mattered was that she was with the man she loved.

But now, for the first time in her life, she knew the proud glow of ownership. Whether it was because of the child growing swiftly within her, or because she had been involved in choosing this house, or perhaps because as a working woman she was helping to pay for her new home, she didn't know. But it was a pleasant thought. She was about to say so to Alex, reading his newspaper at the other side of the table, when he suddenly gave a startled exclamation.

'What is it?'

'This can't be right, surely!'

'What can't be right? Let me see.' Rose held a hand out for the paper, but instead of passing it over, her husband read aloud, '"Mr and Mrs Martin Brodie of The Elms, Paisley, are pleased to announce the engagement of their only son, Mr John Brodie, to Mrs Fiona Chalmers, only daughter of Mr Alexander MacDowall of Glasgow."'

'What? No!' Rose shot to her feet and almost ran round the table to snatch the newspaper from him. 'Where is it? Oh, I see . . .' She read the brief notice several times before lowering the paper to stare at him. 'John – and Fiona? I can't believe it.'

'They wouldn't put it in the Glasgow *Herald* if

it wasn't true.' Alex got up and went into the hall. By the time Rose joined him, her cooling tea forgotten, he was dialling his father's number on the telephone.

Fiona herself answered. 'Alex, how lovely to hear from you. I take it that you've just seen the *Herald*.'

'Is it true?'

'Of course it is.'

'Why didn't you tell us?'

She giggled. 'We thought it might be fun to surprise everyone.'

'You certainly did that,' Alex said grimly.

'Aren't you going to congratulate me?'

'Yes, of course. Rose and I both hope that you'll be very happy,' Alex said, ignoring the faces his wife was pulling at him.

'Thank you, Alex, I knew that you would both be pleased for me. I must go – the telephone has been busy all morning. Tell Rose I'll see her this afternoon – I've just made an appointment with Harlequin. I want them to design a lovely new frock for my engagement party,' Fiona said, and rang off.

'It's all true,' Alex reported. 'She going to Harlequin this afternoon to be measured for a new frock for her engagement party.'

'Poor John!'

'Why poor? He's getting married, not executed. I must go.' Alex began to put his coat on.

'But to Fiona!'

'I imagine that it's from choice.'

'I wouldn't be too sure,' Rose said darkly.

'Don't be so suspicious, Rose. They're in love and they're getting married, that's all there is to it. See you tonight.' Alex kissed her and then collected his hat and gloves and hurried out.

Rose returned to the dining room and began to gather the used dishes together, frowning as she worked. Her lovely, gentle, honest friend John – and Fiona? There must be more to that strange union than love; she was sure of it. But not sure, as yet, just what it might be.

She put the pile of dishes she had just collected down again. She must go to Paisley as soon as she could, to break the news to Caitlin and Mary.

# 23

The phone on Mary's desk rang just as she walked into the office that morning and she pulled her gloves off hastily, frowning. She made a point of always arriving at Harlequin a good five minutes earlier than required so that she could get herself settled before her working day started.

'Harlequin.'

'Caitlin? Oh, it's you, Mary,' a familiar voice said in her ear. 'Fiona Chalmers here.'

'Good morning, Mrs Chalmers. Can I be of assistance?'

'You're such a prim little mouse, Mary — why can't you call me by my Christian name? After all, we're family.'

Mary closed her eyes for a moment and gave

a brief, inward sigh of exasperation. 'I prefer to call our clients by their titles when I'm in the office, Mrs Chalmers. I'm afraid that Rose isn't in yet – she's beginning to cut down on her time here, what with the baby coming. But Caitlin will be in soon; I can easily ask her to telephone you then.'

'Don't trouble her. I only want to make an appointment to discuss a new frock.'

Mary reached for the appointments book and flipped it open with one hand. 'Would next Tuesday at eleven suit you?'

'Dear me, no! I need to have this frock as soon as possible, and I want it to be something special. It's for my engagement party,' Fiona trilled.

'You're engaged to be married? Rose didn't tell us.'

'She doesn't know yet. It's all happened very suddenly. You could say that I've been swept off my feet – very romantic. The announcement's in today's Glasgow *Herald*, so no doubt Rose and Alex will find out very soon.'

'Congratulations, I hope that you and your future husband will be very happy.'

'We will,' Fiona said confidently. 'As a matter of fact, you know him. It's John Brodie.'

'John . . .' Mary started to repeat the name without thinking, then as it suddenly registered, the opened appointments book in front of her seemed to slip to one side for a moment before moving smoothly back to its original position. 'John Brodie, you said?'

'You sound surprised.'

'I didn't realise that you knew each other that well.'

'As I said, my dear, I was swept off my feet. A whirlwind romance.' Fiona's laugh bored through the ringing sound in Mary's ear. 'You wouldn't think it of a stolid fellow like my John, would you? But there you are – or rather, there I am. Shall we say three this afternoon?'

Mary's normally neat hand scribbled Fiona's name clumsily into the book. 'Yes, Caitlin could manage three o'clock this afternoon.'

'Good. You must come to my engagement party,' Fiona said, and rang off.

Mary felt as though an invisible hand had punched her in the stomach. She gave a little gasp and clutched at the edge of the desk, trying to breathe slowly and steadily. After a minute she pulled open the drawer where she kept a small bottle of sal volatile. Mothers of brides sometimes felt quite overcome the first time they saw their precious daughters in their wedding finery, and the little bottle had come in useful on several occasions. She took the top off and breathed in deeply, then choked and jammed the stopper back into place. It was the first time she had ever been in need of a stimulant, and she hadn't realised how effective it was.

She put the bottle away, dabbed carefully at her watering eyes, then made herself reach for the ledger and get on with her work.

As it happened, Rose drove into the courtyard just as Caitlin was going up the steps to the old mill. She beeped the horn and Caitlin swung round, then waited as the car drew up and Rose switched off the engine then leaped out.

'My dear, you'll never guess – John's got himself engaged to Fiona Chalmers!'

'John? Our John? Surely not!'

'Alex saw the notice in the Glasgow *Herald* this morning and telephoned his father. Fiona answered – and it's true! Let's go and tell Mary.' Rose hustled her sister-in-law into the building and into Mary's office.

'Mary, I have the most amazing news!'

'And I,' Mary said, 'have just taken a booking for you for this afternoon, Caitlin. Fiona Chalmers wants you to design a special dress for her engagement party.'

'But did she tell you who the happy man is – that is, if he is happy.'

'Yes, she did, Rose. It's John Brodie.'

'How can you be so calm about it? Aren't you surprised?'

'People get engaged all the time,' Mary said.

'But what does a woman like Fiona Chalmers see in John Brodie?' Caitlin wanted to know. 'I think that he's a very nice, kind man, but he's so quiet. I would have thought that Fiona would prefer a man who likes parties, and travel.'

'He's the son of wealthy parents, and that would certainly please Fiona. The question is – what does John see in her?' Rose countered. 'Don't you agree, Mary, that they're an unlikely couple?'

'Surely that's their business, not ours,' Mary suggested quietly.

'We're women, Mary, nosiness is in our nature.'

'Not in mine, Rose.'

'No, not in yours, but that's because you've got more sense than most. A fitting this afternoon, did you say?'

'Three o'clock. I thought we should find time for her, since she's Alex's other half-sister.'

'We'd better be prepared to make a fuss of the bride-to-be,' Rose sighed.

Caitlin nodded, then said, 'I wonder if Ella would like to work on Fiona's new outfit.'

'Good idea. It would start her off, and keep Fiona out of our hair.' Rose ran a hand through her shorn locks, then said, 'I don't know why

Samson made all that fuss when he was shorn by Delilah. He should have been eternally grateful to her.'

'I must get on,' Mary said, and was relieved when the other two went upstairs to break the news to Grace.

She had quite forgotten that John often came in on a Monday morning to go over the ledgers and invoices with her in his unofficial and purely voluntary capacity as financial adviser, so it was a shock when, an hour later, she recognised his voice out in the foyer. Mary bent lower over her desk, her pen skimming across the pages as she added and subtracted and carried forward with feverish haste. When the door opened she winced, but it was Caitlin, smiling and relaxed.

'Come to Rose's office, Mary, John's here and we're toasting his future happiness.'

'If I leave this I'll have trouble picking it up again. Give him my best wishes,' Mary said, and went back to work, relieved when Caitlin left without further argument, closing the door quietly behind her.

The babble of voices receded as the others crowded into Rose's office, leaving her free to work on. For a good ten minutes she was left in peace, then someone knocked on her office door.

'Yes?'

The door opened and John Brodie came in, carrying two glasses of wine.

'I know you're busy, but I didn't want you to miss out on the celebration.' He placed a glass on her desk, on the exact spot where he had once laid a small bunch of beautiful, sweet-smelling violets, then sat down, smiling at her.

'You've heard the news?' His eyes were bright, his face flushed with excitement.

'I have indeed – wonderful news, John.' Mary picked up her glass, surprised and relieved to find that her hand was steady. 'I hope that you and Mrs Chalmers have a long and happy life together.'

'I can't believe it – it all happened so suddenly. It was the last thing I expected – I mean, she's beautiful, and charming, while I'm . . . well, look at me!'

Mary took a sip of wine and then said, 'There's nothing wrong with you.'

'I'm – ordinary. Nothing much to look at, not very good in social circles, while Fiona could talk to the king and queen without turning a hair. I can't think what she sees in me.'

'You're a very nice, honest, sincere man, John Brodie. Mrs Chalmers must be pleased to be engaged to you.'

'You're such a good friend, Mary,' he said, and raised his glass. 'To you,' he said. 'To friendship.'

The wine was pleasant, but all at once it seemed to turn to vinegar in Mary's mouth. She set her glass down. 'John, I'm exceptionally busy this morning, and I don't think there are any points that need to be discussed today.'

Fortunately, John was so elated, he didn't even realise he was being rebuffed. 'There rarely are, for you're an excellent bookkeeper,' he said cheerfully.

When he had gone, humming a cheerful tune to himself, Mary stared down at the letters piled neatly on her desk, awaiting her attention. John and Fiona . . . Fiona and John . . . Mr and Mrs John Brodie . . . Fiona Brodie . . . The words marched across her mind's eye. John had never once acted or spoken in a way that might make her believe he saw her as anything other than a companion for his Sunday walks, or, perhaps, some lonely soul he pitied and was trying, in his own kind way, to help. He had seen her, as he had just said, as a good bookkeeper and a friend. But she had been foolish enough to make more of the friendship than he had. She had been silly enough to start caring for him, when all the time Fate had earmarked him for Fiona Chalmers.

She put both hands over her face, the fingers pressed so tightly against her closed eyes that the darkness began to fill with flashing lights, then, after a few minutes, she lowered her hands, straightened her back and took a deep breath. Life held its disappointments, but there was always work, and to Mary, work was a consolation. The only consolation left to her.

She swallowed the last of her wine in one gulp, choked, recovered and picked up her pen.

Fiona Chalmers swept into Harlequin that afternoon, glowing with self-satisfaction and looking immaculate in a cream crêpe de Chine dress with a matching waist-length cape, trimmed with thick black fringing. The glow disappeared, to be replaced by a petulant frown, when she was invited into Rose's office to be told that Caitlin was still closeted with another client.

'But I've got so much to do – a big party to organise. I can't afford to waste time!'

'Mrs Forsyth's a regular and respected client. We can't hurry her just because you've arrived,' Rose said sweetly.

'Am I not a regular and respected client?' Fiona twitched the cape from her shoulders and tossed it over the back of a chair.

'Of course you are, but your appointment is for three o'clock, and it's only ten to three now. We've brought in a second designer, Ella Morrison – perhaps you would like to speak to her,' Rose offered.

'A new designer? Business must be doing well.'

'It is.'

'Really? That's interesting.' Fiona seated herself in the armchair provided for clients and helped herself to a cigarette from the box kept on the desk. 'How much experience has she had?'

Rose lit the cigarette, pleased to see that the hand that longed to slap Fiona was quite steady. 'Ella went to Glasgow School of Art and then trained at one of the city's fashion houses. She has excellent references and an impressive port-folio.'

'If she's so talented, why is she willing to waste her time in Paisley instead of in one of the big Glasgow houses?'

Rose, who had never smoked in her life, suddenly regretted it. 'She feels, rightly, that she'll have more to do here and she's looking forward to the challenge. She's a pleasant young woman, a good addition to Harlequin.' Rose glanced at the door, longing to see Caitlin come through it.

'How many clients has she had since she came here?'

'Not many, but she's not been with us for long. Caitlin has every confidence in her.'

'Mmm. I think that I'll let this wonderful new designer of yours practise on more of your clients before I let her work for me.'

'In that case, would you care for some refreshment while you're waiting?'

'I might as well. Tea, China, weak and with lemon.'

When Rose returned from delivering the order, Fiona eyed her up and down, blowing a plume of smoke from pursed red lips, then said, 'You look so fat. It must feel dreadful.'

Rose patted her bulge with satisfaction. 'Actually, it feels rather good. Strange, considering that I used to look on pregnancy as something nasty. No doubt you'll change your mind, too.'

'Oh, that won't happen. I have no intention of letting children ruin my figure and disrupt my life.'

'Does John know that?'

'It's not any of his business,' Fiona said, and then, as Rose raised an eyebrow, 'Since women have to do the childbearing, I think the decision lies with them. I'm surprised at you, Rose. I thought you were more interested in Harlequin than in being a mother. I know I prefer business to domesticity. We women are so much better at business than men,' she was saying complacently when the tea arrived. She sipped at hers, and then sipped again, unable to come up with any criticism.

'I believe that I can look after Harlequin and still have a family.' Rose found herself on the defensive. 'To be honest, Fiona, I'm beginning to wonder why you're bothering to get married.'

Fiona gave her a small, almost catlike smile. 'Marriage can have its uses,' she said, and then glanced at her neat wristwatch. 'It's three o'clock.'

'I'm sure that Caitlin will be with you any minute now,' Rose said just as Caitlin hurried in to sweep Fiona off to the fitting room.

Alone at last, Rose gave a quiet scream and patted her rounded stomach. 'Poor little mite, having an aunt like that. And poor John – what on earth possessed him to ask Fiona to be his wife?'

It occurred to her that rather than John going down on one knee to propose, it was far more likely that Fiona was the one who had decided on the engagement. But why? There had been a time when their mothers were keen for Rose and John to marry, and John himself had been just as keen, but as far as Rose was concerned he was too placid and steady for her. Surely the same reasoning applied to Fiona, who, unlike Rose, was beautiful enough to have her pick of men more handsome and exciting and even wealthier than John. So why choose him? What did John have that Fiona wanted?

Rose stared at the opposite wall, trying to find an answer. She was still pondering the mystery when Grace came in to talk to her about something, which meant that the problem had to be shelved for the time being.

But she knew that it would not go away. Fiona was up to something, and Rose would not rest until she found out what it was.

Sandy MacDowall's large flat only just managed to accommodate all the guests gathered to celebrate Fiona's engagement to John Brodie. Fiona wore a striking peacock-blue silk dress beneath a black net wraparound overdress embroidered with large flowers in peacock-blue threads, with glass beads outlining each petal. Her stockings and elegant, pointed shoes were black, and her golden hair was decorated with a spray of bird-of-paradise feathers.

John's eyes followed her adoringly as she moved from group to group, showing off the magnificent sapphire and diamond engagement ring that almost looked too large for her slim finger.

'He thinks the world of her,' Caitlin said wistfully to Rose.

'No wonder – she looks superb. That gown has to be one of your greatest achievements.'

'It's easy to design lovely clothes for a lovely woman. And Fiona is one of the loveliest women I've ever seen.'

358

'But do you think that she cares as much for John as he clearly cares for her?'

Caitlin glanced around to make sure that they weren't being overheard before murmuring, 'I don't think Fiona can care for anyone more than she cares for herself.'

'Neither do I. That's why I keep wondering – why John?'

'His parents have a lovely big house, and his father will probably retire quite soon. Then John will take over the business. Fiona will be mistress of the most beautiful home money can buy, with servants to order ab—' Caitlin stopped short as Fiona began to move through the crowds towards them.

'Isn't this a lovely party?' Her brown eyes sparkled and her face was flushed with pleasure. 'Are you both getting enough to eat and drink?'

'We are. You look wonderful,' Rose said. 'I was just complimenting Caitlin on that dress.'

'She's done well, hasn't she?' Fiona's engagement ring sparkled as she smoothed the overdress skirt. 'Several people this evening have asked me who designed my clothes.'

'I hope you told them?'

'Indeed I did. After all, you're my sister-in-law and Caitlin's a sort of half-sister, isn't she? And once I marry John I'll have an even closer interest

359

in Harlequin's fortunes. I intend to gain more clients for you then. Needless to say,' she swept on graciously, 'I will be asking Harlequin to design my trousseau.'

'We'd be delighted,' Caitlin said warmly, while Rose murmured, 'Most kind.'

'Where's Mary?'

'She sends her apologies – she developed a dreadful headache and had to go home early this afternoon. Is it to be a long engagement, Fiona?' Caitlin enquired.

'Goodness, no. We plan to marry as soon as we find somewhere suitable to live.'

'In Glasgow?'

'I think we might take a leaf from your book, Rose, and find our new home on the city limits so that John's near his office in Paisley and I'm near Father and the emporium.'

'You're looking for a house near us?' Rose asked nervously, horrified to think that she and Fiona might become neighbours.

'I doubt that – your new house is very sweet, but on the small side, don't you think? There are some very elegant properties around Barshaw Park that might suit us. Please excuse me, I think that Father's about to make his speech. I must find John,' Fiona said, and hurried off.

'On the small side?' Rose was outraged. 'How

dare she criticise my lovely new home? And how dare she assume that we want to do her blessed trousseau!'

'We do, of course. She can afford to pay us well for it – and we can't afford to be selective,' Caitlin warned.

'I realise that, but did she have to be so condescending? My left hand had to hold back my right hand because it wanted to tug my forelock. And what does she want a large house for in any case, when she's already told me that she doesn't intend to have a family.'

'Does John know that?'

'I doubt it. She doesn't seem to think that a husband has any rights in that direction. Do you think I should warn him? Poor John!'

'You can't, Rose. This is between John and Fiona.'

'I suppose you're right.'

'I wish you would stop calling him "poor John".' Alex arrived, one of the waitresses hired for the evening following him. 'We're about to drink to the happy couple's future.' He took two glasses of champagne from the tray and handed them to his sister and his wife before taking another for himself. 'John doesn't look in the least poor – in fact, he seems to me to be quite overcome by his own good fortune.'

'That's because he hasn't realised exactly what

he's let himself in for,' Rose snorted. 'Do you know, Alex, that she has just had the cheek to tell me that our house is on the small side? She intends to buy something much larger – so that poor John can fill it with servants eager to obey her every whim.'

'If you don't know Fiona by now, you never will. Of course she wants a larger house than ours – it will make her feel superior to us.'

'As if she ever could be!'

'Exactly.' Alex took his wife's hand and kissed it. 'So there's no harm in letting her have her dreams. In any case, I like our house – if it was much larger we might not see so much of each other, and that would be terrible.'

'I might not see much of you in a larger house, but,' Rose said, smoothing her dress over her belly, 'I doubt if you could miss seeing me these days.'

# 24

'The way Alex looked at Rose was more loving than the way John looks at Fiona, and John's besotted,' Caitlin reported to Mary a few hours later. 'Rose is so fortunate!'

'The nice thing about Rose is that she knows she's fortunate.' Mary was sitting up in bed, her knees drawn up to her chin and her arms wrapped around them. 'And the really nice thing about her is that she wants everyone else to be as happy as she is, whereas Fiona Chalmers doesn't care about anyone but herself.'

'I don't think she even cares about John. That's why Rose keeps calling him "Poor John". Is your headache coming back?' Caitlin asked as Mary winced.

'Just a stab – it's nothing. So Fiona's dress looked well? I thought it would. You're a talented designer, Caitlin.'

'And you're a very clever bookkeeper, Mary. But when is it going to be our turn to fall in love?'

'I've already told you that I'm set for spinster-hood. And you're already in love, aren't you?' Mary's brown eyes, direct and straightforward, with none of Fiona's feminine, thick-lashed appeal, held her sister's gaze so firmly that Caitlin was unable to look away. 'You're madly in love with Murdo.'

'Not any more!'

'You are too, and don't try to deny it. Folk don't choose to fall in love, it just happens, like tumbling into a deep pit. And once they're in it they don't find it easy to climb out again.'

'You know an awful lot about it for someone who claims that it's never happened to her.'

'I read romantic novels now and again. As I was saying – you're still in love with Murdo.'

At last, Caitlin managed to look away from her sister's steady stare. 'I'm treating it like the influenza; I might still have it, but as time passes I'll get over it.'

'You might get over it faster if you face up to him and make him tell you why he's been treating you so coldly.'

'I don't have to ask him – it's because he's stopped loving me.'

'But why?' Mary persisted.

'Mebbe he never did. Mebbe I took too much for granted and forced the poor man into that deep pit you were talking about, then jumped down on top of him and knocked the wind out of him.'

'That's nonsense and you know it, Caitlin Lennox. He still cares for you – I see it in his face all the time. The man's as miserable as you are.'

'He's not.'

'Don't start that again, we're grown women, not weans.'

'He was the one who turned cold,' Caitlin protested. 'I shouldn't have to sort things out, he should.'

'Och, now you're just being daft! When did men ever take the first step where women are concerned? Talk to him, Caitlin!'

'I don't know . . .'

'I do. At least think about it – and stop picking at that blanket hem, you'll have it all frayed in no time. Go to bed,' Mary ordered. 'I want to get to sleep and we've both got work to do in the morning.'

But instead of turning the light out when Caitlin had gone, she drew a thick exercise book from beneath her pillow and began to turn the pages, studying the pressed flowers within. Each held a special memory; each was caressed gently with a fingertip. Their names and the date they had been plucked were written beneath them in Mary's neat handwriting. She mouthed the names silently and when she had worked her way through to the last flower and the couplet John had written out for her, about being as happy as birds, she closed the book, replaced it beneath her pillow and dabbed at her eyes with a corner of the sheet before she turned out the light.

Just as Mary was putting away the book of pressed flowers, Rose sat bolt upright in the smart bungalow halfway between Glasgow and Paisley, staring wide-eyed into the dark. Beside her, Alex snapped out of a deep sleep.

'What's the matter? Darling . . .' He reached for her, his voice suddenly urgent, 'What's wrong? It is the baby?'

'I'm fine.'

'You're not.' He sat up, putting an arm around her shoulders.

'It was just a touch of cramp.' She swung her long legs out of the bed and paced about the floor.

'D'you want me to telephone the doctor?'

'For cramp? Certainly not. I think I'll go and heat some milk.'

'Come back to bed,' Alex urged. 'I'll fetch the milk for you.'

'I'm better doing it myself; it'll work the cramp out of my muscles. Go back to sleep.'

'I'm not tired,' he protested, and was immediately caught out by a huge yawn.

'I'll be back in a minute.' Rose escaped to the kitchen, where she poured milk into a small saucepan and lit a ring on the gas cooker. She opened a cupboard door and took down a china mug then stared unseeingly at the painted flowers twining round the rim, so engrossed in her thoughts that she forgot all about the milk until it bubbled over the rim of the saucepan and sizzled on to the clean stove.

'Oh, blast!' She put the mug down hurriedly and hunted for a cloth. It took several minutes to clean the stove and wash and dry the pan. When everything had been set to rights she put the mug, unused, back into the cupboard and went to bed.

Alex had fallen back into his deep sleep, but as she crept into bed he reached out and put an arm around her. Grateful for his company, she snuggled against him, sleep forgotten and her mind working feverishly.

She knew now why Fiona was so determined to marry John Brodie.

Rose arrived at Harlequin early the next morning in order to go through the books, all of them kept up to date in Mary's neat, clear handwriting. The war years had indeed been lean; they had barely managed to pay the wages and Rose herself had had to depend on her parents for financial support. At one point, when she was convinced that Harlequin was about to go under, she had turned to John Brodie for advice.

John had already tried to help the company out financially and on that occasion Rose had refused, knowing then that he hoped eventually to marry her and she could not afford to be beholden to him. She herself was in love with Alex, though at that time there seemed little chance of her love being returned.

When she had asked for his help though, John had offered to give her one thousand pounds, 'With no strings attached,' he had said. 'I want to help you as a friend who admires what you have achieved and would hate to see it all come to nothing. You can look on it as a loan or an investment – the decision is yours.'

Rose had accepted the money gratefully on condition that it be invested in the form of shares in the business. 'That way, you might with any luck be able to make money from us as well.'

There was no doubt that John's generosity had saved Harlequin. His investment had allowed them to pay their creditors, and the surge of orders just after the war ended months later had made them solvent again. Rose was fortunate to have him as a friend – but with Fiona wearing his engagement ring the investment that had once saved Harlequin now threatened to destroy it. She knew beyond any doubt that once Fiona became Mrs John Brodie she would use her husband's shares in the fashion house to her own advantage, and to Rose's detriment.

This knowledge meant that Rose had no option but to buy the shares back as quickly as possible. Half an hour with the ledgers showed her that a little money could come from the business itself, but not nearly enough. She would have to find at least eight hundred pounds from somewhere else.

'Oh – Rose!' Mary said from the doorway. 'I didn't expect to find you here so early.' Then, coming into the room and eyeing the ledger on the desk, 'Is there something wrong?'

'Not at all, I just decided to get an early start for once.' Rose closed the ledger. 'You do a grand job, Mary, and I really appreciate it.'

★

'Did you know that Lachie's mending a window frame across at the gatehouse?' Mary asked her sister. Caitlin, working on a design, glanced up, her mind still filled with colours and shapes.

'What about it?'

'I was just wondering why he's back at work there, when you say that you and Murdo aren't going to get married after all.'

'The place still has to be put to rights, hasn't it?'

'Is that what you think it is?'

'What else could it be?'

'Mebbe,' Mary suggested, 'Murdo's regretting what happened between the two of you. Mebbe he's hoping that you'll have the sense to go over there and ask him why Lachie's back at work.'

'And mebbe I'll just not bother. If he's got anything to tell me, let him come over here and say it.'

'In front of all the women?'

'Go away, Mary, I'm busy.'

'D'you want me to ask him?'

'I do not,' Caitlin snapped, aware that Grace and the sewing women were beginning to glance across at her. She returned to her work and was relieved when, after waiting for a moment or two, Mary said, 'Oh well, I just thought I'd mention it . . .' before drifting off.

When the design was completed Caitlin wandered over to a window overlooking the courtyard. Right enough, Lachie was half-in and half-out of one of the upper windows – the window of the room that should have been the main bedroom, Caitlin noted with a pang – hammering at the side frame.

She placed the sketch in a folder and then went downstairs. The front doors were open and sunlight dappled the stone flags outside. Caitlin went out on to the steps and drew in a breath of fresh air, then, without quite realising it, she found herself marching across the yard towards the gatehouse. All at once she was tired of avoiding Murdo and lying awake at night wondering why he had suddenly turned cold towards her. Perhaps Mary was correct; she had the right to know why he was behaving so strangely.

As she neared the building, she halted, tilting her head back and shading her eyes with one hand as she looked up at Lachie. He was perched on the window sill, legs swinging, holding on to the frame with one hand and wielding the hammer with the other.

'Be careful, Lachie.'

He stopped work to peer down at her. 'Och, I'm fine,' he said, and went back to his hammering.

Murdo was immersed in his task, and for a

moment she stood unnoticed in the doorway, watching him and realising that he was still the only man she would ever want. She had been fooling herself when she said otherwise. If he no longer wanted her there was little she could do about it, but as long as there was a chance, she was going to fight for him. She stepped into his line of vision and the loom's clacking stopped as he looked up at her.

'Caitlin – have ye come to look at the new cloth?'

'I've come to talk to you. In the kitchen,' she said, and turned on her heel.

She had to wait for a few minutes, becoming more convinced with each tick of the clock on the wall that he was going to stay where he was. Then to her relief the door was pushed open and he took a few steps into the room.

'What is it?'

'I see Lachie's working on the house again.'

'Aye. Mrs MacDowall was on at me to get the place finished.'

'And about me moving in?'

'Aye.'

'It's none of her business.'

'I didnae like to say that to her, seeing as she owns the place and I work for her.'

'It's not her business, Murdo, but it is ours,'

372

Caitlin said steadily, though her heart was thudding so hard that she was sure he must hear it across the few yards separating them, 'and I think we should settle it once and for all. I want to know why you've changed your mind about marrying me.'

'I've not . . . I mean . . .' he blurted out, and then, both big hands plucking at his canvas apron in agitation, 'Och, Caitlin, can we not leave it for now? We've both got work to do, and Rowena'll probably be on her way over from the school . . .'

'We've left it for long enough. I need to know why, Murdo. You surely owe me that much,' Caitlin insisted and then, catching his swift glance at the mantelshelf, she turned and saw the framed photograph of his long-dead wife and child. And she finally understood. 'It's her, isn't it? Your Elspeth. You're still in love with her.'

'Of course I love her, and I always will—'

'I wish you'd told me that you can't face the thought of replacing her, Murdo. I'd have understood – I do understand.'

'You don't! I took an oath, to her as well as to the minister, that she'd be the only woman in my life for as long as we both lived, but she's gone now – gone where I can't follow, for all that I wanted to when I heard that I'd lost her. I'll never forget her,' he said passionately, 'but I know that she'd not

373

want me to live out the rest of my life on my lone, any more than I'd want that to happen to her if I'd gone first.'

'I don't understand – if she's not come between you and me, then who has?'

'Me!' he almost shouted at her. 'Can you not see for yourself that you'd be daft to marry me?'

'No, I can't. All I can see is that I'll be miserable if I don't.'

'You're wrong, Caitlin! I carry death around with me. I loved Elspeth, and she died. I loved my son Dougald, and he died too. I'll not be responsible for your death as well.'

'Is that what it's all about? You think that your wife would still be alive if she hadn't married you, and your son would have been better off if he'd never been born?'

'I know it. I was far away when Dougald drowned – fighting the Boer. I wasn't there to watch over him,' Murdo said in a voice thick with years of guilt and despair. 'And when Elspeth died of heartbreak over his loss I was still in South Africa. I wasnae there to save her and give her a reason to go on living. I can't bear to think that I'll mebbe fail you as well. I can't bear it!'

'Murdo, you won't do it to me and you didn't do it to them. My wee brother was killed when

374

he ran into the pend in Espedair Street and fell under the carthorse's hooves. My mother blamed herself for a long time, but she came to understand that she couldn't have watched over him every second of his life. Old Mhairi told me that you had to go away from Dougald and Elspeth because you couldn't find work and joining the army was the only way you could provide for them. You were looking out for them all the time, Murdo. You were sending money home so that Elspeth could pay the rent and feed and clothe herself and the wee one.'

'I can't take the risk!'

'I'm not asking you to do that. The risk is mine – I'm responsible for my own life, and my life,' Caitlin stormed at him, 'is no pleasure to me if you're not part of it. I'd rather have one week as your wife, Murdo Guthrie, than ninety years without you.'

He ran his hands through his dark hair. 'But—'

'But nothing! I promise you,' Caitlin said, 'that if you agree to marry me as soon as it can be arranged, I will live for at least fifty years, and I will love you more and more with each day that passes.' There was a pause, then she said, 'I'm going now, for Rowena'll be here any minute. I'll come back this evening for your decision.'

She moved towards him and was disappointed

when he stepped aside to let her pass instead of standing his ground. She walked along the hall and out of the door into the sunshine, but then turned as he said from the dark coolness of the hall, 'You're right, I've been a daft fool, and I can't bear to be apart from you.'

'You never will be,' she said, 'not for one single day.' They each took a step forward and met in the doorway; how long they stayed like that, holding each other tightly, Caitlin had no idea. It wasn't until Lachie said from the stairs, 'Och, I'd not have come down if I'd known that I was interrupting something,' that they broke apart.

'So . . .' the young Highlander glanced from one flushed face to the other '. . . you two have decided to stop behaving like fools, have you?'

'Aye, we have – not that it's any business of yours.'

'It is indeed my business. Am I not waiting for you to name the day when I'll stand beside you as your groomsman?'

'I'm waiting for Caitlin to tell me the day first.'

'As soon as this house is ready,' Caitlin suggested.

'You have your answer, Lachie. Now get back to work,' Murdo ordered, 'for the sooner this house is fit for my Caitlin, the sooner you get to be groomsman.

'You'll come back this evening?' he queried

when Lachie had sprinted back upstairs. 'The two of us have lost time to make up.'

'We have, but I think it would be best if you come to Espedair Street, so that we can tell them the wedding's back on. We'll have plenty of time to spend together,' Caitlin hurried on as his face fell. 'We have all the rest of our lives. Not a word to Rowena until tonight. I have to go.' She kissed him swiftly, then ran down the steps and across the yard, her feet skimming the ground and her heart so light that it seemed to be soaring above the old mill roof.

Mary was standing in Harlequin's doorway, arms folded and a great grin lighting up her normally solemn face.

'You made a right exhibition of yourself in that doorway, Caitlin Lennox. It's just as well we've no clients in this afternoon. Can I take it that we're all going to a wedding?' she asked as Caitlin reached her.

'Aye, you are. And you'll be my bridesmaid — you and Rowena.'

'I'm glad the two of you finally saw sense.'

'There's just one thing, though. Lachie's to be groomsman. Will that bother you?'

'Not a bit of it. Me and Lachie can get on fine together.'

'Murdo's coming to the house this evening so

that we can tell everyone. So not a word until then.'

'Not a word. Now,' Mary stepped aside, 'upstairs with you, so that you can start thinking about that bonny wedding dress you're going to need.'

# 25

'I'm going to be a bridesmaid, I'm going to be a bridesmaid!' Rowena skipped round and round the kitchen table, singing the same phrase over and over again, until Todd protested, 'Hold on there, lassie, you're makin' me dizzy!'

'Oh.' She paused for a moment, then set off round the table again, this time in the opposite direction, singing, 'I'm going to a wed–ding!' until Murdo reached out a long arm to block her way.

'You're not going to any wedding and you're not going to be a bridesmaid if you don't know how to behave yourself,' he warned her, his voice solemn and his face expressionless.

'I'll behave myself,' she said at once.

'Good.'

'Can I come and live with you and Auntie Caitlin at the gatehouse when you get married?'

'I don't think it would be fair to take you away from your grandma and your granddad. What would they do without you?'

'They've got Auntie Mary, and I'll visit every day,' she suggested.

'There's a lot to be done before we get to that stage,' Mary said briskly. 'A wedding dress to make, and bridesmaids' dresses, and the gatehouse to finish—'

'You can leave that part of it to me,' Murdo said. 'Me and Lachie'll get the place ready in no time.'

An hour later, out in the dark pend with Caitlin, he said, 'I've wasted enough time with my daft imaginings. Now I'm going to make it up to you by getting the house ready as soon as I can.'

She nestled close to him, reluctant to let him go now that they had found each other again. 'Promise me that we'll never quarrel again.'

'I promise,' he said, and sealed the bargain with a kiss.

Rowena, who had had to be dissuaded from accompanying the happy couple out to the pend, had been despatched to her bed by the time Caitlin returned to the kitchen.

'Though she's so excited that I'll be surprised

if she manages to get to sleep for at least an hour,' Mary said. 'She can't wait to tell Cavan in the morning about being a bridesmaid. She wants to know if Cavan can be your bridesmaid too.'

'I don't see why not. The more the merrier.'

'Has Harlequin got time to make dresses for three bridesmaids as well as your wedding dress? The appointment book is quite full for the next month or two.'

'Why don't me and Jean and Teenie help out?' Kirsty suggested. 'Harlequin could make a wedding dress for you and a bridesmaid's dress for Mary, and we could make something for the lassies that matches in with what the two of you are wearing.'

'Are you sure, Mam? D'you have the time?'

'We'll make the time. Jean and Teenie'll be pleased tae help with your wedding. And they'll be that pleased tae hear that it's goin' tae happen after all.'

'We all are,' Todd said, knocking his pipe out and heaving himself from his chair. 'Murdo's a decent man and I'm grateful tae him for puttin' the life back intae those bonny eyes of yours, Caitlin. Now then, I'm off tae my bed, for I've had enough excitement tae dae me for one day.'

While the Lennoxes celebrated Caitlin's good news, Joseph McCart was having a bad evening.

381

He had been swinging along the road towards his home, whistling to himself, when Geordie Marshall, the man who had recommended him to Todd as his replacement, came limping towards him, leaning heavily on his walking stick. The older man's face broke into a broad grin when he saw the Irishman.

'It's yersel', Joe. How's life treatin' ye?'

'Not too badly, and yourself?'

'Ach, the rheumatics are bein' a right pest, so they are. Ye'd think that they'd let up in the summer, would ye no'? But some days it's as if someone's trying tae carve me up like a Christmas turkey, an' usin' a blunt knife intae the bargain. I saw yer wee lassie's name in the paper not so long ago. She was doin' some sort of dancin' demonstration.'

'That's right.'

'That's a clever wee lass ye have right enough. And a bonny yin, tae. Ye never come down tae the pub for a wee drink, Joseph. Have ye signed the pledge?'

'Nothing like that. It's just that I'm not much of a drinker.'

'Wise man — best tae keep yer money in yer pocket. But some evenin's a wee glass o' whisky's the only thing that eases my bones. Gettin' old's a right pest, I'm tellin' ye.' Geordie had turned round and was walking slowly back the way he had come. Impatient though he was to get home to his family, Joseph slowed down his steps to accommodate the older man.

'So how are ye gettin' on wi' Todd Paget?'

'Fine. He's a good employer.'

'Aye, he is that. A fair man, and kindly intae the bargain. I knew ye'd suit each other. Wait a minute,' Geordie said in surprise, 'is this no' my close we're at?'

'Aye, it is.'

'Dammit, I was on my way tae the pub for a wee dram. I must've turned mysel' aboot without noticin'. I'll say goodbye then, Joe, an' get on my way again.' Geordie leaned all his weight on his stick and held out his right hand, gnarled as an old tree. Then as Joseph shook it he said, 'Here, I suddenly minded – have any Irish friends o' yours come tae Paisley recently?'

'No.' A prickling sensation suddenly ran down Joseph's spine.

'I was in the pub yesterday an' there was a man came in for a drink. He said he was new over on the boat from Ireland and lookin' out for a friend o' his. Then he gave me your name. A fellow aboot my own height,' said Geordie, who between age and the disease that ravaged his skeleton and stooped his shoulders must have lost as much as

383

nine inches in height, 'an' thin. Secretive lookin'. I didnae take tae him.'

'He knew my name? What did you tell him?' Joseph asked when Geordie nodded.

'I said I didnae ken the name at a', an' there were nae Irish folk living in this district that I knew o'. I thought it best.'

'Did he ask anyone else?'

'There wis only me an' the landlord in at the time, an' he's never seen ye, since ye never go in for a drink.'

'Thank you, Geordie, I'm grateful to ye.'

'Aye, well, we all have our own secrets an' I never took tae strangers asking aboot folk in pubs,' Geordie said, then began to shuffle back along the street.

Before turning in at the close mouth Joseph stopped and glanced round the street. It seemed quiet enough, and free of loiterers, unless the mysterious Irishman who had been asking about him was skinny enough to hide behind a lamp-post. Joseph melted into the dank darkness of the close and hurried upstairs, straining his ears all the while for the sound of footsteps at his back.

All was calm in the kitchen. Cavan was working at the table on her schoolbooks, the ould yin was dozing in her chair by the range as usual and Shelagh hummed quietly to herself as she saw to the dinner.

'It'll not be long,' she said as Joseph came in, then after one glance at his face, her smile faded. He put a swift finger to his lips and then jerked his head in the direction of their bedroom.

'Cavan, listen for the potatoes boiling over.' She wiped her hands on her apron. 'I'll not be a minute.'

When she reached the bedroom he was at the window, staring down into the street below. Shelagh closed the door, the blood suddenly cooling in her veins. 'Joseph?'

He turned to face her, and even though his back was to the window and his face in shadow, she could sense the tension in his lean body.

'It's time, Shelagh,' he said huskily. 'Time to move on.'

'When?'

'Now,' he said.


It wasn't like Joseph McCart to be late for work, but on that Saturday Todd and his apprentice had been busy for the best part of an hour before the Irishman arrived.

'There ye are, Joseph,' Todd greeted him amiably. 'I was beginnin' tae wonder if I should send Kenny along tae see if there was anythin' wrong.'

'Can I have a word, Mr Paget?'

'O' course ye can.' Todd took one look at the younger man's drawn face and went on, 'Kenny, just keep an eye on that glue pot while I step outside for a minute. Come on, Joseph, we'll take a look at the timber in the yard tae make sure it's well seasoned.' Then, once the workshop door was shut and they were well out of earshot, 'What's troublin' ye, man? If it's anythin' I can help with, I will.'

'Nobody can help us. We have to go from Paisley, Mr Paget, and we have to go today. Cavan and Shelagh are putting our things together right now. I just came for the wages owing to me, and to tell you that I'm sorry to be doing this to ye, for you and your family have been kind to us.'

'Ye cannae just go like that, without a word. What about wee Rowena? She's made a good friend in your wee lassie.'

'I know,' Joseph's voice was wretched and he kept twisting his cap between his strong fingers, 'but there's nothing else for it.'

He glanced towards the pend, as though he half-expected to see someone there, and then jumped as Todd put a hand on his arm.

'See now, son, why don't ye come intae the kitchen an' tell me what's goin' on? If ye're set on leavin' I'll no' stop ye,' Todd went on as Joseph began to shake his head, 'but I'll be sorry tae see ye go, and so will the rest of my fam'ly. Come intae the hoose for a minute. It's all right,' he added swiftly as Joseph drew back, 'the women-folk have all gone out and we'll have the place tae ourselves.'

In the kitchen he seated Joseph at the table and poured out two cups of strong tea from the pot simmering on the range. Then he took a bottle down from a cupboard and poured a generous dram of whisky into each cup.

'There now, that's better. Now then, lad,' he took a deep drink from his cup and licked his lips before finishing with, 'tell me what's troublin' ye, an' let's see if I can help at all.'

Joseph took half of his cupful in one swallow and choked slightly. He was unused to drinking spirits, but once he had caught his breath again the whisky gave him the courage to start talking. Having got started, he found it hard to stop. Todd Paget and his family had treated Joseph more kindly than anyone he had ever known, and now, under the man's concerned gaze, the words poured out. He told the story of the bitter feud between his father and the Doyle clan, how it had resulted in his father's murder, and how his mother had never forgiven him for not taking up the feud and avenging her husband's death.

'I was never a man of violence, Mr Paget – my da despised me for my weakness, and so does the ould yin – my ma. But I only ever wanted a decent life for me and Shelagh and our wee Cavan. It would have ended there, with my da's death,' Joseph said wretchedly, picking up his cap again and wrenching it into a rope between his hands, 'if Liam Doyle hadn't tried to take advantage of my Shelagh one day. I came home from work and found her in a right state, weeping her heart out. She'd got away from him and she didn't want to tell me about it, but I made her. As I said, I've never been one for violence, but . . .' he choked again over the memory, and Todd heard threads ripping in the tortured cap . . . 'that night a red rage took hold of me. I mind goin' out of the house with Shelagh tryin' to stop me, and me throwin' her hands off. I found the man on his own, workin' the wee bit field they had, and I don't mind much more – I don't want to remember it – until I was back home with my hands all bloody and hurtin', and Shelagh and me were throwin' things into bags. We took Cavan and the ould yin and we ran off to stay with a cousin in another county, but then we heard that Liam Doyle had died of his injuries. God forgive me, Mr Paget, I killed the man! And then we knew that the Doyles would be out lookin' for me, and not just content with findin' me and killin' me either. They'd have hurt my Cavan, and as for Shelagh . . .' He swallowed hard, then said, 'Why do folk keep hurtin' each other, Mr Paget? And why did I do what I did? I'm no better than my own da!'

'It's human nature, lad. I got close to it myself once, when some braggart ran off with the lass I was tae marry just weeks before our weddin'. If I'd known where to find them I'd mebbe have done tae him what you did tae this Doyle fellow,' Todd said, 'but they were well away, so I lost mysel' in drink for a while. Kirsty was the savin' o' me. Her and me wed and the man I hated died in the war, poor soul. As to the lass – I don't know where she went. But what you've told me happened back in Ireland. I still don't know what's made ye want tae leave Paisley?'

'Last night Geordie told me that an Irishman's been askin' for me in the pub. He never let on that he knows me, but it's the Doyles' man as sure as anythin'. We have to go.'

'Where to?'

'I don't know yet, and you're better not knowin' at all.'

'Ye'll need money.'

'I'd be grateful if ye could see yer way to payin' me what I'm due, Mr Paget.'

'Wait here, I'll no' be a minute.'

While Todd was gone, Joseph looked round the comfortable, quiet room and wondered if he and Shelagh and Cavan would ever know a safe haven like this one. They would, if he had his way of it!

'Here ye are.' Todd returned and handed an envelope over. It felt bulkier than it should and Joseph peered inside, puzzled.

'This is more than I earned. I can't take more than my right.'

'Aye ye can. Think of the extra as a wee gift for yer wife and the lassie that's given Rowena such pleasure. And if ye can ever let us know how ye are, we'd like tae hear from ye.'

'If anyone comes askin' for me—'

'They'll get nothin' from me, or from any of my family. An' I'll see tae it that Kenny holds his tongue, tae,' Todd said firmly, then held out his hand. 'Good luck tae ye, lad. Ye deserve it.'

'God bless ye, Mr Paget, ye're a good man.' Joseph wrung Todd's hand until it ached and then jammed his cap, now looking even shabbier than before, on his dark head. A few minutes later Todd stood at the open street door to watch the young Irishman hurry down the road. He waited until Joseph had turned the corner and disappeared from sight before stepping back into the house, his heart heavy. He had lost a grand worker, and the lives of Joseph and his innocent wife and child might well be warped for ever just because some men were daft enough to hold tight to resentments and bitterness instead of letting go.

He would tell Alex just enough to let him understand why Joseph deserved his wages even though he was leaving them in the lurch by hurrying off without warning, and he would tell Kirsty the whole story because he never kept anything from her. He knew that she would share and keep the secret with him and that she would understand why he had dipped into the little nest egg the two of them kept hidden in their bedroom.

He rinsed out the mugs they had used and placed them on the draining board to dry, then checked the money in his pocket before returning via the back door to the workshop. He had enough to buy Kenny's silence should anyone come around to ask about Joseph McCart – and just to make sure of the boy's silence, he would add a wee threat of his own.

Kirsty, her two daughters and Rowena had spent a happy morning helping Rose to hang the last of the curtains in her new house. When they got off the bus at Paisley Cross in the early afternoon Kirsty hurried off to help out in Jean's second-hand clothes shop while Mary and Caitlin decided to take Rowena window-shopping before walking back to Espedair Street. She was trotting through the Cross between her two aunts, happily sucking at a striped lollipop Mary had bought for her, when she suddenly screamed, 'Cavan!'

'Where?' Caitlin scanned the busy pavement.

'There – there!' The lollipop flew unnoticed from Rowena's hand as she pointed at a passing bus. 'It's Cavan – Cavan!' she screamed at the top of her voice, causing heads to turn.

Cavan, sitting by the window at the back of the bus, had seen Rowena. Her nose was pressed against the window and both hands were plastered flat against the glass on either side of her dark head. Her face was pale and her eyes, usually sparkling but now huge and sorrowful, were fixed on her friend. As the bus began to draw away one palm moved from the glass to be pressed against Cavan's down-turned mouth. Then it was clamped against the window again in a final kiss.

'Cavan!' Rowena shouted again, and ran out into the street, intent on following the bus. Caitlin screamed while Mary lunged after her niece, but it was a man passing by who reached the little girl first, sweeping her up into his arms and out of the way of a bicycle only inches from colliding with her.

'Mind yersel', pet,' the man said cheerfully, handing Rowena over to Mary while the cyclist, a messenger boy with the big square basket before him piled high, wobbled dangerously into the kerb and only just managed to stop before the machine fell over.

'Daft lassie!' he snapped.

'You mind yer tongue, son,' the man told him while Rowena struggled against Mary's grasp and the bus disappeared along the road to Glasgow.

'Cavan!'

'She's just going to Glasgow with her mother.' Mary took a firm grip of her niece's hand. 'She'll be back this afternoon.'

But Rowena had recognised the desolation in her friend's dark eyes. She was young, but she knew a final farewell when she saw one. 'She won't . . . she won't,' she sobbed. 'She's gone!' And then she buried her face in Mary's coat and cried as though her world had come to a sudden end.

The offer of another lollipop and some extra sweeties did no good. Nor did the promise that if she cheered up they would buy her a new doll. Finally Caitlin said in despair, 'We'll walk to Cavan's house right now, then you can see for yourself that she's just gone with her mother to do some shopping, same as you're doing with us.'

'She's not coming b-back,' Rowena insisted, her face now swollen and red, but at least she allowed Mary to mop the tear tracks away with her handkerchief, and then she took their hands as they walked down St Mirin Brae.

As they climbed the last few steps to the flat where the McCarts had briefly lived, Rowena squeezed past Mary, who was in the lead, and got to the door first. She knocked on the scarred panels and Mary and Caitlin, standing behind her, glanced at each other in sudden consternation as the unlatched door swung slowly open before the weight of Rowena's small fist.

'Mebbe I should go in first,' Caitlin started to say, but Rowena had already hurried inside. They followed, to find her standing in the kitchen. The room was shabbily furnished, and dishes were on the table, left over from the last meal. The single armchair was drawn up close to the range, which Mary discovered was unlit and cold to the touch. The chair's cushions held the outline of a large body, and as Caitlin passed it to open a corner cupboard, her nose caught a whiff of stale urine. The cupboard was empty, as were the drawers in the other two small rooms – one little more than a cupboard, with a narrow cot in it. The former inhabitants had taken their clothes and everything they could carry.

The three of them gathered together again in the kitchen, where Rowena looked up at her aunts with blue eyes that were dulled, and suddenly quite old.

'I told you,' she said, her voice a wisp of sound

in the empty room. 'I told you that they weren't coming back. And I never got to tell her that we were going to be bridesmaids together . . .'

# 26

'Alex,' Rose said, and then again, as her husband continued to read his newspaper, 'Alex!'

'Hmmm?'

'I need some money.'

The newspaper was slowly lowered until Alex was looking over the top of it at her. 'I thought that now the nursery's finished we didn't need to put any more money into the house.'

'It's not for the house. I need eight hundred pounds.'

'What?' Now she had his full attention. 'What on earth do you need that amount for? A gold–plated perambulator?'

'I want to buy John Brodie's shares in Harlequin.'

'Why?'

'He's getting married, and I happen to know that Fiona's looking for a grand house. It will cost John all the money he can get hold of.'

'He's asked you to buy his shares?'

'No, it's my idea. A sort of wedding present.'

'Wouldn't something along the lines of a good dinner service be better?'

'The thing is, he invested a thousand pounds in the business during the war, and now that we've taken on another designer at Harlequin I can only raise about two hundred at the moment. So I have to find the other eight hundred from somewhere.'

'You don't have it in your own bank account, I take it?'

Rose shook her head. 'I sank some of the money I inherited from my grandmamma's will into improving Jean's wee shop, then there was Harlequin to set up, and what was left went into buying this place. I wondered if you might be able to help me?'

'My darling wife, I spent every penny I had on buying this house and furnishing it, and today I discovered that Todd and I are going to have to find a good time-served man for the Paisley workshop. Joseph McCart's taken his family and disappeared from Paisley, just when he was beginning to settle in, too. I've got enough on my mind without trying to help you raise money to buy

John out. If I were you I'd settle for the dinner service. He might not want to lose his shares – shouldn't you find that out before you start making plans?'

Rose hesitated, on the verge of telling him the truth, as they had promised to do – always – but then deciding that he would probably accuse her of overreacting, she shrugged. 'I suppose you're right.'

'Of course I am,' Alex said comfortably, picking up his paper again. 'It was a daft idea in any case – why should you worry about John? He's an only child, remember – his parents will probably want to help to buy a suitable house for him and Fiona to live in.'

He twitched the newspaper in a way that indicated that he was settling down to read an article and shouldn't be disturbed. Rose chewed absently at a fingernail, once again going over the list of possibilities she had drawn up in her mind. Sandy MacDowall would no doubt be happy to lend money to the mother of his first grandchild, but he might mention it to Fiona and in any case, it wasn't fair to involve him in her fight to defeat his beloved daughter. Her own parents still disapproved of their youngest daughter becoming a businesswoman, and they would want to know why she needed the money, and as all her wealthy relatives were in good health, there was little chance of another inheritance in the near future.

She got up and went into the hall where she could heave a gusty sigh without fear of Alex hearing it. There was nothing else for it – she would have to throw herself on the mercy of the bank manager.


'What's that noise?' Miss Flora Dalrymple wanted to know, somewhat irritably. Grace, down on her knees in order to pin the hem of the young woman's wedding dress, mumbled something through a mouthful of pins.

'What did you say?'

'It's coming from the gatehouse,' Caitlin interpreted swiftly, concerned in case Grace swallowed the pins in her attempt to be heard. 'My fiancé and a friend are trying to get it ready in time for our wedding.'

'Really?' Miss Dalrymple, middle daughter of a wealthy businessman with a large home in Paisley and a thriving business in Glasgow, raised a carefully plucked eyebrow. 'You're going to live over there, are you?' And then, when Caitlin nodded, 'That's like a grocer living above the shop, isn't it?'

'I suppose it is, but it will suit me very well. I won't have far to travel between home and workplace.'

'When's the wedding to be?'

'That depends on how long they take to get the house ready. Not long, I hope.'

'We had to book Paisley Abbey as soon as we became engaged. It's very popular. But I don't suppose that you'll be getting married there.'

'No, we won't. There you are, Ella,' Caitlin said with relief as the young woman came into the fitting room. 'Miss Dalrymple, this is Miss Morrison, our new designer. Ella, could you assist Miss Dalrymple and Grace for a minute while I attend to some urgent business?'

Once outside the room she paused to draw a deep breath before hurrying out of the mill and across the courtyard to the gatehouse. The door was open to the mild September day and Lachie was again working on one of the upstairs windows. Murdo, nailing down a loose tread on the stairs, stopped work when she went in, and sat on the step below, reaching for her hand and drawing her down to sit by him.

'I had to get out for a minute – Miss Dalrymple's being fitted for her wedding dress and she's such a terrible snob. I left poor Ella with her and fled. I can only stay for a minute.' She inhaled the smell of timber and fresh paint. 'You and Lachie are getting on well.'

'The sooner it's done the sooner we'll be

together.' Murdo slipped an arm around her and she leaned against his solid body. 'I was a fool, Caitlin, to try to fight my feelings for you. I'll always be grateful to you for bringing me to my senses.' He kissed her, then as she drew away reluctantly and began to get to her feet he urged, 'Stay a wee while and let me show you what we've finished today.'

'I have to get back – she's sure to be asking where I am, and it isn't fair to leave poor Ella to deal with her. And Rowena'll be here any minute now. Murdo,' Caitlin said hesitantly, 'how do you feel about her coming to live with us? She keeps asking if she can, and my mother and Todd aren't getting any younger. They've earned some time on their own.'

'As long as she's happy and you're happy, so am I,' he said easily as he followed Caitlin to the door. 'There's plenty of room.'

'You're a good man, Murdo Guthrie, and I'm fortunate to have found you.'

'The good fortune's mine,' he said. 'I lost my family but now I've been blessed with another one.'

'This time it's a family you'll not lose,' Caitlin promised, adding as they went out on to the steps, 'There's Grace looking for me.'

'You'll come over tonight?'

'Of course.'

As he turned back into the house Caitlin hurried towards the mill building, her spirits lifted by the few minutes spent with him.

'She's makin' a fuss about you not bein' there,' Grace said as she reached the steps. 'Poor Ella's havin' a right time of—' Then she screamed, her gaze moving beyond Caitlin.

Caitlin turned in time to see Lachie tumble down the stretch of roof below the window where he had been working. His fingers clawed briefly at the guttering but failed to get a grip. He screamed as his body hurtled into space, arms and legs scrabbling for purchase on thin air; a scream that cut off suddenly as he was dashed on to the paving stones.

Just then Rowena rounded the corner of the gatehouse, swinging her school satchel in one hand. Caitlin saw her stop short, frozen to the spot, and then the satchel fell to the ground as her hands flew to her face. Shriek after shriek began to pour through her widespread fingers.

'Oh dear God!' Grace slumped against one of the elegant posts that Rose had installed at either side of the door. 'Dear God, he's dead!'

Caitlin had begun to run back towards the gatehouse when Murdo erupted from the door, taking the steps in one bound. He paused briefly by the

402

huddled shape on the ground and then jumped over it to scoop Rowena up in his arms and carry her at a run to meet Caitlin.

'Here . . .' He thrust the hysterical child into her arms, brutally ripping Rowena's arms and legs free as she struggled to wrap herself round him. 'Get her out of here!' And then, looking beyond her to Harlequin's door, where people were beginning to gather, he roared, 'Someone send for the ambulance wagon – now!' before turning around and rushing back to where Lachie's broken body lay looking more like a rag doll discarded by a large, irritable child than a flesh and blood man.

Caitlin and Ella both worked at calming Rowena down while Rose and Grace administered sal volatile and brandy to Flora Dalrymple, who kept threatening to faint but never quite managed it. So it was left to Mary and Murdo to tend to Lachie while they waited for the ambulance wagon to arrive.

Not that there was much they could do. The young man was unconscious and it was clear from the way he lay that his legs, at least, were badly damaged. Murdo, his face grey, fetched a blanket from the house and laid it gently over his friend. 'Should we mebbe try givin' him a sip of brandy?'

'Best not.' Mary gestured towards the blood trickling down Lachie's white face. 'He's hurt his head. Wring a towel out in cold water and bring it here.'

While she waited she covered one of Lachie's hands with her own. It was warm, and she detected a faint rise and fall of his chest.

'Lachie, can you hear me?' she said, bending over him. 'It's Mary. You've had a fall but you're going to be fine. The ambulance wagon's comin', Lachie. Just lie quiet and you'll be all right.' She took his hand again, and to her surprise she was aware of a very faint movement as though his fingers were trying to curl around hers.

'He's alive, and I think he can hear us,' she said as Murdo dropped to his knees by his friend. 'He's trying to hold my hand. Wipe the blood away, very carefully.' While he did as he was told, she kept talking to Lachie, telling him what had happened and assuring him that help was on its way.

The ambulance wagon arrived swiftly, but to Mary and Murdo the seconds seemed to drag by before they heard the welcome sound of its bell. Lachie's fingers had managed to curl a little further round Mary's, though his eyes were still closed and he made no sound other than a faint groan as the men began to lift him carefully into the wagon.

Mary went with him to the Royal Alexandra

Infirmary, and when he had been borne off into the deeper recesses of the handsome building she sat down as instructed on a wooden bench in a waiting area, unwilling to leave until she found out how he was.

Nurses, doctors and porters came and went, the doctors solemn and clearly aware of their own importance, the porters harassed, the nurses sweeping past gracefully in their snowy-white starched aprons and their elaborate caps. Other members of the public shared her bench; men and women of all ages, some with wide-eyed, bewildered children in tow. They all came in looking strained, waiting for a nurse or, on occasion, a doctor to come and seek them out. They were taken aside and spoken to in low voices, and then they left, some relieved, some in tears, some taken through the door that led deeper into the hospital, others left to make their own way to the exit.

A middle-aged couple came in and sat behind Mary, who could tell from their low voices that they were Highland folk. After a moment she rose and went to join them. 'Are you Lachie's parents?'

'Aye, we are,' the man said while the woman clutched at Mary's wrist and asked, 'Do you know something about him, miss?'

'I'm Mary Lennox. I've known Lachie for a while.'

'You're the lass he used to walk out with,' Lachie's mother said. 'Mary Lennox – I mind the name.'

'Yes, that's right.' Mary squeezed on to the bench beside them. 'He was helping Murdo at the gate-house, working on one of the upstairs windows, when he fell.'

'You were there?'

'I didn't see him fall but I was with him before the ambulance wagon arrived, and I came to the infirmary with him.'

'Did he say anything?'

Mary shook her head. 'He was unconscious, but when I touched his hand I think I felt his fingers moving.'

'Did they say he'd be all right?'

Lachie took his looks from his mother; he had her long thin face, but while he was always smiling she looked as though she went through life dreading the worst. And today, it had happened. Mary wished that she could give the poor woman some comfort, but she could only explain that nobody had told her anything as yet.

'It was kind of you to come here with him,' the man said with an anxious glance at his wife, who, with no comfort to cling to, had suddenly retreated into white-lipped silence.

The three of them waited while the minutes

dragged by and hospital staff and townsfolk came and went. This must be happening all the time, Mary thought; during all those days she had spent in her beloved little office at Harlequin, or the peaceful evenings with her family in Espedair Street, human dramas were being played out in this infirmary not far away, and she had had no knowledge of them at all.

For some reason her Sunday walks with John Brodie came into her mind. She missed them, and she missed John. She would have given anything to have him with her there and then, comforting her with his quiet dependable presence. She wondered, with some bitterness, if Fiona would ever appreciate the man's worth. She doubted it.

'Mary?' For a few seconds she thought that it was John who stood over her, calling her name, then she looked up to see Murdo. 'How is he?'

'We're waiting to hear. D'you know Lachie's parents?' She indicated the elderly couple by her side and Murdo turned to speak to them in the Gaelic language native to all three. They responded eagerly and she gathered from his gestures that Murdo was telling them what had happened to their son. As she listened, the woman put a hand tightly over her mouth and fresh tears sprang to her eyes. While they were still talking a nurse arrived and drew the couple aside. After a moment or two they began to follow her through the inner door, then Lachie's father turned back.

'They say he's hurt badly, but they think he'll mend. We can go to see him now. Thank you for your kindness,' he said hurriedly. Murdo said something in his native tongue and the man nodded before following his wife and the nurse.

'I said I'd visit them later, to find out how he is. Come on,' Murdo took Mary's arm, 'I'll walk to your home with you.'

She arrived to find Kirsty in an armchair by the kitchen range with Rowena, her face swollen with weeping and still streaked with tears, fast asleep in her arms. The girl was swaddled in a shawl that Kirsty had wrapped around the two of them, as women tied their babies against their bodies. Caitlin was seeing to the evening meal, with Todd trying to help.

'She'll not go to her own bed,' Kirsty said quietly. 'This was the only way we could quiet her. Poor wee lamb, she saw a terrible thing today.'

'I'll take her into my bed with me tonight,' Mary offered, sinking into the chair that was usually Todd's. 'I've just come from the infirmary – Lachie's still alive but that's all I know. Murdo came to the infirmary and walked to the corner with me but he'd not come in.'

'I'll go to the gatehouse later.' Caitlin spooned

potatoes and mince on to plates and Todd set them on the table. 'Mam, how are you going to manage to eat? Let me take her.'

'No, leave her be, we don't want to disturb her. Bring that stool over and put my plate on it. If you cut the potatoes up for me I can manage fine with one hand.'

'Are you sure?'

'Lassie, I've raised my own weans, and you all fell sick at one time or another – I'm used to eatin' with one hand,' her mother said robustly.

Mary, traumatised by the day's events, opted to go to bed not long after she had eaten. Rowena was in such a sound sleep that Kirsty was able to carry her upstairs and put her into Mary's bed without wakening her.

'If she rouses in the night, call me and I'll make her somethin' tae eat. We'll not bother tryin' to put her into her nightdress – let her sleep as she is for once,' Kirsty said, and before leaving the room she reached out a gentle hand to brush a glowing brown curl from the child's cheek. 'Poor wee soul, she's had a lot tae put up with, losin' Cavan and then seein' that poor laddie fall today. It's no' fair!'

'If there's one thing I've learned in life, lass,' Todd whispered, afraid of waking the child, 'it's that nob'dy promised the likes o' us a fair life. It's up tae us tae make the best of what we've got.' And putting an arm around his wife's shoulders, he led her from the room.

Caitlin had half-expected Murdo to come to the house, but when eight o'clock came and went with no sign of him she walked round to Harlequin. It was the middle of September and night was beginning to close in. As she neared the gatehouse she heard the sound of hammering – the same sound that had caused Flora Dalrymple to complain about the noise.

She hastened her steps, realising as she rounded the gatehouse that she was taking the same path that Rowena had taken that afternoon after school. The hammering stopped as she hesitated at the corner before forcing herself to walk on towards the front steps, past the area of paving stones that had obviously been scrubbed clean. She skirted the lighter patch where Lachie's broken body had lain only hours before, then as the hammering began again she looked up at the window Lachie had cheerfully waved from and saw to her horror that Murdo was perched on the sill, one leg inside and the other outside as he pounded at the frame.

The blood seemed to freeze in Caitlin's veins. She opened her mouth to scream his name, then realised that she might startle him and cause him to look down, lose his balance and fall as his friend had fallen to break himself on the hard flags below. Instead, she sped into the house, along the hall and up the stairs as quietly as she could.

Murdo was so intent on his work that it wasn't until she grabbed at his arm with both hands and pulled back as hard as she could that he knew she was there. He shouted what she took to be a startled curse in his own native tongue and the hammer slipped from his hand and went rattling down the slates to fall to the ground while he tumbled into the room and collapsed in a heap at Caitlin's feet.

'Ye daft—What are ye doin'? I could have gone over the edge just like Lachie!'

'I thought you were going to do just that – what possessed you to do such a thing?' she raged at him. 'And you on your lone, too. If I hadn't arrived when I did you could have fallen too, and lain there with nobody to see you or . . . or to help you . . .'

'I was fine until you came and frighted the life out of me,' he said indignantly, scrambling to his feet. Then, as he saw the rush of tears coursing down her face, he took her in his arms. 'Och, Caitlin, don't take on, lass, it's all right.'

'I thought . . . I thought I was going to lose you,' she wept into his shoulder.

411

'Hush now.' He rocked her as though soothing a child. 'You'll not get rid of me that easy.'

'I almost did, before, when I thought you'd stopped caring for me.' She gulped and drew back slightly, scrubbing fresh tears away with one fist. 'Oh, look what I've done to your shirt, it's soaked!'

'It'll dry. Come on now . . .' He led her downstairs and into the kitchen where he sat her down in the armchair and damped the corner of a clean towel before using it to wipe her face. 'Sit quiet for a minute while I make some tea,' he instructed her, and picked up the kettle simmering on the range as usual. 'How's Rowena?'

'She was sleeping when I left. She'd been in a right state, my mother said.'

'Poor wee lass, she should never have seen . . . what she did see.'

'Murdo, what possessed you to work at that window just hours after Lachie fell from it?'

'The job had to be finished. I was doing it for him.'

'How is he? Mary said that you were going to see his parents this evening. Can I come with you?'

'I've already been there. He'll live,' Murdo said, his broad back towards her, 'but his legs are hurt bad.'

'You mean he might not be able to walk?'

412

'They don't know. His mother said that he was awake at least, and able to talk to them.' He turned to face her, his eyes dulled. 'It's my fault, Caitlin. I was hurrying him along, wanting the work done quickly so that you and me could get married. My fault again.'

'No!' She jumped up and took the large teapot from his hands. He had filled it to the brim as though making tea for a whole host of folk instead of just the two of them, and it was so heavy that she only just managed to put it on the table before it began to tip, causing some of the scalding tea to spill out. Then she took both his hands in hers.

'If it was anyone's fault, it was Lachie's. Heights never seemed to bother him – every time I shouted to him to take care at that high window he just laughed down at me.'

'He wouldn't have been there if I'd let Mrs MacDowall do as she wanted and bring in workmen to see to the place. I wanted to get it ready for you myself, and when Lachie wanted to help I let him because I knew he needed the wee bit money I could afford to pay him.'

'You were doing it for me, so that makes it as much my fault as yours,' Caitlin insisted, terrified that he was once again beginning to blame himself for everything that went wrong around him.

'Murdo, don't let this come between us, not when we've just found each other again!'

'What?' He stared at her, puzzled, and then understanding dawned. 'You think that I'm going to change my mind again about marryin' you?' He reached out and pulled her close. 'What's happened to Lachie's made me all the more determined to marry you as soon as I can, and keep you close to me for the rest of my life,' he said into her hair. 'It's made me realise how much I need you to be with me.'

Caitlin clung to him, the tears returning. But this time, despite all that had happened, they were tears of relief, for she knew now that she was not going to lose Murdo.

## 27

Lachie's bed was halfway up the long ward, and as all the beds and all the men lying in them seemed to look exactly the same to her, Mary had to ask a nurse to point him out.

A large curve under the bedclothes showed that a cradle was keeping the weight of the blankets from his shattered legs. His eyes were closed and he seemed to be asleep. She sat by the bed in the chair provided and waited for a few minutes, unwilling to disturb him, then jumped as a voice said from somewhere behind her, 'Ye should speak tae him, hen.'

'What?' Mary turned and saw a tired-looking woman, some ten years older than she was, seated at the side of the next bed.

'Speak tae him.'

'I think he's asleep,' Mary half-whispered. 'I don't like to waken him.'

'He can sleep when ye're no' here. Visitin' hours are important tae them. He's unconscious,' the woman said almost proudly, nodding at the silent man she sat beside. 'He'd an operation three days ago an' he's no' wakened since then, but I still have tae speak tae him. They,' she jerked her head at a nurse hurrying along the ward between the two rows of beds, 'say that it's important tae talk tae him because he might know what's goin' on for all he doesnae seem tae be awake. So I just talk about the weans, and what the neighbours are gettin' up tae, and the messages I bought this mornin'. Anyway, if your man's only sleepin' he'd be disappointed tae waken an' hear that he'd missed ye. They need their visitors while they're in here. So speak tae him.'

'Oh – right.' Mary turned back to Lachie and leaned towards him. The bed was high and the chair was quite low, which meant that their heads were on the same level. 'Lachie,' she touched one of his hands lightly. 'Can you hear me, Lachie? It's Mary, come to visit you.'

He stirred and muttered something. His fingers twitched beneath hers, much as they had done immediately after his fall, and his eyelashes fluttered.

416

She had never noticed his eyelashes before but now she saw that they were long and silky — longer and silkier than her own stubby lashes. She was studying them enviously when they fluttered again before suddenly sweeping up to reveal his grey eyes.

'Mary?' His voice was a faint croak. He cleared his throat and then tried again. 'Mary — you're here!'

'Murdo said that you wanted to see me.'

'Aye, I did. I didn't think you'd come, though.' His voice was stronger now and his smile as bright as ever. He had looked very pale when she first arrived, but now colour had come into his face.

'Why wouldn't I come?'

'You're a good soul, Mary Lennox. You were there, weren't you, after I fell? I knew you were there,' he went on when she nodded. 'I heard your voice, and you touched my hand.'

'I thought you were unconscious.'

'I felt as if I was halfway between this world and another one. It was strange, Mary — I knew who I was, but I didn't know where I was. I could hear you and Murdo and I could feel your hand on mine, but I couldn't open my eyes. It was as if there was a wall between us. Murdo says you went with me in the ambulance wagon too. I'm grateful.'

'Someone had to be with you — someone you knew, in case you woke up.'

'I'm glad it was you,' Lachie said. 'I didn't deserve it, though.'

'Why not?'

'Not after I . . .' he glanced away from her and fiddled with the edge of the coverlet . . . 'not after the way I just decided to stop walkin' out with you.'

'Och, that! We were just good friends, you and me. I was pleased when I heard that you'd met someone special.'

'I was a daft fool. She's not even been to see me since I came in here.'

'Mebbe she's busy. She'll come as soon as she can.'

'My mother went to see her and told her about my legs — about me mebbe not bein' able to walk again. That's why she's stayin' away.'

'Surely not!'

'Och, she was losin' interest before the accident.' He moved slightly and his face creased with sudden pain.

'D'you want me to call a nurse?'

'No, just give me a minute.' He reached out his hand and without hesitation she took it in hers and held it tightly. After a moment his face relaxed. So did his grip, but their hands remained linked. 'I knew she was losin' interest in me,' he said, picking up the conversation where it had been

418

left off, 'but it doesnae matter. I'd rather see you here than her.'

'I brought you some juice.' Mary, anxious to change the subject to something less personal, fumbled in her bag with her free hand. 'I didn't know what else to bring.'

'That's grand, thanks.' He released his hold. 'Put it on the table there, will ye?'

'If there's anything you need,' she said as she sat down again, 'just tell me and I'll bring it next time.'

'You mean you'd come back to see me?'

'Of course I will, if you want me to.' She nodded at the cradle over his legs. 'Do they hurt?'

'Aye, 'specially at night, but they give me stuff to take the pain away.'

'Mebbe this'll teach you to be more careful in future.'

'I don't think I'll get the chance to do daft things any more. I'll not be able to dance again, Mary.' He had always loved the ceilidhs.

'You can still enjoy the music, and the chat.'

'It'll not be the same, though.'

'Now don't go feeling sorry for yourself,' she said sharply. 'That'll do no good at all. And don't be so sure that you won't be able to walk, or to dance. Tell yourself that and it'll come true. You need to make up your mind that you'll get back

419

to the way you were. Bones heal, but you need to help them by holding that thought in your head.'

'What if they don't heal?' There was no mistaking the fear in the eyes fixed on hers.

'If that happens – and it's only "if", mind, then your life'll have to take another road. You'll still be alive, and you'll still be you.'

'And mebbe I'll be a helpless cripple.'

'Crippled mebbe, but forget about being helpless,' Mary ordered briskly. 'And stop looking so far ahead, there's no sense in that. For now you have to do as the doctors and nurses tell you, because that's the only way to get better and get out of this place. Once you've done that, we can decide what happens next.'

'We?' His eyes were still holding hers, but now hope was creeping into them. 'You'll help me?'

'Of course I'll help you, every step of the way.' Mary used the word deliberately.

As she left the hospital she wondered if she had made a mistake in committing herself to helping in Lachie's recovery. It would be a long hard road for both of them, but for him in particular. However, the least she could do was help him as much as she could.

And after all, she reminded herself as she walked back to Espedair Street, it wasn't as if she had anything else to occupy her spare time – not now that John Brodie was going to marry Fiona Chalmers.

Perhaps, when all was said and done, helping Lachie to cope with what had happened to him would go some way to helping her get over her own loss. For loss it was; in the most private depths of her own mind Mary had come to accept and admit that what she had always looked on as a friendship with John Brodie had been more, much more. What she felt when she thought of him, which was more often than she would admit even to herself, was a deep and secret grief; a painful burden that she seemed doomed to carry for ever. Once, someone – perhaps John himself – had quoted a line of poetry to her, something so touching that she had never forgotten it. '*It's better to have loved and lost, than never to have loved at all.*'

Whoever said that was probably dead by now, which was a pity as Mary would have liked to tell him that he was wrong. It was better never to have known the joy of love and the pain of losing that loved one.

Fiona Chalmers had found the house she wanted, exactly where she wanted, near to Barshaw Park and on the road leading from Paisley to Glasgow.

'More of a mansion than a house,' Alex said as he and Rose drove home after attending a family viewing at Fiona's behest.

'It's certainly grand compared to ours.' Rose bit off the comment about that being just what Fiona wanted to achieve, for fear that Alex would think her catty. She *was* catty when it came to Fiona, unashamedly catty. It was difficult not to be, but a man would never understand that.

'It must have cost a lot more than ours,' her husband agreed. 'But then, John can afford it. Do you ever think of that, Rose?'

'Of what?' She tooted the horn at an un-accompanied dog crossing the road. The animal paused, looked at the oncoming motorcar already slowing down, then continued unhurriedly towards the pavement.

'Do you ever think that it might have been you marrying John and living in a handsome house, with servants to look after the two of you?'

'Lord no — what would I want with a barn of a place like that? I'd rather live in a shed with you than a castle with anyone else.'

'Good. I don't know if I'd settle for a shed,' Alex said thoughtfully, 'but I'd far rather live in our neat little house with you than anyone else, so we're both well pleased with our lot. Did you hear Fiona talking about all the plans she has for

422

the place? She could well cost John the price of the house all over again.'

'That's his problem,' Rose said lightly. She had decided that rather than put any financial pressure on Harlequin she would ask her bank for the full thousand pounds, and only that morning the bank manager had approved the requested loan. The next step was to find a way to cajole John into selling his Harlequin shares to her.

'It's kind of you to think of my well-being, Rose, but I can afford the house,' John said as Rose handed him a glass of sherry.

'That's good.' She settled herself behind her desk. 'So now that the place is definitely yours there's nothing to stop you from setting a wedding date?'

'Fiona wants to make some changes so it probably won't be before the spring. She's organising builders to knock down walls and so on, and while that's going on we'll choose carpets and furniture and see to all the other things that have to be done. Women know more about setting up home than men. We just earn the money to pay for it.'

'All the more reason for me to buy your Harlequin shares from you,' Rose coaxed. 'From what Fiona said when she showed us round the place, the refurbishment's going to cost a lot.'

'I'm not worried. Her father's already offered to help out, and so have my parents, but I don't think we'll need to ask them for help. Even if we did need extra money I wouldn't want to put you out of pocket, Rose. I know how hard you've worked to build Harlequin up, and how much of your own money you've put into it.'

'It's been worth every penny. What's the point of keeping money in a bank when it can be put to good use?' Longing though she was for a glass of good dry sherry, Rose had decided to forgo alcohol for the remainder of her pregnancy, so she was making do with a glass of lemonade. She sipped at it, trying to find another way of persuading John to let her buy back the precious shares before they, together with John, fell into Fiona's hands.

'I admire you so much, Rose – I always have. It's refreshing to find a woman with more on her mind than the latest fashions. I count myself very fortunate to know two such women – and to be marrying one of them. Fiona's just as interested in business as you are.'

'You think she'll have time for business when she has such a large house to run?'

'She says she will. It's all a matter of finding the right housekeeper, she says. And we wanted a house large enough to take her father as well, should he decide that he doesn't want to live on his own any more. And in time there will be children to fill the place,' John added, smiling happily at Rose, who found it hard to smile back. She longed to tell him, before it was too late, that his future wife had no intention of saddling herself with his children and that she could bring him unhappiness, but at the same time, she sensed that he was too deeply in love to heed her. So she had no option other than to keep quiet. However, he had given her an idea, and she seized on it.

'Actually, John, that's the real reason why I would like to buy back your shares in Harlequin. I want to put them in my child's name, when he or she arrives and acquires a name. I like the idea of the little one being part of the business from the very first.'

'What an excellent idea!' His face lit up and he leaned forward in his chair. 'Why don't you let Fiona and me give your child the shares as a christening gift? That way you don't have to find the money yourself.'

'No! I mean . . . I really want them to come from me. I don't know why, it just feels important to me,' Rose said hurriedly.

'But can you afford it? I still check the books every month, and I know that you're not taking as much out of the business for yourself as you should.'

'I still have some savings,' she lied. 'I didn't put all my grandmother's inheritance into Harlequin. I couldn't pay you much more than the thousand pounds you paid for them – though I could manage another hundred if you want . . .'

'I wouldn't dream of taking more money from you, Rose – and if you're so set on buying the shares for your child, then of course I'll not stand in your way.' He drained the last drops of pale sherry from the glass. 'I'll draw up the papers today and bring them in tomorrow.'

'Could you make it this afternoon? I might not be in tomorrow.' She couldn't give him time to mention the transaction to Fiona.

'Of course,' said John obligingly.

It was as well that the shares were handed over and paid for that same day, for on the following morning Rose and Alex found themselves suddenly plunged into making plans for an unexpected trip to Edinburgh.

The bombshell arrived in the form of a crumpled, shabby envelope in the morning post. Alex turned it over in his hands, puzzled. As well as being crumpled it was stained, as though whoever sent it had found it in a forgotten pocket, or pushed to the back of a drawer. His name and address were written in large, uneven block capitals by a pen with a nib long past its best; in places the ink had left clumsy blots.

'For goodness' sake open it!' Rose had been watching him, and now her impatience overflowed. 'What's the point of studying it from every angle?'

'I can't think who'd be sending me a letter like this.'

'The best way to find out,' she said sweetly, handing him the letter opener, 'is to open it, don't you think?'

He shrugged, then slit the envelope and withdrew a single sheet of paper written in the same uneven, blotchy capital letters. As he scanned the words swiftly Rose was alarmed to see the colour drain from his face.

'Alex, what is it? What's wrong?'

'It's Beth.' His voice was husky, his eyes, as he lifted them from the letter to look at her, were dazed. 'She died.'

'Oh, Alex! What happened?'

'I don't know. Her employer − a Mrs Brown,' he said after another quick glance at the letter, 'or mebbe Brawn − Brown probably − just says that Beth died and she needs her room and doesn't know what to do about the funeral. She wants me to go there to arrange everything.'

'Poor Beth. You must go, Alex.'

'I suppose so.'

'She was your stepbrother's wife and Rowena's mother, when all's said and done. Of course you must go. What about her own family? Do you think they'd want to know about this?'

'I doubt it. They disowned her when she ran off with Ewan and they refused to have anything to do with Rowena when she arrived in Paisley. I'll have to telephone my father and Todd – and the Glasgow workshop.' Alex pushed his chair back from the table, his half-eaten breakfast forgotten. 'I'll be away for what – three days or so?'

'That anyway. What are you going to tell your father – and Todd? Will you tell them the truth?'

'Best not, at least not until I get there and find out what happened. Beth caused enough trouble for Todd and my mother and I don't want them, or Rowena, upset.'

'I'm coming with you.'

'No,' he said at once. 'Not in your condition.'

'Oh tosh, I'm only having a baby – women do have babies quite often, you know.'

'My darling Rose, you've just had your thirty-second birthday,' he reminded her. 'You probably need more rest than younger mothers-to-be. If you ask me, you should be thinking of giving up Harlequin until after the birth, let alone travelling to Edinburgh.'

'I'm not exactly in my dotage and I feel very

428

well indeed. Don't argue, Alex, I'm coming and that's final. Harlequin can manage without me for a few days – they're already getting used to the thought of doing without me for a few months once the child arrives.'

'That lodging house is no fit place for you.'

'Then we'll stay in a hotel. There are bound to be several – it's Edinburgh, the capital of Scotland we're going to, not Outer Mongolia. It must have decent hotels. Now then, I'll pack and then drive over to Paisley to tell Todd and your mother and Mary and Caitlin, while you telephone your father and get hold of a train timetable. What should we tell them all, since they can't know the truth?'

'Er – we've just sent some furniture to Edinburgh. I could say that there's a problem with that and I have to go and sort it out.'

'Good. And I'm going with you to do some shopping and have a look at the Edinburgh fashions. By the way,' Rose added as she headed for the door, 'I'm not giving up my work until I feel that I need to.'

Once in Edinburgh they booked a room at a comfortable hotel close by Waverley station before going to the lodging house. Their arrival in a cab, which was then booked to wait for them, roused more than a little interest.

The landlady Alex remembered vividly, the woman with small, hard eyes and thin lips, opened the door to them, her gaze travelling swiftly over Rose, who smiled at her.

'Mrs Brown, I'm Mrs MacDowall. It was very good of you to take the trouble to write to my husband about poor Beth.'

'I didnae want the trouble and cost o' buryin' her, and there's things o' hers that need takin' away by folk that ken her. I'm no' a thief – I'm no' one to take advantage o' the dead. Here . . .' the woman dug into the pocket of her filthy apron and produced a ring '. . . take this.' She dropped it into Alex's hand. 'I found it round her neck on a bit o' string. I kept it for ye because ye never know who might be lookin' around for somethin' tae take. Nob'dy would want any o' the other things she had.'

'Is she . . . ?' Rose indicated the house.

'O' course no', she's in the hospital mortuary. Are ye wantin' a room while ye're here?'

'We've booked one near the station. We'll take her things now, and then arrange the funeral,' Alex said, then as they followed the landlady into the hallway, 'What happened to her?'

The woman shrugged. 'She just fell sick and since she couldnae work I had her sent tae the hospital. She died the very next day. I found your address when I went through her things. I'm glad o' that, for she was a decent enough woman and a good worker. I'd no' have wanted tae see her havin' a pauper's funeral. It's the attic room at the back,' she added, then disappeared through a doorway, clearly determined not to become involved any further.

By the time they reached the room, more of a cupboard, at the top of the tall narrow building Rose was glad to subside on to the narrow cot so that she could catch her breath. Alex eyed her anxiously, asking, 'Should you not go back to the hotel?'

'Not at all, I'm fine,' she wheezed. 'And I don't want you to have to go through this business on your own.

'Poor Beth,' she added some fifteen minutes later as they looked at the dead woman's possessions. 'She didn't have very much, did she?'

'She'd a husband but she left him. And she's a bonny daughter but she chose to forget about her as well. If she'd had more sense she could have had a good life with Todd, or even with Ewan. I suppose we should just put these clothes in a bag and get the landlady to throw them out.'

'Or pass them on to any poor soul who might be in need of them.' Rose picked up the ring the woman had given Alex – a thin band of gold. 'At least she kept her wedding ring.'

431

'I can't think why, unless it was so that she could pawn it if things got really bad.'

'Alex, the woman's dead – show more compassion.'

'If you'd known Beth and what she put folk through, you'd understand.' He put the ring into an inner pocket of his jacket. 'One day we'll give this to Rowena – but not yet. Not until she's old enough to be told a little about her mother. But never about this place, or what Beth came to in the end.'

Two days later the remains of Beth Lennox, once the beautiful, wayward Beth Laidlaw, were laid to rest with Alex and Rose as the only mourners. As the plain coffin was lowered into the ground, Alex watched it, his face pale and expressionless. It seemed to Rose that although they were only inches apart, he had suddenly moved far away from her, in time rather than in terms of space. He was back in a period before she entered his life, when his handsome, charming stepbrother Ewan had coaxed lovely Beth Laidlaw out of Todd's arms and into his, causing two lives to be stripped of their early promise, ending in tragedy.

He bent and picked up a handful of soil. It burst as it landed on the coffin lid, scattering over the surface. Rose took off her glove then realised that her pregnancy wouldn't allow her to stoop far enough to take a handful of the earth piled by the grave. As she stood there, vexed and annoyed, Alex scooped up some earth and gave it to her.

The gravediggers, standing only feet away, watched with indifference and as soon as the two mourners and the minister turned away from the open grave, the men moved in, anxious to be done with their work.

As Alex and Rose walked away, they could hear the steady swish of spades digging into the loose earth, then the thump of soil covering Beth Laidlaw Lennox's final resting place.

Within the hour they were at Waverley station, ready to begin their journey home.

# 28

'It's open,' Todd Paget shouted irritably in answer to the heavy knocking on the workshop door. He was still short of a skilled man and although Alex had promised to find someone to take Joseph McCart's place, he and Rose had suddenly taken themselves off to Edinburgh on some ploy or other, leaving Todd with more work than he and the apprentice could handle.

The door opened just wide enough for a thin man to slide through the gap. He closed it behind him and stood with his head raised, as though sniffing the air with his long nose while his eyes darted about, taking in everything.

One glance told Todd that this wasn't a customer about to bring money to the business.

'What d'ye want?' he barked, continuing with his work.

'Would you be the master of the place?' The man's voice was so soft that it was almost a whisper.

'I'm Todd Paget, the cabinetmaker. Who are you?'

'I was lookin' for a friend of mine, Joe McCart. Someone told me that he works here.'

Todd kept his eyes on the timber he was planing. 'I know the man ye mean, but he doesnae work here.'

'Are ye sure of that, now? I was told that a man called McCart worked for you.'

With a jerk of his head Todd indicated the small workshop. 'I've no' got so many men here that I cannae mind all their names. An Irish fellow called McCart or some such name did work here, for a wee while just. But he left a good two or three weeks back.'

'Left?' The word dropped softly into the space between the two men and Todd let it lie. Eventually the stranger said, 'And why would that be? Was he movin' on to another place, d'you know?'

Todd blessed the fact that Kenny, the apprentice, had been sent out on business. Knowing Kenny, he would be slow in returning.

'I don't know and I don't care. The man got

his place here by claimin' tae be a cabinetmaker, but when it came to it I found that he was a lazy creature with no proper idea of what he was supposed to be doin', so I turned him off. And I've no interest at all,' Todd added, lifting his head to look fully at the stranger for the first time, 'in where he went or what he might be doin' with himself now.'

'Did he have a family? A wife and daughter, and an ould mother?'

'I wouldnae know about that. All I'm interested in is seein' that the folk that work for me earn their wages. He didnae do that and now he's gone.'

The man's eyes continued to flicker about, peering into every corner. 'That's a shame, for I've got news for him – news that would please him.'

'Mebbe ye have, but I'm busy and I've told ye all I know. There's no more tae be said.'

'You've got a loft, I see. What's up there?'

'Furniture – what else would you find in a cabinetmaker's?' Todd walked deliberately to the foot of the stairs, picking up a hammer on his way. 'I've told ye all I know about this man McCart, and I've told ye that I'm busy. Ye'll have tae ask elsewhere if ye want tae find yer friend.'

'The thing is – I've got other friends. Friends that don't like to be crossed or denied.'

'Is that right? By the sound of ye, I'd say that

ye're a visitor from another country, an' I never pay any heed tae folk other than my own kind. That's why I sent McCart packin' as soon as I realised what a lazy idle man he was. Now I don't know why ye're so anxious tae find him, but whether ye mean him good or ill it's none of my business. And when it comes tae friends, ye'd best mind that ye're in my home town, and I've got friends o' my own. So . . .' he took a step forward, hefting the hammer easily in one hand '. . . ye can either believe what I tell ye or ye can suffer the consequences. For all I know this man McCart's gone back tae his own country. Mebbe ye'd be as well tae seek him there. From what I mind of him, he didnae fit in here in Paisley. We're particular as to who we give room to,' he finished levelly.

The man put a hand on the latch. 'I might be back.'

'Best not,' Todd advised, taking another step forward.

As the door closed behind his visitor he gave a sigh of relief, then moved to the window. The Irishman hesitated as he drew level with the back door and for a moment Todd thought that he was going to try his luck there. His grip tightened on the hammer, then eased again as the stranger kept going, through the pend and out of sight.

Todd followed, but when he looked out into

the street the man was not to be seen. He returned to the workshop, rubbing his hands against his jacket as though they had touched something unclean.

He was glad that Joseph and his family had got out of Paisley when they did, and hoped, for their sakes, that the stranger would never find them.

As soon as she returned from Edinburgh Rose, glad that she hadn't had to touch the extra money in the Harlequin bank account, used some of it to pay a builder to help Murdo with the work on the gatehouse, and by mid-October the task was completed. Murdo had decreed that Caitlin must stay away until the work was finished, and the waiting had almost been more than she could bear. But at last the day came when he took her on a tour of the house, starting with the front room on the opposite side of the hall from the weaving room. The furniture Murdo had been using was still there – the narrow cot, a cupboard for his clothes, a table and chair – but the room itself had a new, sturdy floor, and the ceiling and walls had been painted, the ceiling white, the walls a pale ivory shade.

'I know that you'll want to decide on your own colours, or mebbe wallpaper,' he said. 'I'll do whatever you want once we're wed; these sticks of furniture'll be put out before then, and better pieces brought in. But I just wanted the place to look nice for you.'

'It's wonderful! I'd not want to change any of it.'

In the kitchen, the old range had been scraped and blackleaded, new linoleum laid on the floor and the walls and ceiling painted white. The walk-in pantry and the water closet were also painted white, and even the coal cellar had been swept and cleaned, ready for its first delivery. Every floor in the house had been replaced, as well as most of the window frames. The creaking treads on the staircase had also been renewed, and the steps varnished. Like the living room downstairs, the two front bedrooms and the smaller rooms at the back had been painted in light colours.

'It's all perfect,' Caitlin said when the inspection ended in the larger of the two front bedrooms, the room that would be theirs. She turned away from the window and wound her arms around his waist. 'Let's decide on a date, Murdo. I want to be married as soon as possible.'

'Ah.' He suddenly looked worried. 'The thing is, when we first agreed to wed I promised Lachie that he'd be my groomsman. And when I saw him the other day he reminded me of it. He's determined to be there, Caitlin.'

'And you want him to be there, but I want to be married before Rose's baby's born.'

'What I want most of all is to make you my wife,' Murdo said. 'But I gave my word tae Lachie before his accident and I couldnae bear tae see the man disappointed – not after what he's been through.'

'We'll wait for a wee while, then, but not too long, Murdo. What about settling on Hogmanay, the last day of the year? That'll give Lachie time to get out of hospital and it should suit Rose, too. And we'll tell Rowena that she can move in with us at Easter. We'll leave her room empty and she can spend the first three months of next year choosing furniture. We'll let her decide on the paint and the wallpaper, and she can help you to get the room ready. Would that suit?'

'Aye, it sounds grand.'

'Come to our house for your dinner tonight,' Caitlin said, 'and we'll tell them all what we've decided.'

Rowena, charmed by the prospect of being able to choose her own furniture and decorate her own room, readily agreed to the idea of remaining at Espedair Street until Easter.

'It'll give me a wee bit longer with Grandma and Granddad. And I'll come to visit you every day,' she added swiftly to Kirsty and Todd. 'You'll not be lonely.'

'We'll be fine, pet,' Kirsty assured the little girl. Although she and Todd would miss having Rowena around all the time, they had agreed between themselves that it would be good for her to be with folks who were the same age as her real parents.

'I just wish that Cavan could have been a bridesmaid too,' Rowena said now, sadness suddenly wiping the broad smile from her face. 'I wish she could be here. I miss her.'

'I know you do, pet. I tell you what,' Mary said, 'when we talked about Caitlin's wedding I was going to be the chief bridesmaid and you and Cavan were going to be my assistants. Why don't we change it so that you and me are equal bridesmaids?'

'Could we?'

'Why not? You can hold Caitlin's bouquet for her while she's getting married, and we'll both wear the same dresses, instead of you and Cavan having different dresses from me. Harlequin could manage to make two dresses instead of just the one, couldn't they?' Mary asked Caitlin.

'I'm sure we can,' Caitlin agreed, and the smile swept back to Rowena's face.

'I just hope that Lachie'll be able to stand by

441

Murdo by the end of December,' Caitlin said when Rowena had gone to bed.

'He's got a lot of courage and determination. Perhaps having something to work towards will help him. I'll have a word,' her sister promised. 'Leave it to me.'

On the following evening Mary marched up to Lachie's bed and laid a large paper bag on his lap. 'I brought this for you.'

He seized on it eagerly and peered inside, then said, 'No sweeties?'

'You'll get sweeties from me when you're back home. Fruit's better for you.'

'I don't like fruit,' he sulked.

'Eat it – it's good for you.' She drew a chair up to the bedside. 'You've got work to do, my lad.'

'I have? What can I do lying in here?'

'Plenty, and you'd better get started now. Murdo's got the gatehouse ready, with help from some other folk, and he and my sister want to get married as soon as they can. They've waited long enough, d'you not think? So, if you still want to be his groomsman you're going to have to get on to your feet and out of here by Hogmanay.'

'You think it's as easy as that? My legs are in bits!'

'That'll teach you to play the fool when you're

working at an upstairs window. D'you still want to stand by Murdo at his wedding?'

'Of course I do, but look at me!' He indicated the cradle over his broken legs.

'I'm looking, and I'm not prepared to be the oldest bridesmaid that Paisley's ever seen. I want these apples and oranges eaten before tomorrow night because I'm bringing in some more then. You have to build up your strength – and I've had a word with the Sister,' Mary swept on as he tried to argue, 'and she says that your bones are healing well. You're going to be started on exercises soon. In the meantime, I've thought of some exercises you can be working on to strengthen your muscles.'

It wasn't easy, but having taken Lachie under her wing she was determined to get him out of hospital and ready to reclaim his life. Although he wouldn't admit it, she could tell by his sulking and his sudden bursts of temper that he was mortally afraid – afraid to let his damaged legs take his weight in case the bones broke again, and afraid, deep down, that he would never be anything but a helpless cripple.

When he sulked she nagged at him, and when he raged at her she simply walked out of the ward and left him to get over it. And she knew that her policy was working when Lachie began to channel his anger and frustration into a determination to regain control of his own body.

Although he didn't know it, Lachie was helping Mary as much as she was helping him. Harlequin was making Fiona Chalmers' wedding trousseau and every time she came in for a fitting she talked about the house she and John were to share after their spring wedding. It was almost more than Mary could bear at times, and driving Lachie on was her way of pushing her own pain away.

Caitlin and Rose also found Fiona's visits hard to take. 'I know exactly where every piece of furniture will stand,' Caitlin complained. 'I know the pattern of every curtain and carpet, and the colour of every cushion. And the most annoying thing is that sometimes I even feel envious of her with her lovely big house.'

'That's probably what she wants,' Mary said, while Rose chimed in with, 'You know that the gatehouse is going to be a much happier place than the big house Fiona's made poor John buy. From the way she talks, I'd say that it's going to be more of a showpiece than a home. And you know that you wouldn't change places with her for all the tea in Chi—' She gave a sudden gasp and clutched at her stomach.

'What's wrong?' Caitlin asked, while Mary was already on her way to the door, saying, 'I'll get Grace . . .'

'No, I'm fine. The baby just kicked.' Rose took a deep breath and smiled at her sisters-in-law. 'It's getting more active by the day, and I don't get much sleep at nights, either. I think it's planning to kick its way out when the time comes.'

'Perhaps you should give up Harlequin until after the baby's born,' Caitlin said anxiously. 'Mary and Grace and I can run it between us, and there's always the telephone if we need your advice or help.'

'Certainly not! Alex and my mamma keep trying to get me to stop work, but it's far too early.'

'Why don't you consider taking every other day off?' Mary suggested. 'That way, you get more rest without having to give up work altogether.'

'I'll think about it. Where were we? Oh yes, I was pointing out that Caitlin wouldn't want to change places with Fiona.'

'No, I wouldn't. John's a lovely man, so kind and so decent, but I wouldn't exchange my Murdo and our lovely gatehouse for Buckingham Palace and the richest man in the world!'

'Quite right,' Rose said.

When the other two had gone she settled herself

445

behind her desk and picked up her pen, then paused, staring at the opposite wall. Each time Fiona came to Harlequin Rose was obliged to spend some time with her, as happened with most of their clients. With some women the duty was boring, with others it was quite pleasant, but with Fiona . . .

Rose knew now that she had been right to suspect that Fiona was intent on getting her hands on the shares John had bought in Harlequin. She walked into the place as though she owned it, and treated everyone, including Rose herself, with a certain disdain. John had been a minority shareholder, but Rose was certain that once married, Fiona would have found some way of adding to his shares. She would have found a way to take over control of Harlequin. Not that she could, now that the shares were back in Rose's hands.

Rose smiled, wishing that she could be there to see Fiona's face when she discovered that she had been forestalled. Then the pen fell from her fingers and she gasped, clutching at her stomach as the baby suddenly kicked again.

'Little pest!' she muttered, half affectionately, half in irritation. Her girth was increasing fast, and the drive to and from work was becoming more uncomfortable every week. Perhaps she should consider Mary's suggestion and only drive to Paisley every other day.

She might even manage to arrange her 'at home' days to coincide with Fiona's dress fittings.

# 29

John Brodie's life had never been complicated. A chap did his best to be a good son and a good friend, treated others fairly, and life was pleasant. But now he felt confused and bewildered and rather as though he had been soaring happily through blue skies and then suddenly been shot down, landing with a painful thud that knocked the wind from his lungs.

Not that John had done much soaring through blue skies before – he was more of a steady plodder. The soaring had started when he suddenly discovered that without quite knowing how it had happened, he was engaged to the most beautiful and most charming woman he had ever had the good fortune to meet. His parents were proud of him and his friends made no secret of their envy. How on earth, they asked bluntly, slapping him on the back, could a stodge like him land a bride like Fiona? What, some of them wanted to know, was his secret? And John, who had no answer to that and was as stunned as they were, just smiled and shrugged and quite liked the way he had suddenly become the object of their envy.

He loved Fiona, there was no question of that, and he had been sure that she loved him. She had told him so, resting her head against his chest and putting her arms around him and looking up at him adoringly with those wonderful gold-flecked brown eyes of hers. She couldn't wait to be married to him, she said, and to live with him in the house he had bought for her – the house she was busy having decorated and furnished. John didn't care what the place looked like, as long as she was happy.

But suddenly, the evening before, he had been brought down to earth with a painful bump. The two of them had been dining with friends of John's and on the way home Fiona had been busy pointing out the flaws in their hosts' home. This, he assumed, was something that women liked to do.

When he stopped the car outside her father's flat she sat in silence for a moment, then said,

'John, what shall I give you as a wedding gift?'

'Do I need a wedding gift?'

'Of course you do. You must think of something. We're to be married in April, so if you want something that has to be specially made I have to know what it is soon.'

'Gaining you as my wife seems to me to be the best gift I could have.'

'That's very sweet of you, John, but we need to have gifts that we can display to our guests.'

'There's nothing I need. Do you have any ideas?'

She sighed, then said, 'What about a set of monogrammed brushes for your dressing room?'

'I already have—'

'I'll get you a silver-backed set – unless you have a better idea?'

'That would be very nice,' John said. 'And I'll have to buy you a wedding gift . . . ?' It was half statement, half question.

'Yes, you will.'

'Jewellery?'

'That would be very nice, but I've been thinking about it, and what I thought was . . .' She reached out in the darkness of the car and took his hand, holding it in hers and trailing one finger of her other hand over his palm. 'Do you know what I would really like, John?'

'Tell me, and you shall have it.'

'You are a darling! When I was having a dress fitting at Harlequin last week it occurred to me that it would be such a joy to be involved in that business. Rose and Caitlin have done so well, and I would like to become part of it, and help them to do even better. Then I remembered your telling me ages ago that you have shares in it so I thought, Wouldn't it make more sense for a woman to have those shares, rather than a man?'

'You want me to sign over my shares in Harlequin to you?'

'It wouldn't cost you a penny, and you know how much I enjoy being involved in business. You wouldn't object to me taking an interest in Harlequin, would you?'

'Of course not, but—'

'You dear man, thank you!' She reached over and with some difficulty, managed to kiss him. 'I can't think of anything I would like more. Shall we go up to the flat? You could have a nightcap with Father before you go home.'

'Fiona, I would sign the shares over to you tonight, if I still had them. But unfortunately—'

'What do you mean, if you still had them? Of course you've got them! Don't be ridiculous, John.'

'I haven't got them. Rose bought them back from me.'

451

'*What?*' The word exploded from Fiona's lips. 'When did this happen?'

'About a month ago.'

'But why did you decide to sell them?'

'It wasn't my idea, it was hers. She wants to give them to the baby when it's born, to make it a part of Harlequin right from the start.'

'And you believed her?'

'Why should she lie? It sounded reasonable to me.'

'Reasonable? You were tricked!'

'I was paid the full price for those shares, Fiona. Rose didn't trick me.'

'She – oh, you don't understand, do you?'

'No, I don't. You're going to have to explain it all to me. As far as I'm concerned Rose made me a reasonable offer and I agreed to it.'

'Has it actually happened? Have you signed?'

'The shares are hers and the money she paid to me is in my bank account. I tell you what – since I can't give you the shares I'll spend the money I got from Rose on your wedding gift. We'll go to Glasgow tomorrow and you can choose whatever you want. Anything at all.'

'I'm busy tomorrow,' Fiona snapped and reached for the door handle.

'Hang on, I'm coming round.' John started to open his own door, but Fiona said coldly, 'Don't

452

bother, I can manage. And I think we should say goodnight here – I'm very tired.'

'Fiona—' he began, but the passenger door slammed so hard that it shook the entire car. He subsided back into his seat, watching as she crossed the pavement and climbed the steps to the door, then disappeared inside the building without looking back.

John waited for several minutes, and then, when she didn't reappear, he drove home to a sleepless night.

Having heard nothing on the following day he called at Sandy MacDowall's flat that evening. Sandy was out and when Mrs Dove showed John in to the drawing room Fiona gave him a cool stare. 'I don't recall making arrangements to meet this evening,' she said as soon as the housekeeper had gone.

'We didn't, but I wanted to clear the air.' She was curled up on the couch; he bent to kiss her and she turned her head at the last moment, proffering her cheek to him instead of her lips. 'I need to know what I did or said last night to upset you. I haven't been able to stop wondering what it was.'

'You don't already know? All I asked of you,' Fiona said, 'was a small wedding gift, and you refused to give it to me.'

'If you're talking about my shares in Harlequin, I explained to you that Rose asked me to sell them back to her, and I did. They're no longer mine to give to you.'

'You could buy them back.'

'No, I couldn't,' John said patiently. 'I told you, she wants to put them into her child's name.'

'You believed that ridiculous story? Imagine giving a baby shares in a business!'

'I thought it rather a nice gesture.'

'For goodness' sake, John! Won't you even *try* to get the shares back from her?'

'I can't do that. Rose worked hard to create Harlequin and build it into a success, and she has more right to its shares than I have. Why do you want them so much?'

'I told you – I've got shares in Father's business and I'd like to have shares in my sister-in-law's company as well, since we're all in the same family now.'

'Why don't you tell Rose that? I'm sure she would welcome you as a shareholder.'

Fiona shot a scathing glance at him. 'You really think so?'

'You've just said yourself that you're both members of the same family. Why would she refuse you?'

Fiona got to her feet and went to select a cigarette from the handsome silver box on the mantelpiece. John, who had not been invited to sit down, picked up the matching lighter and lit the cigarette for her. She shrugged away from him as soon as she could, blowing a plume of silvery smoke into the air.

'Sometimes, John,' she said, 'you can be such a fool.'

He felt his mouth fall open. This was an entirely different Fiona from the sweet, adorable woman he loved and wanted to marry. For a moment, watching her stalk away from him and back to the couch, he was tempted to turn on his heel and walk out. It was a notion that went against his natural courtesy though, and he was to spend the rest of his life regretting that instead of following the sudden impulse, he stood his ground, saying levelly, 'If that's what you really think, then perhaps you feel that our engagement was a mistake.'

'Perhaps I do.'

'I see.' He swallowed, then went on, 'Since all I want is your happiness, I'm willing to release you from any promise you made to me. And of course, I will take any blame that may come my way.'

Fiona turned and regarded him for a long moment, her eyes narrowed in thought. Then she lifted the cigarette to her perfect mouth again, inhaled, and blew another stream of smoke into the space between them.

'I know you would, John. That's the sort of man you are. However, your gallant gesture won't be necessary, for I have no intention of ending this engagement. I've found the perfect house and I've already spent hours and hours making sure that it's going to look just the way it should be. Why would I want to give all that up?'

'So you still want to marry me.'

'Yes, I still intend to marry you, John.' She came to him then and reached up to kiss him. Her lips were soft, and her skin smelled of the expensive perfume she used. He put his arms around her and would have prolonged the kiss, but she drew back and said briskly, 'Now that that's decided, I think I'll have a bath before I go to bed. I'll think of another wedding gift for you to give me – something very expensive, as you suggested. Goodnight, John.'

On the way downstairs he encountered Sandy MacDowall returning home. 'John, I didn't know you were going to be here this evening.'

'It wasn't planned, sir. I just decided to call on Fiona.'

'I'm glad of that. She's been out of sorts all day – I even wondered if I should cancel my plans for tonight, but she insisted on my going out. If you ask me,' Sandy said cheerfully, 'she can't wait to get married and become mistress of that grand house you've bought for her. Goodnight, then, John.'

The two men continued on their way: Sandy MacDowall going upstairs to his flat and his adored daughter, John Brodie going downstairs to his car, where he sat for a while before starting up the engine.

He still loved Fiona, but tonight, having seen an entirely different side to her, a side that filled him with distaste, he was beginning to wonder if he had made a mistake.

'I've found the perfect house . . .' Her words floated through his confused brain. 'Why would I want to give all that up?' Was the house more important to her than John himself?

His background made it impossible for him to end the engagement. Sandy MacDowall would never forgive him for spurning his daughter and his own parents would be humiliated. If Fiona decided to sue him for Breach of Promise, the scandal would be bad for the family legal business.

John drove home feeling that he was caught in a trap of his own foolish making.

★

'Todd, look at this.' Kirsty spoke quietly, positioning herself so that her back was to Kenny and the new journeyman Alex had found to take Joseph McCart's place. 'It's a letter for Rowena – the postman just delivered it.'

'A letter? For our Rowena? But who would write to her?' Todd took the envelope from his wife and peered down at it. The name and address were written in large, rounded writing.

'We won't know that without opening it, and how can we do that . . .' Kirsty glanced round and saw that the other two were watching, though trying to pretend that they weren't '. . . when it's not addressed to you or me?' she lowered her voice to a whisper.

'Rowena doesnae ken anyone but us.'

'I wondered about . . .' Kirsty began, and then, unable to say it aloud, she mouthed the word 'Beth' at him.

'Why would her mother want tae write tae the wean after all these years? And how would she know to write to her here?'

'She'd probably know that Ewan wouldn't be able tae look after the wee lass, so he'd ask me tae do it. And mebbe she's realised that Rowena's getting to the age where she could be earnin' a wage. If it's her, it'll mean trouble, you can be sure of that. Mebbe I should put it on the range and say nothing.'

Kirsty took the letter from him and whisked out of the workshop before he could stop her.

'Get on with your work,' he barked at the apprentice and the journeyman, then hurried outside, catching up with Kirsty as she reached the back door.

'Ye cannae burn a letter meant for someone else, Kirsty.'

'Beth Laidlaw's caused enough heartbreak to this family already. D'you not mind the state Rowena was in when she first came here? I'll not let her mother do that to her again!'

'Listen to me, lass.' They were in the kitchen now and he took the letter from her, putting himself between her and the range. 'Rowena's got the right tae see it, but that doesnae mean that we can't protect her from bad news. When's she comin' home?'

'Right after school. Murdo's got a lot of work on, so she's not going to the gatehouse today.'

'Then I'll come tae the house when she gets home and we can give her the letter then. We'll both be there for her if it turns out tae be anythin' bad. Will that do?'

She glared, but then sniffed. 'I suppose it'll have to do since you're not going to let me burn it, are you?'

'No, I'm not. Ye're a good woman, Kirsty, and

I promise you that I'll not let anythin' hurt our Rowena.' He kissed her cheek and went back to work, tucking the letter into his jacket pocket as he went back down the yard – just in case.

'A letter? For me?' Rowena's blue eyes widened with astonishment. 'But I've never had a letter in my whole life!'

'Ye have now. See there . . .' Todd's blunt finger reached over her shoulder and traced the letters. 'Miss Rowena Lennox, it says. Is there any other Rowena Lennox in Espedair Street?'

'Who's it from?'

'There's one way to find out, pet.' Kirsty could not bear the suspense or the worry any longer. 'Why don't you open it?'

Carefully, Rowena inserted a finger under the flap and eased it open then drew out a folded sheet of paper, clearly torn from an exercise book. She unfolded it, smoothed it out on the table and bent to read it while Kirsty and Todd, scarcely daring to breathe, eyed the tumble of shining chestnut curls. Then they both jumped as Rowena let out a piercing shriek.

'Lassie, what's wrong?' Todd yelped, while Kirsty swept her granddaughter up in her arms, crooning, 'It's all right, pet, we're here. We'll look after you, don't be frighted!'

'I'm not frighted!' Rowena struggled free of the embrace, her eyes sparkling like a summer sky and her face split by a huge grin. 'It's from Cavan – I've got a letter from Cavan! Listen . . .'

She held up the page, which they now saw was covered by the same large, careful writing they had seen on the envelope, and read out in a voice shaking with excitement, '"Dear Rowena, I miss you and I will never forget you. Thank you for being my best friend. I will always remember our solemn vows. One day when I am old enough I will come back to see you. Keep dancing. Your loving friend, Cavan McCart."

'It's Cavan – she's not forgotten me – and one day she's coming back to Paisley. I'm going to put this letter with my daddy's photograph,' Rowena said, clasping it to her chest, 'and I'm going to keep it for ever and ever!'

'You don't think that Fiona and John have had a falling out, do you?'

Mary looked up at her sister, who had just drifted into her office carrying two cups of tea. 'How on earth would I know?' She took one of the cups from Caitlin and sipped her tea.

'You see John from time to time when he comes here. And you like each other, don't you? I just wondered if he had said anything to you.'

'What makes you think we like each other? Just because we're civil to each other, it doesn't imply anything like liking!' Mary smoothed back a lock of hair that had managed to work loose from the severe, swept-back style she always favoured. 'As for him confiding in me, he hasn't been in here for more than a week, and even if he came here every day I doubt if he would want to tell me about his private life. Nor would I listen if he attempted it.'

'What's wrong with folk today?' Caitlin wanted to know. 'Grace and I have just had a dreadful time with Fiona finding fault with everything and scowling like a-a spoiled child, and now you snap at me because I ask a simple question.'

'Sorry, but I've got a headache, and a lot of work to do. And I'm not really interested in Fiona – or John Brodie.' Mary devoted all her attention to her tea. Caitlin knew her sister well enough to know when Mary was lying, but she also knew when to stop prying. Fiona, however, was another matter.

'There's something up with Fiona, I'm sure of it. I've never seen her so— sorry,' she said as her sister fixed her with eyes that had suddenly become quite hard. 'What I really came in to say was that Grace wants you to try on your bridesmaid's dress before you go home today. Rowena's coming to the gatehouse after school, so I'll fetch her over so that the two of you can try on your dresses together. She'll like that – it'll make her feel grown up.'

'What about your dress?'

'Almost ready.' Despite the limited space in the room, Caitlin managed to spin round in an excited pirouette, almost spilling her tea in the process. 'Oh, Mary, I can't believe that soon I'm going to be Mrs Murdo Guthrie!' And then, sobering, 'How's Lachie?'

'He walked five steps last night. With me on one side and a nurse on the other, but even so, he did it,' Mary said proudly. 'He's going to be able to stand by Murdo at your wedding, I'm sure of it.'

'Murdo says it's all down to you. He says that according to Lachie, you're making all the difference.'

'Och, it's nothing. All that's needed is a bit of bullying when he feels sorry for himself, and some nagging as well. And a bit of encouragement now and again,' Mary was saying airily when the door opened and John Brodie walked in. He stopped short when he realised Mary wasn't alone.

'Caitlin – am I interrupting something? I can come back later.'

'No, we were just talking about my wedding.

Marriage is in the air today,' Caitlin said. 'Fiona was in earlier, having a fitting for her own wedding dress. You just missed her – but on the other hand, it would be bad luck for you to see your bride in her wedding dress before the day.'

'So I believe.'

'Would you like some tea?' Mary offered, and Caitlin noted that her sister was relieved when he shook his head.

'I brought back the receipts from last month.' He held up a sheaf of papers.

'Well, I have another fitting to organise,' Caitlin said, and whisked out, going upstairs.

As soon as the door closed, leaving them alone, John laid the receipts on the desk, then said, 'I brought these as well.'

Mary stared at the small sheaf of golden blossoms wrapped carefully in tissue paper. 'Roses, at this time of year? November starts next week.'

'Some of our bushes at home are still flowering. These are special favourites of mine.' He held the little spray out to her, but she drew back, staring at it as though suspecting him of playing some unpleasant trick on her.

'Mary?'

'I don't think you should be giving me flowers.'

'I've done it before, because I know you appreciate them.'

'It was different before. Why don't you give them to Fiona?'

'Fiona wouldn't appreciate them. She prefers gifts that come from expensive shops, while you appreciate the natural beauty all around us.' He swallowed, then said, 'To tell you the truth, Mary, I miss our Sunday walks. I was wondering – could we not meet next Sunday, the way we used to?'

She shook her head. 'Things have changed since then. You're engaged to be married.'

'But surely we can still be friends. Mary,' he said, 'I need to talk to someone, and you're the kindest, most sensible person I know.'

Mary looked up at him and realised that Caitlin had been wrong when she described him as looking tired. He was unhappy, deeply unhappy. Her heart went out to him and at that moment she would have given anything to help him. Then her strong, inborn sense of right and wrong asserted itself.

'John, we can't be alone together now. You must know that,' she said gently.

'Yes, I do know it.' He swallowed hard for the second time and passed his free hand across his brow. 'I should never have . . . I must go,' he said, laying the flowers on the desk.

Once she was alone Mary drank the rest of her

tea, which was now cooling, as she stared down at the perfect yellow blossoms. They were just opening out, and already she could smell their scent. She didn't know what had happened to cause John such unhappiness, but her heart ached for him. She wanted so much to spend time with him as he had asked. She longed to help him but, as her mother would say, he had made his bed and he must lie on it — no matter how unhappy he, Mary and, for all she knew, Fiona too, might be.

She unwrapped the roses, poured some water into her empty teacup from the jug she kept on the top of a cabinet, then put the roses into the cup.

For the rest of the day their fragrance haunted her.

# 30

Rose objected strongly to having a wedding outfit designed and made for her.

'I could wrap myself up in a tent or a very large bed sheet,' she protested when Grace and Caitlin insisted on taking measurements. 'Where's the sense of taking up time and using yards of expensive material when I'm going, God willing, to get back to my usual shape after this child's born?'

'You're going to look good at my wedding,' Caitlin insisted, and Rose, standing in the middle of the fitting room while the other two crawled around her, sighed heavily.

'At least make something that can be taken apart and used again afterwards, then it won't be such a waste. You'll probably be able to make at least three ordinary-sized dresses out of the material.'

'Do stop complaining, Rose, Grace and I are busy.'

Rose sighed again, then mourned quietly to herself, 'To think that I used to hate being shaped like a broomstick. I didn't know how fortunate I was. Grace?' She peered down, but could see nothing other than her own belly, swathed in bronze-coloured silk. 'Are you there, Grace?'

'I'm here,' Grace said indistinctly through a mouthful of pins.

'Have I still got feet? I haven't seen them for months.'

'What do you think you're standing on? Honestly, Rose,' said the bride-to-be, 'I'm really glad that you're not one of our regular clients. You're being worse than Fiona.'

'Grace, are you sure that I'll get back to looking like a broomstick once this child arrives?'

'Of course you will, pet. I've raised three weans and lost another four before they got birthed, and look at me,' said Grace, who was as thin as a rake.

'That's the problem – when you're kneeling at my feet I can't look at you. I wish this baby would hurry up.'

'Och, ye've a good wee while tae go yet,' Grace

said complacently, while Caitlin ordered, 'Don't you dare have it before my wedding. I don't want all this work wasted.'

Alex's jaw dropped when his wife came into the living room on the wedding day. 'You look – wonderful!'

'I look huge.'

'All the more of you to appreciate. And you're not as large as you think you are.'

'You're probably right – nobody could possibly be as large as I feel. Do you really think I look fit to be seen in public?'

'Of course you do,' he said, and meant it. Caitlin had designed a comfortable, loose-fitting dress in bronze silk beneath a wraparound coat of turquoise lace embroidered in gold thread, and with dolman sleeves. Rose's hat was a bronze silk turban to match the dress.

The doorbell rang and the housekeeper came in to announce that the cab had arrived to take them to Paisley.

'You look beautiful, Mrs MacDowall, if I may say so.'

'She does, doesn't she? Take a warm coat, darling.'

'It's a surprisingly mild day for Hogmanay. I'll be fine.'

'I'll bring coats in case it gets cold later. Are you sure that you feel strong enough for this wedding?' Alex worried as he followed his wife into the hall. 'I'm sure that Caitlin would understand if you'd rather stay home and rest.'

'She wouldn't understand at all. She would never forgive me, and I'd never forgive myself if I wasn't there. I might not be able to dance at her wedding,' Rose said, taking his arm, 'but I certainly want to see it happen — at long last!'

Caitlin and Murdo's marriage ceremony was a private affair, held in the house of the Gaelic Church minister with only the bridal party and Kirsty and Todd present. Everyone else gathered in the hall where the ceilidhs were held, ready to greet the bride and groom when they arrived.

Lachie, home from hospital the week before, was only able as yet to walk a short distance with the aid of two sticks; when he wanted to travel around, he was learning to propel himself in a wheelchair. On his wedding day Murdo went to fetch his groomsman and wheeled him to the minister's house. The two of them were waiting outside when Caitlin arrived with her mother, stepfather and two bridesmaids.

'Murdo!' Rowena squealed as soon as she saw him. 'Look at me!' She rushed towards him and he picked her up and whirled her round. 'Don't I look beautiful?' she asked as he set her back on her feet.

'Ye do indeed.' She and Mary wore simple dresses of pale green crêpe, which went well with Rowena's rich chestnut hair and creamy skin, and Mary's brown hair and pale colouring.

'Look at my lovely flowers.' She held up her small posy of artificial cream and green flowers. 'Look, Lachie, aren't they pretty? And I've got silk flowers in my hair as well. Can you see them, Murdo?'

'Aye, I can. Ye're . . .' His voice trailed away as he looked over her head and saw Caitlin coming towards him. A sudden puff of wind caught her waist-length veil and blew it across her face; she put up one hand to lift it aside and gave him a smile so radiant that it made the breath catch in his throat. '. . . the bonniest sight a man could ever hope to see,' he finished the sentence, his eyes fixed on Caitlin, everyone else forgotten.

Then they were all gathered together, talking and laughing, with Kirsty anxiously organising them.

'You and Lachie go in first, Murdo, and then you, Caitlin, with Mary and Rowena, and me and Todd last. No, Rowena, you can't walk with Murdo, not on his wedding day. You just do as you're told, miss. Come on, now, the man'll be 'waiting,' she added as the door opened and the minister's wife came out on to the top step, smiling and beckoning them in.

'I'll walk in,' Lachie insisted, struggling to get out of the chair.

'What about the steps?' Kirsty eyed them doubtfully.

'I'll manage.'

'I tell ye what, Lachie,' Murdo suggested, 'why don't I carry you into the house and then you can walk once we're past the steps? I don't want ye to tire yourself out too soon.' He handed Lachie's sticks to Todd and then scooped his friend up in his arms and strode ahead of the party and into the house.

Grace, Kirsty, Jean, Teenie and the women from Harlequin's sewing room had worked together to provide and organise the wedding breakfast. They had decorated the hall as well, and it was bright with coloured paper streamers, bows of ribbon and bunches of greenery supplied by John Brodie, who had also provided Caitlin's wedding bouquet of orchids from his father's hothouses.

On leaving the minister's house Murdo made sure that Lachie was comfortably settled in his chair and took hold of the handles, only to find himself eased aside by Todd.

'I'll see tae the lad, Murdo — it's your duty tae give yer new wife yer arm on yer first outin' together,' he ordered.

Arm in arm, Murdo and Caitlin walked the short distance to the hall, halting every few steps to speak to well-wishers. Rowena was so keen to get to the next stage of the celebration that Kirsty and Mary had to hold her back, but as they neared the hall they let her go and she rushed past the bride and groom in an excited whirl of pale-green skirts and burst into the hall shouting, 'They're coming, they're coming!' And moments later, the bride and groom — she laughing, her turquoise eyes sparkling, he shy but bursting with pride — were surrounded by friends anxious to wish them well in their new life.

When the time came for the tables, once loaded with food and now almost empty, to be cleared away to make room for the dancers, the band had to do without Murdo, who took to the floor with his wife for the first dance, a waltz.

'I'm not much of a dancer,' he apologised as Caitlin moved into his arms.

'You'll do for me. Are you not wishing you could be up on that wee platform with the others, instead of down here on the dance floor?' she teased, smiling up at him.

'I'm thinking what a fortunate man I am to be

473

here with you. And what a fool I've been to keep you waiting for so long.'

'Put the past behind you, Murdo Guthrie,' she said softly, 'and think of the long future we're going to have together.'

Tears weren't far from Kirsty's eyes as she watched her daughter glide over the worn wooden dance floor. Caitlin's gown was of her own design – cream silk cut at the neck in a V shape, back and front, and with short cap sleeves. The straight skirt was gathered at the back, where it swept down to a short train that, as she danced, was held clear of the floor by a cord hooked round her finger. The bodice, sleeves, wide sash and hem were all decorated with a silver bead flower motif. Her dark auburn hair had been drawn softly back in a loose bun and her veil fell from a beaded headdress with loops of cream ribbon at each side. The simple lines of the dress fitted her slender body perfectly. As she smiled up at her husband, it seemed to Kirsty that the room was lit by her happiness.

'Is she not the bonniest lassie ye've ever seen?' she whispered to Todd.

'Aye,' he agreed, and then, putting a hand over hers for a moment, 'Well, tae be truthful, she's the second-bonniest lassie I know – next tae her mother.'

'Och, you!' Kirsty choked as the tears made a

bid for freedom and began to flow down her cheeks. 'Now look what ye've made me do!'

It was still early when the newly-weds slipped away from the hall to walk to the gatehouse. Scarcely anyone noticed them leave, for by then everyone was having a great ceilidh. The floor bounced and shuddered beneath stamping feet and the roof rang to the dancers' voices as they whirled and spun and wove intricate dance patterns. Now and again, when even the most vigorous dancers were in need of a rest, Rowena was persuaded to dance on her own, and each time the applause almost made the walls bulge.

'I should take her home,' Mary murmured to her mother. 'She must be exhausted.'

'Och, leave her be,' Todd said. 'The lassie's enjoyin' hersel'. I'll carry her home if she's too tired tae walk.' Then, nodding over at Lachie, 'but I think I'll take that laddie home now, for he looks as if he's had enough.'

Lachie, not long out of hospital, was glad of the offer of help. 'Will you walk home with us, Mary?' he asked as she bundled him into his coat and made sure that his scarf was fastened around his throat.

'If you want me to.'

'I do. It was a grand wedding, was it no'?'

'A grand wedding,' Mary agreed.

Once Todd and Mary had left with Lachie, Kirsty, who had been watching Rose, moved over to sit by her. 'You look a bit flushed – are you all right?'

'The place is rather warm, that's all.'

'Come outside for a minute – but put this shawl round your shoulders first, for it'll be cold.'

Together they made their way through the revellers to the door, where they stood looking out into the night. Normally, at this time, most of the local folk would be in their beds, but tonight almost every window they could see was lit, as the householders waited to welcome in the New Year.

'It's been quite a year,' Kirsty said, thinking of Caitlin, now a married woman, and the McCart family, who had come into their lives from nowhere and then vanished without trace.

'Yes, it has.' Rose, for her part, was marvelling over forthcoming parenthood for herself and Alex and grateful for having foiled Fiona's attempt to gain a hold on Harlequin. And she also thought with pity of Beth Lennox, lying in an Edinburgh graveyard, forgotten by everyone but herself and Alex.

'We'd best go back in before ye catch a chill,' Kirsty was saying when the younger woman tensed and gasped, reaching out blindly to find and hold Kirsty's arm.

'I-I think I should go home . . .'

'Is it the wee one? Hold on to me, pet, and try to breathe nice and slow.' Kirsty waited until the contraction was over, then led Rose back into the hall and lowered her carefully on to an empty chair. Then she caught sight of Alex making his way towards them. 'I think the baby's coming,' she said low-voiced when he reached her.

'Rose?'

She smiled up at her husband. 'I'm fine, but I think we should go home now. Don't make a fuss, though – let the folk go on enjoying themselves.'

'I'll fetch the driver.' He had insisted on hiring a cab for the night, just in case of emergencies such as this, and had invited the driver in to enjoy the party.

As he went in search of the man Kirsty asked, 'Would ye be better to go to your mother's house? It's nearer, and she could be with ye while the wee one's coming.'

'Goodness no, my mother would hate to be present. From what I've heard it was only with great difficulty that she was persuaded to be present at her own confinements. I've often wondered if she was present during the conceptions,' Rose said with her usual flippancy. 'I'd much rather go back to our own house.'

They saw the driver leave the hall and then Alex arrived, shrugging himself into his coat. 'The man's bringing the car to the door. We'll be home in no time.'

'Would you like me to come with you?' Kirsty offered, and Rose's face lit up.

'Would you mind? What about Rowena?'

'Of course I'd not mind – I'd like to be there when my grandchild takes its first breath. I'll just have a word with Jean and Teenie while Alex is getting you to the car. They can keep an eye on Rowena until Mary and Todd come back. My,' Kirsty said, beaming, 'this is a year we'll never forget!'

When she woke on the morning of the first day in 1921, Caitlin couldn't understand why she wasn't in her little room over the pend in Espedair Street. Then, as her eyes fell on the chest of drawers, each drawer with its decorative painting of pink roses and blue forget-me-nots, she realised she was in her new home, looking at part of Alex and Rose's wedding gift. Turning over, blinking sleep from her eyes, she saw Murdo smiling at her from the neighbouring pillow.

'Good morning, Mrs Guthrie,' he said softly.

★

At exactly the same moment Rose was gazing down at the baby asleep in her arms.

'Isn't he beautiful, Alex?' she whispered, and then, looking up at her husband in horror, 'Would you listen to me – he's red and bald and tooth-less and I'm calling him beautiful! What's happened to me?'

'You're a mother,' Kirsty told her. 'Our own babies are always beautiful, no matter what. But this one really is bonny – aren't you, my wee man?' she crooned as the baby opened dark blue eyes and stared up at the three of them.

'And he's clever too,' Alex said proudly. 'Born on January the first – he's going to get birthday presents as well as Ne'erday presents.'

'Clever right enough, to work that out for himself,' Kirsty agreed drily as the nurse hired to look after Rose and the baby bustled into the room.

'Time you had a rest, Mrs MacDowall.' She removed the warm, shawled bundle from Rose's arms. 'And it's time this wee one was back in his own crib.'

'Time I was home too,' Kirsty said.

'I'll get a cab for you, and then I'll have to let my father and Rose's parents know about the baby.'

'Och, I can get the bus – there's a stop just along the road.'

'You will not get a bus – you've been up all night.'

'I'll just fetch my coat then, and see the wee one settled in. I'll say cheerio for now, Rose, and let you get your sleep.'

'Come back in once you've got your coat. I'm too excited to feel tired,' Rose said, but when Kirsty and Alex looked in on her less than five minutes later she was sound asleep.

It was a perfect March day with blue skies, sunshine and a breeze rather than the usual chill wind when young Fergus Alexander MacDowall paid his first visit to Harlequin. Rose, as lean and angular as she had been a year earlier, drove her car to Paisley with the baby and his nurse travelling in the back seat.

Everyone had been waiting impatiently for their arrival and when the car drew to a halt outside the doors, Caitlin, Grace and the rest of the staff spilled out to greet them.

'Give him to me.' Rose had jumped briskly from the driving seat and now she leaned into the back of the car and emerged with her son, well wrapped in warm shawls, with a tiny woollen hat on his still-bald head. 'Here we are, Fergus, this is where Mother is going to work when you're a month or two older.'

As they crowded round, making all the usual cooing noises women make when they see babies, Fergus's interested gaze moved from face to face and he waved a mittened hand at the throng, then favoured them with a toothless smile.

'Here, let me have him.' Grace held out her arms and, when Rose had laid the baby in them, said, 'Come inside, everyone, we don't want the wee laddie tae catch a chill.'

'Little chance of that,' Rose said as she and Caitlin followed the group, which now included the nurse, into the old mill building. 'The poor wee soul's been put into a good three layers of clothes. How are things?'

'Harlequin's doing well. We're managing without you, but we'll all be glad to see you back, when you're ready. You still want to come back, don't you?' Caitlin added anxiously.

'Of course I do. Fergus is lovely, but I couldn't give up Harlequin, you know that.'

'I'm pleased to hear it, for I might,' Caitlin whispered, her eyes dancing, 'need to take time off myself, towards the end of the year.'

'Really? Oh, Caitlin! Are you sure?'

'Almost sure, but I want to wait a wee while longer before saying anything to anyone. I've not even told Murdo, so you keep quiet about it.'

'I will.' Rose put an arm around her sister-in-law and best friend, asking as they followed the others, 'Where's Mary?'

'Finishing off some bookwork. She said she'd be out in a minute.'

'We stopped off at Espedair Street on the way here. Your mother says that Lachie's got a job.'

'Aye, as a storeman, thanks to Mary. She coaxed him to apply for it, and taught him how to present himself. She's worked really hard with him, Rose. I'm sure he'd still be an invalid if she hadn't kept on at him.'

'D'you think there's a romance being rekindled there?'

'I have a feeling that Lachie hopes so, but you never know with Mary. She doesn't say much.'

Alone in her office, Mary was staring at a ledger, open at a blank page. She was steeling herself to go out and join the others, and wishing that she could just stay where she was, alone in her small, familiar space.

Someone tapped at the door and she only just managed to snatch up her pen before it opened and one of the sewing women looked in. 'Mary?

Mrs MacDowall's here, with the baby. He's the bonniest wee thing you ever saw! Are you not comin' out to join us?'

'In a minute — as soon as I've finished this,' Mary said, then put the pen down as the door closed.

She could hear the women outside in the foyer, twittering and chirping and cooing over wee Fergus. It was a sound that reminded her of a warm June day, and a walk in the countryside with John. It was the day he had found a clump of wild violets, and had picked one for her. Even now, she could recall the delicate scent of the tiny, perfect flower, and she could hear, inside her head, his voice saying, '"Then the Parson might preach, and drink, and sing, And we'd be as happy as birds in the spring."'

'It seemed to me,' John had said, 'that birds are happy because they live for the moment and accept whatever may come into their lives.'

He was right, Mary thought, rising from behind her desk, smoothing down her skirt and looking into the small mirror on the wall to make sure that her brown hair was, as always, neat and tidy and that a smile was pinned to her face.

Then she went to join the others.

# THE SILKEN
# THREAD

I had a dove and the sweet dove died.
And I have thought it died of grieving,
O, what could it grieve for? Its feet were tied,
With a silken thread of my own hand's weaving.

JOHN KEATS

# PART ONE

# Chapter One

FOR THE THIRD TIME SINCE they left Beith Meg's stomach began to rebel at the cart's lurching progress. She tried hard to fight down the queasiness, both hands squeezed tightly against her stomach beneath the shelter of her shawl. But finally she had to twitch at Duncan's sleeve until he moved his blue eyes from contemplation of the farmland to her white, apologetic face.

'Duncan, I'm feared I'm—'

'Not again!' her husband said impatiently. 'D'you want us to take two days to this journey?'

'I can't help it—' She pressed her hand over her mouth and made to jump from the moving vehicle in her haste to get out before she disgraced herself, and him, completely.

'You'd best stop.' Duncan tapped the driver on the shoulder and he, without a backward glance at his passengers, drew the horses to a halt and waited, back hunched. The animals immediately began to tear at the dry dusty grass fringing the road, twitching their ears and flicking their tails to ward off flies.

With Duncan's help Meg scrambled down from the cart and stumbled over the springy turf. She reached the shelter of a whin bush just in time and knelt on the grass, vomiting miserably and wishing she was back home in the farm kitchen with her family.

It had seemed such an adventure when they first planned it. Duncan, a weaver to trade, was young and ambitious, and in 1745 the flourishing Renfrewshire town of Paisley, some twenty miles away, was the ideal place for a young man willing to work.

Meg was the envy of her sisters. To be a married woman, with a handsome husky young husband like Duncan – she knew herself how fortunate she was. But now the first sweet shyness of marriage had passed and she had begun to realise that this dark confident man was hers, and she his, for the rest of her life. She was bound to follow him wherever he chose to lead. The thought, which had excited her as she danced with him at her wedding beneath the familiar smoke-grimed beams of home, now made her shiver despite the warm May sun above.

What if they didn't fare well? What if she hated Paisley yet had to go on living there, homesick and wretched?

She stood up and glanced at the cart waiting on the track a short distance away. Duncan had stepped down to stretch his legs. The driver, a man of few words, sat hunched on the cart, a sombre figure against the blue sky beyond.

Another spasm dragged her back to her knees. All at once she wanted her mother – though she had been glad enough to escape her sharp eyes a few hours earlier.

'If you have your wits about you you'll see that there are no babies until you're settled,' her mother had advised as she brushed Meg's hair on her wedding morning. 'You've chosen a wild man – see that he makes enough silver to put food for your belly and a roof over your head before you think further.'

Meg, breathless with loving anticipation, had promised easily enough. She never disobeyed her mother, who was not slow to show her displeasure with a clout on the ear that could send even a full-grown son or daughter flying across the room. But common-sense had no chance when she was safely wedded and bedded and Duncan's youthful passion was sweeping them both headlong on the course they had longed to take since they first set eyes on each other.

When the first signs of nausea and giddiness appeared within a few weeks of their wedding day Meg had done her utmost to hide them from the older woman, and had eagerly agreed to Duncan's proposal that they join the growing army of people lured by Paisley's expanding linen industry. She had succeeded in her deception, for her mother still had no inkling of her condition.

Meg spat to rid her mouth of a bitter after-taste, and walked back to the men.

'You took your time, lady,' Duncan greeted her impatiently. 'Early afternoon, I said we'd be there. D'you think we have a whole day to waste on one short journey?'

'I couldn't help it—' she said faintly, apologetically, as he handed her up to her seat and swung up beside her. His round, handsome face was marred by a scowl. Like his mother-in-law, Duncan felt that their first child should have had the sense to wait a little longer for its conception, and he was inclined to blame Meg for her haste.

The driver had lit his pipe during the wait. Meg's insides quivered as a whiff of strong-smelling tobacco drifted back to her, and panic swept over her. Duncan would never stand for another delay! She squirmed into a position that put her tiptilted nose out of the way of the smoke and sniffed at the grass-scented air with great determination.

Duncan took the slight move away from him as a sign that his wife was annoyed. Compassion flooded his heart as he looked at the soft curve of her cheek and the corner of her kissable mouth. He loved her in his own irresponsible way, and his spirits rose with every turn of the wheels that carried them to their new life. An orphan, raised by an elderly aunt who cared little about anything but her Bible, he had found Meg's large, noisy family oppressive. He wanted to be independent, to look after his wife and make his own decisions. If he couldn't make his way in Paisley – well, he'd go elsewhere. But wherever he went he wanted Meg by his side.

It was almost two o'clock when the driver raised his whip and pointed.

'There's where you're bound.'

They craned their necks to see. Paisley was tucked snugly below the Gleniffer Braes – the Muckle Riggs as they were known locally. The main features to be seen from a distance were the High Church steeple and the ruins of the Abbey, once a great monastic house but now in a state of disrepair.

Smoke from the chimneys smudged the green of the surrounding hills. The River Cart was a shiny ribbon curling through the town, passing beneath the Abbey walls.

Duncan put his arm about Meg.

'There's where we'll find our fortune!'

'You think so?' she asked doubtfully.

'I know so! Paisley's growing, and we'll grow with it. We'll have our own place before long, and our own looms – and sons to carry the trade on after me.' His voice was strong, his optimism catching. 'You'll see, Meg – you'll see!'

The fields and hedges blossomed with great stretches of linen as the cart neared the town. These were the bleachfields, where newly-woven linen was brought to whiten. Then the first cottages, some thatched and some with slate roofs, appeared on either side of the low rutted road.

Duncan fingered his plain jacket as he looked

at the young men strolling along the pathways of raised earth, stylishly clad in blue and green coats, nankeen britches and flowered waistcoats. Meg's eyes widened as she stared at the women's colourful dresses. Obviously, Paisley was the very place for an ambitious young couple like themselves.

The sound of hammering came to them as they passed through the town's fringes, where new houses were being built. Paisley was growing fast and there was plenty of work for builders – hard work, if they were to keep up with the demand from the constant stream of incomers.

At last the cart jolted into the rutted main street, busy with carts and carriages. Housewives hurried along the footpaths or stood gossiping in tight groups. A crowd of young men laughed and joked outside a howff – and judging by the state of one of them, kept on his feet by his companions, they had been inside sampling the landlord's wares. Bewhiskered businessmen paced solemnly, brushing barefoot children aside like flies, too involved in their own fat-bellied importance to notice their surroundings. Dogs, cats and pigs were amiable company for each other as they nosed among the refuse at the sides of the road.

After the pure country air they had just driven through the travellers found the smell of rotting rubbish offensive, but they knew that they would quickly get used to it. It wasn't any worse than the dungheap that sat just outside the farm door in Beith.

'Here 'tis,' the driver announced. With a final squeeze of Meg's hand Duncan jumped briskly down and rapped at the door of the three-storey building. While he waited for an answer he handed his wife down from the cart and she looked timidly at the buildings crowding in on the narrow street. Had she been alone she would have turned round there and then and ordered the driver to take her home again, but being a married woman she could only clutch the bag that held her worldly possessions, and swallow hard.

The door burst open suddenly and a small tornado whirled out of it, almost knocking Meg over with the force of its passing. With a squeak of alarm she clutched at the cart for support while the tornado, which turned out to be a red-headed infant no higher than her knees, recovered its balance and headed in determined fashion down the street, skipping nimbly over holes and hillocks.

'Stop that wean!' a voice shrieked from inside the house, and a plump young woman, her own head topped with glowing red hair, came hurrying along the passageway.

'Get a hold of him, quick!' she shrilled, and Duncan, who had been standing open-mouthed, shot off down the street after the child.

'The wee imp!' The woman leaned on the door frame to catch her breath. 'The times I've told these men to make sure the door's not left on the latch! Do they think I've nothing to do with my time but chase after him?'

9

Then Duncan was back, a screaming kicking bundle of fury held at arm's length before him.

'You rascal, you!' the woman scolded, taking the child and administering an automatic smack on his plump legs. Then she kissed his rosy cheek.

The child stopped screaming at once and settled himself comfortably astride her hip. He rammed a thumb into his mouth and looked at the visitors with round blue eyes. His face was dirty and his head a mass of tangled curls, but even so it was easy to see how beautiful he was.

'You'll be the Montgomerys? I'm Mistress Todd.' The woman transferred her attention to the couple standing before her. 'Come away in – you must be fair worn out after your journey.'

'So am I – am I to stand here all day waiting to get my cart unloaded? I've work to do,' the driver said sourly from behind them.

Mistress Todd's wide green eyes flashed scathingly. 'Poor man, are your arms wasted away, that you can't unload a wee cart by yourself? Well, well, I suppose Mister Montgomery'll help you while we go into the house.' And leaving him at a loss for words she led Meg into the passageway.

'We live above the weaving shop – here it is—' She threw open a door to disclose a large sunlit room noisy with the clack of looms and the hum of deep voices. Peering over her shoulder Meg could see men working at two of the four looms, swaying rhythmically as they threw the shuttles from side to side.

'I'll not tell you again – the next one to leave the door on the latch gets his ears warmed!' Mistress Todd bawled. 'The wean's wild enough without any help from you!'

Then she slammed the door shut on the shouted replies and went on upstairs, remarking over her shoulder, 'They're not a bad lot, but they need an awful strong hand to keep them in order.'

And a strong hand was what Mistress Todd had, Meg thought as she followed her red-haired guide up the narrow dark stairway and into a large spotless kitchen, fragrant with the smell of home-made bread.

'Sit yourself down and I'll make some tea.' Mistress Todd deposited the baby on a rag rug and handed him a wooden spoon. He immediately began to bang it on the floor.

'That's right, my mannie, you give these lazy men below a good fast rhythm to work to. This is our Jamie – a wild ragtail of a boy if ever there was one. He's for a soldier for sure, unless he finds himself beneath a horse's hooves first,' his mother said cheerfully. 'You've got it all unloaded, then?' she added as Duncan came in.

'There wasn't much to unload.'

Her eyes twinkled. 'Best to start married life light. Not that I did, for Peter's first wife died and I came to a ready-made home when I wed him. He had two grown lads too – now he's on his second family.' She nudged the baby with her toe. 'And Peter says this one's more bother than

11

Matt and Colin put together. You'll have some ale, Mister Montgomery?'

'I wouldn't mind,' he said gratefully, and drained half the tankard in one thirsty swallow when she handed it to him.

The tea was being poured out when Peter Todd himself arrived.

'So you're here already? I'd have been home to greet you, but I had some linen to deliver—'

'—and you got talking.' His wife finished the sentence for him, nodding at Meg. 'They say women enjoy a gossip, but you'll find that in Paisley the men know how to do their share of tongue-wagging.'

Peter Todd let the remark run off his broad shoulders as he studied the couple before him. He was a big handsome man with a head of thick white hair and shrewd eyes of the same vivid blue as his son's.

'So – this my new man, is it? Well, we'll get on together if you're prepared to work. We all work hard in this house.'

'You'll find nobody more willing than Duncan,' Meg said sharply. 'Mister Brodie was fair vexed to lose him.' Then she coloured as Duncan shushed her.

Peter nodded calmly. 'I know that, lass, for Mister Brodie himself recommended your man to me. I see a spinning wheel downstairs – is it yours?'

Now it was Duncan's turn to boast. 'Meg's as good a spinster as anyone.'

'I'll be glad of her help, then, for this wee skelf keeps me away from my wheel often now that he's found his feet.' Kirsty disentangled Jamie's groping hands from her hair and handed the child to her husband. The little boy buried his face in his father's shoulder and Meg watched, amazed. Her father would never have allowed anyone, even his wife, to see him making a fuss of a child.

'This one's going to be a weaver,' Peter boasted. 'Matt chose the army and Colin's a grocer now. He had to give up weaving because the fluff bothered his chest. Mebbe I'll be spared long enough to teach Jamie how to work the loom.'

'Of course you'll be spared!' his wife hectored. 'Show Mister Montgomery the weaving shop while we see to the meal. And you can tell these men down there to stop leaving the street door on the latch!' she shouted after him as he led Duncan downstairs.

As she and Meg got the meal ready Kirsty chattered on without waiting for a response. She talked glowingly about Paisley, as proud of the place, Meg thought, as if she had built it with her own capable hands.

'Bragging about the town again, Kirsty?' her husband asked dryly when he and Duncan arrived back upstairs.

'That one comes from Dumbarton—' She jerked her head in his direction, '—and nothing I say'll convince him that this side of the Clyde's better than the other bank.'

'What's wrong with Dumbarton?' Peter wanted to know.

'Nothing – though you were pleased enough to wed a Paisley woman. I'm Paisley born and bred myself,' she confided to her guests.

'I think they realised that,' said her husband, poker-faced.

After supper Jamie was put to bed in the attic room he shared with his parents and the adults were free to sit round the fire, Kirsty's fingers flying nimbly over a pile of mending. Meg offered to help and soon she too was working busily, letting the men's talk flow over her bent head.

Finally, Peter knocked his pipe out against the chimney-head and stretched his arms.

'We rise early and sleep early. And before we go to bed we have a verse or two from the Holy Book.'

His wife put away her mending and rose to fetch the big family Bible from the corner cupboard. Peter took it from her and placed it carefully on the table.

'D'you want to read tonight's passage, lad?'

Duncan's face, flushed by the fire, deepened in colour. He glanced at Meg for encouragement, then burst out, 'To tell the truth, I'm not much of a hand at reading.'

'You can't read?'

'A wee bit – I learned at the school. But I never took to it. Meg sees to that side of things.'

'Learning's a fine thing,' Peter Todd said mildly.

14

'And there's a lot a man can find in books whether he's a scholar or a weaver.' Then he opened the huge tome and began to read in a slow, clear voice. Kirsty folded her hands in her lap and nodded agreement with the words now and then.

The scene reminded Meg so vividly of the final ritual of the day at the farm that she was homesick and comforted at the same time.

When the book was closed and put away again Peter and Kirsty stood up.

'Good night to you,' he said with grave courtesy. 'We rise at five o'clock.' Then the Todds departed up the winding staircase that led to the attic.

In their own bedroom, a tiny apartment that had little space for anything but the bed, Meg snuggled up to Duncan's warm body, but resisted his attempts to make love to her.

'Sssshhh! They'll hear!'

'But we're wed! I'll be quiet as a mouse – come on, lass!'

But she couldn't bring herself to make so free of their new employer's bed on such short acquaintance, and Duncan was finally forced to turn over, grumbling to himself.

Meg lay wide-eyed. The room was very dark, and all at once she was grateful for Duncan's presence, protecting her from the ghosts and bogles of the night. She lifted herself onto one elbow.

'Duncan?' she whispered. 'Duncan – I'll learn you to read, then when we have our own house

15

you can read from the Book every night like Mister Todd. It's easy.'

He heaved himself over onto his back and she felt his fingers tangle themselves in her soft loose hair.

'My wee Meg—' his voice was already thick with drowsiness. 'You're a good lass, Meg. You'll see – we'll have a fine home, and our own looms. I'll look after you, Meg.'

Wrapped in his arms she slept at last, certain of the fine future they had mapped out for themselves.

# Chapter Two

MEG AND DUNCAN WERE QUICKLY caught up in the rhythm of Paisley life. There were two other weavers in Peter Todd's shop besides himself and Duncan – one was an irrepressible young man who saw humour in everything, the other a studious man who kept a pile of books by his loom and loved to hold forth on any subject under the sun. The men's tongues worked as swiftly as their looms.

Each morning Meg and Kirsty saw to the house-work, baked, visited the market, and looked after red-headed Jamie, a day's work in itself. Any spare time they had was spent spinning coarse thread for the looms. Their wheels were placed close to a trapdoor that allowed communication between the kitchen and the weaving shop below. When the trap was open the women could join in the conversation, and the pirns or reels of spun thread could be passed down to the weavers as they were needed.

When Jamie tired himself out with his continual toddling around and his occasional forays into the street when the door was left open he was lifted into the big wooden cradle, then Kirsty slipped her foot into the rope looped to one rocker, and rocked him as she tended her wheel.

As well as domestic duties, Kirsty and Meg, as the women of the household, were responsible for the upkeep of the long garden at the back of the house. It was stocked with sweet-scented flowers for the benefit of the bees in the two skeps, and there were plenty of bushes where the washing could be spread out to dry.

Meg was happy with the Todds, but she longed for a home of her own, where she and Duncan and their coming child could be a real family. Kirsty was sympathetic.

'I mind when Jamie was on the way – Colin was still living here and I was fair fretting for him to find a place of his own, the soul. Not that I ever let on to him or to his father.' She deftly guided thread onto the spinning wheel as she spoke. 'Then he and Lizzie wed and moved into the rooms behind the wee grocer's shop. I sometimes think he'd have been better staying here with us.'

Then she bit her lip and added swiftly, 'Not that it's any of my business. He chose Lizzie, and if he's content that's all that matters.'

Colin Todd, the grocer, had his father's good looks, but was of slighter build and had none of the older man's vitality. Soft fair hair helped to give him a fragile air, but when he smiled, which happened rarely, his thin face lit up and Meg was charmed.

When she first met his wife Lizzie she found it hard to understand why Kirsty, one of the most generous women she had ever known, disliked the girl. Colin's wife was mouse-like, quiet-voiced, her brown hair tucked beneath a clean white lace cap, her eyes lowered.

It wasn't until Peter and Kirsty held a gathering for their friends that Meg saw the other side of Lizzie's nature; then she knew why Kirsty had her doubts about Colin's choice of a wife.

When she worked in the shop Lizzie wore a grey dress, high in the neck and long-sleeved. But for the social evening she appeared in a white cambric dress sprigged with yellow, red and blue flowers. It was cut low enough to reveal the swell of surprisingly full breasts, and her slim arms were bare. Long brown hair, stylishly curled, fell about her shoulders, and for the first time Meg noticed, and envied, Lizzie's tiny waist. The head that was usually lowered was now held proudly on a long slender neck and her eyes, smoky grey with an Eastern slant to them, were raised boldly to Duncan's handsome face when they met.

'You don't take snuff, Mister Montgomery?' Even Lizzie's voice was different now, self-possessed and attractively husky.

Duncan looked puzzled. 'I don't.'

'That's why we haven't met before. The women and bairns are in and out of the shop for provisions every day, but the men only come in if they want snuff.'

'Mebbe I should think of taking the habit up,' he said with clumsy gallantry and Meg, hovering by his side, felt a flicker of unease run through her.

'You'll do nothing of the kind, Duncan Montgomery – we've enough to do with our money as it is!'

The smoky eyes left Duncan's face and flowed over Meg. It was as though Lizzie was seeing her for the first time, and assessing her.

'I hear you're anxious to find a place of your own before your bairn comes.' Her gaze moved to rest, briefly, on Colin, who hovered by her side. Somehow she managed to make him look insignificant and frail in his brown coat and plain vest. 'We have no family – yet. All Colin's energy goes into caring for his shop.'

There was calculated malice in the remark. Colin flushed and Duncan looked puzzled. Then, mercifully, Kirsty interrupted them and the moment was gone.

As the evening wore on the children were carried to the attic bedroom to sleep, packed tightly together on the Todds' bed, until their parents were ready to go home. The men went downstairs to talk around the fire in the loom shop and the women stayed in the kitchen, most of them with knitting or sewing in their hands.

Meg noticed that Lizzie reverted back to her mouse-like nature once the men had gone. She retired to a seat in a shadowy corner, her face hidden by a curtain of hair, her fingers toying with the looped earrings in her small lobes.

She brightened noticeably when the menfolk came stamping back upstairs for the musical part of the evening. She stood in the centre of the room, eyes bright and cheeks glowing, and sang in a sweet, strong soprano. Meg turned to look for Duncan and caught him watching Lizzie with a frown tucked between his brows, as though he was trying to decide what to make of her.

Suddenly uneasy, Meg made a small movement towards him, and was relieved when he turned his head and slowly smiled at her as though wakening from a dream.

'Are you content with me, Duncan?' she asked later when they were in bed together.

His hands explored her body tenderly. 'What a thing to ask, and us wed these four months past. Of course I'm content with you!'

'I wish I could sing like Lizzie Todd – and look like her.' She waited for his reaction, holding her breath, but he only laughed.

'I'd not have you any other way – my bonny Meg,' he murmured into the valley between her breasts, and Meg was happy.

Two days later Lizzie Todd, busy at the shop counter, looked up from a list of figures as the door opened. She took in the newcomer at a glance then went on totalling prices. Neat as a sparrow in her grey gown and white cap, she completed the list, took money from wee Tommy Burns's hot fist, handed change over, and bundled parcels into his arms.

'Mind that money,' she said automatically as he went out. Then she smoothed her skirt and tilted her chin to survey the customer who stood, hands planted on the counter, awaiting her attention.

A faint smile curved the corners of her mouth and gave added lustre to her smoky eyes. 'And what can I do for you, sir?'

'I was thinking—' said Duncan Montgomery '—that I might buy myself some snuff.'

Matt Todd, Peter's eldest son, came home on leave from the army soon after the Montgomerys arrived in Paisley.

Tall and broad and handsome, he was very like his father, with Peter's boundless energy and extrovert nature. Even Meg, who knew that Duncan was the handsomest man in the town, felt a flutter of excitement when she first set eyes on Matt in the tartan plaid and blue feathered bonnet of the Fusiliers.

His coming was the signal for one gathering after another. Everyone wanted to hear of his adventures, and Matt was more than ready to entertain them. His tales of the life a soldier led had the men roaring with delight and the women blushing. When a story became too embarrassing Kirsty would reach up to slap his curly head and order, 'That's quite enough of that – you'll not be bringing any more of those lies into my house, thank you!'

'Lies? Lies?' Matt's blue eyes opened wide and as often as not he swept Kirsty off her feet as though she was a child. 'Would one of His Majesty's brave soldiers tell his little old mother lies?'

Then Kirsty, struggling in vain, would shrill, 'I am not your little old mother – I'm only six months older than you. And you're still young enough to get a slap on the ear if you don't put me down this instant!'

It was then that Meg was most aware of Colin, sitting quietly in a corner, smiling at the fun, but outside it. Lizzie, too, was quiet when Matt was around, which surprised Meg more than a little.

It was Matt's idea that he and Colin should ride in the annual Silver Bells horse race, due to take place in a few days' time.

'Man, it's a grand event!' he enthused one night when the Todds and Montgomerys were together in the kitchen above the weaving shop. 'Everyone comes to the Silver Bells race – in the old days the three of us used to ride in it.' His eyes blazed blue fire. 'We could all enter for it again—'

'Not your father,' Kirsty said at once. 'He's not as young as he once was.'

'Aye, my day's past for racing,' Peter agreed reluctantly. 'It's a sport for younger men.'

To Meg's relief Duncan declined to take part. He was no horse rider, but she was well aware that

23

although he was now a married man, soon to be a father, there was still a reckless, restless side to his nature and for a moment she had been afraid that he would take up Matt's suggestion.

'Then it's you and me, Colin – just like the old days, eh?'

'No!'

They had almost forgotten Lizzie was there, sitting silently beside Colin. Her chin was up and she was glaring at Matt.

'Risk your own neck if you want to – but leave Colin alone!' she said with startlingly open antagonism.

His face was suddenly stiff. 'I didn't realise you cared so much for your man's safety.'

Lizzie shot him a look of pure venom. 'Colin's got responsibilities. He's not a thoughtless fool!'

'Then he can speak for himself,' Matt said coldly, and turned away from her. 'What d'you say, Colin?'

Meg saw Lizzie's hands clench on her lap. Colin's eyes flicked over his wife's face, then lifted to Matt.

'I'll ride with you,' he said, and Lizzie's hiss of rage was almost drowned by Matt's triumphant, 'Good for you, man – we'll bring the Bells home!'

The town's looms clattered late into the night before the Silver Bells race, so that the weavers could take the next day off. Long after she was in bed Meg could hear the faint thump of the shuttles racing to and fro and she pictured the men, red-eyed and weary, working in the lamplight. When Duncan finally came upstairs he was asleep as soon as he crawled in beside her warm body.

Matt had hired two horses from a local farmer, and had invested enough money in wagers to ensure that if either he or Colin were among the first riders home he would not be out of pocket. Kirsty and Meg scrubbed the spotless house in readiness for the gathering to be held there after the race.

'I hope you've plenty in for our guests,' Peter said anxiously and his wife tossed her red head.

'When have you ever known this house to lack refreshments? Well I know the celebrations you'll have whether your own lads win the Bells or not, and there'll be plenty for everyone, never you worry.'

As she walked with Duncan and the Todds to Love Street, where the race was to begin and end, Meg felt the festival atmosphere stirring her blood. Children ran through the thick crowds, squealing like piglets in their excitement, men congregated in groups to place wagers on the outcome, women wore their best and brightest clothes.

Street vendors had set up stalls at the Cross, strangers flocked into the town from miles around – it was as if the whole of Scotland had congregated in that one small town for the Silver Bells horse race. The Council members massed importantly at the starting point, bearing with them the wooden casket which held the silver bells that gave the race its name.

Duncan held Meg's arm as they picked their way carefully down the street, skirting refuse heaps. Peter was well known and had no difficulty in finding a good spot for his party, where they could see the start and finish of the race.

Many Fusiliers were home on leave like Matt, and their uniforms added an extra splash of colour to the scene. The local gentry were in attendance, gazing loftily over the heads of the crowd from their fine carriages.

Kirsty nudged Meg's arm. 'There's the Laird of Dundonald,' she murmured, indicating a richly dressed young man. 'A wild, wild laddie – they say there's nothing to be done with him at all.'

'Too fond of fighting and womanising,' Peter added bluntly. 'And he's taking a lot of Paisley's lads on the same track as himself.'

Colin and Matt were already at the starting post. Their father eyed their mounts critically.

'Fine animals. You've still got a good eye for a horse, Matt.'

The soldier grinned. 'There'll be no stopping us.' He leaned from the saddle to thump his brother on the shoulder. 'A pound says I'll cross the finishing line afore you.'

Colin's thin face was flushed and handsome, the fragile air gone. Even his voice was stronger, more confident, as he said, 'You'll lose your money!'

'Not me!'

'Pride goes before a fall,' Kirsty reminded Matt, hoisting Jamie more securely on her hip. 'Just you do your best, my bonny soldier, and don't be so sure you're always going to be a winner!'

Colin laughed and nodded agreement, then his eyes moved beyond Meg's shoulder, and she saw a cloud come over his face. She turned and saw that Lizzie had arrived, demure in white linen bonnet and russet gown. The girl's lips were set in a thin line and splashes of colour in her cheeks matched her short scarlet cloak. She looked at her husband unsmilingly, then turned away to scan the crowd. Colin's shoulders slumped for a moment, then he straightened in the saddle, his mouth as firm as Lizzie's.

Nobody else seemed to have noticed the angry, wordless exchange between husband and wife.

'Colin should have found someone better,' Meg thought, and realised that she was sharing Kirsty's misgivings.

The senior Bailie raised his hand and the crowd hushed at once. The riders jostled their mounts into position, the Town Officer bawled, in a surprisingly high thin voice for such a brawny man, 'Mind these bairns! Clear the way, now!' then the signal was given and the horses were off, their riders yelling like savages, the crowd screaming encouragement.

Meg had a brief final glimpse of Colin sweeping past, mouth open in a full-throated roar, eyes glowing. Matt followed, crouching over his horse's neck.

There was a mad flurry of hooves and noise, and the riders were gone, plunging in a tight-packed bunch down the narrow thoroughfare and round the corner into St James' Street. From there they had to go onto the Shambles Road, then circle back to the Love Street starting point.

'My certies, what I wouldn't give to be one of them!' Peter boomed as the last horse swept out of sight and the yells of the crowd in St James's Street drifted back to them.

'No doubt, but it's time you realised that you're too old for such ploys,' Kirsty said mercilessly.

'But not too old for everything, eh, lass?' Her irrepressible husband slid an arm about her shoulders and she fended him off with a scandalised, 'Peter Todd – will you mind where you are?'

He took out a small box and helped himself complacently to a pinch of snuff. 'I'm at the Silver Bells horse race – and the Bells'll belong to the Todd house tonight. It's grand to be the father of sons, Duncan. Before we know it Jamie here'll be riding for the Bells.'

Kirsty rubbed her chin against her son's head. 'Mebbe, for he's as wild as you and Matt ever were. But there's time enough, is there not, my wee mannie? You'll not be in a hurry to grow up.'

'Don't cosset him, Kirsty,' Peter cautioned, but Meg, feeling the child in her womb flutter at that very moment, knew what the other woman meant. She longed to hold her own baby in her arms, and when that day came she would be in no hurry to see him – or her – grow up and away from her.

Small boys as often as not inarticulate with excitement deftly stitched their way through the crowds, carrying the latest news.

'Will Robb in front – Geordie Ogilvie's horse went lame on him – Matt and Colin Todd are well up—' The messages were passed from mouth to mouth and Peter almost danced with anticipation, craning his neck to see the end of the road, where the first riders would soon appear.

The full-throated roar was a dull rumble at first, swelling as it swept nearer. Even Lizzie was caught up in the tension, standing on tip-toe to see the winner come in. Peter scooped Jamie from Kirsty's arms and held him high; Meg gripped Duncan's arm as she heard someone shout, 'Here they come—!' Then the ground shook beneath her feet as the horses pounded back into Love Street, their red-faced riders clinging on for dear life.

Lumps of dried mud sprayed up on either side as they galloped past the line, a huge bay in front with three others fighting for second place behind it.

'Pat McGregor – it's Pat!' a man yelled as the winner, a jovial Paisley cobbler, whooped and threw his bonnet in the air.

Peter Todd stood aghast. 'Would you credit it? They're not there – not a sign of them! What the blazes do they think they're up to, the pair of knuckle-headed, clumsy—'

'Now, now, Peter,' his wife, admonished. 'It's only a race. They did their best, I'm sure.'

'Not a very good best—' he was beginning, when one of the Bailies came hurrying over, an urchin at his heels.

'Peter, this lad says there's been an accident just round the corner. One of your boys – they've sent for a physician—'

But Peter was already shouldering his way through the throng. Kirsty thrust Jamie at Duncan and followed, snatching at Lizzie's wrist as she went and towing the girl along behind her.

'Duncan—?' A chill had taken hold of Meg's limbs.

'Come on, lass, we might be needed.' He put his free arm about her and helped her along, stumbling through the dense crowd, pushing against the flow of people, for everyone else was flocking to the winning line.

They rounded the corner and found a knot of men standing in the middle of the road. Some horses, steaming after their frantic gallop, were being held by wide-eyed gawping boys.

In the middle of the group Matt knelt beside Colin, who lay in a careless, oddly boneless heap as though a giant hand had picked him up then tossed him aside. His eyes were closed and his fair hair was bloody over one temple.

As the Montgomerys arrived Kirsty dropped to

her knees and lifted her step-son's head onto her lap. Peter's hands moved carefully over Colin's limbs. Lizzie stood looking on.

'I'd not move him too much, lass,' Peter said quietly. 'It looks bad.'

Matt rubbed both hands over his paper-white face. 'It – it happened so fast.' He stumbled over the words as though the language was new to him. 'We were out in front and he'd just shouted to me that he'd take the Bells for sure. Then his horse must have put its foot in a hole – the daft gowk, why couldn't he have been watching out for it—?' he added in a burst of anguished fury. 'He went over its head and landed – on his back – on the dyke.'

They all looked at the low wall, at its hard, sharp stones.

'God help us!' Kirsty whispered, stroking Colin's bloodied hair.

Jamie, sensing that something was wrong, began to weep and punch at Duncan's shoulder. Meg took him, clasping the wriggling little body close for comfort.

'It was so quick—' Matt said again, then reeled back as Lizzie broke out of her trance and flew at him, her hands clawing for his eyes.

'It's your fault!' she screamed at him. 'It's always you! Why did you have to come back here and spoil everything, Matt Todd? Why did you have to come back?'

31

# Chapter Three

COLIN TODD SURVIVED THE ACCIDENT that marred that year's Silver Bells Race, but his back was broken and he was paralysed from the waist down. In the space of a few seconds he had become a ruckle of skin and bones lying on a cot in the kitchen behind the grocer's shop.

Peter and Matt were ghosts of themselves, weighed down by guilt.

'Colin's a grown man after all,' Duncan protested miserably to Meg during that bleak time. 'He made up his own mind to race. It's wrong of Lizzie to blame Matt for encouraging him, but the woman's out of her mind with grief.'

But instinct told Meg that Lizzie's claim on Colin was possessive rather than tender. The attack on Matt had been prompted, she felt, by fear of what would become of Lizzie herself if anything happened to her husband. And it went deeper – she was quite sure that Lizzie harboured a bitterness against Matt Todd that went beyond any consideration she might feel for Colin's welfare. But she kept her thoughts to herself. This was no time to air them, even to Duncan.

Colin had heard the physician's verdict quietly – indeed, he scarcely spoke at all. But his eyes held a look of trapped anguish that tore at Meg's heart each time she saw him. She and Kirsty did what they could to help, sitting with Colin to let Lizzie have a rest, making delicacies to tempt the invalid's appetite, helping in the shop. But both Colin and Lizzie seemed to have locked themselves away behind set, pale faces and tight lips.

When Meg called in at the shop the day before Matt was due to rejoin the Fusiliers she found Janet, the girl who had been brought in to attend the counter, dealing with a handful of customers.

The kitchen beyond was empty apart from Colin, lying in the box bed. His head was turned away from the door and he made no move when Meg went in. Quietly she put her basket down and took her cloak off. She was reaching up to hang it on the nail hammered into the door that separated the kitchen from the 'best room' when she heard voices from beyond the wooden panels.

There was no mistaking Matt's deep tones – 'You'd expect that of me, you slut?' – or Lizzie's voice – 'Why not? D'you think I'm going to spend the rest of my life like this, with a man who's no use to any woman? You weren't ashamed to touch me before, Matt Todd!'

The voices came clearly to Meg, but it was a moment before she glanced at the bed and saw with sick horror that Colin was awake, his blue eyes fixed on the ceiling, his fists gripping the blanket that lay over his useless legs. She took a step towards him as the door to the inner room was swept open so hard that it crashed off the edge of the dresser.

Matt stood in the doorway, eyes blazing in an angry face, his move into the kitchen checked as he saw Meg. Lizzie's face bobbed round his arm.

Cold anger, the first intense rage that Meg had ever experienced, gripped her.

'Have you no shame?' she asked Matt. 'Have you no feeling for the man at all?'

His eyes immediately went to the bed and she saw the colour drain from his skin.

'Colin! Colin, lad, it was a misunderstanding—' He stumbled over to take his brother's hand in his own. 'I would never—' His voice died away as Colin looked at him, a look that made Meg shiver and sent Matt stumbling from the room.

Lizzie stepped cat-like to the bed and Colin's eyes moved to meet and hold hers. But the gaze that had destroyed Matt held no fears for her. She matched it until his eyes closed against the sight of her and he turned his face back to the wall.

Then she gave Meg her attention. 'You wanted something?' she asked flatly, as though attending to a customer in the shop.

'I came to sit with Colin—'

'I can see to him.' Lizzie's voice was cold, dismissive.

The anger that gripped Meg gave her courage. 'I came to help – I didn't expect to find you and Matt—'

'You never know what you'll find in life,' Lizzie cut through her words. 'I went looking once, and I didn't find what I wanted. You'll learn.'

'Not your way, Lizzie Todd!' said Meg, and walked out before her fingers gave way to an impulse and buried themselves in Lizzie's neat brown hair.

She avoided Matt until he left Paisley; it was a relief to her when she knew that he was away. She couldn't even bring herself to tell Duncan what she had seen and heard, and he began to worry over her pallor and her depression.

'It's been the shock of Colin's accident,' Kirsty told him. 'What she needs is some good country air.'

When he suggested that Meg should go back to Beith for a few days she seized the idea eagerly, longing to escape for a while from Colin's misery and Lizzie's cold, secretive face. Duncan travelled down with her on a cold, drizzly day that gave them an excuse to cuddle together under a plaid rug as the cart carried them away from Paisley.

'I'll miss you,' he whispered, and she hugged him.

'I'll be back soon. You'll keep at your reading while I'm gone?'

He sighed, but nodded. Meg had been a hard task-master since that first night in Paisley, but her bullying was paying dividends and Duncan's reading and writing skills had greatly improved.

Meg fell back into the ways of the farm with surprising ease. It was comforting to be a daughter again, ordered about by her mother, giggling with her sister Mary, treading blankets in the big tub in the farmyard.

In Paisley, Duncan eased his loneliness by spending most of his free time with some of the young married weavers. He hadn't realised before how interested the Paisley men were in world affairs and he learned a lot from listening to them.

He had the sense not to join them in the howffs, for he couldn't afford to spend hard-earned money on drink, but he went with them on their long walks, argued with them, bowled with them, and on more than one occasion fought beside them when they had differences of opinion with men from other districts. Their cheerful rowdiness appealed to that part of him that hadn't yet resigned itself to marriage and its limitations. He enjoyed the life of a bachelor once again; it was only at nights, alone in bed, that he hungered for his wife's soft, warm body, her willingness, her loving.

'It's time for Meg to come home,' Kirsty said shrewdly one evening when Duncan had gone out to meet Davie. 'It's not natural for a young man to be parted from his wife for too long.'

Lizzie, sitting in a corner of the kitchen with her sewing on her lap, looked up from under pale eyelids. The quiet older weaver who worked in

Peter's loom shop, had offered to sit with Colin and free her for a while.

'Meg'll be back soon enough,' Peter said easily. 'I've no doubt she's missing Duncan as much as he's missing her.'

Lizzie's long fingers folded the material she had been working on. 'I'd best get home,' she said.

Duncan, bored and restless, was wandering home when he turned a corner and bumped into Lizzie. The books in her arms would have gone flying if he hadn't caught them deftly.

'I'll carry them for you,' he offered. She said nothing, but let him take the rest of the books from her.

'How's Colin?'

'No different.'

'It must be hard for you.'

She lifted her head for the first time and looked fully at him. 'It's not easy. But folk don't seem to understand what it's like to be young and wondering what's to become of me for the rest of my life!'

Taken aback by the bitterness in her voice he stammered something, but she ignored him.

'Just because I say little they think I don't bother – but I do, I do!' she went on fiercely. 'Night after night I lie there, beside him, and I look into the future, and I'm frightened—'

Her voice broke and she clenched her hands into small, knotted fists. They came to a pothole in the roadway and Duncan took her elbow to steer her safely round it. A strong tremor seemed to run through Lizzie's body and into his hand. He snatched his fingers away as though they had been burned, then slowly, deliberately, took her arm again and guided her along the rough road as though she was made of fine china.

She said no more until they reached her door then she turned and took the books from him, tilting her chin defiantly. 'I've shocked you.'

'No, no—!'

'Aye, Duncan Montgomery, I have.' Her voice had taken on a soft lilt. 'I've shocked you and I'm not sorry for it. You're mebbe the only one who can understand how I feel. I had to speak out to someone. Meg's far away in Beith – you know as well as I do what it's like to lie alone at night, wanting – hurting—' The words hung in the dusk between them. 'I'm not ready to finish with life yet,' she added, low-voiced. 'Not yet! Thank you for listening, I'll not ask you in.'

And with a nod she was gone.

Duncan walked home slowly, thinking over her words. His final thoughts before he fell asleep that night weren't of rounded, loving Meg, but of slender, pale Lizzie with her brilliant eyes and her lilting voice.

He wondered if she was thinking about him at that moment as she lay awake beside her silent, crippled husband.

\*　　\*　　\*

Lizzie Todd was as intoxicating as strong drink. She haunted Duncan's mind over the next two days. He avoided the shop but on the third day, his work finished and a lonely afternoon before him, he met her in the street.

Her grey eyes held his. 'I'm going to the moors for a breath of air – mebbe you'd like to accompany me,' she said softly.

He hesitated, but only for a moment. 'I was thinking of going there myself,' he said, and allowed his hand to brush hers as he turned to walk by her side.

The grass on the moors at the foot of the Muckle Riggs was short and springy and warmed by the sun. They found a little hollow sheltered by bushes, and Lizzie picked daisies and made a chain while Duncan watched her, drinking in each movement she made. She slit the final stem with sharp finger-nails, tucked a daisy head through it, then put the completed circlet on her hair and smiled up at him.

'What do you think?'

'You look bonnie. Like a queen.'

Her slanted eyes laughed at him. 'I never thought to hear such a compliment again.'

'It's the truth.'

'You're a fine-looking man yourself, Duncan Montgomery.' She reached out to take his hand in hers and again he sensed that tremor flowing between their fingers. It tingled through him, exciting him, and at the same time warning him of danger.

'We should get back.'

Lizzie shrugged, then let herself fall back on the grass, her eyes mocking him. 'It's early yet. Are you scared of me?'

'Mebbe I should be.'

She laughed. Strands of her hair fell across the tiny white flowers that starred the grass beneath her. Her teeth gleamed white and sharp between parted lips. His body burned with his need of her.

'Then why don't you take to your heels and run home, where you'll be safe?' she suggested silkily.

He knew well enough that he should do just that – run over the moors and back to the streets; run all the way to Beith and to Meg. But he was infected by Lizzie. He couldn't rest until he possessed her.

'You know why—' he said hoarsely, and caught at her shoulders, raising her up to where he knelt above her, bringing her mouth to his own hungry lips.

Her kiss excited him, made him want to take her swiftly, fiercely – and yet he must delay the moment of taking as long as possible, because with Lizzie there were so many delights to explore first. She twined her fingers in his hair, then she was writhing like a wild thing against him, her mouth warm and moist, as he bore her down again onto the springy turf.

\* \* \*

They had three further meetings before word of Meg's return reached him.

The letter lay in Duncan's hand like a stone. Meg's goodness and love, and her trust in him, shone from those few scrawled words. Like a handful of icy water thrown into his face they brought him back with cruel haste to his real purpose in life – making a home for his wife and his child.

He felt weak, like a man who had just recovered from a consuming fever. His burning lust for Lizzie ebbed away as he read the letter again, and in its place came a longing to hold Meg in his arms once more. The illness had almost been fatal, but now he was cured. Then he remembered that he still had to face Lizzie, and his limbs trembled anew.

Mercifully, she was alone in the shop when he went in. She looked sharply at him when he stepped through the doorway.

'What's amiss?'

'Meg's coming home – tomorrow.'

Her eyebrows lifted slightly, her eyes mocking him. 'And you'll go back to being the perfect husband, is that it?'

His mouth was dry. 'I must. Lizzie, it was never meant to last – we needed each other for – for comfort, that was all.'

'And after tomorrow you'll have no more need of me?'

He swallowed, and longed for a mug of ale.

'You knew as well as I did that there was no future to it.'

A strange light flared into the grey eyes that surveyed him, and he braced himself to face her rage, then the look was gone, and she shrugged. 'So we'll just have to make the most of this afternoon?'

'No!' His voice was so emphatic that she frowned and put a finger to her lips.

'Ssshhh! The girl's in the kitchen with Colin.'

'I'll not see you this afternoon, Lizzie. It's finished.' He hadn't meant it to sound so blunt but he didn't know what else to say. For a moment her lips parted to speak, then she shrugged again.

'Please yourself. There's other men,' she said deliberately. The contempt in her voice stung, but Duncan welcomed the cleansing, absolving pain of it. He walked out, towards the nearest howff. It was over.

As the time for her baby's birth approached Meg became happier than ever before. Shortly before Christmas she and Duncan were able to move round the corner from the Todds' home into a two-roomed ground-floor house in Lady Lane, scantily furnished, but a palace as far as they were concerned.

Duncan kept well away from the grocer's shop, and didn't see Lizzie at all as the weeks passed. It seemed that their affair had only been a passing dream – then at the very moment when he began to let himself relax he was summoned one night to Peter Todd's house.

'Is there something wrong?' Meg asked anxiously when a boy knocked at their door and delivered the message. 'Should I go with you?'

'No, it's probably to do with the loom-shop.' Duncan shivered as a handful of rain spattered against the window. 'You stay here, by the fire. I'll be back soon.'

But when he walked into the warm kitchen and saw Lizzie, wild-eyed and bitter-mouthed, he knew that his shameful secret was out. His knees dissolved and he had to catch at the back of a chair to keep himself upright.

'No doubt you know what this is about?' Peter asked in a harsh unfamiliar voice.

'Did you have to bring them into it?' Duncan asked Lizzie, indicating the Todds with a jerk of the head. Her eyes narrowed, no longer luminous and inviting.

'I wanted them to know what their fine new weaver's brought to their door!'

'That's enough!' Peter's face was old and drawn, and Duncan was reminded of the day the man had looked down at his son, bloodied and unconscious in the mud. 'What's done can't be cured by harsh words. We have to think of what's best for – the child.'

Duncan cursed himself for a fool. He might have known that their passionate loving would bear fruit. Hadn't Meg fallen pregnant right after their marriage?

'Meg mustn't know—' he said automatically.

'Oh – so Meg mustn't know?' Lizzie mocked shrilly. 'She'll know all right! You've got me with child and now you'll have to acknowledge it! You'll have to set up house with me!'

'Leave Meg for you? But I – I love her!'

'You should have thought of that before you gave Lizzie a child!' Peter made a move forward and Kirsty put a restraining hand on his arm.

'I wish to God I had! But I'm thinking of it now – and I'll not leave Meg! I'll pay for the child's keep, Lizzie, but I'll not leave my wife!'

Lizzie made for the door. 'We'll see what she thinks when she's heard about it—'

Duncan's hands caught her shoulders and spun her round. He shook her until her head flopped on its long neck.

'You dare to go near Meg – you dare to say a word to her, and I'll kill you—!'

'For God's sake, man!' Peter dragged him away and Kirsty pushed Lizzie, spitting defiance and threats, into a chair.

'It's you and me'll have to sort this out,' she told her husband bluntly. 'These two hadn't the sense to leave each other alone, and they've not got the sense now to decide what's best.'

'I'll not leave Meg!' To his horror Duncan heard his own voice thicken with the threat of angry, frightened tears. He had never wanted or needed

Meg's loving arms more than at that moment. 'I'll see you right for money, Lizzie, but that's all. I'll take Meg away, back to Beith – I'll tell her that I can't settle in Paisley—'

'And you'll get out of it that way, will you?' Peter almost snarled at him. 'What about my son? God – this'll be the finish of him!'

'And what about me?' Lizzie screeched. 'A child I don't want, no man to look after me—'

'Wait a minute.' Kirsty's quiet authority cut across the girl's rising hysteria. 'It's too late to start blaming each other. What's done's done, and we're here to decide how to make some sense out of it. Lizzie, how far on are you?'

'Eight weeks,' the girl said sullenly, and as another gust of wind drove rain against the house walls Duncan recalled those sunny afternoons in the little hollow. In the weeks since then he had known more contentment with Meg than ever before. He would have plunged a knife into his heart willingly if he could only obliterate his affair with Lizzie.

'A few weeks here or there wouldn't make much difference,' Kirsty thought aloud, swiftly. 'The child could have been conceived just before Colin's accident. It could be his.'

'It's not!' Lizzie almost screamed at her. 'It's his!' One long finger stabbed at Duncan.

'I'm saying that for all anyone knows – for all Colin knows – you could be further on than you are.'

'You'd let Colin think he'd fathered another man's child?' Peter asked, aghast. 'I'll not have it!'

'Now listen for a minute before you say another word,' his wife ordered. 'Colin's always wanted a family, and the poor soul's never going to father children now. Would it be such an unkindness to let him think it's his?'

She watched her husband's face, and saw understanding dawn in the blue eyes.

'But there's me to consider – what about my wishes?' Lizzie said sourly.

'You might as well face up to it – Duncan's admitted responsibility but he'll not leave Meg for your sake,' Kirsty said flatly. 'You'll either be alone with the child or you'll let Colin think it's his and have a roof over your head. And I daresay Peter would be willing to pay Janet to stay on and see to the shop for you. Eh, Peter?'

'You think I'll be content with that?' Lizzie sneered.

'I don't see that you have much choice, Lizzie. It's that, or manage on your own with a child to birth and raise. Is it worth breaking Colin's heart? Surely the poor man's got enough to contend with.'

'I'll not agree to it!'

Peter caught his daughter-in-law's wrist with strong fingers. 'You'll do what's best for Colin – whatever that might be!'

Kirsty let out her breath in a sigh, eyes bright with relief as she realised that her husband, at least,

46

was beginning to give her his support. 'This is the way I see it—' she began with a new briskness.

Lizzie wrangled for another hour before she accepted that Duncan wasn't going to leave his wife for her sake. Then she sulkily agreed to Kirsty's plan, and slammed out of the door and down the stairs.

For a moment the three left in the room were silent, then Peter said, 'You're mad, woman! It's a daft ploy – the whole town'll see through it!'

'Not unless Lizzie tells them,' Kirsty argued. 'And a crippled husband's better than no man at all to the likes of her. Pay her well and she'll hold her tongue.'

Duncan straightened and felt his joints creak. He was certain that he had aged twenty years since leaving Meg by the fireside.

'I'm sorry, Mister Todd.'

'Well you might be! Colin lying helpless and your own wife carrying her first child, and you—'

Duncan's face drained of colour, then flamed. 'You can't say anything to me I haven't already said to myself.' He picked up his cap, twisted it tightly in both hands. 'And now I've to face Meg.'

'Poor lass – does she have to know about Lizzie? It'll kill her, Duncan,' Kirsty said, her mind already busy with another scheme.

'She'll never know about that, for it's my guilt, not hers. I'll tell her—' he swallowed, thinking of her pride in their first proper home. '—I'll tell her I can't settle here. I'll tell her tomorrow.'

\*       \*       \*

47

'And they'll go back to Beith and you'll lose a good weaver,' Kirsty said as they listened to Duncan's footsteps, slow and heavy, stumbling down the stairs.

'There's other weavers.' Peter's voice was hard.

'But Duncan's better than most, is he not? Admit it, Peter, he's more like a son than an employee already.'

'You see more than your fair share – and talk more than your fair share too!' he said angrily, but she shrugged the reprimand off.

'And there's Meg, too – they both fit well into Paisley. You're angered just as much by the way Duncan's betrayed your trust as by the way he's betrayed Colin.'

'Kirsty, I've never raised my hand to a woman before, but if you don't guard that tongue of yours—' her husband howled, goaded beyond endurance.

'Let them stay, Peter.'

His jaw dropped. 'Let them stay?' he repeated incredulously. 'Let him stay in the same town as Colin after he and Lizzie – after they—'

'Just hear me out before you go jumping around as if you've met up with a flea—' She put a firm hand on his arm. 'It's over between Duncan and Lizzie, you must see that for yourself. The lad's got a good future here. He'll never make a fool of himself again, that's for sure.'

'Keep him on in my employ after—' Peter made

for the door. 'I'm going to my bed.' Then he swung round and snatched his jacket from the back of his chair. 'No, I'm going out for a drink. You're the one that should be going to your bed. It's late, and your mind's addled with all this trouble!'

'Peter, if Duncan suddenly goes it'll cause more talk than if he stays. And you'd not want Colin to wonder at his going, would you? The poor man's crippled, not stupid.'

'D'you think I could go on working with Duncan Montgomery, knowing the truth about him and – and—?'

Kirsty took the jacket from his hands. 'I think you're an honest, just man, Peter Todd. I think you've got a good heart. And if you'd just give yourself a chance to ponder over what I'm saying you'd know I'm right.'

There was a long pause, then Peter said, 'I'm away to my bed.'

'Do as the Book says, Peter—' Kirsty said as he touched the latch. 'Cast your bread on the waters. As far as Duncan Montgomery's concerned, it'll come back to you. You'll see.'

He went out without speaking or looking at her. Kirsty listened until she had satisfied herself that he was going up to the attic and not down to the street, then she went about her duties with hands that shook very slightly, making sure that the room was tidy and putting oatmeal to soak for the morning's porridge.

When she went into the attic bedroom he was sitting on the bed staring into space.

'Mebbe you're right,' he said gruffly. 'Mebbe I'll talk it over in the morning with Duncan.'

Kirsty beamed at him. 'Mebbe you should, Peter.'

'That's not to say he'll stay.'

'I think he will.' She didn't tell him that she, too, would have a word with Duncan.

'But I'm damned if I know why I let you talk me into things against my better judgement, woman,' Peter grumbled.

It was only then that Kirsty allowed herself to believe that her plan was going to work out. Duncan and Meg would stay, Colin would have his child, Lizzie would hold her tongue. Slowly, aware of his eyes on her, she untied her white lacy cap and released her fiery silken hair from the pins that confined it by day. Then she went to sit by her husband, her arms about him, her lips against his face.

'Because I'm always right,' she said demurely.

# Chapter Four

Meg's son was born one January afternoon just as the last of the grey daylight was ebbing and the weavers were setting tapers by the looms so that they could continue their work. Kirsty, summoned that morning when the pains began, had ordered Duncan off to his loom as usual.

'A first baby can take a while, and you'll just be in the way,' she'd said, pushing him out of his own street door. 'I'll let you know when you can come back.'

All day he blundered through his work, and when word finally came for him to go home he jumped to his feet, almost knocking his taper into the loom.

'Will you watch what you're about!' Peter roared at him, then added, as he looked at the knotted threads Duncan had been trying to unravel for the past half hour, 'Ach, mebbe you'd be as well to burn the lot after all!'

But Duncan was already away, his boots clattering along the passageway then skidding on the hard-packed, ice-rimed earth of the footpath.

The kitchen was warm and peaceful when he burst in; Kirsty was putting on her cloak and Meg lay in the wall bed, her face radiant when she saw him.

'There's food on the table, and I'll look in later,' Kirsty said briskly, and went out as Duncan stared down at the baby, plump and smooth-skinned, with a thatch of dark hair.

'He's like you,' Meg said contentedly. 'Give him to me.'

Duncan lifted the warm, solid bundle from the cradle, balanced it carefully in his two hands, and settled it in the curve of his wife's arm. Then he hid his face in Meg's warm, soft shoulder.

'I promise I'll be a good husband to you for the rest of my life—' he whispered into her hair. 'I'll take such care of the two of you—'

Surprised by the damp touch of his tears on her skin, she reached up to stroke his face.

'But Duncan,' she said, puzzled, 'You've always been good to me.'

Robert Montgomery took to life as a weaver's son without any misgivings at all. Each day Meg scooped him into a shawl and took him out and about with her, and wherever they went people responded to his lop-sided, toothless smile and his large blue eyes.

Everyone, that was, except Lizzie Todd. If Meg was helping Lizzie in the shop or about the house she tucked Robert in at the end of Colin's truckle bed and the invalid, now propped up on cushions, watched over him. But Lizzie ignored the child and Meg wondered uneasily what sort of mother she would be to her own baby when it arrived.

'She's such a cold creature,' she fretted to Duncan. 'A wee one needs love—'

He got to his feet abruptly, pleasure in his own fireside suddenly gone. 'D'you have to talk so much about Lizzie Todd?' he asked sharply.

Hurt, Meg kept her thoughts about Lizzie to herself from then on. But it was hard, especially when Lizzie's baby was born in May. The girl went into labour after a fall from the step-ladder in the shop and had a long and hard labour before William was born, a frail, passive little boy.

'He's dark, like you,' Meg said cheerfully when she went along to visit mother and child. Lizzie, still confined to bed, shrugged, then shook her head and drew back when Meg bent to give the child to her.

'I can't be doing with his crying – put him in the crib.'

'In a minute.' Meg straightened, reluctant to put down the tiny mite that nestled against the curve of her breast. 'A crib's a lonely place for such a wee thing.'

Colin called from the parlour, where he lay on his cot. As she went in he held out her arms. 'Give him to me—'

She handed William over and watched as Colin stroked the small face gently with one finger.

'He'll strengthen fast enough,' Meg assured him. The difference between William and her own chubby, healthy child, now four months old, was frightening.

'I know. I'll keep him by me for a wee while, Meg.'

Going back into the kitchen, looking at the woman who lay like a ramrod in the bed there, Meg was glad that Colin and his son had each other for warmth.

Further north, and almost in another world as far as Paisley was concerned, the Jacobites and the Government troops were locked in a struggle to the death.

On the whole the Paisley folk supported the King and disapproved of the hot-headed clansmen and their loyalty to a young man who, when all was said and done, was 'more a Frenchie than a Scot, and not the man for the crown at all,' in their view. The packmen kept them abreast of the latest news, and where two or more people met there was always some lively argument going on about the situation. Often Kirsty got so caught up in a disagreement with the men in the shop below that her spinning wheel almost whirred right off its mounting, and Peter would be goaded into bellowing up at her, 'Ach, why don't you content yourself with pots and pans and bread making, woman, and leave the opinions to the menfolk?'

To which Kirsty, face crimson, would yell, 'If

you wanted some mealy-mouthed skivvy who'd keep her mouth shut and your belly filled, Peter Todd, you should have stayed in Dumbarton and not come to a place where the women have minds of their own!'

Then she would kick the trap shut and, eyes gleaming and red curls bouncing, say triumphantly, 'That's one argument he's lost, big man that he thinks he is. Never let them have the last word, Meg!'

After a while Peter would bang on the hatch, Kirsty would open it and, with a sweet smile, pass down the old top hat which she kept the loaded pirns in – and the argument would be forgotten, until the next time.

Matt came back home, his old vigorous self again, spilling over with tales of the Battle of Falkirk a few months earlier. Seated in his father's kitchen, a pipe in his hand and Jamie asleep on his knee, he held court to a crowd of wide-eyed listeners, chilling their blood one minute, throwing them into laughter the next with a malicious and hilarious word-picture of poor John Renfrew, who in the noise and confusion had dashed straight into a hedge and stuck fast.

'We'd not have bothered with him, but he was the colour-bearer, and we weren't going to let those Highlanders get their hands on Paisley's standard.' He winked at the ring of faces. 'Man, you should have seen Johnny – head on one side, fat rump on the other, bellowing like a stuck heifer – and his hands clamped round the banner all the time with a grip like death itself. It took three of us to pull him free.'

Meg noticed that Lizzie didn't attend any of those gatherings. The only time she appeared in the Todds' kitchen was when Matt went along to see Colin.

A terrible suspicion began to form in Meg's mind. She could say nothing to Duncan or even to Kirsty, so she had to keep her thoughts to herself until one day when she had to work at home because Robert was teething and too fretful to take out.

Duncan had arranged to call round for the finished pirns, but when the door opened Meg saw Matt's tall figure outlined against the light beyond, his head stooped beneath the lintel.

'I told Duncan I'd fetch the pirns,' he said and she felt warmth rise in her face. She hadn't been alone with him since that day in Colin's kitchen.

'They're in the corner there.'

He closed the door behind him, shutting out the street. 'You've got a fine home since I last was here.'

'Aye,' she said shortly, eyes on her wheel, willing him to go away. Instead, he sat down opposite her.

'Meg—'

Reluctantly, she slowed the wheel and looked up at him – to be stunned by the lost look on his handsome, normally confident face.

'I have to talk with you – about Lizzie.' He put

out a hand as she started to speak. 'Listen to me! I know what you think about her and me, but you're wrong! We walked out together before I went into the Army, but I had no thought in my head then but soldiering, though it turned out that Lizzie had her heart set on marriage.'

His big, capable hands knotted into fists as he spoke. 'God, she had plenty to say when she realised that I was set on going away. She flew at me like a she-devil and near tore my face open with her nails. But I went all the same so she set her cap at Colin instead. When I came back they were wed. And from that day I've never treated her as anything other than my brother's wife.'

'You can say that to me, when I heard with my own ears—'

'What you heard – and, God forgive me, what Colin heard – was Lizzie's doing, not mine!' Matt spoke with a sudden surge of energy. 'I wanted to crush her as if she was a flea on my arm – I still do. It would please me if I was never to set eyes on the bitch again. I've done enough to Colin, making him ride with me that day. D'you think I'd do more?'

'And William?'

'As God's my witness, Meg, he must be Colin's, for he's not mine!'

She studied him for a long moment, then nodded. 'I believe you, Matt.'

Relief lit his handsome face. 'I'm glad that's settled between us. I'll take the pirns to Duncan,' he said, then hesitated at the door.

'Meg, will you keep watch over Colin and the wee one?'

'We'll all look after them—' Meg broke off as the baby started to cough. She went quickly to the cradle, and Matt, whistling, left for the loom shop. Walking up and down with Robert muttering fretfully in her arms, Meg thought of Lizzie and those strange grey eyes of hers, the way they changed when they looked on men such as Matt and Duncan—

She stopped, and Robert squeaked a protest as her arms tightened. Meg kissed his sweat-damp hair and rocked him soothingly, her thoughts in sudden turmoil. As Lizzie and Duncan's names linked in her mind panic caught at her heart, then she forced herself to calm down, to be sensible.

Lizzie looked at all men, other than her husband, in the same way. It meant nothing, particularly to a man as sensible as Duncan. Besides, he never looked the road Lizzie was on, never even encouraged Meg to talk about her.

'You've got a silly mother,' she said shakily to Robert, and made up her mind once and for all, as she laid the baby back in his cradle, that never again would she allow such foolish ideas about Duncan to enter her head.

By the time his son reached his first birthday Duncan had joined the Society of Weavers, and he and Meg had become members of the Baptist Church, attending meetings in the Abbey Close.

To Meg's intense pride Duncan was even invited to speak at a church meeting, an occasion fraught with nerves for them both. Duncan's hands gripped the lectern before him, his face red with effort; Meg sat in the front row, her lips moving in unison with his, leaning forward to prompt audibly if he faltered. When the ordeal was finally over she almost split in two with pride.

A month after Robert's birthday his sister Margaret was born, and six weeks later Kirsty Todd gave birth to a daughter, Kate. In June, when the tiny white flowers were beginning to star the grass on the moors, the whole town was rocked by a piece of scandal.

The gossips were out in force at once, eyes gleaming, tongues wagging. 'Lizzie Todd's run off wi' a farm-worker! Have you heard about it? That poor man – and that poor bairn!'

Meg, who heard the story at the market place, hurried at once to Kirsty's kitchen, Margaret tucked into her shawl, and Robert running alongside as fast as his fat little legs could carry him, complaining breathlessly.

'It's not true!' she said as she burst into the kitchen.

Kirsty, rocking in her chair with Kate in the crook of one arm and William in her lap, was stony-faced.

'It's true. Hell mend the woman, for she's done a terrible thing this day!'

'How's Colin?'

Kirsty shook her head. 'Determined to fend for himself and the boy, though there's no way he can run the shop. There's room here for them both, and food enough, but he's being that thrawn about it – Peter's near out of his mind.'

At that moment an idea came to Meg, such a daring idea that it caught the breath in her throat. She said nothing to Kirsty, or even to Duncan, but the thought stayed with her. When she couldn't stand it any longer she called on Colin, still living in the rooms behind the shop, though Kirsty was looking after William.

The woman waiting to be served eyed her with open curiosity as she went round the counter with a brief nod to Janet. She heard their voices buzzing as she closed the house door behind her.

Already there was an air of neglect about the place, though Kirsty had been in that morning, Meg knew, to see to the housework. But there was something undeniably depressing about a house without its proper housewife.

Colin was propped up on a pile of pillows, staring at the opposite wall. His face, gaunt since his accident, was no more than skin stretched over sharp bones, his eyes, when he glanced up at her, were sunk in their sockets, without any hope in them at all.

'I'm in no mood for visitors – or sympathy!' he said harshly.

'I'm not a visitor. And I've more to do with my

time than pity you.' She sat down on the chair by the bed and stared at him defiantly. He glowered back at her, then turned his face to the wall.

'Go away, Meg – leave me be!'

She steeled herself, recognising his frustration, his despair, his desperate need to be whole in himself.

'We have things to talk about, you and me. Colin, I want the shop,' she said bluntly, and saw his head turn, the grim set of his face slacken with sheer surprise.

'You what?'

'I want the shop. I've worked in it often enough and I managed fine. I could run it with Janet's help. But I'd need this house as well.'

Anger flared in his eyes, and she was glad to see it there.

'And I just take my son and move out to suit your convenience? By God, Meg Montgomery, you know how to take advantage of a man's misfortunes to line your own nest!' He almost spat the words at her. 'I'll chain myself to the grate before I'll move from here!'

Meg tucked her hands beneath her shawl in case Colin saw how they shook. 'Tuts, man, d'you have no sense in your head at all?' She had to speak loudly to quell the tremor that conveyed itself from her fingers to her voice. 'You can't manage the shop by yourself. But I can, if Duncan and me move to these rooms where I can see to the children and the counter at the same time. I'm offering to run the place for you, with financial gain for us both.'

'And what about me and William?'

'You've got brains, Colin. Use them,' she rapped back at him. 'Peter has a storeroom across the passageway from the weaving shop, I'm sure he'd let you turn it into a room for yourself and William. Kirsty can keep an eye on the two of you and you can help Peter to sort out wages and accounts. You could mebbe teach some children their letters too, if you had the time.'

'And what do you get from this daft idea?'

'A home, rent-free, so that we can save up and build our own house one day. And something of my own to do. It's not such a daft idea, Colin, if you'll just think of it.'

She leaned forward, enthusiasm giving weight to her argument. 'I like working in the shop – I like it more than anything else. Ever since I came to Paisley I've wanted to be part of the place in my own way. Now I can be.'

'What does Duncan say?'

'He doesn't know. If you refuse I'd as soon he didn't hear about me making a fool of myself, and if you agree you can help me to persuade him that it's a good idea.'

There was a short silence, then to her surprise Colin laughed, a genuine peal of amusement. 'God, Meg, but you're a breath of fresh air!' he said, and it was settled.

With Colin won over, it was easy to persuade

THE SILKEN THREAD

Duncan to give his approval. Within two weeks
Colin and the baby were settled in the Todds'
former storeroom, under Kirsty's eye, and the
Montgomerys had moved into their new home.

With Janet to help her in the shop Meg was able
to combine the roles of shop-keeper and housewife
efficiently. The dwelling-house was adequate, and
there was a garden where she kept bees and grew
vegetables. It was as though Lizzie, with her final
act of betrayal, had somehow bestowed the gift of
peace on those who had known her.

Meg was too busy to travel to Beith, so her parents
came to Paisley to see her new home and her little
daughter.

'I don't know how you can live in such a crowded
place,' her mother said nervously as she picked her
way along a footpath.

Meg laughed and skipped nimbly aside as a
passing cart sent water flooding up from the rutted
road. 'You get used to it.'

'I never could!' the older woman said with
feeling. But she was proud to see the recognition Meg received as they walked along. A
gentleman standing at the door of his establish-
ment, resplendent in knee britches, tall hat and
tail coat, bowed to them and Meg, pink with
pleasure, whispered, 'That's Mister Robertson –
one of the biggest cloth manufacturers in the
town.'

'Imagine!' gasped her mother and stepped into a

63

puddle in her excitement. Then she stared. 'Mercy – who's that?'

A crowd of young men, some dressed in the height of fashion and others in weavers' working clothes, stood on the opposite path. In their midst a good-looking young man held court.

'That's the Earl of Dundonald – a rapscallion, they say. The Council are always complaining of the disrepute he brings on the town.'

Her mother tutted disapprovingly. Like most people of her class she was willing to give the gentry their place, but only if, like the working people, they had the sense to keep in it. Rowdies were rowdies, be they lords or apprentices, and she had little time for them.

Meg was secretly shocked at the relief she felt as she watched her parents clamber aboard the cart for Beith at the end of a week's stay. Despite her new-found maturity she was still wary of her mother's sharp tongue, and to her secret annoyance she had reverted a little during the visit to the role of submissive daughter. Confidence flowed back as she watched the cart jolting away, and she hugged Duncan's arm tightly as they turned back into the shop.

She had chosen her path, and it was one that more than pleased her.

# Chapter Five

'WILL YOU HOLD STILL, YOU wee scamp? Duncan, get out the back this minute and bring Robert in. He'll be black as the heathens by this time, and us supposed to be at Kirsty's long since! We'll be the last there, and I promised I'd give her a hand before the other guests arrived!' Meg lamented, holding onto Margaret with one hand and wringing out the flannel with the other.

'But I'm—' Duncan stopped, sighed, and made for the back door. Let his shirt be unbuttoned and let his slippers get wet. There was no arguing with Meg when she was in that mood.

His son was at the bottom of the garden, as usual, and climbing the apple tree – as usual.

'Out of it!' Duncan ordered, and grabbed at Robert when he reluctantly slid down the trunk. 'Your mother'll skin you alive!' he fretted, brushing leaves and bark off the boy's jacket with a large but gentle hand. 'Get into the house quick, before she comes out here after the pair of us!'

Robert gave him a gap-toothed conspiratorial grin, and scuttled up the path. Duncan fastened his shirt as he followed. It seemed only yesterday that he had been the wildest boy in Ayrshire, and now his own son was a four-year-old miniature of himself.

Time was moving on, he thought as he stepped into the kitchen. The first dusting of grey could be seen on his dark temples and his waist had that slight thickening that tells of prosperity and contentment.

'I'll have to let out your trousers soon,' Meg said at that moment with uncanny perception.

He patted his stomach defensively. 'A man needs a bit of muscle.'

'There?' She poked him in the midriff, then squealed as he swept her off the floor and kissed her. 'Duncan! The wee ones are watching!'

He let her go, grinning down at her laughing, pretty face. 'Ach, a show of affection'll do them no harm.'

Margaret toddled after him as he went to fetch his jacket, her eyes huge after her afternoon sleep. He held his arms out and she rushed into them.

'Now don't get her into a mess,' Meg cautioned. She scrubbed at Robert's rosy face and he stood uncomplaining, knowing that if he opened his mouth to protest it would be filled with wet flannel.

'And you didn't even see the bonnie flowers, did you?' Duncan was asking Margaret, who had slept in his arms all through their afternoon walk in the Hope Temple Gardens.

Meg smiled to herself as she recalled their promenade round the flower-beds, the pleasant moist warmth within the glass enclosure, the snug fit of her new leather boots, the way the senior magistrate's wife had bowed to them when they met. The memories gave her such pleasure that Robert's features were almost scrubbed off his face.

'There – you'll do.' She released him and he rushed to join his father and sister, who were romping on the box bed.

'Keep tidy, now!' Meg called automatically, and went into the shop to make sure that everything was in order. The outer door was closed and bolted, the floor swept clean, the sacks tied tightly, the scales shining. She stood for a moment, one hand on the counter, and inhaled the rich smell of meal.

She had been in charge of it for two years, and had enjoyed every minute of it. She and Duncan had just put down the first payment on a piece of land on the west fringes of the town. There, in a few years, they would build their own house. She smoothed her skirt, letting her palms linger for a moment over the bulge caused by the coming baby, then called Duncan and the children, and put her cloak on for the walk to the Todds' house.

The place was in a turmoil when the Montgomerys arrived. Kirsty, crimson-faced from the heat, was stirring a huge pot of broth while trying to soothe John, the baby. Kate, Jamie and Willie were chasing each other up and down the stairs, and Peter could be heard from the bedroom, demanding to know where his best shoes were.

'I'm glad you're here!' Kirsty greeted Meg. 'I'm in a right pickle – would you take the wee one for me? Duncan, keep an eye on that broth. And as for you—' she swooped on the older children and deposited them on a settle by the fire '—sit there and hold your tongues for two minutes while I see what that handless man wants. Where are your best shoes always kept?' she yelled as she vanished. 'Seven years, and you still don't know where to look for them!'

By the time she reappeared a minute later, tucking a stray wisp of glowing hair beneath her cap, Meg was setting the table, the baby whimpering fretfully on her shoulder.

'He's not so grand today.' Kirsty took her son and rocked him. 'He's been coughing since morning. I'll try to settle him down before the others arrive.'

She stroked the child's flushed cheek with one finger and John moved his small head against her sturdy arm. By the time he was in his cradle the visitors had begun to arrive, and the kitchen was soon filled.

Duncan and Billy Carmichael, the packman, carried Colin upstairs and put him on a chair by the fire and William, a quiet little boy, immediately climbed onto his father's knee and fell asleep, one thumb jammed into his mouth and his head nestled under Colin's chin.

After supper all the children were taken to the attic where they were packed into bed like sardines to wait for their parents. Billy took his fiddle from his pack, and the evening got off to its proper start.

In an hour or two the house was bouncing with music and the babble of voices, yet the sound of a child in distress broke through the noise easily. First one woman, then another, fell silent, listening to the dry, painful coughing from up in the attic room, fearful in case they recognised their own child. It was the sound of croup, that lung-torturing illness that dogged infants in Paisley's low-lying, damp atmosphere.

Half a dozen anxious women followed Kirsty upstairs. When she came back to the kitchen she carried John, his face crimson, his little lungs crackling and wheezing as he tried to suck in air.

Someone put a kettle on the fire to make steam to ease his labouring lungs, someone else heated a blanket to wrap him in, then they all gathered their children and left. The party was over, and Kirsty would probably be up all night with John, waiting for the attack to pass.

Duncan had scarcely left for the weaving shop the next morning when he was back, white-faced.

'Kirsty needs you. I'll fetch Janet, she can see to the bairns and the shop today.'

Meg didn't stop to ask what was wrong. She didn't need to. In a few minutes she was in the

Todds' kitchen which was no longer the warm, noisy place it had been only a few hours earlier. Instead it was frighteningly silent and Kirsty sat huddled by the fire, oblivious of Peter's arms about her and the bewildered faces of the children who hadn't yet learned to understand the meaning of sudden death.

While Peter went off to make the necessary arrangements for his little son's burial, Meg fed the children and sent them down to Colin's room, then made tea and wrapped Kirsty's cold, stiff fingers about the cup before setting about the housework. The kitchen had to be spotless, and there was a baking to do in preparation for the people who would start arriving as soon as word of John's death spread.

Kirsty sat motionless, scarcely heeding the visitors. She didn't even pay attention to Mistress McKenzie, one of the first callers.

'The Lord giveth and the Lord taketh away,' that lady announced almost as soon as her foot was over the lintel. 'Your bairn's been chosen to reside with his Maker, Mistress Todd, and it's not for poor mortals like us to question or to lament. I'll try one of these scones, Meg.'

'Are you trying to say that Kirsty should rejoice?' Meg heard herself say in a strange, hard voice.

The black ribbons on Mistress McKenzie's bonnet rustled dryly with the force of her nodding.

'Just so. Children belong to the Lord, not to us. It's an honour when one's chosen from among our

THE SILKEN THREAD

number. It's not for us to question the ways of the Lord.'

Meg swallowed hard and glared at the woman who sat with her skirts hitched up to let her heavily veined legs soak in the fire's warmth.

'It seems to me that if the Lord knew more about the work that goes into caring for a baby, and the mortal love that goes with it, He'd have a bit more compassion for mothers!'

It was the other woman's turn to gape, and a half-chewed chunk of scone almost escaped past her teeth. She gulped, choked, and muttered something about Baptists knowing no better.

Meg set her lips over an angry retort. This wasn't the time to quarrel.

'But I could have taken her by the hair and dragged her out of the kitchen and down the stairs,' she stormed to Duncan when she was home again. 'The besom! Her with no children of her own – talking about honour and rejoicing!'

And she hugged Margaret so tightly that the little girl's lower lip began to tremble.

A few days later Kirsty and Peter saw John's tiny coffin buried in the churchyard, then they went back home and set about their usual day's routine.

There was little time to spare for mourning in a thriving town like Paisley. Water had to be fetched from wells, bees had to be tended and living children cared for, and thread had to be

71

spun for the ever-hungry looms that beat out a steady rhythm for the townsfolk to live by.

As the time for her own baby's birth drew near Meg found it more and more difficult to cope with all her duties. Janet was a dreamy girl, not to be trusted in the shop alone if there were more than two customers. At times Meg longed to shake the girl hard, just to see if there was any life behind that vacant face. Her temper grew short, and it was as much for his own sake as for hers that Duncan suggested asking her sister Mary to help with the chores until the baby arrived.

Mary arrived within a few days, delighted with the opportunity to leave the farm. With an ease that stunned her older sister she familiarised herself with the shop routine and her happy nature and pretty face, with its sparkling brown eyes and its frame of dark curls, made her a great success with the customers. She even had an impressive effect on Janet, who began to take an interest in her appearance and her work.

'How did you manage to waken that ditherer?' Duncan demanded to know one day after he had found Janet, neat and tidy, chatting animatedly with Mary as they restocked shelves.

His sister-in-law leaned across the table and wiped crumbs from Margaret's chin. 'She just needed a firm hand. Nobody's ever encouraged her to take an interest in the way she looks, that's all.'

Mary was the beauty of the family. Meg was

plump and maternal, but Mary was slender and elegant. They had the same dark hair, but Mary's was glossy. Her manner was confident, her bearing almost regal. Somehow she managed to make even the plainest dress look stylish.

The town's young bachelors flocked to the shop and the snuff jar had to be replenished once every day; but to Meg's astonishment her sister wasn't interested in romance.

'A wee flirtation can be entertaining, I'll grant you,' she said carelessly. 'But I'm not interested in marriage.'

'What else is there?' Meg asked, and Mary threw a scathing glance at her.

'Plenty!'

She was fascinated by fashion, and always willing to take the children to the Hope Temple Gardens where she could study the ladies' clothes. She bought silks and ribbons and made her own bonnets, and on Meg's first outing to the Baptist rooms after her baby, Thomas, was born, she wore a hat made by Mary's nimble fingers.

Duncan's eyes shone when he saw his wife's rosy face framed by the new bonnet. 'You'll be the loveliest woman in the place!'

Meg laughed and blushed. But it was true. Nobody else had such a fine hat.

'Though it's wicked to think such vain thoughts in the Lord's House,' she whispered to Mary, who whispered back, dimpling, 'Mebbe the Lord's too

EVELYN HOOD

busy admiring my fine bonnet to notice the vain
thoughts underneath it.'

If the Lord did admire the hat He wasn't the
only one. Within a short time quite a number of the
townswomen, including Mistress MacLeod, wife of
one of the town's councillors, had asked Mary to
make bonnets for them, and the little spare time she
had was spent surrounded by ribbons and lace.

One day she came back from delivering a bonnet
to Mistress MacLeod with shining eyes and an extra
bounce to her light step.

'Meg, it's the grandest place I've ever been in –
we sat in the parlour, but she calls it a withdrawing
room, and the maid served tea just as if we were
two ladies visiting! And I'm to make another bonnet
for her!'

She seized Meg's hands and whirled her round.
'And she's going to pay me more money than I
would have asked for myself!'

It was fortunate that Meg was back to her former
energetic self, for Mary became too busy to give
much time to the shop. The kitchen was a riot of
colour as she stitched away at her bonnets by day
with the children, festooned in ribbons, playing
happily beside her. At night, when Duncan and
Meg needed the peace of their own fireside, Mary
worked in her tiny room.

When the time came for her to return to Beith,
she announced that she had decided to settle in
Paisley.

'But—' Meg looked helplessly at Duncan. The

house behind the shop was already crowded and Mary's millinery was taking up more room than they could afford.

Mary's sharp eyes saw the look. 'You've nothing to worry about. I'm going to set up a wee shop at the Sneddon and live on the premises. It's all arranged between Mistress MacLeod and me,' she swept on as Meg opened her mouth to protest. 'We talked about it today, when I delivered her new bonnet. I'm to be a milliner!'

'Hold on there, Mary—' Duncan finally made himself heard. 'It's all very well talking of wee shops, but where d'you expect to find the money for all this?'

She gave him a withering look. 'D'you think I haven't thought of all that? Mistress MacLeod's going to pay the rent of the place, and pay me to work for her. And I'll see she gets her money back as soon as I can give it to her. The woman's got more money than she knows what to do with, and it'll pleasure her to help me. At least she'll not be throwing her silver away.'

'What about the farm?' Visions of angry parents swooping down on her and accusing her of tempting Mary away from her proper place in life floated before Meg's eyes.

'I'll see to that – and I'm not going back, whatever they say!' Mary tossed her sleek dark head. 'I was never afraid of hard work, but I'd as soon be doing something I want to do. And I know now that it's got nothing to do with farm work!'

There was no arguing with her. Mary had found her vocation in life, and within the next few weeks she had scrubbed out the Sneddon shop and the rooms behind it, and had settled in. From then on she was often to be seen tripping about the town with a box in each hand, delivering wares to her customers. Almost every time Meg called in at the shop there was a carriage waiting at the door. Mary, like Meg, was a born businesswoman, and her shop thrived.

'That sister of yours has a good head on her shoulders,' Kirsty approved when she and Meg were spinning thread together.

Meg sighed. 'I suppose she's right when she says farm life's not for her. But I wish she would take a husband.'

Kirsty snorted with laughter. 'Why should she? She's managing fine on her own. It was a good day for Paisley when the Montgomerys arrived, Meg. There's you seeing to Colin's shop for him, and Mary doing the same for Mistress MacLeod. And Duncan's the best weaver Peter ever employed. You're all making your mark on the place.'

Meg said nothing, but she smiled at the thread smoothly winding itself onto the pirn. She wouldn't have changed places at that moment with the King himself.

Working silently beside her, Kirsty marvelled at her own words. The ugly wound caused by Duncan's affair with Lizzie had healed. She had been right to persuade Peter to keep Duncan and Meg in Paisley.

Colin was content, and nobody could wish that William, a quiet and lovable little boy, had never been born. For his part, Duncan had learned his lesson and would never stray again, she was sure of that.

'It's an ill wind—' Kirsty thought to herself with a trace of justified smugness as she added another loaded pirn to the old top hat by her side.

# PART TWO

# Chapter One

THE GROCER'S SHOP IN NEW Street was Margaret Montgomery's whole world, and she loved it.

True, there was more world outside its doors – narrow muddy streets, carriages and horses and people, rutted footpaths to walk on, houses leaning above her in friendly curiosity, the weaving shop where her father worked – but the grocery was the main part of her existence.

She loved the thick dusty smell of meal, the way the rough sacks tickled her palms, the exciting sensation of grain shifting and yet resisting when she punched the sacks with small knotted fists. She loved the counter, though at five years old she was still too small to see over it and all she knew of it was the feel of its flat surface beneath her fingers and the sight of raw grained wood at eye-level. She loved the way her mother's voice changed from loving or irritable to brisk and efficient when she was waiting on customers.

Everyone came into the shop, thus proving what Margaret already knew – that it was the hub of the town. So she loved the customers too, because the shop gave them a reason to exist.

With the open-hearted trust of one who had never been betrayed she loved the ladies with their rustly clothes, the housewives with their ready laughter, the deep voiced, snuff-buying men, the children struggling with large unwieldy baskets and reciting sing-song lists dinned into their heads by busy mothers. She even loved old Mister Lyle and his dog – and not many people loved them. They both smelled, and she had heard people calling Mister Lyle an old rascal, no better than he should be. Whenever he came in for his groceries Margaret deserted her post by her mother and slipped out to stroke the dog, waiting patiently by the door for its master.

When Mister Lyle came out he smiled at her and patted her on the head with a dirty hand. A lot of people would have found the smile terrifying, a drawing back of cracked lips to reveal gums and a few black teeth, but Margaret saw only its gentleness and its friendship. Then Mister Lyle would go off down the street, his dog at his heels, the two of them old and stiff and unloved by anyone else but Margaret.

Her capacity for affection was vast. It even included her brothers, though Thomas, still a baby, could be a great trial and Robert bullied her if she gave him the chance.

There were times when she could do nothing with Robert. Today was one of those times, she realised wretchedly as he dragged her along the crowded High Street, ignoring her pleas.

'I want to go home!' she repeated again and again, each time raising her voice a little more. But there was such a crush and noise about them that her voice made little impact. She had never known the street to be so busy, and the forest of legs and skirts she was being towed through unnerved her. She dragged back, but Robert merely tightened his grip on her hand and forged ahead, towing her behind him.

Margaret hadn't wanted to go out that day; she had burrowed into her mother's skirts and whined to stay in the shop, but Meg had pushed her at Robert and ordered her in a new, sharp voice to stop being a nuisance and do as she was told.

'You're supposed to be taking me to Aunt Kirsty's house!' Margaret pointed out, but Robert only jerked harder on her hand and she yelped with fright as she almost lost her footing.

William Todd, on her other side, steadied her.

'It's all right, Margaret, I'll look after you,' he whispered, and she squeezed his fingers in gratitude. William wasn't like Robert or Jamie – he was kind, and she felt safe with him. She often wished that grey-eyed, brown-haired William was her brother.

'Come on!' Robert's face glowed with excitement and he plunged into the thick of the crowd, dragging poor Margaret along.

The atmosphere reminded her of the Fair days,

though this wasn't one. Voices clanged in her ear or whizzed past and vanished, leaving half-finished, confusing sentences for her to puzzle over.

'Going to the hanging – the hanging – hanging—' The word was on everyone's lips. She had heard her parents mention it that very morning.

'Today's the hanging,' her father had said and Margaret, supposedly asleep in the truckle bed which by day was pushed beneath her parents' big bed, opened one eye to see him put an arm about her mother.

'Don't cry, Meg – there's nothing you or me can do about it.'

'But, Duncan, he's an old man! And all he did was take some kail from someone's garden—'

'It wasn't his only theft – or his first. You know that, Meg.'

'But he doesn't deserve—' Her mother pressed the back of a hand against her lips to stop the words.

'Why don't you close the shop for once and take the children to the braes for the morning?'

'No!' Her mother's voice was unusually sharp. 'The shop'll be open – though no doubt most of the customers'll be off for some entertainment instead of going about their lawful business!'

Then they had seen that she was awake, and had said no more. She and Robert were hurried through their breakfast and bundled out of the shop with orders to go round to Aunt Kirsty's at once. Instead they had met up with Jamie and William and now, like it or not, Margaret was on her way to the Cross with most of Paisley's population.

Jamie's red head acted like a beacon ahead of them, but they didn't catch up with him until they had reached the site near the river where the stalls were set up on market days. He and Robert burrowed their way to the front of the mob with Margaret and William following.

Margaret felt a little better when she found herself at the edge of a big open space with the bulk of the people behind her. Now the only legs in front belonged to the militia lining the open area. Beyond them stood a queer wooden arrangement of ladders and platforms that she didn't recall ever seeing before. She was trying to puzzle out what it could be when a cart was driven into the empty square, and an expectant sigh rustled through the crowd. The cart drew up before the wooden structure and a group of men clambered out.

Margaret eyed them idly, then her attention was caught by the figure in the middle. She tugged at Robert's sleeve.

'It's old Mister Lyle. What's wrong, Robert? Is he ailing?'

Mister Lyle was being helped along by two of the men. His old legs seemed to have lost their strength, and he lurched against his helpers, almost falling twice. He was escorted to the wooden contraption then the men began to help him up a ladder.

'Robert, why are his hands tied? Is it a game?'

Ignored by the three boys, Margaret ducked down to peer between the legs of the soldier standing directly before her. While the crowd buzzed with anticipation, the old man was heaved onto a small platform. A plump man in a long black coat was hoisted up the steps in his turn, but with his hands free, then he began to talk long and earnestly to Mister Lyle, as though scolding him. The old man stood abjectly before him, a pathetic, defeated figure.

Something grimly purposeful about the rest of the men on the platform, something helpless and shrunken about Mister Lyle's stance, struck an uneasy chord in Margaret's mind. She reached out to William, her only ally.

'I want to get out of this place! I want to go home!'

But the crowd's excitement gripped William fast now. He spoke hurriedly, without taking his eyes from the scene before him. 'Ssshhh, Margaret, we'll go home in a minute—'

Fear began to whisper in her ear. She closed her eyes then opened them again as the rumble of a drum cut across the babble of voices behind her.

The man in the long black coat had stopped talking to Mister Lyle and had stepped back. Then someone else looped a rope about the old man's neck. Completely bewildered, Margaret craned her own neck to see what happened next.

To her horror the platform beneath Mister Lyle's feet broke and he dropped through the hole, to be caught before he touched the ground by the rope about his throat.

His legs kicked and he swung to and fro like a doll. The crowd hushed for a second, then moaned, a sound that reached eerily to the sky. But nobody went to help Mister Lyle. Appalled, Margaret watched him swinging, kicking, choking – while the militia, the crowd, and everyone on the platform just stood and watched. Her hands went up to her own chubby neck in an instinctive effort to relieve the hempen grip on the old man's windpipe. His body swung right round then lost momentum as the legs stopped kicking.

Margaret, too, spun round, gripped by unspeakable horror, searching the faces behind and above her for some sign of compassion. But they all bore a look of rapt fascination, like babies watching a toy dangle before their eyes.

'Robert—' She tugged frantically at her brother's sleeve. 'Robert, what's happening to Mister Lyle?'

He watched the old man's last gyrations on the end of the rope. 'He's hanging, Margaret.' His voice was filled with awe. 'He was a bad man.'

'He wasn't!'

'He was so!' Jamie Todd interrupted her sharply. 'That's why he had to be hanged. He was a bad man – and now he's dead!' There was no mistaking the satisfaction in his voice.

'Dead?' Margaret whirled back to the scene in the middle of the empty square. She suddenly realised that Mister Lyle would never again walk on the ground that lay a tantalisingly short distance below his shabby boots. He would never come into the shop again, never pat her head or walk along a footpath with his old dog again. The enormity of it descended on her like a threatening cloud. She felt a sudden terrible need to get home to her mother—

Her dash for freedom brought her up against one of the soldiers lining the square. The man, almost thrown to the ground by the impact of her sturdy little body against the backs of his knees, caught her shoulder.

'Lassie, what are you doing in a place like this? Someone take the bairn away!' he appealed to the crowd. Margaret, seeing his tall uniformed figure stooping over her, feeling his hand on her arm, took his interest as a sign that she was to be the next victim.

'I'm not bad – I'm not for hanging!' she shrieked with the full power of her lungs, and flailed her arms until she managed to wriggle free. Then she eeled round and dived into the crowd before any of the boys could catch her.

Screaming for her mother she fought her way along, bumping painfully into knees, tripping over feet, half mad with terror and convinced that at any minute a rope would slip about her neck.

When the ground dropped away and left her feet kicking in mid-air as Mister Lyle's had done she shut her eyes tight and redoubled her screams.

'Here, here, lassie, no need to take on like that.'

Billy Carmichael the chapman wrapped his arms about her to still her struggles. 'It's Margaret Montgomery, isn't it?'

Margaret refused to open her eyes. 'They gave Mister Lyle a hanging and I don't want one!' she bawled, kicking and punching at the hands holding her. Then she felt herself carried swiftly along while a deep warm voice rumbled overhead.

'Nobody's going to hurt you, lassie. See, I'm taking you home. You mind me, don't you? Say hello to me like a good wee girl—'

When she finally prised her eyelids open and recognised him she threw her arms about his neck and demanded loudly to be taken to her mother at once.

'We're going, lass, we're going, for this is no place for you. I'd just be grateful if you'd neither smother nor deafen me on the way,' Billy said, and fought his way through the people pressing forward for a glimpse of the still figure swinging on the rope.

Margaret quietened down once she realised that they were leaving the crowd behind and heading for home, but at the sight of her mother and Mary in the shop her terror and outrage returned in a fresh well of tears.

Meg sank down in a chair, clutching her weeping daughter, while Billy explained.

'The hanging? Oh, my poor wee lamb! And I thought they were safe at Kirsty's. Wait till I get a hold of Robert—!'

'And Mister Lyle's hands were t – tied and he fell and no – nobody would help him,' Margaret roared. 'And Robert said he'd been b – bad and it was a hanging, then the soldiers took me for the hanging t – t – too—'

'See now, Margaret, wee lassies don't get hanged.' Mary's practical voice broke through the noise. 'They might get smacked if they need it but they never get hanged. The soldiers wouldn't do a thing like that to anybody.'

Margaret raised her swollen red face from her mother's shoulder.

'They gave Mister Lyle a hanging,' she retorted with as much sharpness as her aunt. 'And he's dead!'

'Aye – well, I'll grant you that, since there's no sense in denying it. Now listen—' Mary lifted her niece from Meg's lap in time to avert a fresh outbreak of sobbing and stood her on the floor, kneeling to wipe Margaret's streaming eyes and nose. 'I'm going to wash your face and then we're going to deliver a new hat to Mistress Black's house. Would you like that?'

Margaret nodded, her body still racked by great tearing sobs.

'But you'll have to stop crying first. Mistress Black'll mebbe have a nice bit cake for you if you're a good girl.'

The sobs were replaced, after a massive effort on Margaret's part, by sniffs and hiccups.

'There's my brave lassie,' Mary said briskly.

'Now come with me and we'll clean your wee face.'

Five minutes later, soothed and washed and brushed, Margaret waited for Mary, one thumb jammed comfortingly into her mouth, the other hand stroking the familiar grain of the shop counter. Billy's voice washed over her as he talked to her mother and helped himself to snuff from the big jar that was always kept on the counter-top.

She felt as though she had had a terrible nightmare and had wakened to find herself safely tucked up in her warm, soft bed. Idly she watched the light catch the thick bottom of the snuff jar as it was lifted up.

Then the jar thudded onto its accustomed place again and Billy's large hand with its square-cut nails rested on the scarred wood, just level with her eyes as she stood on tiptoe, her nose pressed against the edge of the counter.

The significance of what she had just witnessed burst on Margaret in a shower of stars. She stood gaping, open-mouthed, then let out a delighted roar. Meg swung round, startled, and Billy inhaled snuff the wrong way and exploded into a huge sneeze. Mary, emerging from the room behind the shop, stopped short with one hand half in and half out of its glove.

Margaret stood behind the counter, her hands white-knuckled on its edge, her blue eyes wide as they peeped over the top.

'I can see!' she crowed. 'I'm not a wee bairn any longer – I can see over the counter!'

'Did you ever see such a change in a lassie? She's forgotten the hanging already,' Meg said with relief when her daughter had skipped out of the shop with Mary.

'Aye.' Billy had his doubts about that, but he didn't voice them. 'You've got a bonny family.'

'Come early tonight and see them all before they go to their beds.' She knew how much children meant to Billy. A big, easy-going man, he had been a cobbler before his wife and three young children were struck down by fever.

Left alone, he had taken to the roads, joining the band of men who peddled their wares from town to town.

'I'd like that. I hear there's been changes in the town since I was last here.'

'Aye.' She folded her hands over her apron, soothed by the everyday comfort of a wee gossip. 'There's always something going on. The new Grammar School's open now, and the flesh market in Moss Row too.'

'And the Council's put a tax on beer and ale, I hear. Bad news travels,' he said wryly.

'The money's needed to deepen the river and put up more new houses, so Peter says.' Meg spoke with all the earnestness and pride of a true citizen. 'You'll have heard that they've made Peter one of the directors of the new Town Hospital? Kirsty says he's hardly ever at home these days. And Colin's as cheery as ever I've seen him.'

Billy's head came up quickly at mention of Colin. 'I heard news of Lizzie Todd last month, up by Dundee,' he said, and a cold hand clutched at Meg's heart.

'What of her?'

'She was living near there with that man of hers until recently. Things haven't been going well for them.'

'She's only got herself to blame!' After more than five years Meg still couldn't think of Lizzie without deep uneasiness. 'You'll not tell Colin?'

The big man shook his greying head. 'It's best left unsaid.'

'Aye.' Meg took up a cloth and rubbed the spotless counter hard. 'That's all over and done with. Best forgotten.'

The town dismissed old Robert Lyle from its memory almost as soon as Jamie, William and Robert stopped smarting from the punishment they received for going to the public execution. Margaret's pain was buried deep, and everyone thought it, too, had been forgotten, although she had bad dreams for the next six months or so.

Winter closed in and Duncan, now Peter's right-hand man, had extra work to handle when his employer took to his bed with a heavy cold that refused to go, but lay on his chest for weeks.

'You might as well admit it, man – the fluff's

got into your lungs. Either that or it's all these meetings you have to attend,' Kirsty hectored. 'I told you, did I not, that you should have stayed home and looked after that bad cough when it started instead of going out till all hours in the chill air. Remember, you're not as young as you used to be.'

'Away with you, woman!' Peter scoffed. But he couldn't disguise the fact that the illness had left him breathless and unable to climb stairs easily.

The cold weather at the end of 1755 took its toll of young and old alike. One of its most disreputable victims, an inmate of the new Poor's Hospital, went carousing in a bothy with cronies one January night then stumbled homewards in a blizzard. He was found the next morning, frozen to death yards from the hospital door.

Mary's benefactress, Mistress MacLeod, succumbed to a severe chill brought on by a charitable visit to the Hospital on a cold wet day.

'She should never have gone out – and her with a cough that's said to have drowned out half the High Church service two days before,' said Mary sadly to Meg.

'What'll become of your wee shop now?' Meg trailed covetous fingers over a fanciful creation on Mary's counter.

'Nothing, for I've already repaid a fair piece of the money to Mistress MacLeod.' Mary looked about her little shop. 'I called on Mister MacLeod to pay my respects, of course, and while I was there we had a wee talk about the rest of it. He's content to take the payments month by month, just as it was when his wife was alive.' Mary's fingers flew among ribbons as she worked on another hat. 'Poor man, he's bad with the rheumatism, and only a parcel of servants to see to him in that big house. He'll miss his wife sorely. I don't know why it's the best of us that get taken every time.'

Spring came at last, and brought with it the realisation of a dream for Meg and Duncan. By the time May brought warm sunny days to replace April's showers, plans for their new house at Townhead had been drawn up, and the house itself was finished in the early spring of 1756.

After the workmen had downed tools for the last time, toasted a job well done, and departed, Meg ran from room to room gazing out of the small windows, peering up chimneys, opening and shutting doors. The children clattered noisily about and Duncan basked in the glow felt by a man of property.

'I told you we'd do it one day, lass.' He caught Meg's hand and drew her to him when they found themselves alone in the kitchen, across the passageway from the loom-shop.

She beamed up at him through tears. 'I never doubted you.'

The memory of a woman with slanted grey eyes came fleetingly to Duncan but he pushed it away.

'I'll not have my own looms yet, of course. But the shop's here and the looms'll come in good time.'

Meg slipped her hand into his and they stood dreaming for a moment before she shook herself and said briskly, 'Time to get back to the shop.'

'Janet can manage fine without you.'

'I'm not so sure, now that new weaver of yours has put stars in her eyes. Young folk in love can be right stupid at times,' Meg shook her head primly, then blushed like a girl when Duncan laughed.

'You're right there. I mind as if it was yesterday the time you got into trouble with your mother for dropping a basket of new collected eggs – all because you saw me passing by in the road!'

'Mary, you can't!' Meg stopped sweeping the hearth and stared up at her sister, her eyes wide with shock.

'And what's the "can't" for, Meg Montgomery? Just because you didn't have a hand in arranging the match, does it follow that I'm not allowed to get wed?'

'But – Mister MacLeod! Mary, he's an old man! Besides—' she floundered, seeking words to express her dismay, 'his wife's not that long in her grave!'

Mary sighed and began to remove her gloves.

'The man's been widowed for more than eighteen months – and he's crippled with the rheumatism and scarcely able to move out of his house half the time. And here's me, back and forth between my shop and his house this past year and more, trying to see to him – for what good are servants when a man's ailing? It's the wisest thing to marry him, then I can see to him properly and save my legs a lot of running.'

'Have you accepted him, then?'

Mary stared. 'What do you mean, accepted him? There was no accepting about it. I just told him plump and plain – if you've any sense in your head, I said, you'll marry me and save me all this to-ing and fro-ing.'

Meg's apron was thrown over her horrified face. 'Have you no shame in you at all? You mean that you proposed marriage to a gentleman twice your age and as rich as a lord? D'you know what they'll be saying about you in the streets?'

'They can say all they like and it'll not stick in my throat,' her sister said calmly. 'His age doesn't come into it, and neither does his money. If he didn't have it he'd be welcome to come and live in my wee room behind the shop. As it is, I'll move into his house and have more room for my work. And don't start that again,' she added ominously as choking sounds came from beneath the apron. 'I'll keep my shop and my independence. Nobody'll be able to say I married Andra MacLeod so that I could be a lady of leisure. Indeed, it's going to be hard work seeing to it that those lazy servants of his earn their keep for a change.'

Meg's flushed face appeared for a moment round the apron.

'D'you want to shame me entirely in this town?' she squawked. 'Rich men's wives don't keep shops!'

'This one will – for no doubt I'll outlive Andra, poor old soul, and I'll need something to keep me occupied in my own old age.'

'Would you not have a word with Duncan first?' Meg appealed.

'What has it to do with him? No, no, Meg, it's all arranged, and a date set. Not that the minister was entirely happy at first, but I soon pointed out that it was a Christian thing I was doing, and he agreed with me – eventually.'

Mary got to her feet. 'And next week I'm taking Andra down to Beith to tell my mother and father.'

'I forgot about them!' Meg moaned. 'Oh, Mary, what are they going to say?'

'Leave them to me. I don't think they'll make half the fuss you have. Anyone would think I was disgracing you, Meg Montgomery. Take my advice and pay no heed to wagging tongues – or tell them to come and wag at me. I'll soon sort them out.' Mary looked round the cosy kitchen as she drew her gloves on again. 'It seems to me, Meg, that the two of us have come a long way since we used to tread the blankets together down on the farm.'

'Mary, are you sure that you're—'

'You'd best see to Thomas,' Mary said from the window. 'The wee scamp's asking to get himself stung, plunging round the bee-skeps waving a stick.' And she escaped in the ensuing domestic panic.

'You're talking as if Mary's going to bring disgrace on us, instead of marrying with one of the most respected men in Paisley,' Duncan argued when he came home that night to be met by an agitated wife.

'But the scandal—!' Meg almost wept.

'Tuts, woman, we both know well enough that she's not after the man for his money, so what does it matter what anyone else says? Even if she was, she's earned it, the way she's tended him since his wife died. There'll be no more weeping over Mary's plans in my house,' he ended firmly, and Meg had to leave matters at that.

Mary married her elderly husband in the Laigh Church, with a gathering in Andrew MacLeod's house afterwards. Andrew was a tall, lean man, stooped and twisted by rheumatism, but retaining some of the good looks he had once had. Quiet and shy, he obviously doted on his vigorous new wife. His home was a big two-storey building on the hill behind the High Street, looking down on the ruined Abbey with the River Cart slipping beneath its walls.

Mary, taking on the role of mistress of the house as though born to it, sat in the parlour dispensing tea for the ladies and something stronger for the men, and supervising the servants with an ease that made Meg and her mother gasp.

The children were less intimidated by the place than their elders, and explored enthusiastically. Margaret's eyes were round when she returned to her mother.

'It's a castle! How many folk live in it?'

'Just Mister—' Meg stopped, blushed, tried again. 'Your new Uncle Andra and your Aunt Mary and the folk who look after them.'

'But this house is too big for them!' Margaret was outraged. 'Half our street could live in it. Why do they need so many rooms?'

Meg hushed her, glancing guiltily round the room. 'Uncle Andra's got a lot of money, so he can afford a big house. Stop your questions, for any favour!'

'But why should rich folk have houses that are too big for them, when—'

'They just do!' She re-fastened Margaret's jacket and tidied her hair. 'Run and find the boys, there's a good lass.'

Margaret did as she was told, but as she scurried along the big dark hall, hung with paintings, a rebellious inner voice that was to be heard many times during her life continued to ask, 'Why should the rich have so much space when the poor have to crowd together in hovels?'

# *Chapter Two*

Mary turned her predecessor's sewing room into a workshop, took on an assistant, and was a devoted wife to Andrew MacLeod. The fact that she now met most of her wealthier customers on a social basis in the evenings made no difference to her business dealings with them during the day.

'But I'll admit, Meg,' she confessed with a dimpling smile, 'that I have a wee chuckle to myself when I go to one of those grand gatherings and see that most of the bonnets in the room were made by my own fingers.'

She also took on the charitable duties expected of the more well-to-do women in the town, fitting them into an over-crowded day without visible effort. The gossips who had predicted that she would play the fine lady and not bother with anything else soon found themselves proved wrong. Busy as she was, Mary involved herself just as much as ever in other people's lives.

It was she who found a replacement for Janet when the girl married a local stonemason and gave up her work in the shop. Mary promptly produced a capable widow with a family to support and talked Colin and Meg into taking the woman on as a shop assistant and letting her have the empty rooms behind the grocer's shop. Then she organised the task of converting the rooms, now used for storage, back into a home.

She swept into the shop dressed in practical working clothes and festooned with cloths and pails. Robert and Thomas, who were unfortunate enough to be there at the time, were despatched to fetch water.

'And go right to the well, d'you hear me? You needn't think you'll take the lazy way out and climb the wall to get to Mistress Pearson's well.'

She handed them each a stoup to carry the water in. 'That bad-tempered old devil of a man of hers can still run, and he'll keep these if he gets the chance. Now then, Meg, tuck your skirts up out of harm's way, for we've a lot of scrubbing to do.'

'It's a bad deed that benefits nobody,' she added as she set to and scrubbed until drops of water flew from her brush. 'You'll not regret taking the widow-woman on, for she's a hard worker and an honest soul. But I think Janet's made a mistake. That new husband of hers is a shiftless creature that broke his first wife's heart.'

Meg sat back on her heels and nodded, brushing a tendril of hair back from her face with one wet fist. 'For once I agree with you.'

'Just because her sweetheart jilted her,' Mary

puffed, 'If you ask me she's gone out and thrown herself at the first man she saw to prove to us all that she doesn't care. I don't know why women have to be so set on marriage! And if you say one word about me proposing to Andra, Meg, I'll empty this bucket of water about your ears, for that's not the same thing at all!'

As time passed it became clear that Peter's bronchitis had become chronic. Duncan took on most of the responsibility for the loom-shop though Peter kept an eye on everything from his big armchair by the kitchen fire.

Duncan was soon trying to persuade him to let one of the looms go over to the manufacture of silk gauze, a new material that was selling well in London. Some of the town's manufacturers were trying it out on their looms, and Duncan saw it as part of Paisley's future.

'Linen isn't going to keep us going for ever,' he argued. 'The town's growing – we need to try new ideas if we want to grow along with it.'

'He's right.' Colin nodded, fingering the sample Duncan had brought in. 'This is a cloth the gentry'll want to buy, father. The weaving trade can't afford to stand still.'

'Humphrey Fulton's contracting weavers to make it for him.' Duncan was referring to another man from Beith, who had become a successful manufacturer. 'He sees a good market for it –

and he knows what he's about. We have to keep up with the times, Peter!'

'Ach, you're new-fangled, both of you,' Peter grumbled, but his eyes were shrewd as he in turn took the material, rubbing it through his fingers. 'Well, go ahead – but if it doesn't pay its way it comes off my loom, mind!'

'Aye, aye, I hear you,' Duncan agreed cheerfully, and went on to prove that silk gauze was a paying innovation.

The restlessness that had led him into the affair with Lizzie was channelled into his work and his plans for the future. He was a man of property, mellowed and content with his life. He rarely thought of Lizzie now; Duncan was one of those people with a talent for closing their minds against memories that shamed or angered them. Not even the sight of William reminded him of that dark secret in his past. The boy and Colin were devoted to each other, and Duncan always thought of the youngster as Colin's son.

When he was summoned to Mary's shop late one afternoon it didn't occur to him that there might be something wrong. He hovered in the doorway, waiting until her customer had gone, uneasy in this feminine haven. When the woman left, he stepped out into the street to let her by, and re-entered the doorway to see his sister-in-law whisk a cloak about her shoulders.

'I'll not be long,' she told her assistant, and hurried Duncan back onto the footpath.

'What fine new idea have you got in your head now?' he asked indulgently.

'None, as yet – but I wish I had, for it's going to take brains to get us out of this pickle,' Mary said crisply. 'I was at the Poor's Hospital two hours since, and I met a woman there who claims to be Colin Todd's wife.'

'Lizzie?' Duncan stopped short and she almost bumped into him. A hand caught at his heart and began to squeeze it painfully. He felt the colour ebb from his face. 'You're certain?'

Irritation touched her voice. 'I spoke to her. She told me enough to make me believe her, for all that I've never set eyes on the woman myself. In fact, she told me more than I'd like my poor sister to hear, Duncan Montgomery!'

A red mist clouded Duncan's vision and he wondered if he was going to succumb to apoplexy. 'Oh God! Dear God!'

'Well might you call on Him for help – though I doubt if it'll do you a lot of good.' His sister-in-law's eyes raked his face. 'No need to ask if she was telling the truth or just trying to make mischief between you and Meg. The guilt's written on your face for anyone to see. Duncan, Duncan – who'd have ever thought you'd be such a fool!'

'What does she want?' he asked, sick with apprehension, his thoughts filled with Meg and the need to keep this from her.

'She has it in mind to take back her old position as Colin's wife. She arrived late last night, it seems, with nothing but the rags on her back. She's in a sorry state. Lucky for you she went to the Hospital instead of going straight to Peter's house.' Mary wagged her bonneted head. 'A right hornet's nest she'll stir up if she gets her way. But I got her to promise that she'd stay where she was for the moment – if I bring you to see her.'

'The bitch!'

'I told her that Peter's ailing and the shock of seeing her's like to kill him. I said nothing more. Not a word about Colin or the laddie. Not that she asked about them – just about you. I don't care how you do it, Duncan, but you'll have to get that woman away from Paisley before Colin finds out about her.'

The Poor's Hospital was a large building not far from Mary's shop. Homeless and penniless townsfolk found refuge within its walls; the children were schooled, the women set to wash and cook and keep the place clean, and work was found for the men and the older children whenever possible. Duncan shivered as he followed Mary through its big doors and across the hall, past faces blank with misery and despair.

The Mistress greeted them in a small bare room on the ground floor. She raised an eyebrow when Mary asked to see Lizzie, but said nothing. Fortunately, she was a comparative stranger in the town, and it didn't occur to her to connect the new

106

inmate, who gave her name as Lizzie Todd, with the prosperous and respectable Paisley family of that name.

Duncan paced the small room, four steps one way, four steps the other, while he waited. He had thought that Lizzie was out of his life for ever, had never dreamed that after all this time she would return to haunt him like a malignant ghost.

Mary sat motionless on a hard upright chair, watching him but keeping her own council.

'You're thinking of the terrible thing I did, betraying Meg,' he blurted out at last.

'Men can do awful daft things. I take it that she never knew the truth of it?'

He shook his head. 'And she never will, supposing I've to—' He broke off as the door opened, the colour leaving his face then rushing back as he stared at the woman standing before him.

Lizzie came into the room slowly, eyes downcast and hands clasped in the same pose she used to adopt when standing behind the shop counter. Then she looked up and he saw that her once pretty face was gaunt, her hair lifeless and threaded with grey, her slanted eyes set deep in shadowy sockets. She was a cruel parody of the girl who had lain beneath him among the little white flowers on the moors. But her boldness, as she looked him up and down, was unchanged.

'Well, Duncan Montgomery? You're a welcome sight.'

'It's you right enough, Lizzie. I never thought to set eyes on you again.'

'Oh? So it was good riddance to bad rubbish, was it?' Her laugh was harsh, mocking. 'Are you not glad to see me after all those years?'

'I never wished to look on you again, Lizzie – and well you know it!'

'Mebbe – and mebbe not.' She twitched a shoulder in a faintly coquettish gesture he remembered. It was as though some ragged crone was slavishly copying the mannerisms that had belonged to the young, vivid Lizzie. It was grotesque, and Duncan's skin crawled.

'I hear Peter's unwell.' Neither of them paid any attention to Mary, who stayed where she was, silent for once, watching this reunion of former lovers with bright, unblinking eyes.

'He is, and you'll do him no good at all by turning up again. Besides, Kirsty would scratch your eyes out of your head for what you did to Colin and the bairn.'

Her tongue flickered over cracked lips. 'I'm still Colin's wife.'

'Stay away from him, Lizzie! He's happy now – he's more of a man than you ever let him be!'

'Since he's become a man, let him speak for himself!' she flared at him. 'And there's my son. I have a right to see him, have I not?'

A churning, sick feeling stirred in Duncan's belly. 'You cared nothing for him when he was little and helpless. Why should you see him now?'

'Because he's nearing an age when he can go out and work for his own keep.' Mary spoke for the first time, and Lizzie whirled on her with a movement full of grace despite the rags she wore.

'I have the right to take him away with me if I choose!'

'You have no rights!' Duncan's voice was a low hiss. 'Colin raised that boy, not you. He's the one to say what becomes of William.'

Lizzie's teeth, discoloured and broken, showed in a sneer. 'So he thinks. Mebbe it's time he learned that it's you and me that have the say in the lad's future, not him. After all, it was you and me that made William, Duncan!'

Her shoulders were brittle beneath his hands. Even in his anger he was careful not to grip her too tightly, aware that he could so easily crush and snap those fragile bones beneath his fingers. Instead, he shook her hard.

'You ever say that again to a living soul, and by God, Lizzie Todd, I'll spill your blood! If you try to see Peter or Colin or the boy, I'll take you out onto the moors where it all started and wring your neck! Who's to care if you're found lying in a burn one morning?'

She swayed within his grip, her eyes wide and bright, her open mouth uttering little whimpering sounds. But she didn't try to break his hold on her. It was Mary who caught at his wrists and tore him away from the other woman.

'For any favour, Duncan, d'you want to get yourself hanged?'

He let go and Lizzie almost fell. She recovered her balance by catching at the back of a chair, the faint little enigmatic smile he remembered playing round her thin mouth.

At the sight of it, and the gleam in her knowing grey eyes, despair choked Duncan. She had won. Now he must pay for the years of foolish complacency. If the two women hadn't been there he might have sunk down on the floor and given way to tears.

'Why don't you go ahead, Duncan?' Lizzie asked, her voice suddenly young and sensuous, with a provocative lilt to it. 'Why don't you put me out of my misery and get yourself hanged? I'm not the only one who betrayed folk, am I? You're no better than I am, if the truth be known!'

'God damn you, Lizzie Todd!'

'He's done that already.'

'Lizzie, what would you take to keep your mouth shut and leave Paisley?' Mary asked briskly, and the other woman laughed.

'You'll not get me away as easy as that. If it was money I wanted, d'you not think I'd have asked for it long since?' Lizzie mocked. 'It's been a long lonely road for me. I want companionship. I want to be cared for. I want Colin – or the boy – or you, Duncan. It's up to you to decide which it's to be.'

If Mary hadn't stood her ground between them

110

he would have killed Lizzie there and then and be damned to the consequences. Instead, he stood helplessly by, fists knotting and unknotting, while Mary forced a reluctant promise from Lizzie to keep her mouth shut and stay where she was until the next morning. Then Duncan was hustled out into the street where he gulped the fresh evening air in.

'She's safe until the morning, and we've got time to think about what's to be done. Say nothing and do nothing until you see me again,' Mary ordered. 'There has to be a way out of this without breaking innocent hearts.'

'You heard her – you saw her! The woman's evil! She's hell bent on destroying lives the way hers has been destroyed.' He ran a big hand over his face. 'I'll have to go with her, out of the town, then—'

'Leave her body in a ditch and end up swinging from a rope? You've not got the sense to escape a hanging,' his sister-in-law said scathingly. 'Listen to me – I'll visit the woman again first thing in the morning, and it's my guess that by then she'll be willing to take enough money to keep her for a while and get out of the town. Away home, Duncan Montgomery, and not a word of this to Meg. Come along to the shop first thing tomorrow and we'll see what can be done. Go on, now!'

He went, shambling along the street instead of walking with his usual confident gait. Watching him, Mary sighed and shook her head.

\* \* \*

Duncan couldn't face Meg right away. He wandered into a howff near the Cross and sat alone in a corner with only a jug of ale for company. By the time he was accosted by a well-known voice the level of the jug had lowered considerably and he was finding it hard to focus. He peered blearily up at Matt Todd through the howff's smoky atmosphere.

The soldier lowered his big frame onto a stool at the other side of the table. 'Everyone's round at our house having a grand wee gathering. I told Meg I'd look for you.' He winked. 'She's none too pleased because you never came home from your loom.'

Duncan tried to say something but the words came out as a slurred mumble.

'By God, she'll have something to say when she sees you like this—' Then Matt took a closer look and his expression changed. 'Come to think of it, I've never seen you in such a state myself. What's amiss, man?'

Duncan couldn't keep his misery and worry to himself for a moment longer. His tongue seemed to start wagging of its own accord while one part of his brain, the sober part, stood by, unable to stop the flow of words.

As Matt heard him out one expression after another moved across his face, but Duncan was too steeped in his own misery to notice the other's reaction.

'What in God's name am I to do?' he finished wretchedly. 'How am I to tell Meg?'

112

'Listen to me—' Matt leaned across the table, his voice low and urgent. 'You're in no fit state to do anything tonight. Go on home and I'll see to Lizzie for you.'

'But I must tell Meg before—'

'You tell Meg and I swear I'll give you a hiding from one end of the town to the other! Do as Mary says and hold your tongue until you see her tomorrow. Come on, I'll help you on your way.'

Duncan shook his head. 'I can – I can manage to walk to my own door,' he said with dignity, heaving himself to his feet. Then he clutched at the table as his knees sagged.

Matt dragged him upright again and half carried him outside, where the fresh air set Duncan's head reeling. With some difficulty the two of them made their way to Townhead, and Duncan was snoring loudly almost as soon as Matt dropped him into his bed.

The soldier looked down at him thoughtfully. 'Man, Meg'll go berserk when she sees you!' he murmured, then let himself out of the house again.

It was still only mid-evening when he presented himself at the Hospital and asked for Lizzie. When she found him waiting for her in the little ground-floor room she stopped abruptly in the doorway, her Eastern eyes widening.

'So – you're home, are you?'

'Aye. You didn't think to see me, did you, Lizzie?'

She smiled faintly. 'No more than you thought to see me. I'm glad you came—' she looked about the room and the smile deepened mockingly '—calling on me.'

'Do you have to stay here?' The place depressed him, made him feel shut in.

'We can go out, unless it shames you to be seen with me.'

He ignored the teasing lilt in her voice. 'I know of a place where we could talk in peace.'

She shrugged, then fetched a worn cloak and they went out into the darkening streets together. Silently he led her to a tenement building by the river and she waited by his side as he paid the landlady for the use of a small room. He left Lizzie there and went out to buy some ale. When he returned she had managed to light the fire and was huddled beside it, fingers spread out to the flames.

'It's cosy in here.' She reached for a mug with a work-roughened hand and drank greedily.

'Duncan tells me you want to see Colin.'

Lizzie tossed her head. 'I'm still his wife.'

'You're no wife to him, for all the church service you went through together. You gave up the right to call yourself wife the day you walked out on him – a helpless cripple! It damned near killed him, do you know that?'

She smiled, her lips wet with ale. 'Did it? So we both nearly killed him, didn't we, Matt?'

The force of the blow threw her off her chair.

She sprawled on the floor, one hand to her face, staring at him. He stood where he was, making no move to help her, and at last she got up and poured out more drink to replace the ale that had spilled.

'D'you think I'm not used to that sort of treatment? It makes no difference, Matt,' she said vindictively. 'You and that horse race took my man from me, and I couldn't settle after that. I'm not the sort of woman who could love a cripple.'

'Because you've never cared about anyone but yourself, you evil bitch!'

Lizzie's eyes flared, then dulled. 'Think that if you want.'

'What else is there to think? First you tried to tempt me, then you fastened on poor Duncan. You'll not cause any more mischief in this town, Lizzie. Leave them alone!'

She laughed, emboldened by the warmth of the drink in her belly. 'What can you do to stop me?'

'You're not dealing with Colin and Duncan now,' he said quietly. 'I'm not a gentleman – so be warned.'

She spat a sulky curse at him, drained the mug and made for the door. He reached it before her.

'Get out of my way, Matt Todd!'

'No, Lizzie!' He grabbed her arm, swung her bodily away from the door and against the damp wall. 'I've had a debt to settle with Colin since the Silver Bells race and now's my chance to pay it. If you try to see him, or get word to him that you're in Paisley, I'll kill you, Lizzie.'

'You're the second to make that threat today.' Her voice was scornful, but a tensing of her body and a sudden heat in her smoky eyes told him that she was keenly aware of his nearness as he held her against the wall.

'I could scream for help.'

It was his turn to mock. 'Lassie, in this building, who'd pay any heed to you? The folk who live here have no wish to call the militiamen's attention to their doings. They know when to turn a deaf ear.'

He was right. In the ramshackle hovels by the river pimps and prostitutes and thieves plied their trades in safety. Nobody would pay attention to a woman's screams, and Lizzie knew it. She let herself go limp and he caught her as she slipped down the wall, holding her to him with an arm about her waist. She tried to push away from him, then suddenly her clawed hands were in his hair, her thin body pressed against him with an animal urgency.

'Matt! Oh, Matt—' she said breathlessly. 'Before Colin, and all the time I was married to him it was you. It was always you I wanted, Matt!'

'Damn you!' said Matt, and released her. She held on fiercely, wrapping her arms about him, pressing herself against him.

'Kill me, if that's what you want to do! Kill me and get it over with! I'd as soon die at your hand as live without you!'

He gripped her arms and she gasped as his fingers bit deep. He looked at the gaunt face just below his, and was suddenly, painfully reminded of the lovely, tantalising girl he had courted long ago, the girl he had left behind when he joined the Army.

There was a tense pause, then 'Will I never be free of you, you Jezebel!' groaned Matt, and dragged her down onto the floor with him.

Their coupling was vicious, an act of hate instead of an act of love. On Lizzie's side there was a deep thirst to be quenched, and revenge for the bitterness of his rejection years before: on Matt's there was all the resentment man had ever felt against woman's ability to tempt and destroy.

Daylight was trying to force its way through the grimy little window before the two of them fell away from each other and slept, exhausted, on the rough wooden planks.

# Chapter Three

WHEN LIZZIE OPENED HER EYES the fire was a pile of cooling ashes and Matt was dressing quickly and silently.

'Where are you going?' She raised herself on one elbow, pain stabbing through her bruised body.

'Out of this place.'

'Take me with you—' She began to scramble to her feet. 'I'll follow the regiment – I don't care where – I'd be true to you, Matt, only you—'

But he shook his head vehemently. 'I'd as soon walk with Old Nick himself as with you. And you'd best mind what I told you – keep away from my brother and from the Montgomerys!'

She caught at his sleeve. 'Matt, don't go!'

His face was bleak as he looked down at her. Overnight, new lines had chiselled themselves downwards from the corners of his mouth. 'You wanted me to lie with you when your own man was helpless. You left him and went off with someone else. You're a whore, Lizzie, and last night I used you as a whore. I used you because I wanted to show you what you are. And if you go near Colin or anyone else in Paisley I'll see to it that they all know what happened between us in this room.' There was triumph mingled with contempt in the look he gave her. 'Colin might have taken you back yesterday – but now he'd not dirty his hands on you!'

Without realising what she was doing she reached up with one broken-nailed hand and drew her torn, dirty gown about her throat in a defensive, feminine gesture. 'That's why you brought me here?'

'Just that. D'you think it gave me pleasure to touch you?' he asked bitterly. 'I felt sick! But I had to do it for Colin's sake.'

Her mouth writhed, cursed him, spat on him. He dug into his pocket and tossed some coins on the floor at her feet.

'I'm a generous man – I pay for favours received.'

Silenced, her venom spent for the moment, she gathered the money then straightened again, her eyes fixed on his face. He hesitated at the door, then stripped his jacket off and tossed it at her.

'It's cold outside,' he said, and went out.

The chill morning air struck through Matt's shirt sleeves as he strode away from the building without a backward glance. Deep in his body a familiar pain gnawed. It was a hunger that had wakened in him when he first began walking out with Lizzie all those years ago, a wanting that only her sensuous, insatiable body could ease. But the military way of life had also demanded his attention, and it had won.

During all the time Lizzie was his brother's wife Matt had subdued his desire. Now, when it should have been sated, it burned within him. No other woman had ever been able to rouse him as Lizzie could. Even now, dirty and half-starved as she was, he wanted her. But because she was his brother's wife, and because of what she had done to Colin, he must turn away from her and suffer his own torment in silence.

He hunched his shoulders and walked to his father's house, his eyes fixed on the ground as he went.

By the time Mary called at the Hospital Lizzie was back.

'Now then – I've been thinking about you, Lizzie, and it seems to me that you'd be better taking charge of your own life than hanging onto some man's coat-tails—' the milliner began briskly, and was interrupted.

'You can forget about the sermon, Mistress MacLeod.' Lizzie sneered the name. 'I've decided that I've no more wish to live among the self-righteous mealy-mouthed Paisley folk than I had before.'

Mary gaped, taken aback for once by the sudden change in Lizzie, then noticed the good warm jacket, several sizes too large, about the other woman's shoulders.

'I've seen that before.'

Lizzie gathered it protectively about her. 'It's mine!'

'Oh aye?' Mary asked dryly, then got down to business. 'You've decided to go back to the man you went away with the last time?'

'Him?' Lizzie spat out a curse. 'I'd die before I'd go back to him!'

'So you've finally found the way of the world? Women are daft if they let their happiness depend on a man.'

'From what I've heard, you managed to find a prize for yourself.'

'Andra's a good husband.' Mary refused to be baited. 'But I had my independence long before we wed, and I can look out for myself if need be. Any woman with her head fastened on properly can do the same. Look at the way you worked in the shop – you could turn your hand to shop-keeping again, could you not?'

'If I had to,' Lizzie admitted grudgingly, her eyes suspicious.

'Tuts, it's not a case of having to, it's a case of wanting to. You've no need of Colin or William to buy your bread for you, and you know that fine. You can earn your own living.'

'With nothing to my name but these?' Lizzie indicated the clothes she wore.

'You've got two good hands, and a brain of your own. I started my business with the help of Andra's first wife, and with a lot of hard work on my own

121

account. If you're willing to put in the work I'd mebbe be prepared to put up some money – as a loan, just.'

It was Lizzie's turn to gape. 'And what's to stop me making off with your precious money?'

'I'd set the militia after you if you did. But I doubt if you'd be that daft. Listen to me – Andra has good business friends in Dumfries. If I was to give you a letter of introduction to them, and some decent clothes and money to get you there and give you a start, you could take a wee shop and set up in business for yourself. Mind you, I'd be looking for my money back. But if you put your mind to it there's no reason why you shouldn't pay off the debt in a few years, the same as I did myself.'

It was a gamble, but during the long night, while Lizzie and Matt writhed together on the floor of the dingy room by the river, Mary had carefully thought over everything she had ever heard about Colin's wife, and had gradually uncovered a pattern similar to her own nature.

True, Lizzie had been selfish and cruel, but Mary recognised her intelligence and determination, and felt that it was high time those qualities were appealed to.

She waited patiently as doubt, suspicion and bewilderment chased each other across Lizzie's drawn face.

'You're willing to risk a lot just to buy safety for Colin and your sister's man.'

'I'm not overly concerned with them,' Mary

scoffed. 'I'm thinking of what's best for everyone, including you, for you'll not let anyone here rest easy until you're settled, Lizzie. If you agree to my proposition we'll go right now to my house and I'll give you a decent breakfast. Then we'll go to Glasgow to buy some clothes and get a legal acquaintance of mine to make out a proper business agreement between us. But if you're set on going to hell in your own way—' Mary rose and went to the door – 'I'll bid you good day right now.'

She put a hand on the latch.

'Wait—' Lizzie said from behind her. 'I'll come with you.'

'I knew you were a woman with a good head on your shoulders,' said Mary, and led the way out of the little room.

Duncan's head pounded from the night's drinking and from the tongue-lashing Meg had given him when he finally woke, wincing as daylight splintered into his eyes. Although he hazily remembered promising to see Mary before doing anything else, he hurried along to the Hospital as soon as he could escape from Meg.

His blood ran cold when he discovered that Lizzie had gone. He recalled meeting Matt the night before and telling him about Lizzie and her threats. What if the soldier had killed her to protect his brother?

With visions of Lizzie floating in the River Cart

passing through his befuddled mind Duncan ran to Mary's house. She came into the entrance hall to talk to him, closing the parlour door carefully behind her.

'Get back to your loom and hold your tongue,' she ordered before he could speak. 'The matter's settled and there's no need for you to stay here.'

'But—'

Mary almost pushed him out into the street. 'Duncan, will you go away? Lizzie and me are coming to an arrangement. She'll be out of Paisley shortly, when she's broken her fast.'

'You mean she's here?' he yelped, suddenly realising why the parlour door had been closed so firmly behind Mary.

'Aye, she's here. Now – you can either stay and ruin all my hard work or you can get back to your loom and thank the Lord you've got a friend like me with all her wits about her. I'll tell you about it when I've got the time.' And she shut the door with a decisive slam.

Totally confused, but weak with relief, he slunk back down the hill to the loom-shop. He had to wait until late in the afternoon before Mary came to the High Street house and gave him a brief outline of her talk with Lizzie, ending with, 'So she's away, fed and clothed and looking more like her old self already, the poor soul.'

'It's not right that you should have to put your hand in your pocket on my behalf. I've some money put by that Meg knows nothing about—'

'Tuts, I didn't just do it for you! There's Colin to think of, and Lizzie herself. And if you're able to put anything by without my sister's knowledge then she's failing in her proper duties,' Mary said dryly. 'Don't you go offering me a penny of it or I'll feel bound to tell her you've got it.'

She went to the door, paused, and returned. 'Duncan – you didn't go back to the Hospital last night to talk to Lizzie on your own, did you?'

'D'you think I could have faced her again? No, I got as drunk as a lord and Matt had to help me home,' he admitted, embarrassed.

'Matt?' Her voice sharpened. 'Did you tell him?'

Duncan's shame deepened. 'As I mind it, I did. But you've no need to be feared of Matt. He'd never speak a word of this to Colin or anyone else.'

Mary's face was suddenly blank. 'I'm sure you're right. See that wee bit of money you were bragging about a minute since? Mebbe you should use it to buy Matt a new jacket. Something tells me he could do with one,' she said, and opened the door.

'Eh? Jacket?' Duncan spluttered, but Mary had gone.

'Women!' he thought. He'd never understand them, especially his wife's sister.

Duncan's prediction that silk gauze would become an important industry in Paisley came true, but Peter Todd only lived to see the first hint of it. One April night in 1760 he died in his sleep, and was laid to rest in the family plot beside his first wife and his infant son.

Colin was a rock for Kirsty to lean on in the first grief of widowhood. Often, after the children were in bed at night, she took to sitting in the downstairs room with her step-son, soothed and comforted by the calm presence that reminded her so much of Peter.

Matt was like a lost soul the first time he came home after his father's death.

'It's as though the heart's gone out of the town,' he told Meg miserably. 'Everywhere I look I expect to see him. But there's nothing – nothing.'

Duncan, much as he yearned to get looms into his own shop, agreed to stop on and run the Todds' weaving shop for Kirsty. Jamie had finished school and had become an apprentice at the looms, though Duncan confided to Meg that the boy wasn't cut out for the work.

'He's more like Matt than anyone. He's restless. He only started his apprenticeship to please Peter. Mind you, I think he'll see it through for Kirsty's sake, but he'll likely be off as soon as he can.'

'Kirsty's got more sense than to hold him against his will, surely?'

There was no reply.

'Duncan!' She tweaked a corner of the newspaper clutched in his fists. 'Come out from behind that paper and let me have a proper talk with you! You've surely heard all the news already?'

The Paisley men usually stopped work and got

together to read the paper as soon as it went on sale. Items from all over the globe interested them deeply; in Paisley they knew more about the world's affairs than most working folk in Britain.

'I like to go over it again when I'm on my own.'

Meg laid her sewing down in her lap. 'Do you indeed? And are you not glad I bullied you into learning how to read all those years ago? Where would you be without me, tell me that?'

'Aye, I suppose I didn't get a bad bargain the day I picked you,' he said casually, then yelled as the paper was whipped out of his hands by his exasperated wife.

Paisley became the acknowledged centre of silk gauze manufacture. The town's weavers could match anyone when it came to texture, quality and cost, and by the end of the year it was quite common for the local people to hear English voices in their streets as more and more London merchants sent representatives north to open up new branches. There was work for all, and the looms in the surrounding villages were pressed into service for the Paisley manufacturers.

Over the next two years Duncan at last got his own looms installed. For Kirsty's sake, he continued to spend most of his working day in the Todds' shop, employing a reliable weaver to supervise the looms in his own shop.

Robert and William both put in a year at the new

Grammar School, then were apprenticed, Robert to a weaver, William to a cobbler. Margaret and Thomas were attending the English School, where they learned to read and write, and were taught grammar and geography.

Thomas, who in his mother's words 'soaked up learning like a cloth in a bucket of water', found his schooling quite inadequate, and persuaded his father to let him have extra tuition from Colin.

Although the space left by Peter's death was never quite filled they all adjusted, and life continued smoothly.

'We're like a sack of barley,' Margaret said to William. 'Poke your finger in it – if my mother isn't looking – and when you take your hand away the grain flows back into the space as though it had never been there at all. We do that. We smooth over things and it's all the same again. Well, almost.'

'Except that my grandfather wasn't a finger in a sack of barley,' he said stiffly, then relented. 'But I know what you mean.'

She smiled at him. William was different from the others. He never laughed at her high-flown ideas or belittled her. She slid her hand into his and squeezed his fingers affectionately.

The sense of injustice she had first known when she demanded of her mother at Mary's wedding, 'Why do rich people have houses that are too big for them?', strengthened as she grew older.

Margaret could never accept a system that decreed that some folk lived in poverty while others enjoyed wealth, and as she grew into her teens she was often to be found at the Town Hospital in Sneddon Street, taking the inmates scraps of food saved from her own meals or warm clothing which she and her brothers had outgrown. Her parents approved of her sense of responsibility towards others, but they had to draw the line when her enthusiasm reached the stage where both shop and house were being raided regularly.

'Colin'll be wondering what's happening to his profits,' Meg protested.

'And if much more goes from this house you'd be as well to move us all to the Hospital so that we can enjoy our own possessions,' Robert added scathingly. So Margaret had to rein her generous nature in a little, though she continued to beg and coax unwanted items from all her friends. Margaret always knew of some poor soul in need.

When one of the young hospital inmates was expelled for giving birth to a bastard child, it was Margaret who fought on her behalf, storming into the building to confront the Hospital Mistress and Master.

'I found Jenny in the street, crouched against the side of a house!' she accused them, while the shamed girl wilted beside her, clutching her baby. 'You can't just put her out like that. Where's she supposed to go? How's she to care for her baby?'

'The lassie's sinned in the eyes of the Lord and the community. Forbye, she tried to hide the truth from us. It's a Hospital rule that she can't stay here!' the Master said coolly. 'You've got a good heart, child, but it's a trifle misguided.'

The baby began to wail and Jenny's white, tear-streaked face crumpled. But Margaret was made of stronger stuff.

'Come on, Jenny—' she put an arm about the girl and marched to the door. 'We'll go to where folk care about other folk!'

Outside the big door she hesitated, baffled. A light patter of rain was falling, and Jenny did her best to pull a tattered shawl over the baby's head.

'We'll go to see my Aunt Mary,' Margaret decided, and the two of them made for the milliner's shop and a lukewarm reception.

'There's times when you vex me sorely, Margaret!' her aunt scolded. 'I might have had some lady in here buying a hat!' She covered her ears as the hungry baby's wailing filled the little shop.

'All the better—' said her unrepentant niece. 'The lady might have had a conscience and taken Jenny in. Since there's nobody here but you, Aunt Mary—?' She paused hopefully.

'You needn't think of my house, for Andra's not at all well at the moment and I'd lose the servants if I walked in with a crying bairn. Why not bother your own mother instead of me?'

'Because my father warned me the last time that there was to be no more of it, and it's too soon to change his mind. Please?' Margaret beseeched her.

Mary sighed and shook her head. 'What am I to do with you, girl?'

'It's what you're going to do with Jenny that matters,' Margaret rapped back at her.

'Well – Mistress Brown's a decent widow woman who's fond enough of bairns, and she could probably do with a hand in her wee shop—' said Mary, and so a refuge was found for Jenny and her child.

Not content with her success, Margaret dared to face one of the Hospital directors in the street and take up the matter with him. The shocked man called on Duncan to complain about his daughter's impertinence.

'If we were all as irresponsible and as soft-hearted as your daughter the Hospital would end up as a refuge for all the feckless poor in the town!' he protested.

Duncan eyed him thoughtfully. 'Is that not what it was built for? She's mebbe hasty at times, and for that I apologise to you. But a wee bit compassion for a young mother and her blameless child isn't entirely out of place, surely.'

The director's face flamed. 'It seems that you have no notion of the right way to care for paupers!'

'Mebbe not,' Duncan said shortly, suddenly sickened by the man's manner. 'I only know how to care for folk – and it's the same with my daughter. Now, sir, if you've said your piece, I've work to do—' and he pressed his foot firmly on the treadle and set the loom into noisy action, turning his broad back on the visitor.

When he went home later he soundly rebuked Margaret for her impudence towards a member of the Hospital Board.

'I wasn't impertinent – I asked him in a civil manner how he'd feel if his own daughter had fallen like poor Jenny and was in need of compassion,' she protested.

'Mercy!' Meg's apron flapped over her reddening face. 'Margaret, how could you speak to a respectable gentleman in that fashion?'

'See here, Margaret, if you're going to defend folk you'll have to learn to do it with a smile and a soft word.' Duncan said patiently. 'That way you'll get more out of others without them realising it.'

He was soon to regret his words, for she took them to heart from that day on and redoubled her efforts to help others. When she left shool she worked in the shop and helped Meg in the house. She was a deft spinner, and as thread was sorely needed to fill the eight looms under Duncan's care she persuaded him to employ some of the Hospital women as spinners.

'She's a nuisance at times, but apart from that,' said Mary smugly, 'the girl's got a lot of my nature in her.'

Duncan sighed and nodded.

'That's what worries me,' he said – but he said it very quietly, so that his sister-in-law couldn't hear him.

\*　　\*　　\*

Margaret bustled down the length of the hospital sick-room, her blue eyes scanning each bed as she passed. She stopped here and there, to pull a blanket round someone's shoulders, to soothe a fretful child, to hold a cup of water to dry lips.

She reached the end of the room and was about to turn back to the door when her attention was caught by a man tossing in a corner bed.

'Billy? Is it you, Billy?'

She approached the cot cautiously, wondering if she was only imagining a resemblance between the big, cheerful chapman who visited her parents each time he was in Paisley and the flushed, delirious creature twisting and turning between coarse grey sheets.

The sick man looked at her without any recognition for a moment, then his glazed eyes managed to focus and his lips twisted into a faint smile.

'Wee Maggie Montgomery! Lassie, it's good to see a friendly face—' His voice was harsh with fever. 'Would – would you fetch some water? I could drink the Cart dry if I just had the energy to crawl to it.'

The jug by his cot was empty. Margaret sped out of the room and was back in no time with water, then she supported Billy's shoulders while he drank greedily. Her hands felt scorched by the heat from his big body. When he had slaked his thirst she helped him to lie back on the mattress.

'What brought you to this place?'

Billy's head moved fretfully from side to side. 'Just a foolish chill that wouldn't leave me. A few days' rest and I'll be right again.'

Margaret looked about the cheerless room, listened to the cries and moans of the sick. 'This is no place for a man who wants to recover.'

'Where else would I go? No use staying at my usual lodgings if I can't fend for myself. All I need's a bed and shelter till the fever breaks—'

A fit of harsh coughing tore at his chest and Margaret took a linen square from her pocket and wiped the sweat from his face. Then she waited patiently while he struggled to get his breath back.

'So now it's you tending to me?' he said hoarsely when he could speak again. 'The years go by too fast. Mind that day I found you down at the Cross, out of your mind with fear, and I carried you back to the shop on my shoulders? Remember it, Maggie? The day your brother took you to see that old man's hanging.'

'I remember.' It had been buried deep in her mind, only surfacing occasionally in nightmares. She forced her mind to reject memories of the sight she had seen at the Cross that day, and concentrated instead on the kindness shown to her by the man lying in the cot. 'I remember, Billy,' she said gently.

'By God, you near burst my ears with the noise you were making.' He managed a faint chuckle. 'I wish my lungs – were as good as – yours were that day—'

His eyes closed and his voice died away. Margaret stared down at him, troubled.

When she left the Hospital William was waiting for her outside, as he often did. She poured out Billy's story as the two of them walked through the busy streets, ending with 'I think he's awful sick, William!'

'I'll ask Aunt Kirsty to visit him tomorrow. She'll know what's best for him.'

'Yes – do that,' she said with relief, smiling up at him as they stopped outside her parents' door. Margaret was quite tall but William was a good head taller, lean and lithe and always dependable. 'He looks awful sick.'

He had an attractive, crooked grin that lit up his grey eyes. 'Don't fret yourself, just leave things to her. Will you go walking on the braes with me tomorrow?'

'Come to the shop when you're finished work, and if I can be spared I'll go. But don't be hammering any more fingers, or your work'll never get done!' She indicated his left hand with its bandaged index finger. He was learning his trade the hard way, and the number of times he arrived home with bruised fingers made him the butt of everyone's jokes.

The grin widened. 'Jamie says it's because I'm a dreamer. He says I'm handless.'

'You will be if you go on like that,' Margaret told him, and slipped into the house.

'Out with William Todd again?' Robert greeted

her as she hurried in. Thomas sniggered, then turned it into a cough as he met his mother's eye.

Margaret looked down her nose at her brothers. 'I was at the Hospital, as you well know. William walked home with me.'

'He always seems to walk home with you,' Robert scoffed. 'I'll wager he asked you to go up the braes with him – and you know what that means.'

Margaret flushed scarlet, and this time Thomas couldn't disguise his snigger. The braes beyond the town were popular with courting couples.

'You've got a bad mind, Robert Montgomery!'

'That's enough, the lot of you!' Meg ordered as her husband came in. 'Sit at the table and mind your manners!'

Later that night, when Meg and Duncan were getting ready for bed, she said thoughtfully, 'He's a nice lad, William Todd.'

'He's civil enough,' Duncan agreed.

'Margaret could do worse than marry with a decent young man like him.'

Duncan stopped in the act of taking his shirt off, his back to her. After a pause he said carefully, 'What nonsense is this you're talking now, woman?'

'It's not nonsense! They've always been fond of each other, William and Margaret – and it wouldn't be the first time childhood friends wed.'

'Are you serious?'

'You'd have noticed it for yourself if you'd taken the trouble to look.' Meg said with unfair scorn, for she herself had only just begun to wonder about a future romance between the young people.

'You're letting your thoughts run away with you!' Duncan said vehemently, and rolled into bed.

'Are you so old that you've forgotten what it's like to have an eye for a bonny lass?' she teased, but he hunched himself up, turning away from her.

'Margaret's too young for that sort of thing!'

'I didn't mean they were crying the banns already. There's plenty of time – but she's old enough to start thinking of her future.'

'Then she can look elsewhere, for I'll not have her throwing herself away on the likes of William Todd!'

'Duncan! He's an upright, honest lad who comes of fine stock!'

'He's not the right one for our Margaret!' His voice was muffled.

'But—'

'For God's sake will you blow the lamp out and get to sleep!' he barked at her. 'I've got work to do in the morning, and no time to lie here and listen to your nonsense!'

Furious, she put the lamp out and thumped down onto the mattress with her back to him. She was soon asleep, but Duncan lay staring into the darkness, mortally afraid, not only for Meg and himself, but for his daughter. When dawn's grey fingers probed into the room and Meg stirred beside him he had only slept fitfully, and had been plagued by bad dreams.

Swinging his feet to the cold floor, rubbing eyes that felt as though they were filled with dry grit, he swore to himself that from now on he would keep an eye on Margaret. And if necessary he would act to put a stop to her growing friendship with William Todd before things went too far.

# Chapter Four

BILLY CARMICHAEL'S EYES LIT UP when Kirsty arrived at his bedside on the following morning.

'It's good of you to come and see me, lass.'

Her eyes scanned his fever-ravaged face. 'I'm doing more than that,' she said flatly. 'I'm going away right now to arrange for a cart, then I'll get you well wrapped up and take you to my house till you're well again.'

'Deed you will not! You've got enough to do without taking a sick man into your home—'

'Wheesht, Billy,' she ordered. 'The matter's all settled. I'd not let a good friend like yourself stay here while there's room for you in my own house.'

His protests were ignored. Within the hour he was jolting painfully in the back of a cart to the High Street house. Between them Kirsty and Duncan managed to get him upstairs and he was soon in bed, with Kirsty spooning hot broth down his throat.

His recovery took longer than any of them had

imagined. His feverish chill had already turned to pneumonia, and Kirsty had her hands full caring for him and tending her family. Thanks to her careful nursing he passed the crisis and found himself on the road to recovery, though as weak as a kitten. By the time he was on his feet again winter was coming in, and Kirsty steadfastly refused to consider his return to the road.

'D'you think I nursed you back to health just so you could get soaked through and catch another fever?' she wanted to know, hands on hips. 'Make up your mind to a winter spent under this roof, Billy, for you're not fit to go back on the road yet.'

He was secretly happy to give way to her, for the weeks spent under her roof had been a warm reminder of the domesticity he had known before the fever deprived him of his wife and children.

To pay for his keep he returned to his old trade as a cobbler, working in a corner of the weaving shop. At night he sat companionably on the opposite side of the fire from Kirsty, in Peter Todd's old chair, or spent long hours downstairs talking to Colin.

Kirsty was equally content with their arrangement. 'It's good to have a man about the house again,' she confided to Meg.

'No doubt. How's Kate faring?' Slim, red-headed Kate had just started work in a dressmaker's shop.

'She's doing fine. Time flies, does it not? I mind the day your Robert was born as if it was yesterday

– and now they're all going out into the world.
There's only Thomas left at school.'

'Aye – Thomas!' Meg laughed and shook her
head. Still as round and rosy as he had been since
babyhood, Thomas seldom had his nose out of a
book. Most of his spare time was spent at Mary's
house, where he was allowed to browse through
Andrew MacLeod's library. His parents marvelled
over his scholastic bent, while Robert and Margaret
openly thought of him as the 'strange' member of
the family.

'Margaret, now – she's a different problem
altogether.' Meg went on slowly, and Kirsty saw
a sudden shadow passing over her friend's face.

'What's amiss?'

Meg shrugged and drove her wheel faster. The
two of them were alone in the Todds' kitchen,
spinning thread for the looms below.

'It's Duncan. I don't know what's amiss with the
man. He's like a cat on hot bricks every time he sees
Margaret and William together – and you know as
well as I do what close friends they've always been.
What harm could it do if they decided to wed?'

Kirsty's hand, deftly guiding the strand of thread,
stilled for a moment.

'Wed? You're not serious, Meg! Margaret's only
just sixteen and William's less than a year older!'

'They're old enough to be thinking of marriage. I
wouldn't be surprised if they came to the idea one
day. They're fond of each other, and what would be
wrong with a marriage between them? William's a

141

fine lad. I can't think why Duncan's suddenly so set against him and Margaret seeing each other. He's started to go on at her, and the two of them are having terrible quarrels over the head of it.'

'That's the wrong thing to do,' Kirsty admitted. 'If Duncan's set against William, Margaret's just the sort of lassie to defy him.'

'That's my own view.' Meg shook her head. 'But why should he be opposed to the boy? William's never done anything amiss in his life – he's a credit to yourself and Colin. I don't know what's got into Duncan at all. He won't talk to me about it.' She sighed, her normally happy face clouded. 'I tell you, Kirsty, it's got me fair worried. I don't know where it's all going to end!'

Duncan himself came to Kirsty a few days later. He closed the trap door then paced the kitchen, his brows knotted with worry.

'Kirsty – I don't know how to begin. The Lord knows I've no wish to rake up the past—'

'Is it Margaret and William? Meg told me,' she said as he gaped at her. 'She can't understand what you've got against the two of them having an innocent friendship.'

'And she'll never know, please God.' He threw his hands out helplessly. 'It never entered my head until I heard Robert teasing her about him, then I realised that they're always together, these two.'

'They always were. It's no more than that, Duncan, and mebbe it'll never be anything else.'

'I can't take that chance, Kirsty! And I can't let them know the truth.' He slammed one fist into the other. 'If I'd had any sense at all I'd have seen to it that they were kept apart from the beginning!'

'You couldn't have done that. All the bairns went about together.'

'I wish I'd never set eyes on Lizzie!' said Duncan for the hundredth time.

'Then you're wishing William away, and that's wrong, for he's a fine boy who's made Colin's life worthwhile.'

She paused, then said slowly, 'If you really think the pair of them'll have to be kept apart, Duncan, Colin must be brought into it.'

'No!'

'Have some sense, man! You know your Margaret as well as I do. Forbid her to see William and she'll fall in love with him just to spite you. And you'll have Colin thinking that his son isn't good enough for your daughter. You'll need his help, can you not see that?'

'It'll kill him!'

'Not now,' said Kirsty. 'He's strong enough and wise enough to take the truth and not let it make a whit of difference to the way he feels about William, at least. Leave it to me – I'll see to it.'

'It's my place to—'

'I know how to talk to him,' she said firmly. 'It has to be done right. How would you like to hear plump and plain from another man that he's your son's real father?'

'Don't make me feel worse than I do already, Kirsty!' he groaned.

'I doubt if anyone could do that.' Her tone was matter-of-fact, but her heart recognised his torment and wept for him. 'Now it's time you got back to your work, for it seems to me that there's more clacking from the tongues than from the looms down there. Go on with you, and leave Colin to me.'

Kirsty turned at the kitchen door to look at Billy, dozing by the fire, a newspaper in his lap. A faint smile touched her lips as she closed the door gently. It was good to see a man by the fireside again. Then the smile faded as she made her way downstairs. She had no stomach for what she must do now.

Colin was working by candlelight when she went into his room, transferring a finished design from rough paper to design sheet. A box of colours stood by his elbow. He looked up and smiled.

'Come away in and sit down. Give me a minute to finish this.'

Before him lay the design paper with a black-leaded page over it. On top he had laid the paper with the design sketched on it, and he was carefully going over the outlines with a blunt steel point. In spite of the furrows which his accident had engraved on his face he was still youthful in appearance and his mop of fair hair was as thick as ever. At last he straightened up and grinned at her, a boyish grin that made him look very like his father and brother.

'I'll colour it tomorrow, then pass it over to Duncan.'

She looked at the simple but delicate pattern of leaves. 'It's bonny.'

'It's a special order. How's Billy coming on?'

'Well enough. He's talking of going back on the road now the weather's turning.'

'You'll miss him,' he said shrewdly, and she flushed.

'I suppose I will.'

He leaned across the table and put a hand on hers. 'Take my advice, Kirsty – keep him with you. Billy's a good man. He'd look after you.'

'Colin Todd!' she blustered, confused and embarrassed. 'I never thought to hear you black-footing like an interfering old woman!'

His grin widened. 'Black-footing's resulted in many a happy marriage. And I know a good match when I see one – where's the harm in putting in a word to help things along?' Then the grin faded. 'But that's not what you came to talk about. What's wrong, Kirsty?'

'D'you think I only come to see you when there's something wrong?'

'No, but you came in that door as if you had the cares of the world on your shoulders.'

Deftly he wheeled his chair round the table until he was beside her. One of the town's carpenters had designed and built the chair for him, and it was

Colin's great delight to be able to move about his room, and even to wheel himself outside in good weather. It had taken a lot of skill to master the chair on rough footpaths, but he had persevered and succeeded.

'Tell me, Kirsty.' His voice was calm, reassuring. His hand touched hers, closed over it. Suddenly she found it difficult to meet his eyes.

'It isn't easy to speak of it—'

'Kirsty, when did you and me ever find it hard to talk to each other?'

She stared into the fire. 'Duncan wanted to see you himself but I'd not let him. It's William and Margaret – Duncan thinks they're getting too fond of each other. He thinks it should be stopped.'

His eyebrows climbed. 'You mean they might be falling in love?' he asked with genuine surprise, then laughed softly. 'And here was me thinking of William still as a bairn. God, Kirsty, the years go by too fast for comfort! But why should it bother Duncan? Is my son not good enough for his—'

He suddenly stopped and she looked up to see the animation ebbing from his face, leaving it strangely blank, like a page still to be written on. She started to say something but he lifted one hand sharply, the hand that had warmly covered hers.

'Wheesht now, Kirsty!' The voice was so like Peter's that she almost expected him to add, 'You're letting your tongue run away with you, woman!' as his father would have done. But when he finally spoke it was in his own quiet voice.

146

'Duncan? It was Lizzie and – Duncan?'

'What do you mean?' Her voice shook, out of control.

'Kirsty, the Silver Bells accident might have robbed me of the use of my legs, but it didn't affect my brain. D'you think you need to tell me anything about my wife that I didn't know already? Lizzie thought she could keep her own counsel, but I always knew what was going on behind those strange eyes of hers. The only thing I didn't know till now was the man's name. All these years,' he said in wondering tones, 'I thought it was Matt.'

'Oh, Colin—' It was her turn to reach out and take his hand. 'Why did you never say anything? To keep such a secret—'

'It was no hardship,' he said swiftly, briskly, looking more like the old Colin. 'Don't go feeling sorry for me, Kirsty. I've got William and he's my son. I raised him, and I'm proud of him. But Duncan's right – the two of them'll have to stop seeing each other. Tell him I'll find something to say to the boy.'

'You should have told me!'

'What sense would there have been in that?' Colin asked her. 'I didn't know that you knew anything of it. It was Lizzie's secret and I'd not have betrayed her to anyone. Now—' he reached over and patted her hand '—off you go to your bed, Kirsty, and stop worrying. What's done is done. We'll say no more about it – none of us. You can tell Duncan that.'

She got up to go. 'What else d'you want me to tell Duncan?'

Colin smiled faintly. 'Nothing. We've been friends for a long time, him and me. It would be foolish to let a friendship go because of something that happened eighteen years ago.' Then the smile widened a little. 'Mebbe I should be grateful to him for the pleasure William's given me. Now go upstairs and let Billy tell you about the stories in his newspaper.'

She opened the door, then turned. Colin sat motionless in his chair, one finger absently tracing the new design. His head was bent, his hair golden in the candlelight. He looked up and saw her standing there.

'I'm glad it wasn't Matt,' he said.

When Kirsty fumbled her way upstairs in the dark and stepped into the kitchen Billy, who had just wakened, was shocked to see tears on her round cheeks.

'What's wrong? It's not Colin, is it?' He jumped to his feet.

'No, it's – just—' She went to him and his arms opened to take her. She sobbed on his broad comfortable shoulder and he held her close, stroking her hair, until the tears finally ceased.

Then gently, unsure of his reception but unable to deny the longing that had grown in him over the past weeks, he lifted her face to his and kissed her.

\*     \*     \*

'But why?' William asked on the following day.

Colin's fingers tightened on the book in his lap.

'You're just an apprentice, and you're young. It's foolish for you to get too friendly with any girl just yet. Later on—'

'To hear you, anyone would think Margaret and me were talking of marriage!' William exploded incredulously. 'I just like her – she likes me – we get on together, that's all.'

'Are you certain?'

'You know Margaret Montgomery well enough! She's not like the other girls – she's not interested in getting wed and raising a family!'

'Still, it's best that you do as I say and leave it at that, William.'

'But why?'

Lamplight cast deep furrows on Colin's face. 'Mebbe you'd be wise not to ask me that again.'

'It's Duncan Montgomery, isn't it?' Bitterness sharpened William's voice. 'He doesn't think I'm good enough for his daughter!'

'It's not that, it's – for other reasons that don't concern you.'

'Don't concern me? You come between me and Margaret then you say the reason's not my concern?' The boy laughed without amusement then threw himself out of his chair towards the door in an awkward tangle of adolescent limbs. 'I'm going to see Duncan Montgomery. I'm going to make him tell me man to man what he's got against me—!'

'No!' Colin's body, trapped in the wheel-chair, couldn't move between William and the door, but his voice managed to stop the youth in his tracks. He swung round to stare at Colin, his eyes dark angry pools in a pale face.

'William, if you care at all for me and for what we've always been to each other you'll agree here and now to do as I ask,' Colin said quietly. 'I swear to you that I'd not look for such a solemn promise if I could avoid it. But I can't. For my sake, William!'

And William, who loved his father more than anyone else in the world, gave his promise – against his better judgement.

It was some time before Margaret realised that William was avoiding her. She was kept busy with her shop duties and hospital visits, and of course Kirsty's betrothal to Billy Carmichael occupied all their minds.

'I thought we'd see it one of those fine days,' Mary said smugly as she sat in Meg's kitchen. 'Billy always had a soft spot for Kirsty, and she needs a man about the house.'

'She's got Jamie and Colin and William,' Margaret pointed out, and her aunt shot her a withering glance.

'I mean a man to be head of the house. Jamie and William are growing up, and Colin always kept himself to himself. Kirsty's the sort of woman who's the better for having a man around.'

'You make marriage sound the same as owning

a dog,' Margaret said, to her aunt's amusement and her mother's embarrassment.

'Take that shocked expression off your face, Meg,' Mary ordered. 'The girl's more like me than you – she's got some fire in her. Now – what about the wedding bonnets?'

It was decided that Billy should take over Colin's room and turn it into a cobbler's shop. The looms were shifted from the Todd house to an empty weaving shop nearby and Colin moved into the loom-shop where he had more space for his books and papers.

'Such a stramash – I wonder at times if it's worth it all,' Kirsty fluttered as she supervised the transfer of Colin's possessions.

Jamie flashed a huge grin at her as he staggered across the passageway, carrying one end of his half-brother's bed.

'Of course it's worth it.'

'Here – watch what you're doing and don't break the leg of that thing off against the door!' she shrieked, following them into the room. While the men struggled with the bed she stood alone, gazing round. Without the four big looms the apartment was vast and desolate.

'It's strange to see the shop so empty.' Her voice was suddenly tremulous. Her ears rang with the beat of the looms and the sound of Peter's deep, warm voice. She was grateful when Jamie put his arm about her and gave her a warm hug.

'The looms aren't far away, and Colin's carrying on the tradition in his own way, with his designing.'

'Aye.' Kirsty swallowed hard and smiled up at her tall son. Then her eyes travelled beyond his fiery head to the trapdoor linking the shop with her kitchen above.

'And I'll be able to call down to him whenever I want to,' she added, and Colin, catching the words as he manipulated his chair through the doorway, had the wit to smother his sudden apprehension before he caught her eye.

When the move was completed William was despatched to fetch a jug of ale so that they could, in Kirsty's words, 'celebrate the wee flitting.'

Drink could be bought at the howff on the ground floor of the new Town House at the Cross. The upper part of the building consisted of the Council chambers and offices, and the cells.

It seemed fitting that howff and cells shared the same building, for often enough the temporary inhabitants of the cells were men and women who had over-indulged in drink, and it was a simple matter to whisk them upstairs to sleep off their stupor. Everyone thus incarcerated for the night was obliged to pay a fee of four pence – two pence for burgesses – to the jailer.

William had almost reached his destination when someone stepped into his path and Margaret's voice said lightly, 'Good evening to you, Mister Todd. Where might you be bound?'

152

Colour flamed into his face and he stepped back.

'Margaret! I'm just – just—'

'—Going for ale,' she finished the sentence for him, eyeing the jug in his hand. Then her clear gaze swept up to his face again. 'I haven't seen you for long enough, William.'

'There's been a lot to do at the house, moving the looms out and—' His voice died away and he moistened dry lips with the tip of his tongue.

'I hear Billy's taking you on as his apprentice. And I see you still have that habit of hammering your fingers as often as you hammer the shoes.' She reached out and touched his bruised thumb-nail, then it was her turn to colour as he jerked his hand away from her.

'What's amiss?'

'Nothing.' He clutched the jug in both hands as though it was a shield between them. A puzzled frown drew Margaret's neat eyebrows together.

'When are you coming to the Hospital again?' Then, as he stood silently before her, she asked with growing suspicion, 'Have you been keeping out of my way deliberately?'

'I'd not do that!' the words poured from him, and were checked. 'At least – I'd not want to!'

Her frown deepened. 'Then you've been told to stay away from me? Was it my father? You don't have to heed him, surely!'

William wished that the ground would give way beneath his feet and let him fall into whatever hell might be lurking underground. But the earthen path remained solid and Margaret's eyes were beginning to glint blue fire.

'I – Margaret, don't ask me to explain it, for I can't. It's just that – mebbe they're right, mebbe we were seeing each other too much—'

She gave a short, angry laugh. 'So that's the way of it, is it? You're scared folk might think I've got my cap set at you?'

'Margaret, listen—' It was his turn to put out a hand, with the intention of drawing her into a doorway out of sight while he explained. But she drew back sharply, avoiding his outstretched fingers. Hurt coloured her cheeks.

'Never mind – I'd not want to make a nuisance of myself. I'll wish you good day, Mister Todd – and if we never speak again I'll be well pleased!' she flared at him, then deliberately sidestepped into a pool of dirty water so that she could pass without brushing against him.

He watched her flounce away, back straight, well-shod feet slamming angrily on the path with each step. For the first time in his life he discovered that a heart could ache. He had lost her, and he didn't know why.

Miserable and confused, he stood for a long moment, clutching the empty jug, before turning towards the howff.

# *Chapter Five*

WHILE MARGARET BEGAN THE LONG bitter process of struggling with hurt pride, life held few problems for her brothers. Robert, still serving his apprenticeship, had taken to weaving as easily as his father had. It was what he had been born to, and he loved the life.

Thomas, on the other hand, had no wish to take up weaving. Every time his father referred to the day when he would be apprenticed the boy winced inwardly. He loved books and studying, and he had already made up his own mind about his future. He lived in a perpetual dream, and only came to life at school, or studying with Colin Todd, or when he was in his Aunt Mary's house in Oakshawhill.

In the mornings before going to school, as he waited his turn to draw water at the street well, he would stand in a daze, his mind turning over something he had recently read, or memorising some homework. His blue eyes stared unseeingly at the tenements across the road while his lips moved soundlessly.

After school there were errands to run for his

mother and then, if he didn't have a lesson with Colin, he was free to scurry up the hill to Mary's house, where there was always a welcome for him. His first five minutes or so were spent in the kitchen, where the cook fed him tit-bits, then he and Andrew MacLeod would have a deeply satisfying academic discussion in the library, after which they both selected books from Andrew's extensive collection and settled into comfortable chairs to read in contented silence.

Thomas didn't agree with his sister Margaret that big houses were sinful, nor did he share his mother's awe of Mary's home. He simply saw it as a treasure cave filled with literature and he wasn't in the least intimidated by its many high-ceilinged rooms.

When Mary came home from the shop the three of them had tea then, if Thomas didn't have to hurry home, they all sat in the parlour, Thomas with his homework, Andrew reading or writing, Mary sewing, one or other of them making an occasional remark.

The childless MacLeods developed a genuine affection for Thomas. Mary and Robert got on well enough but saw little of each other. Margaret was so like her aunt in nature that they frequently sparked against each other, but Thomas's placid belief that everyone had a right to live as they pleased made him a relaxing companion.

'Your mother tells me you've had a good report from the school,' Mary said one evening, her needle flying deftly through the material in her hands. Thomas raised his head from the book on the table before him.

'It wasn't bad.'

'You'll soon be finished at the school.'

'Aye.'

'And taking your place at the looms, no doubt.'

There was a pause, then 'I've no mind to be a weaver,' said Thomas. She raised her eyebrows at Andrew, who had looked up from his accounts.

'Indeed? And what does your father have to say about that?'

Thomas swallowed. 'He doesn't know yet.'

'Have you decided what you want to do with yourself, then?'

'Mister Paterson at the school says I could mebbe get a place in Glasgow Academy.'

'That would take money, laddie.'

'I know. But I'd work hard. I have it in mind to be a physician.'

Andrew dropped the pen he was holding and Mary's embroidery needle stabbed into her hand.

'Tuts, I think this thing's got a life of its own!' she said irritably, sucking the wound. 'A physician, did you say?'

'That would mean going to the University,' Andrew put in gently.

'Aye.' Thomas's dark blue eyes glowed in his round face.

'And that's what you're going to tell your father when the time comes?'

'Aye.' The glow dimmed somewhat.

'It's not just what he has in mind for you, Thomas.'

There was a mild warning in Andrew's voice, and the glow dimmed further.

'I know that,' said Thomas, and sighed heavily.

'Well—' Mary's voice was brisk, 'you haven't read all those dry books of Andra's just for the sake of something to do, I'm sure. Plenty weavers read, but I've never seen one that eats books the way you do. You'd probably be too busy with your reading to turn out a decent piece of cloth. Your father'll surely see the sense of that.'

'I hope so,' said Thomas, but without much conviction.

Mary shot a quick glance at him and opened her mouth to say more, but a slight clearing of the throat from the writing desk where her husband sat cautioned her to close her lips again. Andrew was one of the few people who could tell Mary when it was wise to hold her tongue.

'No sense in worrying the boy further – or raising his hopes,' he said when Thomas had gone clattering home in the warm summer evening. 'He's a clever lad, Mary – but he'd make a poor weaver, for sure.'

'Try telling Duncan that,' she said with a sniff, and Andrew looked at her thoughtfully.

'I'd not dare. It might come better from you. As I see it, my task is to keep my mouth shut and my

purse at the ready,' he said; then, elderly and frail
as he was, he endured his vigorous young wife's
grateful kisses with both courage and pleasure.

Mary wasn't one to let an idea simmer for long. A
few days later she found Meg and Duncan alone by
their fireside and settled herself on a chair, untying
her bonnet strings.

'Your Thomas wants to be a physician.'

'A what?' Their two faces stared at her.

'A physician. He has it in mind to go to the
Academy in Glasgow, then to the University to
study. He doesn't want to be a weaver.'

'And just who—' Duncan began ominously, then
collected his wits. 'Mary, it seems you know more
about our son than we do.'

'I should, since he spends so much of his time
with me and Andra. He's a fine boy, Duncan, and
if you take my advice you'll let him have his head
over the matter. Meg tells me he does well at the
school.'

'Aye, but—'

'When did you hear this nonsense, Mary?' Meg
could never get used to her sister's habit of organising each and every one of the family without so
much as a by-your-leave.

'Just the other day – and it's not nonsense.
Thomas never wastes his time talking nonsense,
you should know that yourself. Now, Andra and
me've been discussing it, and it seems to us that we
should see to the cost of it—' She held up a mittened

hand as Duncan shot upright in his chair. '—Since we've no children of our own – Andra being too old and me being too busy anyway – and we're so fond of the boy.'

'Just a minute—' Duncan had rallied and begun to fight back. 'Before you say another word, Mary, I'd always had it in mind to make the lad a weaver, like Robert and myself.'

'I know that, but think about it for a minute. He'd be useless at a loom, for his heart's not in the work and you know better than I do that a weaver needs to be single-minded. Now, Duncan, you'd not want one of your lads to be in a trade he didn't enjoy, would you?'

'Mebbe not, but—'

'Mind you, he still has to prove that he's able, but I'm sure he can do it—'

'To hear you speak anyone would think he's about to open his own surgery already,' Duncan said sourly, and was ignored.

'—So when the time comes for him to go to the Academy in Glasgow, and then the University—'

'The University!' Meg said faintly, and was also ignored.

'We'll pay what's necessary. It would be worth it to have a physician in the family.'

'Aye, that would get your nose in the air, would it not?' Duncan said meanly.

'Yours and all, when it comes to it, Duncan, yours and all. You don't have to mention this wee talk to him, by the way. Let him tell you himself when he feels that the right time's come. I'm just smoothing the way for him.'

She rose to leave, and Duncan made one last attempt to assert himself as the head of the house.

'Before you go, Mary – I'll remind you that I've not given my consent for this daft idea you and Andra have dreamed up between you. I'll have to – Meg and me'll have to give it our serious consideration, you understand.'

She smiled sweetly. 'You do that, Duncan. You think about it, and let me know what you decide.'

At the door she turned and beamed on them both again. 'It pleasures me to know that one of my own flesh and blood kin's to be a physician. We'll all be that proud of him!'

When she had gone they sat in a stunned silence for a while, Duncan carefully re-lighting his pipe, Meg lost in a happy dream. She agreed with Mary – it would be grand to have a physician in the family. But she knew that she daren't get excited about the idea until Duncan had had time to get used to it.

Finally he cleared his throat and spat into the flames.

'I know your sister's always right, Meg,' he said, almost plaintively, 'but does she have to be just as plump and plain about it every time?'

Margaret's pride wouldn't allow her to look for the reasons behind William's betrayal. Something had been knocked awry in her safe, happy world, and she coped with it by putting the blame squarely on William and slighting him whenever she got the opportunity.

Then her fortunes took a turn that swept William from her mind. Mary was in the shop with Meg when Margaret burst in, eyes shining.

'The Chaplain called me in when I was at the Town Hospital just now and – and I'm to be taken on to teach the children!' She grabbed Meg and waltzed her round, then collapsed onto a sack of barley. 'Every morning I've to go along and teach them their letters! Me – they asked me!'

'Oh – Margaret!' Meg clapped her hands to her flushed face, giggling like a girl, but Mary was unruffled.

'I don't see why you should look so surprised, Meg. The girl's the best person to ask, is she not? You'll be an asset to the place,' she told her niece warmly. 'I'm right pleased for you.'

Margaret picked up her apron then threw it down again, too excited to keep still. 'Can I go out for a while? There's so many things to think of—'

'Off you go – I can manage for an hour or two on my own.' Meg felt sudden tears at the back of her eyes as she watched her daughter. It seemed only yesterday that she herself had been on the threshold of adulthood. But in her case it had been the prospect of marriage that brought stars to her eyes.

At the doorway Margaret stopped, darted back

and hugged her mother then her aunt. 'I'll work hard – you'll see—' she said, and was gone.

The sisters smiled at each other when they were alone.

'It's good to see her happy again. For a while there she was awful downcast.' Meg shook her head. 'It doesn't take long for moods to change at that age.'

'Margaret's got the sense to know that bitterness is needed as well as sweetness to make life worth the tasting,' Mary said briskly. 'I'm glad she's found the sort of work that suits her temperament best.'

A sudden thought struck Meg. 'Mary, you didn't—?'

'Didn't what? Arrange the post for her? The very idea! Of course not!' Mary lied virtuously. 'Sometimes, Meg, you vex me sorely with your suspicions. You're getting as bad as that man of yours! You can just measure out the pound of meal I came in for, instead of standing there letting your imagination run away with you.'

Margaret was stifled by the crowded streets. Her feet scarcely seemed to touch the ground as they carried her towards the moors at the edge of the town; then she halted abruptly as William's tall lean figure stepped from a doorway ahead.

Her first instinct was to spin on her heel; she started the move, then checked it. She had to tell someone her news. Until recently she would have gone straight to William. Perhaps this was the time to forget disagreements and start anew—

But even as she began to walk towards him William glanced up and saw her. His head ducked in an involuntary movement and he swung away, presenting his back to her.

Margaret stood where she was, a red tide surging over her neck and face. Jamie, perched on a passing cart, had to hail her twice before she saw him.

'D'you want to come up the braes with me and walk back down?'

'Yes!' It was just what she needed. He caught her upstretched hand and hauled her onto the cart where, sure-footed, she stood beside him on close-packed bales of linen, above the heads of the pedestrians. The cart lurched and Jamie's arm looped about her waist, holding her securely against him.

'Jamie – I'm to teach the children in the Town Hospital!'

'Teach them what?'

'Their letters, you daft loon! I'm to go in three mornings a week and – oh, Jamie, I'm going to teach them such a lot!'

As they left the town behind she dropped down onto the lumpy bales and closed her eyes tightly against the sun's light. Her lids seemed to be made of beaten gold. Beside her, Jamie was propped on one elbow, whistling tunelessly.

At the Bonnie Wee Well, where a spring gushed cold and clear from the rock-face, the carter stopped and they scrambled down onto the grass. By the time the sun's dazzle had cleared from Margaret's eyes the cart was disappearing over the slight rise that lay between them and the bleachfields.

She cupped her hands at the spring and drank its icy water, then rinsed her face and arms. Jamie drank his fill and wiped his mouth with the back of one hand.

Margaret opened her arms to the warm air and danced over the grass, twirling like a leaf in an autumn wind, her skirt twisting about her legs. Finally she dropped to the ground, laughing up at Jamie when he reached her.

'Aren't we lucky to be alive and living in a town as fine as Paisley?'

He sat down, arms clasped about his knees, staring down to where the smoke rose lazily from dozens of chimneys. 'You think so? There's a lot more to life than working a loom and going bowling or cock-fighting. The world's out there—' his hand swept the horizon. 'That's what I want to see.'

'Go for a soldier, you mean? Like Matt?'

'Mebbe. I don't know—' he said restlessly.

'Jamie, what would you do if you could do anything in the world?'

'I'd get onto a cart and ride until the horse was too tired to go any further,' he said promptly. 'Then I'd get another cart and another horse.'

She giggled. 'You could go all the way to the end of the world and come back if there were enough carts!'

'I might. I'd not mind coming back as long as I could say I'd seen the rest of the world.'

'Not me – I've got plenty to do right here.' She stretched her arms above her head. 'Oh – I'm so lucky!'

He looked at her, and saw that the sun had turned her hair into a halo about her pretty, happy face.

'And so bonny,' he said, then leaned forward and kissed her, his lips warm and hesitant on hers.

Sheer surprise made her heart skip a beat. As Jamie's lips left hers she stayed motionless, looking at him with startled eyes. Emboldened, he put his hands on her shoulders and kissed her again, a longer embrace this time.

She liked it – but even her first kiss had to take second place to the excitement the day had already brought her.

'Come on, Jamie—' She jumped up. 'We've got a long walk ahead of us and I've to get back to the shop.'

'Margaret, will you—' he began, but she had started running, and only the warm air heard the last few words '—walk out with me again?'

'Come on, Jamie!' She stopped at the foot of a slope, slipped her shoes off, and ran on without waiting for him, down the hill towards the town below.

The gathering held to celebrate Kirsty's wedding to Billy Carmichael gave proof to the boast that in 1763 Paisley's working class were the best dressed in the country. Most of the women had lace trimming to their vividly coloured gowns and there were plenty of earrings and finger rings in evidence. A few wore the figured silk dresses which were coming into fashion, and the men were dashing and stylish in ruffled shirts and knee britches, with silver buckles shining on their shoes.

Mary's contribution to the occasion was the finest collection of bonnets ever seen at one gathering. Kate and Margaret were highly amused by her little approving nods each time another of her creations swept into the room atop a head.

'You'd think she'd arranged the wedding just to get the chance to show off her bonnets,' Kate whispered, blue eyes dancing.

'You're right – and you and me are next on her marriage list, so we'd best watch our step,' Margaret prophesied darkly.

'Oh, I don't know about that – I'd like fine to have a wedding,' her friend sighed, and Margaret shook her head in disgust.

The house was packed to the rafters, yet everyone managed to sit down to the wedding feast of broth, beef, mutton and fowls followed by puddings swimming in cream, with bread and cheese for those who still felt hungry. After the food had been washed down with generous mugs of ale the furniture in Colin's room was pushed back against the walls and the floor cleared for dancing.

The first person Margaret saw when she went

into the room was William, leaning against the wall, watching the door. When she appeared he pushed himself upright and began to ease his way across the crowded floor.

Then – 'Come on, Margaret—' Robert's hand claimed her and whirled her into a group of dancers. Over her shoulder she saw William stop, as though it had been his intention all along, by Kirsty's side.

It was a grand gathering, a testimony to Kirsty's and Billy's popularity. Half-way through the evening, exhausted and hot, Margaret slipped out of the room and escaped into the coolness of the back yard.

As she walked up the hard earth path by the kail-bed a figure stepped out from the shadows under an apple tree. Startled, she gave a cry and stepped back, almost tripping over a brick by the side of the path. A hand held her arm, steadying her.

'Margaret—?'

She pulled herself free, embarrassed. 'I – I didn't know there was anyone else out here.'

'You mean, you didn't know I was out here.' William moved back in his turn, indicating the distance between them. 'Don't worry, I'll not come too close.'

'No need to make it sound as if you've got the plague!'

'No?' he said bitterly. 'The way you've been avoiding me I thought I must have.'

She looked fully at him for the first time in weeks. His eyes were shadowed, his mouth unhappy.

'It's you that started this nonsense, not me.'

'And I'd finish it,' he said at once, 'if I only knew what to do.'

She darted a glance at the lighted doorway, wishing she had never come through it. 'Mebbe you just have to grow up, William, and stop letting your father make all your decisions for you.'

Even in the dusk she could see his face redden. 'It's not as easy as that.'

'I don't see why not.' Looking at him, talking to him for the first time in weeks, she wanted so much to knock down the wall that had begun to grow between them. 'All you need to do is face your father and make him tell you why he's come between us.'

'I've tried! He says he can't tell me.'

'Can't, or won't? You're not a child any more – you don't have to spend your life pleasing him! When my own father made a fuss about us I soon told him what I thought!'

'But I've never gone against him,' William said wretchedly. 'You don't know how things are between us, Margaret—'

She reached out and took his hands in hers. 'I know you're fond of him, but has he the right to expect so much of you? Is it fair to make you turn away from me when I've done nothing and said nothing to anger him?'

'William? Colin's asking for you,' Jamie called

169

from the doorway, and she felt William's hands flinch, then loosen in her grasp.

'Well?' she asked in an undertone, 'Are you going? Or are you man enough to stay here, with me?'

She felt his fingers slide from hers.

'Wait for me – I'll come back and we'll talk about it—'

'We'll talk now or never,' she said angrily, then, as he remained silent, she went on, 'Best run in and see what he wants, like a good little boy.'

She stepped aside to leave the path free. He hesitated, then brushed past her and went down the path and into the house.

Margaret kicked angrily at an innocent cabbage and bit her lower lip.

'What's amiss with him?' Jamie reached her side. 'I've never seen William with such a bad-tempered look. Were the two of you quarrelling?'

'I'd not waste my breath quarrelling with the likes of him!' Margaret stormed, then it was her turn to push her way down the path and into the house, slamming the door in Jamie's surprised face as she went.

It was late when the evening drew to its close. As was the custom they all stood to sing the 127th Psalm before going off to their own homes, and the wooden beams rang with their voices. 'Except the Lord to build the house, the builders lose their

170

pain; Except the Lord the city keep, the watchmen watch in vain.'

When the guests had gone William helped his father back to his room and saw him settled for the night, helping him to undress and easing him back onto the pillow with a woman's gentleness.

'It was a grand wedding,' Colin said contentedly. 'And it's good to see Kirsty so happy again.' Then he looked sharply at his son's closed face. 'What's worrying you?'

William hung his father's jacket carefully over a chair, smoothing the material. 'The same thing that's worried me for weeks. I still want to know what you've got against me seeing Margaret.'

The light went out of Colin's eyes and he slumped back against his pillow. 'I've told you – I've nothing against her! I just think you're both young, and it would be a mistake to see too much of each other.'

'There's more to it than that.'

'I've told you all that I'm going to tell you!' There was an edge to Colin's voice that William had never heard before. 'For pity's sake will you take heed and stop pestering me!' Then he added sharply, 'Where are you going?'

'Out for some fresh air!' William snapped.

'Wait—!'

But the boy had gone. Colin fell back onto the bed, one clenched fist pounding helplessly at the sheet over his useless legs.

\* \* \*

The cool quiet darkness did nothing to ease William's mind. It seethed with pictures of Margaret, laughing as she danced, angry when they faced each other in the garden. And there were bitter memories of that meeting in the street a few months earlier, when she had walked towards him and he, honouring the stupid promise his father had wrung from him, had turned away, only to see her go off with Jamie.

'Mebbe you'll have to grow up, William, and stop letting your father make all your decisions for you.' Her voice echoed in his head.

Four large, sturdily shod feet blocked his path, and he looked up and recognised two of his fellow apprentices.

'Will! Come and have a wee dram with us,' one of them coaxed. He shook his head. Colin didn't approve of drink, and he himself had never felt the need of it. But the apprentices were insistent. Unwilling to pull away from the friendly arms draped about his shoulders, William allowed himself to be steered to a nearby howff.

The door opened, sending a shaft of light, a cheerful hum of voices, a thick aroma of smoke and alcohol to where he wavered on the threshold. The two youths urged him on.

He compared the loneliness and bewilderment he had known recently with the warm unquestioning friendship of the young men on either side of him. All at once his need to belong somewhere was more than he could bear. Let his own people reject him – there were others.

Without looking back William made his choice, and stepped through the doorway.

# PART THREE

# Chapter One

'PAISLEY—' MARY MACLEOD SAID BREATHLESSLY to her companions as she elbowed her way to the front of the crowd '—is for all the world like a drystane dyke. The big stones are the special occasions, and the wee bits holding them in place are made up of the gossip and the scandals.'

She gained a place right on the edge of the road, pulling Margaret and Kate to either side of her, and added with satisfaction, 'Speaking for myself, I have a great fondness for the wee bits. But there's nothing wrong with a big occasion like this now and then.'

Even Margaret, impatient to be back with her charges in the Town Hospital, felt her blood stir as the shrill piping of fifes and the rumble of drums signalled the approach of the procession. Kate quivered with excitement, her lovely red hair shimmering in the June sunshine.

'I've never seen so many people in the town, even for the Silver Bells race. D'you think King George knows that we're doing all this in honour of his birthday?'

'D'you think he'd care even if he did know?'

Mary's sharp elbow delivered a reprimanding nudge that would have sent Margaret staggering into the roadway if she hadn't been wedged against a stout woman.

'There's an unseemly dryness in your voice, Margaret. Whether His Majesty knows or not it's a grand spectacle for the folk and they've a right to enjoy it.'

'It's too crowded!'

'Havers! A procession's best when you can get a good sight of it, and hear it – and smell it,' her aunt added with relish.

They could certainly smell it. Piles of refuse rotted all along the gutters, and on this day, when the street was crowded, the usual aroma was enriched by the smell of humanity itself. Margaret thought longingly of the braes outside the town, where the air was sweet and fresh and scented by flowers that grew wild among the hedgerows and on the grass and in crannies in the drystone walls.

Then she looked up above the heads of the people opposite and found herself gazing directly into William Todd's serious grey eyes. He was at Kirsty's kitchen window, together with his father Colin, Kirsty herself, and her husband Billy Carmichael.

The other three were craning their necks to see the procession, held as a loyal display for His Majesty King George in this year of his reign 1768. But William stared down at Margaret as though she was the only person in that thronged street.

She looked away quickly. In the past five years she and William had never met informally, never been alone together. Hurt pride and misunderstanding had built an insurmountable barrier between them during those years, but Margaret still regretted the end of their deep friendship, though she would have died rather than let William or anyone else know it.

Mary caught at her arm. 'They're coming! Oh, aren't they bonny lads? See – there's your father!'

The parade was headed by the local militia, their tartan plaids and blue feathered bonnets contrasting with the scarlet cloaks worn by many of the women in the cheering crowd. The officers were on horseback, silver buckles at waist and instep catching the sun.

Duncan and Robert Montgomery walked with the Paisley weavers, the largest contingent in the long procession. They were followed by men from the neighbouring communities – Kilbarchan, Renfrew, Beith and Elderslie, and miners from the Thorn village, each group with its own silken banner carried proudly before it. A breeze caught the banners and filled them till they looked like land-locked sails slashing bold colour against the grey and brown stone tenements on either side of the street.

The men stamped along stolidly to the beat of drums and the chirruping of fifes.

A vivid blue gaze met Margaret's as the Paisley men swept by. Beneath it a wide grin almost split Jamie's face in two, and above it his red head added its own contribution to the colourful parade.

After the weavers came their apprentices, a tousled, cheerful barefoot lot.

'Jackie!' Margaret waved, and her father's new apprentice, a skinny orphan recently hired from the Town Hospital, blushed with pleasure then stared grimly ahead, sticking his bony little ribcage out in imitation of the older boys.

In the wake of the official parade danced the children, ragged and over-excited, some of them tormenting the apprentices who marched in front of them, others cheering squeakily for a King who, in Margaret's opinion, probably cared nothing at all for them.

Then the parade was by, and the onlookers surged after the marchers to the Cross to hear the speeches.

Once the formalities were over, they were all free to mingle, and meet friends who had come into the town for the big occasion.

Jamie arrived at Margaret's side. 'Come down to the river with us – I'm supposed to keep an eye on Kate and Archie, and they want to go for a walk.' He nodded to where his sister was gazing into the eyes of a young uniformed lieutenant and added hurriedly as Margaret opened her mouth to refuse. 'They'll be wanting to be together, and that'll leave me looking like an old nursemaid if I'm on my own!'

They had no sooner reached the water's edge than Kate and Archie wandered off together on the pretext of having a closer look at an interesting flowering bush. Jamie guided Margaret to a spot where a log by the river made a comfortable seat.

'I thought you were supposed to watch out for Kate? They're nearly out of sight.'

'Ach, she's fine,' Kate's brother said with a sudden lack of interest in her welfare. 'We'll sit here and have a talk, you and me.'

She settled herself on the log. 'Talk? We talk nearly every day – there's nothing left to say.'

'There's always something—' His voice trailed off and he worried at a twig, plucking the leaves from it one by one.

There was a short silence, then – 'You're not saying much,' Margaret pointed out with some exasperation.

'I'm just – thinking it out first.'

'There's no thinking needed. Just open your mouth and let your tongue clack on the way it usually does.'

'Och, Margaret!' he rapped at her in a sudden irritated burst, 'It's not easy to ask someone if they'll wed you!' Then his face flamed. 'I mean – I should have said – d'you have to gawp at me like that?'

For once Margaret found herself at a loss for words. Finally she said weakly, 'Wed? Are you asking me to wed you, Jamie Todd?'

'Well, I'd – if you – I—' Jamie gazed around as though hoping to find the right phrases hanging from a tree, then sat down suddenly on the grass and stared at the slow-moving river, avoiding her eyes.

'Yes.'

'You're daft!'

'No I'm not!' Jamie argued hotly. 'I'm a master weaver now, and we've been walking out together for a good long time—'

'But not like sweethearts – like friends!'

'I've heard of friends who've wed each other before this!' he almost shouted, exasperated. 'I know you've a fondness for me. Every woman has a fondness for someone, Margaret. Kate, there—' he gestured to the two figures a considerable distance away, '—she's fond of Archie—'

'I'm not Kate!' Margaret was outraged. 'Just because I like someone it doesn't mean that I want to wed with him. I don't want to wed anyone!'

'Don't be daft, Margaret, every woman wants to get married.' Without realising it Jamie went on adding fuel to the fire. 'Is it William?'

She jumped to her feet. 'Is what William?' she asked in a cool voice.

'Is it him you're fond of? Oh, we all knew you liked each other well enough once, but for years now you've scarcely looked at each other. So I thought that – but mebbe I'm wrong. Mebbe he's the one you care for.'

Then he looked at her face and prudently scrambled to his feet. It didn't seem wise to stay on the ground.

'I've never heard such a foolish notion!' Margaret exploded. 'Of course I've no feelings for William!'

'In that case what's to come between us?' he persisted. 'Margaret, will you wed me?'

'No!' She started to flounce past him but he caught at her hand.

'I'd be prepared to wait while you thought it over.'

'You've got your answer!'

His own temper came to the surface. 'My God, woman, you're stubborn! D'you think I've stayed here in Paisley because I wanted to? It was because I thought you and me might settle down together.'

'I've no intention of settling down with any man!' Margaret snapped, and began to walk back to the town, yelling for Kate as she went.

Jamie fell into step beside her. 'If you turn me down I'm leaving, Margaret. I'll go off to be a soldier.'

'Good fortune go with you. Kate, it's time to go home!'

'I might be gone for years.'

'We'll hold a gathering for you when you come back,' said the light of his life grimly.

'Mebbe I'll never come back. Soldiers can get killed.'

She stopped and gazed up at him as he loomed above her. Jamie was a well-made man, and at that

183

moment, blue eyes aflame and red hair raked by exasperated fingers, he looked invincible.

'Tuts, Jamie Todd, who'd ever be so bold as to kill the likes of you? You'll be back, and we'll all be glad to see you. And isn't it time you attended to your sister instead of leaving it all to me?'

But Kate, pretty mouth twisted in a petulant scowl, was approaching them with Archie in tow, and Jamie had to bite his tongue and give Margaret the best of the argument.

Nine people sat down to dinner in the Montgomery kitchen that night. A babble of voices filled the place, led by Mary's. Since Andrew MacLeod's death a year earlier his widow spent a lot of time in her sister's home, rather than 'rattle around', as she put it, on her own in the big house on Oakshawhill. Robert's sweetheart Annie was another frequent visitor, and so was Gavin Knox, a young surgeon who lived in lodgings in Glasgow and often came to Paisley with Thomas, who had attained his ambition and was now a medical student at Glasgow University.

Jackie, the little apprentice, sat at a corner of the table cramming food into his mouth with the dedication of one who was not used to getting enough. Above his busy cheeks he surveyed the company with two round solemn dark eyes which were hastily lowered whenever anyone looked in his direction.

With his pale face and high-domed head, sparsely

covered with fine straight black hair, he looked more like a small middle-aged man than a child of thirteen, Margaret often thought.

She herself had no appetite and no interest in the talk that flew about the table. She pushed a potato about her plate and looked up to find Gavin's clear hazel eyes studying her. She glared back at him and was pleased when he blinked in embarrassment and looked elsewhere.

She didn't have much time for Gavin Knox. The first time he had come to the house he had tripped on a stool and knocked over a pile of pirns she had just spun, and ever since she had dismissed him as a clumsy slow-moving oaf with little conversation. She could never understand why such a ham-fisted man should wish to be a surgeon.

When the meal was over and the dishes cleared away she escaped to the garden to collect the sun-scented clothes that had been spread out on bushes to dry.

Bees making their final forays of the day droned contentedly as they carved a path through the air between the scented blossoms planted specially for their benefit, and the three skeps sitting in a niche in the stone garden wall. With practised ease Margaret folded the clothes, breathing in their fresh summer fragrance. The tight angry knot within her began to loosen.

'It's a grand evening.'

The knot tightened again as Gavin ducked his

dark head under the lintel of the kitchen door and stepped into the garden.

'It was—' she began ungraciously, then added swiftly, 'Mind where you put your—'

It was too late. As they righted the basket and gathered up the spilled clothes she asked in exasperation, 'D'you walk about the wards like that? It's a wonder sick folk ever get better with the likes of you bumping into their beds and knocking them to the floor! Not to mention the harm you probably do with your cutting!'

'So you've got a tongue in your head after all? I was beginning to wonder.' He picked up a sheet and tried clumsily to fold it. 'It's my personal experience that women are only silent when they're mortally ill or already dead.'

Impatient fingers whisked the sheet from his grasp. 'It's well seen you've got no sisters, then! I can attend to the clothes – is it not time you and Thomas were getting back to Glasgow?'

'We're setting off now. Robert and Annie are walking part of the way with us. I thought – we thought you'd like to come as well.'

'I've other things to do. There's been enough time wasted as it is.' She threw the words over her shoulder as she reached for a cravat that had fluttered to the far side of a bush. Gavin's long arm stretched past her and scooped up the errant garment easily.

'The parade? It meant a day off work for the folk – you'd not grudge them a rest now and again?'

'No, but they could surely find a less frivolous cause.' She twitched the proffered cravat from his hand and dropped it into the basket. Gavin fidgeted with a bush that dropped frothy golden sprays almost to the path.

'You think the King's frivolous? So you're no Royalist?'

She shook out a sheet, making it crack in the still warm air. 'I've no objection to the man, but he lives far away in London. We're hard-working folk in Paisley, and it's only other working folk we understand. If the King was to come here and build a house or plant a field or weave a good stretch of linen I'd see the sense in holding a parade to honour him. But as far as I can make out he does nothing useful at all!'

He was still digesting her comments when she added crisply, 'And you'd best leave that flower alone, for I just saw a bee crawl into it. If the poor thing's forced to sting you it'll be the end of it, and we need our bees. You can carry the basket into the house for me, if you've a mind to be of use.'

Jamie's proposal of marriage irritated her like a stone in a shoe. She slept badly that night, and her usual enjoyment in her work at the Hospital was lacking the next morning. The large gloomy apartment set aside as a schoolroom was even more forbidding than usual; a shaft of sunlight venturing in the high, narrow window only served to emphasise the bleakness of the children's surroundings.

'We'll have a botany lesson!' she announced abruptly, and the solemn, pale faces before her brightened noticeably.

Inside the Hospital walls, surrounded by regulations, the children were always solemn and silent, reminding her, as Jackie did, of small careworn adults. But once they were out in the fresh air they started to chatter, and when they reached the fields near the Hospital they raced around happily, freeing Margaret, the lesson forgotten, to return to her thoughts.

Instead of hurrying off to help her mother and Janet when her morning's work was done she called in at her aunt's shop. Although the two of them were so alike in nature that they wrangled continually Mary was the only person Margaret could safely confide in.

She was alone, and in fine fettle, having just succeeded in selling an expensive bonnet to a difficult customer.

'And she took the one I chose for her, not the one she'd have bought herself,' she said smugly. 'A lacy, frippery thing she wanted, and her with a face like a cow looking over a gate at milking time. Not that I told her that, mind you. I put it a shade more politely, and she's fair pleased with what she bought. So am I, for she's a hard one to please. What news is there from the Hospital?'

'Alexander Orr's in the cells again, they tell me.' Margaret said absently. 'He's got the madness.'

'D'you tell me?' Mary tutted. 'Poor Alexander,

I mind what a fine figure of a man he used to be before the smallpox got him.'

'And wee Geordie Lang's in the sick-room again with a fever.'

Margaret thought of the child as she had last seen him, tossing restlessly in his cot. 'He needs fresh air. The Mistress says he gets enough, for he's apprenticed out to run errands for a tailor in all weathers when he's able. To hear her, you'd think these fevers were Geordie's own fault. But what the laddie needs is to run wild for a few years, the way I did – the way you did yourself, living on a farm.'

'We can't all be hearty.' Mary was busy working on another bonnet.

'The Hospital Mistress would agree with you there. She says he's just suffering from the usual fever, the one that often visits folk in that place.' Margaret felt her mouth twist into a wry smile. 'I asked if she thought it was a sort of poverty fever – and she agreed with me!'

'Now, Margaret, there's a lot done in this town to help the poor – and I should know, for I work as hard at it as anyone.'

'But it's never enough! They need good nourishing food, and more care in the sick-room.'

'And where's the money to come from, may I ask? We all give handsomely as it is. I keep telling you – your grand ideas are all very well, but some folk are born to be poor, just as some are born to be clever, or healthy,' Mary lectured. 'You're only flying in the face of Providence when you try to change the natural way of things. Now that we've dealt with the Hospital – what's amiss with you?'

'Nothing.'

'I'd like fine to think you'd just happened by to exchange a word or two, Margaret, but you never put a foot inside my door unless you've got something important to say. So out with it before another customer arrives. Besides, the lassie's due back any minute from making the deliveries. And that's a bonnet for a councillor's wife, not a chicken waiting to be plucked—'

Deftly she whipped a half-made bonnet from beneath her niece's restless fingers.

Margaret sighed heavily and shot a sidelong glance at her aunt, 'Jamie's asked me to wed him.'

'Has he, indeed?' Mary asked without surprise, 'And what did you say to that?'

'I told him he was daft.'

'Daft for asking or daft for thinking you'd have him? I could have told him to save his breath, for there's more ahead of you than marriage to Jamie. But he's a fine young man, and there was no need to be hard on him.'

'No need? And him with the impertinence to think I'd fall into his arms and thank him for the honour he was doing me?'

'Men always think that, poor simple creatures that they are.'

'And then he said – he said—' Margaret almost

choked at the memory, '—that I'd only refused him because I'd a liking for William!'

'Have you?'

'Aunt Mary! You know fine that I've scarcely said two words to him in years. How could I have a liking for any man who spends all his time drinking himself into a stupor?'

'Poor William,' Mary sighed, her fingers smoothing a piece of ribbon. 'Colin's fair out of his mind with worry over him. I never thought the lad would come to this – going from howff to howff with a bunch of ne'er-do-wells.'

'He needn't have, if he'd any backbone at all.'

'You're too hard on him, Margaret.' But Margaret's mouth was set stubbornly, and Mary changed the subject.

'Have you told your mother about Jamie's proposal?'

'And have her planning a wedding? I have not!'

'That was wise of you. Well now, Jamie's proposed, and you've said no, and that's an end to it. Mind you, it's nice to be asked.'

'Hmphh!'

'Is there no romance in your soul at all, Margaret Montgomery? Oh, you'll come to it one day, when you find the right man. Independence is a fine thing – but when all's said and done, there's nothing like the love of the right man,' said Mary with relish.

'I thought you had more sense than that!'

'Oh, Margaret – when the good Lord created you

he was short on the sweetness and heavy-handed with the thorns.'

'Mebbe so, but I've the sense not to want to spend all my days sitting by some man's fireside,' her niece said sharply, and Mary sighed, shook her head, and said no more.

# Chapter Two

ONE AFTERNOON IN OCTOBER, AS autumn bronzed the ferns on the braes and the chill promise of winter made itself felt in the evenings, Mary MacLeod made her way up the Waingaitend and past the Town House. Along the High Street she bustled, stepping high to avoid muddy spots and giving a sharp kick to two dogs who tried to start a fight on the footpath just as she approached on her way to see her sister.

Arriving in the grocer's shop she rattled off a list of provisions, finishing with '—and I've decided to hold a Hallowe'en gathering for the young folk.'

Meg looked at her pityingly. 'Hallowe'en? Who in Paisley would want to know about such daft games?'

'All the young folk. Have you forgotten the times we used to have on the farm?'

'We were just children then.'

'I still recall the state you got into with the three caps, Meg – and so do you.'

For the first time in many years Meg thought

of those Hallowe'en nights at home – the smoke-blackened walls of the farm kitchen and the three wooden basins, one holding pure water, one with dirty water, the third empty. And she herself, on the brink of womanhood, standing blindfold with a rod in her hand. She had just started walking out with Duncan, and the game's outcome was vitally important to her.

She remembered her brothers' and sisters' muffled laughter, the scraping sound of the tubs being shuffled about, the slap of water against wood. She remembered her fear, as she blindly pointed the rod, that in the 'best of three' result she would touch the empty basin, which forecast no marriage, or the tub of dirty water, which represented a dishonourable match.

The breathless excitement of that moment held her spellbound for a few seconds, then she came back to the present with a sharp, 'Och, it was only a bairns' game!'

'I mind you picked the dirty water,' Mary said thoughtfully, and was rewarded when her sister flashed, 'I did not – I picked the clean tub!'

'And made a good marriage, so who are you to sneer at Hallowe'en?' Mary seized her advantage. 'As I was saying – there'll be refreshments for the older folk if they care to come along too. We might as well make a proper evening of it.'

'I'm telling you, Mary—'

'No, I'm telling you, Meg – and I'm never wrong. Just one thing – see and get Margaret to come. She needs a bit of magicking to balance that deplorably practical streak she has. I can't for the life of me think who she takes it from,' Mary said airily, and went off to plan her party.

As she had predicted, her house was filled with people on the last evening in October. Instead of turning up their noses at country customs the young folk clamoured to be taught the old courting games.

'The place'll be like a mire in the morning,' Mary said happily as she shooed them all outside into the darkness to 'pull the Castoc'.

They bobbed blindfolded about her kail-yard, grubbing up the greens; then they trooped back into the kitchen, pink-cheeked and blinking in the light, to where Mary waited to examine each root. The comeliness of the future partner depended on the amount of earth clinging to the roots, and the shape of each vegetable.

'Well, he might be cabbage in shape and a dour-looking man, going by all that dirt, but he'll have a good heart,' she said blandly as she inspected Margaret's offering. Then she looked up at her niece, a wicked gleam in her eye. 'On the other hand, he'd make a good rich broth, and that'll please your practical heart. Now – if you leave it by the door, you'll find that the first man who comes in'll have the same initials as your future husband.'

'Keep your black-footing for the likes of Robert and Annie, or Kate and her lieutenant,' Margaret told her crushingly. 'They've already chosen their partners. Speaking for myself—'

'There's someone coming in right now—' Mary interrupted, and Margaret dropped the cabbage and fled to the safety of the parlour.

Under Mary's supervision the young people roasted peas on live coals to test the strength of future unions, cast apple peel over their shoulders to find out the initial of their loved ones, and enjoyed themselves to the full.

Even Thomas and Gavin Knox threw themselves into the make-believe with enthusiasm; the only two on the outskirts were Margaret and William, who had forsaken his usual drinking friends to attend the party at his father's urging.

For the final test Mary bustled the girls into a line in the hall, each clutching an apple and a comb.

'You go into that wee room there one at a time. Comb your hair before the mirror and eat the apple – mind and hold each piece over your left shoulder before you eat it. Then you'll see your future husband's image in the mirror.'

'I'll not look!' Kate shivered. 'I might see someone I don't like!' But she allowed herself to be pushed into the room, and came simpering out after a few moments, refusing to say what she had seen.

'You too, Margaret—' Mary put an apple and a comb into her niece's reluctant hands when the other girls had finished. 'You have to take your turn.'

'It's all nonsense!'

Mary's eyes widened. 'It takes a foolish tongue to say such a thing at Hallowe'en! This is the night the witches and warlocks have their bit of fun, and who are we to deny them? In you go!' She pushed the girl in, closed the door, and went back to the parlour where all her other guests, young and old, had gathered to hear ghost stories.

The small room was lit by one candle. Shadows flickered in the corners and Margaret's face floated in the mirror like a water lily against a dark background. She heard Mary's footsteps clicking across the hall; a babble of voices rose then sank to a dull murmur as the parlour door opened and shut, and Margaret was alone.

She made a face at her reflected image and decided that she might as well follow the rules of the game and get it over with. She drew the confining pins from her hair and combed it out, letting it drift about her shoulders, then she bit into the apple, daring Mary's witches and warlocks to do their worst.

But no male image, strange or familiar, peered over her shoulder to threaten her future. It was as she had already planned – she would walk through life alone, unencumbered, free.

Margaret pinned her hair up neatly and finished the apple, her mind drifting away from the party and the people waiting for her in the parlour, to the lesson she intended to set the Hospital children in the morning.

Then, suddenly aware that time was passing and

she would have to rejoin the others, she glanced up – and saw a dim figure reflected in the mirror, hovering in the shadows behind her shoulder.

With a stifled gasp she whirled round, the apple core falling from her fingers to spin into a corner of the room.

'Margaret—' the man half-way between the door and the mirror moved forward. 'I didn't mean to fright you. I wanted to talk to you—'

'William!' She jumped to her feet, one hand clasped to her throat where a pulse hammered against the soft skin. 'You – you daft gowk! Has the drink addled what brains you ever had?'

The thoughtless words, born of fright and anger, were out before she could stop them. In the flickering light from the candle she saw his face twist as though a sharp pain had lanced through him.

'William—'

But he was already turning away from her, towards the door. He stopped as it opened and light from another candle flooded the room. Gavin Knox stood there, looking from one to the other of them.

'I thought I heard you cry out, Margaret—'

'I didn't,' she said quickly. 'We were just – talking—'

William brushed past Gavin without a word. She followed in time to see the front door close behind him.

'Did I do something wrong?' asked Gavin from just behind her. She looked up at his rugged, puzzled face.

'No, but I did,' she said, and led the way into the parlour.

On the last day of 1768, two months after Mary's Hallowe'en party, Robert Montgomery and Annie were married.

The most striking figure at the wedding feast was Jamie, resplendent in the green tartan plaid and blue feathered bonnet of the 79th Fusiliers.

'Now do you believe I meant what I said?' he asked Margaret belligerently when he first appeared in his uniform. 'If I can't have you, I'll settle for soldiering.'

She smiled sweetly up at him, relieved that at last the matter was settled. Jamie's proposals had begun to be wearying.

'I always believed you – the trouble was that you would never believe me,' she pointed out, and he scowled.

'You'll grow to be a sour-faced old woman if you don't come to your senses!'

'Mebbe so – but if I do you'll thank providence that you're wed to someone else, and not me,' she said but for a fleeting moment, as she watched him moving about the room, tall and broad and handsome, she wished that she could have been an empty-head like Kate, and happy to settle for marriage.

Then she caught sight of William standing behind his father's chair, his eyes on her, and all thoughts of Jamie were swept away in a wave of irritation.

Why couldn't William be the one who was leaving
Paisley? Life would be easier if she knew that there
was no danger of meeting him and being reminded
how drastically his appearance had changed in the
past year or two.

Habitual drinking had dimmed his clear eyes
and given his fair skin an unhealthy sallow tinge.
His shoulders were rounded and his brown hair,
once touched with rich gold lights, was lank and
untidy. His mouth never curled into the crooked
grin she remembered so clearly – instead, it had
a bitter twist to it.

'Poor William,' Mary said into her ear. 'He looks
as if he's in sore need of a friend.'

'From what I hear he's got friends in every howff
and drinking den in the town.'

'You know what I mean, Margaret. For someone
who cares about folk, you've an awful indifference
towards him.'

Margaret's face felt warm. 'The people I care
about can't help themselves! William Todd's
brought all his misery on his own head. He
could easily have decided to live his own life, as
Jamie's done, and me – and the rest of us. Instead,
he's chosen to do everything his father orders him
to! What sort of a man would do that?'

Mary's eyes were surprisingly unsympathetic as
she studied her niece. 'Mebbe it takes a special
sort of son to follow his father's wishes without question and go against his own feelings.
Mebbe you should remember that you don't know

the whole story. You're lacking in compassion, Margaret.'

Hurt anger set Margaret's eyes ablaze. 'If you're so sorry for him why don't you go and keep him company instead of wasting your time with the likes of me?'

'Because it's not my friendship he's hungering for – and anyway, he's just gone out,' Mary said calmly, and a wave of relief swept over Margaret. She felt more comfortable when William was out of the way. No doubt, she told herself, still stinging from her aunt's criticism, he had gone to join some of his drinking cronies.

Outside, William hunched his shoulders against the chill wind and turned towards Pit Land, a tenement in Broomlands Street with a cock-fighting pit at the rear. It was a popular place, and the room was crowded with men when he got there. Weavers and masons and carpenters and merchants rubbed shoulders, for every man was equal at Pit Land as long as he had money to wager.

Here and there were clusters of brawny, unsmiling men with coal dust etched deeply and permanently into their skin – miners from the nearby Thorn Village, opting to spend their few hours above ground in this airless room, gambling their hard-won wages away.

Tobacco smoke hung like pools of treacle in the lamplight. In a sanded circle at the centre of the room two cocks danced towards each other, necks and wings outstretched, then in a united movement they locked, a tumble of bronze and blue-black feathers and sharp eager talons.

William dug into his pocket and tossed some coins onto the ground. Then he leaned against a post and watched with dulled eyes, little caring what the outcome of the fight was.

Blood sprayed suddenly from the black cock and sprinkled the men immediately beside the ring. The red bird went in for the kill amid a chorus of jeers from onlookers angry at the speedy conclusion to the bout. A hand scooped up William's wager and he threw down more money. The victor and its victim were removed and two more birds, bloodlust in their glaring eyes, were loosed on each other.

The white cock, owned by an Elderslie man, was well-known in Pit Land. It was an undisputed champion, but it was getting old and the challenger had ventured his best bird against it, a gamble that paid off that day.

After a preliminary skirmish to assess its opponent's abilities the other bird, younger and stronger, began to shred its adversary coolly and scientifically. The white cock, covered with blood, retreated almost at once but its humiliated owner, with an angry wave of the hand and a curt 'Let it stay!' deprived it of its right to a swift neck-wringing end. A few minutes later it was a sodden red heap and the owner of the new champion swept up his exhausted bird with a whoop of joy and kissed it, smearing blood from its feathers onto his face.

The scene suddenly came into sharp focus for William. The place reeked of death; the man's bloody face and the bird's bright, hard eyes were demonic in the hazy lamplight. His stomach heaved and he pushed his way out roughly, leaning against the tenement wall and breathing in great mouthfuls of air when he gained the street. Then he wandered into the night, not knowing or caring where he went.

He didn't realise that his feet had carried him out of the town and onto the moors until the splash of a small waterfall reminded him that his mouth was dry. He followed the sound through the dark night, slid down a steep bank and plunged his face into the icy stream, sucking water up greedily.

He was tempted to stay where he was, in that quiet empty place far from the town and its inhabitants. But William hadn't entirely opted from his past. Deep within the bitter shell he had become he still cared for his father, and he knew that Colin would be sick with worry if he didn't go home.

With a sound that was half-groan, half-sigh he resisted the impulse to curl up among the reeds and sleep to the lullaby of the waterfall and began to scramble up the banking.

He was almost at the top when a clump of grass gave way beneath his hand and he slid back, twisting and turning in an effort to stop his descent. His head struck a fair-sized stone by the water's edge; he cried out in pain, then lay still, one arm in the cold water.

Margaret plunged along the footpath. Chill droplets sprinkled her ankles as she splashed into a puddle but she ran on without pausing to inspect the damage to her skirts.

Behind her she heard Jamie call her name, but she rounded the corner into High Street, unheeding.

'William's hurt bad – bad—' The words pounding in her head kept time with her flying feet. People turned to stare at her as she sped by, wisps of dark brown hair escaping from under her bonnet to blow round her pale face, blue eyes seeing nothing of her surroundings.

'Margaret!' Jamie caught up with her as she reached Kirsty's street door. 'It was your mother I was sent to fetch, not you! You should've stayed in the shop and let her come back with me.'

'D'you think I'd be content to stand there giving out pokes of meal when William's mebbe dying?' she stormed, and pulled away from him, into the passageway. He stood where he was, watching her disappear up the stairs, then, shoulders slumped, he went slowly into the room where Colin waited for news of his son.

The kitchen was ominously quiet. Kirsty's spinning wheel lay idle, and its owner was bending over the wall-bed in the alcove.

'Meg?'

'It's me.' Margaret went to the bed at once, her eyes dark with fear of what she might find there.

William lay motionless, his body scarcely mounding the covers, his face whiter than the pillow and even thinner than usual, as though the flesh had collapsed in on the bones. A bloodied cloth was wrapped round his head. To Margaret's terrified gaze he looked as though he was already dead.

'Is he—?'

'He's still with us, though the dear Lord knows how he survived that cold night on the braes.' Kirsty straightened her aching back. 'A carter found him this morning – his head's cut badly and it looks as though he's been lying in a burn all night. He was chilled through. When's your mother coming? I'll need her help with the nursing—'

Gently Margaret lifted one of William's hands. It lay passively in hers. 'I'll do it.'

'Best leave it to Meg and me,' Kirsty insisted but Margaret's head lifted sharply.

'I said I'll do it – night and day if need be! If anything happens to him it's my fault, d'you not see that?' She stroked the inert fingers that lay in hers. 'If I hadn't been so cruel to him for doing as his father wanted, he'd never have turned to drink the way he did – and he'd have stayed at the wedding party instead of going off on his own. If he should die—'

Her voice broke and she bent her head over the still hand clasped in her own grip.

'Margaret Montgomery, your tongue's running away with you! I didn't raise him all those years just to see him put into an early grave.'

'I want to help!'

Kirsty gave her a long level look. 'Very well, but if you're so set on caring for him you'll have to stop crying all over him – he got wet enough last night to do him for a lifetime! Now – dry your face and help me to heat more stones to put against his limbs.'

It was a long hard fight. In spite of her brave words Kirsty thought for several days that they weren't going to save William. The soaking he had endured brought on a rheumatic fever, with swelling and tenderness in every joint. Every movement was agony, and Margaret grew hollow-eyed and pale as she listened to him moaning and babbling in a semi-conscious stupor. The physician prescribed one remedy after another and William was bled, purged, treated with hot poultices and cold poultices, and dosed with everything the man could think of.

'I think that man's killing him with his cures,' Kirsty said unhappily. 'What's wrong with warm flannel next to the skin, and good broth – and peace of mind?'

'There's nothing at all wrong with it, for that's what cured me when I was near death's door.' Billy looked down on the grey-faced man in the bed. 'You should try it, Kirsty.'

'You'll have to do something,' Margaret begged.

'I can't stand to see him slipping away from us like this!'

Kirsty hesitated, looking from one to the other.

'If Colin agrees to it, I will. I'll not see William tormented with that man's cures any longer!'

Slowly, so slowly that it was a few days before they noticed the difference, William began to respond to Kirsty's treatment. Margaret was the first to see it taking effect.

'Speaking for myself, I've viewed healthier corpses many a time,' Mary said bluntly when she called to inspect the invalid.

'He's getting better,' Margaret contradicted her. 'He spoke to me this morning. And it wasn't delirium this time. He's on the mend.'

'I'll just have to take your word for it,' said Mary, but once she was settled by the fire in Colin's room she told him cheerfully, 'The boy's looking better every time I see him. I brought some of my best brandy for him, but he's so well cosseted up there that I decided to give the most of it to you instead. In fact, we'll have a sup of it now to cheer ourselves up.'

His eyes followed her gratefully as she bustled about his room. During the dark days when it seemed as though William was going to die, only Mary had realised how bad the waiting was for Colin, unable to walk upstairs and take his turn at watching over his precious son.

She had taken to visiting the invalid every day

and then going downstairs to report on his progress. Now she handed him a cup of brandy then settled herself on the other side of the fire.

'See and enjoy that now. The Honourable James Erskine and his Honourable wife were in for their dinner last night and I opened this bottle for them. My Andra's finest brandy – but d'you think they appreciated it? Not them! "My," says the Honourable, "a real treat, Mistress MacLeod." And down his throat it went in one swallow before I could get a word of thanks out of my mouth. His wife was no better – the two of them were sitting there going at my good brandy as if it was nothing more than water from the street well. So I winked at the maid-servant to bring out the claret instead and put the brandy by for you. I'd have been better giving these two the sour-tasting elderberry wine Andra's sister sent from Melrose last year, for all the taste their tongues have.'

For the first time since William's accident Colin's rich chuckle was heard, and Mary smiled down into her brandy, well pleased with herself.

# Chapter Three

JAMIE JOINED HIS REGIMENT SHORTLY after William began to recover from his illness. On his final day in Paisley Margaret took time from her nursing to walk with him across the moors where they had all played as children.

'It's a shame, you going away without a proper farewell gathering.'

'I'd not want one with William still so poorly.' He gave her a sidelong glance from beneath his lashes. 'I'll miss you, Margaret.' Then, as she walked on without answering, he asked impatiently, 'Will you miss me?'

'I've known you all my life – of course I'll notice when that red head of yours isn't around!'

'Can you not find a gentler way of saying it?'

'Jamie—' she said, exasperated, 'You know fine I'll miss you, without me having to say it!'

His eyes brightened. 'Does that mean—'

'No, it does not.'

'You don't know what I was going to say!'

'Yes I do. You were going to say that if I miss you and I don't have to say it because you know it already, it might mean that I feel strongly for you and that's why I don't say that either. But it doesn't work that way.'

'Och – Margaret!' said Jamie, thoroughly confused.

Braving the January cold, she sat down on a flat rock and pulled her gloves off. She had picked some reeds on the banks of a burn, and now she began plaiting them as she had done as a little girl. The moors had their own bleak beauty under the winter sun, and the air was sharp and clear.

'How can you bring yourself to leave this place?'

'That's easy enough.' He paced restlessly round her, kicking at dry dead clumps of grass. 'It's the folk I don't want to leave – some of them.'

'You'll meet other folk. The world's full of them.'

'Will you write to me?'

'If you write back.'

'Me? You know I was never one for letters.'

'It's not hard,' she assured him. 'Just let your fingers do the work. If they wag as much as your tongue does you'll have no trouble.'

Then her work on the reeds was finished, and it was time to go back home. Margaret searched the grassy area round the rock, but there was no sign of her second glove.

'I'll keep your hand warm,' Jamie said daringly, taking the ungloved fingers in his. She clicked her tongue disapprovingly, but let her hand stay in his warm clasp.

'Can I kiss you goodbye?'

'You can not!'

'Surely a soldier has the right to a kiss before he goes off to the wars?'

'What wars?'

'Margaret,' he wheedled, 'I promise I'll bear in mind that we're just friends. One farewell kiss, that's all I'm asking for.'

She couldn't deny a request from someone who might be on his way to the other end of the world. She reached up and put her arms about his neck, her face lifted to his.

Jamie, resigned to the prospect of a swift peck as Margaret's idea of a kiss, was pleasantly surprised. As her lips met his they softened and parted. For a long moment they clung together, and when they drew apart they were both breathless. Before Margaret could move from his embrace Jamie claimed her mouth again.

Her heart began to flutter and she wondered for a moment why she had so often denied herself the pleasure of Jamie's kisses in the past. Then her practical everyday self took over and she drew back, flushed and breathless.

'Well, that's that,' she observed briskly, as though she had just tossed the dirty dish-water out onto the midden. 'We'd best be getting back now.' And she set off for the town at a rapid pace.

Jamie, striding to keep up with her, was content. He could still feel the soft pressure of her mouth against his, and the warmth of her body in his

211

arms. And her lost glove nestled in his pocket, a fitting keepsake for a brave soldier.

Once William was well on the road to recovery a continual stream of visitors tramped up the stairs to see him; Robert and Annie, flushed with the joy and self-importance of their marital status; Kate, perching on the bed and chattering like a bird about her own approaching marriage to her young lieutenant, unaware that each enthusiastic bounce sent waves of pain through poor William's tender joints; Thomas, the gravity of a medical student sitting strangely on his round young face; Mary's sharp, witty tongue bringing the gossip and scandal that made up the 'drystane dyke' of Paisley life.

But his favourite visitor, and the most frequent, was Margaret. By some unspoken agreement neither of them spoke about the misery of their separation. They behaved as if nothing had ever come between them and Colin and Duncan, both shaken by the young man's brush with death, left them in peace.

It was mid-March before William was well enough to go out, walking slowly up and down the garden with his arm about Margaret's shoulders for support, his pale face lifted to the spring sky. The only reminder of the rheumatic fever that had almost killed him was a slightly crooked left elbow.

When he was fit enough to travel, he went down to Beith to convalesce on the farm which was now owned and worked by Meg's brothers. As she watched him go Margaret felt a sudden pang that she hadn't experienced when she waved goodbye to Jamie. William was part of her life again, and his going left an empty space in her days.

But an epidemic of influenza in the Town Hospital soon gave her plenty to do. Hours spent nursing William had given her the patience to work with sick people, coaxing them to take nourishment, watching over them in their delirium, soothing them when they were weak and afraid.

Those who died were immediately replaced by new inmates grateful for the opportunity to walk through the big doors even as the bodies were carried out the back door for hasty burial. Poverty was like the River Cart itself – it flowed endlessly, and filled every available space. But while the river gave Paisley new growth and a reason for its existence, the flow of unwanted humanity contributed nothing.

There were plenty who saw the Hospital as unacceptable, humiliating charity and preferred to beg in the streets and sleep huddled under walls rather than apply for a place.

'More fools, them,' Meg said irritably as her way along the footpath was hinderered by one of those unfortunates one day. 'Littering the public way when they ought to be in the Hospital – I don't know what they think they're about!'

'Have you visited the Hospital?' Margaret asked. 'It gives shelter, but it's a cheerless place – and some poor souls still have enough pride left to want to manage on their own.'

'Pity they don't have the pride to look for honest work.' Meg had worked all her life, and she had little time for folk who didn't earn their own way.

Margaret's eyes flashed blue fire. 'There's not enough work for them all – and some of them are sick. Have you forgotten poor old Rab Dalrymple?'

Meg had the grace to look embarrassed. Rab, an old shepherd, had been forced to give up his work during the winter because of increasing blindness. No work meant no home, and Rab had gone to the Town Hospital. But hunger for the fields and hills where he belonged gnawed at him, and one bitterly cold day he went out, feeling his way along the house walls and out into the countryside, where he was found the next day, frozen to death.

Margaret was haunted by memories of Rab and people like him who were sacrificed because they didn't fit into the community. But there was little she could do about it except work longer hours at the Hospital, helping where she could.

During the epidemic she was sometimes joined there by Thomas and his friend Gavin Knox, the 'clumsy physician', as Margaret always thought of him.

The clumsy physician arrived at Margaret's side one evening as she left an old woman's bedside in the big sick-room, her cloak in his big capable hands.

'Put this on and I'll walk back with you. Thomas'll be a wee while yet.'

She pushed a strand of hair back from her forehead. 'So will I. I've still to—'

'You've done enough for tonight,' he interrupted crisply. 'You'll make yourself ill if you keep working at this rate, and that'll not help anyone.'

She opened her mouth to argue, then shut it again. He was right – her very soul ached with exhaustion. Meekly, she allowed him to put the cloak about her shoulders and lead her out onto the Hospital steps, his hand beneath her elbow.

'Lift your chin up and breathe deeply,' he ordered, retaining his hold on her arm. 'I find it the best way to recover when I've been working too hard on the wards.'

'I've not been working too hard.'

'Yes you have. Your colour's gone and your eyes—' He halted suddenly and scooped her chin into his free hand, turning her startled face up to his. '—You've got nice eyes, but they're shadowed. You should pay heed to what I'm telling you. It was foolish to spend weeks nursing William Todd back to health then go straight to the Hospital sick-room without giving yourself a rest.'

She pulled her chin free of his grasp, and would have freed her arm too if he hadn't held it in such a grip that it would have meant an undignified struggle.

'No need to lecture me! It's those poor sick folk back there who need help, not me.'

'They're getting it. You're not stepping out as I told you.'

'I'm tired!' she snapped at him, and regretted the words as soon as she saw his eyebrows climb towards his untidy dark hair.

'Isn't that just what I said earlier?'

She could have kicked him. Instead she asked icily, 'Did you never think of joining the militia, Mister Knox? You'd have made a grand officer with your fondness for giving orders.'

He grinned, unruffled. 'You can call me Gavin. I might have gone for soldiering if I hadn't set my heart on medicine instead. Mebbe you're not the only one who wants to help folk. D'you like dancing?'

'Dancing?' The abrupt change of subject took her by surprise.

'Dancing. You've surely heard of it? Folk do it sometimes, to music.'

'Folk that have nothing better to do with their time!'

'So you don't care for it? That's a pity, for there's a public dance to be held in the Saracen's Head in three weeks' time. I'd be honoured if you'd agree to be my partner.'

Sheer surprise brought her to a standstill. As it happened, they were outside the Saracen's Head, the main assembly rooms in the town.

'Well?' Gavin prompted.

'But I – I don't know how to dance.'

'You can learn. I'm told that a Mister William

Banks has just opened a dancing school in Waingaitend.'

Panic seized Margaret. 'I'm – I've never felt the inclination to go in for such frippery.' She lied. Part of her wanted to go to the dance, to wear a fine new dress and learn the social arts. But the other part of her was terrified in case she made a complete fool of herself in front of a man who was, after all, a stranger to her. He fell into step with her as she walked on.

'If you feel that you'd not have the skill to master the steps there's no sense in agreeing to go to the dance with me,' he murmured.

'I didn't say I couldn't master the steps if I put my mind to it! I just said that I – I wasn't sure if I'd enjoy the dance.'

'Have you never been to a dance before?' he asked, and she had to shake her head, like a bumbling country girl who knew nothing of society, she thought angrily.

'Then you must let me partner you to this one,' he insisted, and Margaret, afire with mixed feelings, gave in.

Kate thought that the new formal dances from England were the height of elegance, but Margaret's worst dreams were realised. She was not a natural dancer and she hated every step and every lesson at Mister William Banks' dancing classes.

'I'm not going back,' she threatened each time she came home, but when Kate called to accompany her to the next lesson Meg thrust her out into the street and off she went, tightlipped. If it hadn't been for the thought of having to admit defeat to Gavin she would never had gone on trying to master the complicated steps.

Her only pleasure in the whole business came when she put on the gown that Kate had specially made for her. Margaret, who had never been over-interested in clothes, possessed a fashionably long, slim figure, and even she was impressed by her own appearance on the night of the Assembly.

Her gown was of pale green silk over a hooped white underskirt embroidered in the same pale green. The over-gown's low neckline was trimmed with white lawn and the sleeves ended at the elbows in a foam of green ruffles. Her shoes were of white satin, and her brown hair was simply dressed and tied with ribbons to match the gown.

When Meg escorted her into the kitchen where Gavin waited, his hazel eyes blazed with surprised admiration.

'You look almost beautiful!' Thomas said in awe, and Jackie, Duncan's little apprentice, stopped in the doorway, mouth agape, the stoup of water he had been bringing in for Meg tilting in his grasp and almost spilling onto the clean floor.

She stood before them, rosy-cheeked under their admiration, feeling strangely unlike herself, yet liking the sensuous kiss of silk against her skin and the whisper of her skirts as she moved.

When they reached the Saracen's Head light was pouring through all its windows, illuminating the area outside, which was crammed with carriages and horses. In the building's main rooms voices and laughter mingling with the lusty music of a Scottish reel.

'Would you care to dance?' Gavin roared over the noise, and led Margaret onto the crowded floor.

At first it seemed that everything was going to go well. The musicians were playing for a Scottish reel, and Margaret began to enjoy herself as she swung round to the beat of the music, her hands tight in Gavin's, her green silk skirt billowing about her. They danced the next dance, a strathspey, then Gavin led her to a seat and went off in search of a cooling drink.

As he came back, weaving skilfully through the crowds, a cup in each hand, she studied him through discreetly lowered lashes. He wore a deep blue coat with silver buttons, a flowered waistcoat, yellow shirt and breeches, and there were silver buckles on his shoes. His own dark hair, unpowdered, was tied back with a ribbon. He was, Margaret had to acknowledge, a fine-looking man. She took the proffered cup and sipped at it. The evening was going to be more bearable than she had supposed.

But the formal English dances proved her wrong. During the first, she managed to be deep in conversation with someone, watching with growing panic as Gavin adroitly steered Kate through the intricate steps, smiling down into her flushed, excited little face. But there was no escape the second time, and her heart sank as he led her onto the floor and the music began.

Three minutes later he caught up with her as she fled outside on to the balcony, to hide her shame in the darkness.

'Margaret?'

'Let me be!'

His hands turned her about to face him. Beyond his shoulder she could see through the lighted window to where dancers circled and bobbed with stylish ease.

'Are you ill?'

'Ill in the head, to try those daft dances!' Her voice shook with humiliation.

'You were doing fine.'

'You didn't think that when I trampled on your foot, did you? I heard what you said then, Gavin Knox!'

'Well – it hurt at the time. But—'

'At the time? You'll probably be lame for a week – and so will everyone else who was dancing near me!' She realised that she was wringing her hands, and pushed them down by her sides. 'I'm going home—'

'No you're not! You came to the dance with me, and I'll take you home when it's over,' he said firmly, his big body trapping her in a corner.

'I'm not one for dancing – I told you that in the

beginning,' she wailed. 'Why couldn't you have paid heed then and found some elegant Glasgow lady to go with you?'

'I didn't want any Glasgow lady – I wanted you to be my partner.'

She felt tears thicken her throat and plunged on in an attempt to finish before they choked her altogether. 'It's that dancing class that's to blame! Mister Banks won't teach men and women together, and I'm taller than Kate so I always had to be the gentleman and – and I'd have been better dancing with the girl Thomas invited, for I've I – learned the steps all the wr – wrong way!'

The final words came out in a sort of wail, then there was silence, broken only by Margaret's sniffs of self-pity. Gavin drew in a deep breath and stared over her head at the wall behind her. 'Are you laughing at me?' she demanded to know. It was too dark for her to make out his expression.

'No!' The denial was too prompt, too abrupt. Margaret put her hands on his shoulders and stood on tip-toe, peering into his shadowy features.

'Am I to believe, then,' she said tartly, 'that you always have a silly grin on your face?' Then she released him and stepped back, chin tilted belligerently. 'Get on with it, then – get it over with!' she ordered, as if he was one of the children in the class at the Hospital.

She had never heard Gavin laugh so heartily. He roared and whooped and gasped for breath, first supporting himself with one arm about her shoulder – for all the world as though she was one of his drinking friends, she thought indignantly – then gathering her into his embrace.

She endured it stoically, her nose pressed against his jacket buttons, waves of mirth rumbling in his chest and vibrating against her cheek. Finally, just as she was wondering if he was ever going to stop, the peals of laughter eased to hiccups, then slowed.

'Your pardon, Mistress Margaret,' he said at last, his voice still shaky with amusement.

'So I should hope—' she began indignantly, then the words died away as she looked up and saw his face just above hers.

'You look beautiful—' Gavin said huskily and bent his head to hers.

'I – I don't approve of kissing men I scarcely know,' said Margaret weakly when she was free to speak again.

'I should have known that. You'll grow to like it—' he said, and kissed her again.

She should have resisted. Indeed, she fully meant to resist, but somehow time passed and she did nothing about it, other than sliding her arms about his neck and letting her mouth soften and melt beneath his.

In the two weeks after the Assembly Margaret made a point of being out of the house when Thomas and Gavin Knox came from Glasgow.

Memories of those moments spent in Gavin's arms tormented her. She had lost her head – she had behaved like an empty-headed female, and she was afraid that he, like Jamie, would leap to the conclusion that a kiss meant more than it should. But as the days passed and the physician made no attempt to seek her out, her confusion lessened and the Assembly faded into the background.

William came home earlier than was expected. Country air and farm food gave him back his health quickly, and he was soon hungering for Paisley again, for the familiar routine of work and above all for Margaret.

She was wandering alone on the braes, enjoying a rare afternoon's freedom, when a cart rumbled past, bound for Paisley. The man on the box grinned when he saw her perched on the bank of a burn, her skirt kilted about her knees and her bare toes splashing in the water.

'It's yourself, Maggie Montgomery,' he called, and she recognised him as a former schoolmate. 'It's a grand day.' Then he jerked the whip-handle over his shoulder. 'William Todd's coming your way.'

She shaded her eyes from the sun and looked up at him. 'William? He's in Beith, surely.'

'I brought him back myself. He got down just over the hill there to walk the rest of the way—' His voice faded as the cart rattled on.

She scrambled to her feet and ran up the rise, not waiting to put her shoes and stockings on.

Her heart jumped as she saw a figure in the distance, a man walking with an easy swing, unhampered by the weight of the bag slung carelessly over one shoulder. A warm breeze brought her the sound of a melodious whistle as he walked.

She cupped her hands about her mouth. 'William!'

He stopped, looked round, saw her, and began to run. Her hair was in a curly mass about her face, her skirt caught about her bare legs as she sped towards him, but it didn't matter. As they met he dropped the bag and picked her up, whirling her round as though she was a feather's-weight.

'William – put me down! You'll hurt yourself!'

'I will not. I'm as strong and hearty as ever I was, thanks to your aunt's cooking.' He set her down but kept her within the circle of his arms. 'She fed me so well I began to fear that she was fattening me for Christmas.'

'You look so – oh, you just look grand, William.'

He did. His skin had taken on an even gold tan and the gold lights had come back to his soft thick hair. His grey eyes sparkled and the body lightly touching hers was strong and firm.

'And I'm—' she tried in vain to smooth her tangled hair, laughing up at him. 'I must look like a tinker child. What a way to welcome you home!'

He shook his head, hugged her close. 'You're even more lovely than I remembered,' he said into her wind-blown curls. 'And it's the best welcome a man could hope for.'

Then he scooped up his bag and they turned towards Paisley, his arm firmly about her.

# Chapter Four

S UMMER BLOSSOMED, THEN GAVE WAY to autumn. Weavers with work to do in the late afternoons had to light tapers to see by. Kate married her young lieutenant and in October Robert's wife Annie gave birth to their first child, a son.

Jackie McNab, the orphaned apprentice in Duncan's employment, decided that the time had come to better himself and plucked up the courage to ask Margaret if she would teach him to read and write 'proper'.

'But I taught you along with the others in the Town Hospital, Jackie.'

His thin little face was crimson, his mouth trembling with the need to say the right things, to convince her of his sincerity.

'But I have to learn more if—' He shuffled his knobbly bare feet and squirmed with self-consciousness, '—if I'm to be a proper master. Now that there's drawlooms coming into the town there's a new need for learning—' His brown eyes begged for her understanding.

Despite Meg's good food, Jackie was doomed to

carry always the signs of a half-starved infancy. He was small for his age, and rickets, that common childhood ailment, had warped his bones and made him look clumsy, though he was agile enough, with a speed of movement learned from the need to dodge blows and keep out of trouble.

'So you want to learn to work a drawloom, do you?'

His face glowed. Jackie's real idol wasn't Duncan, but Robert, who wove cloth on one of the big new drawlooms with an intricate overhead harness that had to be worked by a drawboy.

'If you'll teach me about letters and numbers I'll learn well—' he said huskily, scarcely daring to hope, and she wanted to take his slight body into her arms and mother him.

'You'll have to work hard, Jackie McNab,' she said instead, with a briskness that was meant as much for herself as for him, and was bathed in a huge smile of gratitude and pure love.

'I will!' gulped Jackie, and was as true as his word. Each evening he studied his books by the light of a taper in the corner of the silent loom-shop where he slept. And whenever Robert called at the house, wreathed in the confident aura of a family man with a son of his own, Jackie tried to be there, tucked into a corner of the work-shop, devouring the talk that floated round his ears with the blue-grey tobacco smoke from the men's pipes.

'Gauze is on its way out,' Duncan would announce firmly above the thump of his loom.

227

'If you're right, there's something to be said for cotton, now they've got that new yarn in England,' his elder son said just as firmly. 'I hear it makes for a better cloth.'

'Let England get on with it, then. We've got our own way of working.'

Robert's fist crashed onto the deep window-sill where he sat. 'Listen to me, man – a Lancashire weaver can make seven shillings in a week!'

'And a Paisley weaver can make the same if he puts his mind to it, without being beholden to anyone. D'you want to see us turning to those manufactories they've started in the south? All the looms under one roof and the weavers working for one employer and not able to call their souls their own? That's not for me!'

'But we have to move with the times!' Sooner or later Robert would come out with Jackie's favourite phrase.

Later, when the day's work was done and he was studying alone in the loom-shop, the little apprentice would clamp his slate-pencil between his teeth in imitation of a pipe, pace the floor, thump his fist on a loom and tell the silent wooden structures about him, each with its half-made cloth stretched between its rollers, 'Man, we have to move with the times, I'm telling you! Move with the times!'

When all was said and done, Jackie had never been happier in his entire life. Every morning he began his day by cleaning and oiling the looms, sneezing as he removed fluff, spiders' webs and, sometimes, snails attracted by the damp dark places beneath the treadles. Then it was time to have breakfast with the family.

Afterwards he brought in water from the street well and swept the back yard, then he took his place in the loom-shop, doing whatever he was bid, and watching the finished cloth gradually take shape between the huge rollers.

If the weavers were keeping pace with the work in hand they very often took the afternoon off, leaving Jackie free to work on his lessons or run off with apprentices from other shops. They bowled, ran races, went to the braes to paddle in cold swift-running burns. Sometimes they went swimming at the Hammells, the River Cart waterfalls close to the town centre, or visited the cock-fighting pit behind the Deer Inn in Broomlands Street. There was always something to do. Ragged and mischievous, rebelliously against authority other than that imposed on them in the loom-shops, the apprentices and drawboys often brought the wrath of their elders down about their uncaring ears, but Jackie tended to be a follower, not a leader.

The market was another popular venue with the apprentices. One of Jackie's closest friends was a carrot-headed drawboy named Charlie Brodie, famed for his ability as a sneak-thief. A walk round the market in Charlie's company usually resulted in some treat or other – pies or fruit or sweets that had magically slipped into Charlie's tattered shirt as he passed a stall.

'Want one, Jackie?' he asked one afternoon as he saw the younger boy's gaze fall on a pile of apples, large and rosy, promising crisp white flesh and sharp-tasting juice that would trickle down a boy's chin.

Jackie's mouth watered. 'I wouldn't mind.'

'Easy.' Casually, Charlie sauntered closer to the stall, looking around, while Jackie watched, his stomach tight with excitement and his tongue already tasting the fruit. Two scarlet globes seemed to glide from the stall into Charlie's grasp. One disappeared into his shift, but as the other one was about to follow a large hand whipped out and caught him by the arm.

'You thief, you! I'll teach you to steal from me!'

Charlie immediately ducked and twisted, but the woman held on and he only succeeded in ripping the sleeve out of his worn shirt. The first apple fell to the ground; he threw the other to Jackie, who automatically put out his hands and caught it. As soon as its firm roundness slapped into his palms he realised his mistake, but it was too late.

'Get that one an' all!' the stall-holder bellowed above Charlie's enraged screeches of innocence. Faces turned towards Jackie, hands reached out to grab him, and he turned and ran for his life. Head down, the apple still clutched in his hands, he butted his way across the market, eeling between stalls until he gained the High Street.

He fled across it, miraculously avoiding the carts and carriages, and ran down Waingaitend with some idea of finding a hiding place in the bushes and trees by the river.

Terror squeezed his heart and all but stifled him. He could have thrown the stolen fruit away and run into one of the tenement entries, protesting his innocence if he had been caught empty-handed. But he could no longer think clearly. All he wanted was to get away, to hide, to be safe from pursuit.

He reached the bottom of Waingaitend and ran by the Town Hospital, too frightened to see Margaret coming down the steps.

She almost fell over him as he fled past, and put out a hand to stop him. Jackie felt her fingers brush his shoulder, and with a thin, choked scream of despairing terror he swerved away, into the roadway and into the path of a large farm cart filled to overloading with refuse collected from a nearby tenement yard.

'Jackie!' Margaret's shriek broke through his panic and he looked up to see the carthorse above him, hooves flailing as the carter dragged back on the reins. Again, Jackie hurled himself to one side, the apple thrown away at last to let his arms curl protectively about his head.

He fell clear of the chopping hooves, which tore lumps of dried mud from the road as they descended, but his bid for safety didn't carry him far enough.

As the cart lurched to a standstill one of its huge

iron-bound wheels ran over his outstretched leg, crushing it as if it was a twig.

With a wrenching scream that echoed in Margaret's ears for the rest of her life, Jackie's thin body arched up then fell back, his fingers clawing into the hard-packed earth.

People came running to group around him as he lay there. Margaret was among the first to reach him, heedless of the unnerved horse's hooves as she dropped to her knees by the boy.

The apple, thrown well clear, had rolled into a puddle of stagnant water. It only lay there for a few minutes before a small child scooped it up and carried it off.

There was little they could do to save Jackie's leg. The weight of the cart, taking refuse to fertilise the fields, had crushed and mangled the bone beyond any hope of repair. It would have to be amputated.

Nausea swept over Margaret when Doctor Scobie pronounced his verdict. Jackie had been carried into the Hospital, where he lay, mercifully unconscious, in a cot in the big sick-room.

'Amputation's the boy's only hope,' the doctor repeated, frustrated by his own uselessness in the face of such terrible injuries.

'And what sort of hope is that for anyone?' Margaret asked dully. 'When will it be done?'

'In the morning. I'll have to find a surgeon willing to undertake it.'

A surgeon. The word penetrated Margaret's misery, bringing with it pictures of a square face under dark hair, a clumsy big body and broad capable hands.

'Gavin's one of the finest surgeons you could hope to meet—' Thomas's defence of his friend echoed in her head.

'Wait – I think I know of a surgeon who'd see to Jackie—' she said, with rising hope, and fled from the Hospital, glad to be out of the place and doing something to help the injured boy.

It was only natural, now, to look to William for help. Within the hour the two of them were huddled in a cart, rattling over the town bridge and through the new streets recently built on the opposite bank, each one called after the trades that had brought prosperity to Paisley. Usually Margaret delighted in those fine names – Silk Street, Cotton Street, Gauze Street – but that day she had no time to spare for them.

William watched her anxiously. 'Margaret, from what you say of his injuries, the boy might not recover even if the King's physicians themselves took on his case. You're mebbe expecting too much of Thomas's friend.'

'I'm not looking for a miracle. I just want to know I've done all I can for Jackie. Gavin might – he might—'

She stopped, fighting back tears, and he put an arm about her and held her close against his shoulder.

233

Dusk was hovering over Glasgow's fine broad streets by the time they arrived at Thomas's lodging house. Margaret scarcely took time to introduce herself to his landlady before hurrying upstairs with William following close behind her. She rattled on the door panels with impatient knuckles, then burst in without waiting for an invitation.

The little room seemed to be overflowing with books. They fell over each other on a shelf on the wall, sprawled in heaps on the table, lay scattered over the floor.

Thomas, in shirt sleeves, was sitting at the table, and Gavin lounged comfortably in a chair by the fire. The two men looked up, startled, then jumped to their feet.

As Margaret poured out the story of the little apprentice's accident the medical student and the surgeon exchanged glances. They let her finish without interruption, then Gavin took her over the details of Jackie's injuries again, interrupting her several times, making her describe the wounds as accurately as possible. When she had finished there was a long silence while he deliberated.

'From the sound of it there's not much I can do to save the leg—' he began and William interrupted him.

'If you're not willing to try, we'll walk the streets of Glasgow till we find someone who is!'

A muscle twitched in Gavin's jaw, and his eyes seemed to frost over as they met William's glare.

'I was about to say that I'll do my best. I'll come to Paisley first thing in the morning.'

'Now! Come back with me now!'

An irritated frown furrowed his brow. 'I'm on my way to dine with friends right now, and it's an engagement I can't cancel. Besides—'

She flew at him and he took a step back under the unexpected onslaught. 'Be damned to your dinner-party!' The oath sprang easily to her lips in her agitation, though it was the first time in her entire life she had used it. 'There's a child lying in the Hospital, needing your care right now!'

Appalled by his sister's behaviour, Thomas sprang forward, but it was William who reached Margaret first, pulling her away from Gavin and into the shelter of his own arms.

The surgeon smoothed his blue embroidered silk coat.

'The child needs to rest tonight – and so do I, for I've been working in the wards all day and I'd not trust my own judgement at the moment,' he said coolly. Then he added, in a kinder voice. 'You have my promise that I'll be in Paisley first thing tomorrow. Go home now, Margaret, and get some rest yourself. We'll all need to be strong tomorrow.'

When Margaret arrived at the Hospital early in the morning Gavin and Thomas were already there, closeted in a small side-room with Jackie. Clear-eyed and calm, the surgeon gave her a brief nod by way of greeting when they came into the Mistress's room with Doctor Scobie.

'There's nothing for it but to take the leg away.'

Despite herself Margaret felt her lips tremble. 'But – all he's ever wanted is to be a master weaver. A weaver needs his two legs!'

'He needs to be alive, too.' Gavin's face darkened. 'It's a matter of trying to save the boy himself now. Thomas, you know what we'll need.' He took his coat off and dropped it on a chair. 'Margaret, do something useful – take the children outside, away from this business.'

Not many people could dismiss Margaret Montgomery as easily as that and hope to get away with it. But Gavin was no longer Thomas's clumsy, amiable friend, or even the man who had kissed her at the dance. He was a professional trained man with an air of authority about him that she had never seen before. Meekly, she did as she was told.

Thomas felt a stab of envy as he watched his sister lead her charges out of the building. It was the first time he had assisted at an operation under such circumstances, and his skin prickled with apprehension as he went into the room where Jackie lay on a large table. Gavin was setting out his instruments, his face mask-like as he concentrated his mind on the work ahead.

Thomas splashed whisky into a cup and lifted

Jackie's head. The boy choked, coughed, then swallowed the liquid that trickled into his mouth. Patiently Thomas fed the cup's contents to him, drop by drop.

When Jackie's eyelids fell and his breathing took on a thick, slow note, Thomas put the empty cup aside and bared the injured leg, drawing in his breath sharply as the shattered mass of bone and bloody flesh was revealed.

The two male inmates who had volunteered their services for payment of sixpence each paled and turned their heads away, but mercifully they both retained their determined grip on Jackie's small body as ordered.

Gavin's eyes were calm and his hand, as it gripped Jackie's thigh just below the groin, was steady. For a second he paused, then the knife descended.

The small paupers, revelling in their freedom, scampered along the river's banks, noses reddened by the chill wind. Margaret found a sheltered area and paced up and down, tormented by thoughts of what must be happening back at the Hospital. Finally, unable to banish the terrible pictures from her mind, she resorted to a childhood trick, thrusting her ungloved hand into a thorn bush, letting the pain of a dozen small scratches shock her back to her surroundings.

The minutes dragged by, and she felt as though she must have aged years by the time the sun

indicated that it was midday and she was able to
gather up her charges and shepherd them back to
the Hospital.

They went willingly enough, their appetites
whetted by the fresh air, eager for the piece of
bread and the small plate of broth that made up
their midday meal.

Gavin, Thomas, and Doctor Scobie were all in
the Mistress's room. Thomas, gratefully sipping at
a glass of brandy, smiled wanly at Margaret.

'He's survived the operation – and a fine job
Gavin made of it,' he added proudly.

'It was that,' the physician chimed in and Gavin,
his shirt sleeves and waistcoat spotted and blotched
with blood, nodded in offhand acknowledgment of
their praise.

'It wasn't a difficult task. But there's many a fine
piece of surgery hidden in a grave.'

Margaret's heart was touched by an icy hand,
'You mean he'll die after all?'

He eyed her thoughtfully. 'Don't expect too
much, Margaret. The boy's not strong and I've
no great hopes for his future.'

Fear for Jackie, the shock of the accident itself,
and the surgeon's seeming indifference suddenly
welded together within her to red-hot fury.

'So you think you've had a wasted journey?
You think we should have got someone else to
cut the boy's leg off – or mebbe we should just
have left him to die in the street, seeing he's only
an orphan and a pauper? I'm sorry if we've taken

you away from the important work of tending to a rich man in a fine Glasgow hospital, but you've no need to worry, for I'll pay your fee whatever the outcome. You'll not be out of pocket – not even if your doctoring kills Jackie!'

'Margaret!' Thomas's face was crimson with anger and embarrassment. Doctor Scobie was scandalised, the Hospital Mistress pursed her lips disapprovingly, but Gavin merely raised one eyebrow.

'You're angered with me,' he said unnecessarily. 'There's no need. I care for the boy's welfare, but it doesn't do to get upset over any patient, rich or poor. If I let myself do that every time I'd not be a good surgeon, you see. And I want to be good at my work.'

'I've no doubt you will be, one day – when you've tried your hand on folk that don't matter to anyone – like Jackie!'

'Margaret!' This time Thomas's voice was a whip-lash, cracking across the small room.

'Leave her be,' Gavin advised him calmly. 'She needs to speak her mind. Though you're being hard on me, Margaret. Best prepare your mind for the worst, as I do in these circumstances.'

'Why not?' she asked bitterly, unable to stop the tirade now that it had begun. 'What chance does he have now, in any case – a crippled pauper!'

Gavin got up unhurriedly and crossed the room, 'Just so,' he agreed, and went out, closing the door gently behind him.

Thomas's fingers ground into his sister's arm, forcing her down on a chair.

'Will you hold your tongue, for the love of God – and take a sup of this, for it seems you need it more than I do!' The cup containing half of his brandy was thrust into her hand, and he stormed out of the room.

He found Gavin outside on the steps, leaning against the Hospital wall, his hands in his pockets.

'Thomas,' he said thoughtfully when his friend tumbled out of the building and arrived by his side. 'The more I see and hear of your sister, the more I think she'd make a grand wife for some ambitious man.'

'If,' said Thomas, his voice tight with rage, 'anyone'd be stupid enough to want her!'

# Chapter Five

FORMALLY, MARGARET PROFFERED GAVIN'S AMPUTATION fee – three shillings and four-pence – on the day after the operation, and formally he accepted it.

She watched the coins disappear into his pocket with stunned disbelief. She had fully expected him to refuse payment on the grounds of his friendship with the family. Then she would have been able to force the coins on him and thus ease her troubled conscience.

She glared up at him, and reddened as she glimpsed a sparkle of malicious amusement in the hazel eyes that met and briefly held hers. Then he was serious again, looking down at Jackie.

'He's survived the shock of the cutting, at least.'

'He seems to be comfortable.' She caressed the sleeping child's face lightly with one finger.

Gavin said nothing, and she knew what he was afraid of. Thomas had taught her that gangrene was the surgeon's greatest enemy. All too often infection set into a wound and killed the patient.

Nobody knew why, Thomas said, his round face perplexed.

'D'you like tending the sick?' Gavin asked as they left Jackie's bedside.

'I like seeing folk getting better. Thomas is lucky to be going into medicine. I wish I could have done that.'

'Hospital work's not for the likes of you,' he said decidedly. 'They can be dirty places – it's a wonder to me that anyone gets well at all in some of them. I've seen dogs running in from the street to forage round the beds for food. And the women that work in the wards – lazy old hags willing to buy drink for any patient who'll share it with them.'

'Mebbe someone should change things.'

He shook his dark head. 'I doubt if that'll ever happen. The folk that care the most are too busy trying to cure the sick to do anything else, and the rest are indifferent.'

In the days that followed he came to Paisley whenever he could to see his patient. Jackie regained consciousness of a sort, though he was too confused to take in what had happened to him. Margaret was glad of that, for she dreaded the day when the boy would discover that he was crippled. In his conscious moments he fretted because they wouldn't let him get up despite his pleas that Mister Montgomery needed him in the loom-shop, but Margaret's presence soothed him a little, so she sat by his bed for hours, listening to him babble about the years ahead, when he would be a drawloom weaver with apprentices of his own.

On the fifth day Gavin came to meet her as she went into the sick-room. His face was pale.

'Margaret, before you go in to him – I've changed his dressings and—'

She knew then that the fight was lost. The poison that had crept into Jackie's wound claimed its victim with hideous efficiency, and when the end came Margaret could only be thankful that Jackie's sufferings were over.

Gavin pulled the dirty sheet over his patient's face and walked out without a word, leaving Margaret to tell the Mistress the news and beg some brandy from her.

She found Gavin in the empty schoolroom, staring at the wall. She put the cup into his hand, and his fingers curled automatically about it.

'You did your best.'

'It wasn't enough.' He drained the cup in one gulp.

'Gavin—' she said awkwardly. 'I was wrong to speak to you the way I did that first day.'

'You said what was in your mind.' His head was bent, both hands gripping the empty cup as though he was warming himself with it. 'I can never accept a death,' he said, more to himself than to her. 'I should have got used to them, but I never do. This one – it was wasteful. The operation went well. He would have lived.'

'He'd probably have become a beggar if he had,

243

poor boy. He'd have hated that – perhaps it was as well it ended this way.'

'I'm not thinking of that!' Gavin said fiercely. 'I don't care what might have become of him. He died because of something we haven't found yet. Because we know how to cut folk, but not how to care for them properly after the cutting. And I can't for the life of me think what we're doing wrong!'

Then he put the cup down and went back to Glasgow and his duties there, without another word.


Jamie came home just when Margaret most needed the sight of his cheerful grin and blazing red head.

'You're sure you've missed me?' he asked jealously during one of their moments together.

She beamed at him affectionately. 'The whole town misses you. You're like a stone in a pond, Jamie Todd – you cast ripples everywhere you go.'

'I'm not talking about the whole town, just about you!' He paused, then added, carefully casual, 'I see you and William are as cosy together as a couple of old women gossiping at a street corner.'

'And why not?'

Jamie scowled. 'Mebbe I should have stayed home. Mebbe if I had you and me would be—'

'Would be quarrelling most of the time instead of enjoying the times we can be together, like this,' she finished the sentence swiftly. 'Admit it, Jamie – you'd not change your soldiering life for anything.'

'I'd not go as far as to say that—' he began, then grinned and shrugged his broad shoulders. 'Well – mebbe you're right. There's things to do and places to see, and the restlessness in me's eased a little now.'

Then, as they rounded a corner and came on a group of sturdy girls, hair tucked under linen caps and round brown arms and legs bared to the chill wintry sun as they gathered water to wash the linen that was spread out to whiten, he added with a wolfish twist to his grin, 'But I'll admit that Paisley has some bonny sights!'

'This is a bonny pattern.'

William, on one of his many visits to his father's room, lifted a sheet of paper that Colin had left lying on his cluttered work table.

Everything Colin needed lay on that table – colours for his designs, volumes he used when he taught his young pupils, sheets of paper scrawled with verses, the half-dozen books that Colin happened to be reading – they huddled together in what seemed to be chaos to the observer, though he himself knew exactly where every item was and resisted all Kirsty's efforts to tidy things up for him.

His thin face flushed with pride at William's praise, though his voice was casual. 'I'm pleased with it – but I'll no doubt have to make some changes before it gets to the loom. The weavers are still complaining that I expect too much of them at times. Mebbe one day some clever man'll invent looms that can take my designs as I mean them to be.'

'Nothing surer.' William sat down on the other side of the fire that kept the December chill at bay, and sprawled his long legs over the hearth rug with the air of a man well-pleased with himself. 'I've been thinking about my future.'

'Aye?' Colin's loving eyes travelled over the younger man's face, noting with relief how well and happy William looked now that he had stopped drinking and found peace with himself and his surroundings.

'Aye. I like working with Billy Carmichael well enough, father, but my apprenticeship's long over now and it's time I started out on my own. See—' he held his hands out, laughing. 'Not a mark on them that wasn't put there by honest toil. Mind when I started work? I was never done hammering my fingers or cutting them instead of the leather. I've mastered my trade at last.'

'How's your arm?'

William punched the crooked elbow, the only reminder of his bout of rheumatic fever, with his other fist. 'It doesn't bother me at all,' he said carelessly, intent on telling his news. 'Now – I was out at Renfrew last week, and there's a wee shop there to rent. It would make a nice beginning for a man setting up in business for himself.'

'What would you use for silver?'

William grinned disarmingly, sure of his reception.

'That's why I've come to you – though you'd always be the first to hear of any plans I might have anyway,' he added hurriedly. 'If you could lend me the money to start off with – it'd not be much, just enough for my rent and my materials, I'll work all the hours God sends to pay it back and get myself properly started.'

'It can be a hard life, setting up a new business. I know, for I did the same when I was about your age.'

William brushed the warning aside with a wave of one hand. 'I know that, but I'm not afraid of hard work. It would do me good – I'm getting too lazy working for Billy, for there's not enough to keep me as busy as I'd like. He could manage with another apprentice, he doesn't need a time-served man, to tell the truth.'

He stopped, eyeing Colin anxiously. The older man deliberated for a few moments, eyes fixed on the flames in the grate, then he looked up and nodded.

'You can have as much as I can afford, and welcome.'

William jumped up and shook his father's hand vigorously. 'I'll only take what I need to see me started, and not a penny more. I want to work for what I get.' He paced the floor, the words tumbling out as he planned aloud.

'I could be in business by February at the latest, and my debt could be paid off by next year at this time. By then I'll know how soon I can afford to find a wee house and get wed—'

Colin's laughter, rarely heard, interrupted him. 'Hold on, man!' he protested. 'One minute you decide to set up on your own and the next you're a married man? You're letting your tongue run away with you.'

'Oh, but I've got it all worked out. I'll not ask Margaret until you've got your money back, but by then—'

'Margaret?' his father interrupted, the laughter suddenly wiped from his face, his hands clutching at the arms of his wheel-chair. 'What Margaret?'

William stopped pacing. All at once it seemed as though the temperature in the warm room had dropped sharply. A gust of wind rattled at the window.

'What Margaret do you think? Margaret Montgomery, of course,' he said, then his gaze hardened. 'Father, you're not going to start all that nonsense again, are you?'

'Have you spoken to her of marriage? What makes you think she'd have you?' Colin's voice was harsh in its urgency and William frowned.

'I told you I'd no intention of asking her until I've got something to offer her. But I think – I hope – she'll accept me when the time comes.'

'You can't marry Margaret Montgomery.'

The bleak words seemed to take shape and stand between the two men like a barricade. William's young face flinched, then set in a cold mask.

'So you're planning on coming between us for a second time, are you? D'you not think that you and Duncan Montgomery have caused enough trouble between Margaret and me? We're grown now – we don't have to heed our fathers any more.' He leaned forward, each word clear and definite. 'I'll not let you tell me what to do with my life now – and if I have to, I'll find the money I need from someone else – so don't think you can try to buy my obedience!'

Colin's face, youthful in his happiness only minutes earlier, was old and drawn. 'Listen to me, William. Believe me. You can't marry Margaret Montgomery!'

William's hands clenched into fists by his sides. 'I'll not listen! And I'll not let you and her father conspire against us this time. I was willing to wait for another twelve month before I spoke to Margaret, but not any more. I'm going to her tonight, and I'm going to ask her if she'll give me her promise that she'll be my wife as soon as I can offer her a home.'

'And if she refuses you?'

William's mouth twisted. 'If she refuses me of her own free will I'll accept that. But I hope she'll say yes – and if she does, father, I'll bring her back

249

here with me and we'll throw your small-minded bigotry right back in your face!'

'William – I'm begging you to leave things as they are!'

'I love her, and I've wasted enough time. If you've got good reason for coming between us a second time then for God's sake tell me what it is—' William strode to the door where he paused, one hand on the latch '—or mind your own business from now on!'

For a moment there was silence, then William's tension was released in a long breath.

'You see? There's no real reason at all, is there? Just some bee you and old Montgomery got in your bonnets. I'm going to Margaret.'

His thumb pushed the metal tongue down, releasing the latch. His wrist tensed to pull at the door.

'She's your sister.'

Even the flames in the hearth seemed to stop moving. William's fingers tightened on the door handle but he wasn't aware of its edge cutting into his palm. He felt as though he had been pushed off the edge of the world and was cart-wheeling through space.

'What?'

Colin's voice was bleak. 'Margaret Montgomery is your sister.'

William opened his clenched hand with difficulty and walked across the room to the window. Kirsty was spreading her washing over bushes to dry. Her rounded arms, damp from the wash-tub, seemed impervious to the bitter wind.

Billy came from further down the garden, a muddy spade in his hand, and said something to her as he passed. The two of them laughed together.

William turned away from the scene, avoiding Colin's gaze, and picked up the design he had been looking at earlier.

'How can she be my – my sister?' he asked through stiff lips.

'Because Duncan Montgomery's your father.'

There was a pause, then – 'Go on!' William's voice was rough, ugly. 'Or am I supposed to try to guess what happened? D'you want to turn this nonsense into a child's game?'

'It isn't nonsense, William. I wish to God it was. Your mother, Lizzie, was my wife, but it was Duncan who fathered you, not me.'

'How did it come about?'

'I don't know the full story of it. I never wanted to know.'

'Well, I do!' The design was crushed into a ball, thrown aside. 'It's my existence we're talking about! Why wait till now to tell me?'

'I thought you were my own flesh and blood until a few years ago, when Duncan saw the danger of you and Margaret becoming too close. It makes no difference to me. You were never his – always mine!'

'"When Duncan saw the danger—"' William

repeated, stunned. 'Duncan saw it? But it was you that came between us – you that used my affection for you to get my promise that I'd not see Margaret again.' He ran a hand over his hair, bewildered. 'You damned near killed me, to cover up what he'd done to you – and to me?'

'He wanted to be the one to speak to you, but you'd not have listened to him, and neither would Margaret. D'you not see that? It had to be me. It was the only way I could think of to protect you and her from the truth!'

'But you've kept your friendship with him! With the man that betrayed you with your own wife!'

Colour flooded Colin's face but his voice didn't waver. 'What's the sense in raking up the past and hurting innocent folk who know nothing about this?'

'It was all right to hurt me, was it? To put me through hell and then do this to me when I finally come out the other side and try to make something of my life?'

'If you hadn't fallen in love with her you'd never have had to know—'

William laughed bitterly. 'I might have realised the fault would lie with me at the end of it!'

Then he asked, low-voiced, 'Is there anything else I should know while we're about it?'

Colin's fingers had teased a thread from the blanket about his knees, and twisted it about his index finger until it was a livid white.

'Lizzie – your mother – she didn't die when you

were small. She went off with another man. I've no idea what happened to her after that.'

'The bitch!'

'You'll not speak of her like that?' Colin flared at him. 'When all's said and done she's still my wife and your mother!'

William's laugh sounded as though it had been blessed in Hell. 'My mother? An hour ago I had no mother! An hour ago I was a happy man!'

'William, it's breaking my heart to see you like this!'

'Is it? Who else knows about – about me?'

'Only Kirsty.' Fear jumped into Colin's eyes. 'You'll not tell Margaret or her mother? It would kill Meg if she knew—'

'You think I'd want to tell anyone about this? You think I'd want anyone to know that I'm the fool that was going to ask his – his half-sister—' William choked the words out '—to be his wife? They'd all have a good laugh over that one in the drinking houses and the loom-shops!' His hands clenched on the back of a chair.

'Go and see Duncan,' Colin urged, at his wit's end. 'Talk to him. Ask him all you want to know—'

'No! If I found myself alone with Duncan Montgomery I'd not be able to keep my hands off him. He's made a bastard of me – he'll not make me a murderer as well.'

'William, listen to me—' Colin implored, but the

hard young voice flowed on, each word striking at Colin's heart.

'"The sins of the fathers shall be visited on the children." Is that the way it goes? I could never believe the Almighty would be cruel enough to make that come true, but He has. My Heavenly Father! That makes three fathers I've got today – and not one of them able or willing to give me any comfort!'

He lunged towards the door.

'Where are you going?'

William looked back at the man huddled in the wheel-chair, a look so devoid of feeling that Colin's breath caught in his throat.

'As far from Paisley as I can,' he said, and went out of the house where, after a lifetime, he felt that he no longer belonged.

'But why go away now, just when – when everything's all right again?' Margaret asked, perplexed.

'Because I'm tired of Paisley, the way Jamie got tired of it. There's other places to see.'

'William Todd, you'd hate soldiering and you know it!'

William's face was set in a stubborn scowl. 'There's more than soldiering.'

'What, then?'

'All sort of things. Don't nag at me, Margaret! I'll go to Edinburgh first, to Unc—' he stopped abruptly, then went on '—to Matt's farm. Then

254

I'll find work in the city, or mebbe I'll take ship for some other country.'

Matt Todd had left the Army years earlier and was farming outside Edinburgh.

'There's something you're not telling me,' Margaret said suspiciously. Then her face darkened. 'Your father's not starting his nonsense about us again, is he?'

'No!' William exploded, then drew a deep breath. 'No, of course not. I just want to stretch my legs. Leave it at that, Margaret – a woman can have no notion of the way a man's mind works!'

There was a ruffled silence while she eyed him narrowly and he glowered at a beetle struggling up a blade of grass.

'I know how your mind works,' Margaret said at last. 'I know you'll not be able to stay away from Paisley for long. You'll be back soon enough.'

The toe of William's boot flicked the beetle off the grass stem. It soared through the air and disappeared from sight into a clump of reeds.

'I'll never be back,' said William. 'Never!'

# PART FOUR

# Chapter One

RAIN FELL STEADILY FROM A grey sky. It pattered on the earthern streets and, with the help of horses' hooves, cart-wheels and feet, turned them to quagmires. March of 1770 had come in like a lamb, blue-skied and rich with the promise of spring; now it was going out like a lion, laying down a grey, damp carpet to welcome April.

Even the red tents sheltering the kail-wives and their wares at the open-air market looked drab and colourless. Customers hurried through their business and turned homewards without stopping to talk. The place was almost deserted.

'You should have stayed by the fire,' Margaret told Gavin as they splashed along the High Street and turned towards the market. He pulled his hat more firmly over eyes half-shut against the rain.

'A wee bit water never hurt anyone. And it looks as if it might be easing,' he said optimistically.

If it had been up to Margaret she would have stayed at home, snug and dry, but her mother needed some vegetables for the evening meal. At least she and Gavin were warmly dressed and well shod.

She went from stall to stall, prodding the merchandise with an experienced finger, bargaining with the kail-wives who were, for the most part, bare-armed and bare-headed in spite of the rain. Gavin followed her patiently. Living in lodgings as he did, he enjoyed the domestic side of life in the Montgomery household.

Margaret finally decided between two large solid cabbages and paid the woman.

'That'll please my mother. You'll be staying for your dinner, I suppose?'

'I will. I enjoy your mother's cooking.'

'I've noticed,' she said dryly, and stopped at a stall to peer at some cheeses.

Gavin stepped across a puddle. 'Mistress Paterson feeds me on herring and potatoes every day. First thing in the morning, then again in the evening with a mug of small beer.'

She looked up at him, blinking against the rain. 'You seem to be thriving on it.'

'I am that,' he agreed cheerfully. 'It's a fine nourishing diet, but a change now and then's more than welcome.'

'Mistress!' An old woman wrapped in a greasy, tattered cloak that had long since lost its original colour and warmth tugged at Margaret's sleeve. 'Mistress, have you mind of Beth Lang?'

'Beth? I mind her fine.'

'You've to come to her right now, for she needs

you,' the woman said, and scuttled off over the wet slippery ground like an aged crab. Without any hesitation Margaret pushed her basket into Gavin's hands and followed her down one of the narrow lanes leading to the maze of alleys and closes and tall houses by the river.

The area was the oldest part of the town and its tall buildings had long since deteriorated into dirty, neglected slums. This was where the poor who could still afford some form of shelter congregated. Rubbish was piled high on footpaths and streets, the gutters flowed with stinking water, many of the windows were empty holes in the walls, open to the wind and rain.

Margaret followed the old woman into a lane so narrow that her shoulders almost brushed the walls on either side. Something squelched underfoot and she recoiled instinctively. When she looked up again her guide had vanished. Just ahead was a doorway, two crumbling steps up from the street. She went through it into a dark ill-smelling passageway, felt her way along the slimy walls, and almost fell through an opening. The stench of the small room caught at her throat.

The place was lit by one tiny window. Half its panes were broken and the gaps stuffed with rags in a vain attempt to keep the wind out. The existing glass was too thick and too dirty to allow much light to filter through.

As Margaret's eyes accustomed themselves to what there was she made out a rough table and a bench. The old crone stood beside a younger woman who held a whimpering baby in her arms. A man snored in one corner, his face to the wall. A pile of rags in another corner moved, and she realised that several children were lying there in a heap.

'There she is—' The old woman pointed to the darkest corner of all, where someone shuddered and trembled on a heap of straw.

'Beth?' She dropped to her knees, heedless of the filthy floor. The girl, in the grip of a spasm that made her entire body shake violently, groaned as Margaret tried to take her into her arms.

'Margaret! In the name of God where are you?' With a wave of relief she heard Gavin's voice from the passageway.

She called to him, and saw the shock on his face when he arrived in the doorway.

'Gavin, it's Beth from the Town Hospital – she's sick—'

'She's been taken with the fever,' the old crone said, though by now Beth's teeth were chattering so hard that they could all hear her, even above the man's snoring and the wails of the baby. Gavin knelt, brushing Margaret's hands aside with an impatient, 'Out of my way till I see to her.'

She stood up. The last time she had seen Beth the girl was employed as a servant in one of the big houses, and doing well.

'What brought her to – to this place?' she asked the women, who shuffled uneasily.

'She'd need of a roof over her head, and enough to pay for her keep,' the younger woman said reluctantly, her voice hoarse and slow. 'But now the money's gone and she's sick. You'll have to take her back to the Hospital.'

She began to cough, a bubbling cough that racked her body. The baby, fearful of falling, caught hold of her hair with tiny grasping hands and cried louder.

'She told us about you.' The old woman took over the story. 'She'll have to get out of here.'

The other woman straightened, spat, and sucked air into her lungs, the coughing fit over. The sick girl's breath whistled in her throat.

'She'll have to get out of here,' Gavin agreed, his voice grim.

'What's wrong with her?'

'She's dying.' He straightened up and tore his coat off. 'And it's no wonder, in this place.' He wrapped the coat about Beth then lifted her in his arms. 'Out of here, Margaret, if you value your own life!'

He pushed past the two women, Beth's tangled fair hair swaying as her head lolled against his shoulder. The old crone, her good deed done, spat an oath at him, but the younger one allowed herself to be elbowed aside without complaint, her gaze fixed avidly on the table where, Margaret saw, Gavin had put the basket containing her mother's cabbage.

'Here – make the children some broth with this—'

she said before she followed him out, thrusting it into the grimy hand that was already reaching out to claim it.

Gavin was waiting in the street, breathing deeply to flush the fetid air from his lungs. In the grey light of day Beth looked as though she was made of grey-blue wax.

'Show me the way out of this rabbit warren.'

'Gavin, will she—'

'Hell's teeth, woman, stop chattering and do as I tell you!' he roared at her.

They made an incongruous trio; Margaret in her good warm clothes, Gavin, his waistcoat and shirt black with rain-water, and Beth, unconscious in his arms, her ragged gown half-covered by the elegant bottle-green coat he had wrapped about her. But few people turned to stare as they passed, for they were in a part of the town where folk minded their own concerns and it was not wise to be too inquisitive.

As they turned into New Sneddon Street a passing carriage stopped and Mary MacLeod's sharp nose appeared at the open door.

'Margaret! What in the world are you up to now?' she demanded of her niece.

'She's saving a life,' Gavin snapped back, wrenching the door open and stepping up into the carriage as though the girl he held weighed no more than a rag doll. 'Drive us to the Town Hospital.'

'No!' Margaret scrambled up behind him. 'I don't

want her to wake up and find herself in the Hospital sick-room. That's where her brother Geordie died of the poverty fever.'

'The – what?' he asked, bewildered. Then Beth began to cough in great harsh spasms that twisted her thin body, and he said tersely, 'I don't care where we take her as long as she finds a warm place to rest.'

'Then we'll go to my own house,' Mary decided promptly. As the wheels began to turn she sat back and murmured to her niece, 'He's mebbe a bit on the sharp side, but I like his style!'

'You might not be able to save the girl, Mistress MacLeod.' Doctor Scobie's long sad face looked longer and sadder as he walked into Mary's parlour an hour later.

'I'll make a brave try at it, though. What ails her?'

He pursed his lips in a way well known throughout Paisley. 'Well, now – her brother was never strong, as I mind. And it seems that she has the same tendency to be affected by humours in the atmosphere—'

'She's half-starved and worn out,' Gavin interrupted from behind him. The older physician looked ruffled.

'Mebbe, mebbe, but even so—'

'But why was she in that place at all, when she left the Hospital to work in Councillor Brodie's household?' Margaret wanted to know.

'Why is anyone in a hovel like that?' Gavin's face was dark with anger. 'Who owns the place?'

'I'll – I'll be on my way,' Doctor Scobie said uneasily, picking up his bag and giving one last regretful glance at the cupboard where Mary kept an excellent Madeira. 'I'll call tomorrow morning, Mistress MacLeod – that is, if the girl's still with us by then—'

'I'll let you know if she should leave,' the lady of the house assured him graciously, and rose to accompany him to the door. 'And I'll make sure Beth's still alive tomorrow,' she added when she returned, 'for I don't believe in giving in to doctors and their opinions. Now – you were asking about these tenements down by the river. All the property down there's owned by Councillor Johnny Brodie.'

'The man that employed Beth?' Margaret asked, stunned.

'The very one. A bad-tempered, greedy wee runt of a man, he is – but a great one for making money and keeping it.'

'Come on, Margaret—' Gavin's hand clamped round her wrist. 'We've got things to discuss with Councillor Brodie!'

'Now don't go upsetting the man,' Mary squawked primly after them, a glint in her eyes.

'I've a feeling poor Johnny's in for a shock,' she added to her late husband's portrait, hanging above the ornate fireplace. 'And it serves him right!'

\*     \*     \*

266

Councillor Brodie lived in a large and comfortable house only five minutes' walk from Mary's. His thin eyebrows rose at the sight of Gavin's dishevelled appearance.

'You find my wife and I enjoying a quiet hour at home. You'll take some claret?'

'Thank you, no.' Gavin ignored the chair he had been waved to, and stayed on his feet. Margaret declined an invitation to sit on the sofa by Mistress Brodie, so the councillor was forced to remain standing with his guests. He was a small man, intended by Nature to be thin but blessed, because of his wealth and self-indulgence, with a pot-belly which, together with his skinny limbs, gave him the look of a beetle that had learned to walk on two legs.

Gavin swept aside the usual formalities. 'We're looking for a girl named Beth Lang. I believe she's in your service.'

Brodie's jaw dropped and his wife looked up briefly from her embroidery. 'I mind the name, Johnny. She came from the Town Hospital, did she not?'

'To take up employment in your house.' Margaret's voice was angry, and Gavin laid a restraining hand on her arm.

'That's her. I dismissed her,' said Mistress Brodie serenely, and returned her attention to her work.

'There you are, then. She was dismissed.' The councillor was clearly beginning to wish that they would go away and leave him in peace.

'Why?' Gavin turned his attention to Mistress Brodie. She looked him up and down, decided that he was a fine looking young man, recalled that she had two daughters as yet unmarried, and smiled on him.

'Theft.'

'Never!'

'Hush now, Margaret,' Gavin reproved. 'And when would this be, Mistress Brodie?'

'Some two weeks since. I thought you'd have seen her back in the Hospital, Margaret, and got the whole sorry tale from her.'

Margaret kept her voice under control with an effort. 'She didn't go back. What's she supposed to have taken?'

'I recollect it now,' the councillor butted in, annoyed at being ignored in his own parlour. 'She's the one who took the ribbon from Lizzie's room.'

Margaret turned to him. 'You found it in her possession?'

'No, but she must have taken it, for it disappeared and the only other servant's from a good Paisley family, so it wasn't her,' the councillor's wife nodded complacently.

'You turned a girl into the street because of a missing ribbon?' Gavin asked slowly.

'It was our Lizzie's best new ribbon!' Mistress Brodie pointed out.

'We could have sent the girl to the cells and had her flogged for theft,' her husband chimed in. 'But we were generous. We just told her to go.'

'Where did she go?' Gavin pressed.

'That's not our concern.'

'I'll tell you anyway. She took lodgings in a house you own by the river, and now she's mebbe dying. There's a whole family still there, living in a way you'd not force on a pet dog.'

The councillor retreated a step or two towards the sofa. 'The girl's a thief – no responsibility of mine. And if you can't be civil to me in my own house I'll thank you to leave!'

'Civil!' Margaret began, but Gavin's fingers bit painfully into her wrist and she stopped.

'D'you ever visit the houses you own by the river, Councillor?'

'I've no need. A man sees to collecting the rents for me.'

'Would you come with us now and see where we found Beth Lang?'

'I will not, for I've important town business to attend to. And I'll have no more of your insolence, Mister Knox!' Brodie retreated right behind the sofa. His wife, who was easily his height and fat all over, rose to her feet as though prepared to defend him with her embroidery needle if necessary.

'We'll leave, since you request it in such a civil manner,' Gavin's voice was suddenly silky. 'Come on, Margaret.'

'That was a fine performance!' she snapped at him when the councillor's door closed behind them.

'Why didn't you let me speak? I'd have given him something to think about!'

'So will I, in my own way. Best leave him to me, for I don't live here and he can't harm me the way he might try to harm you or your father.' Gavin looked up at the afternoon sky, which was beginning to clear, then said again, 'Come on, Margaret,' and set off along the road, her hand clasped firmly in his. 'We've got work to do before night falls. We'll go to the Hospital first.'

In the next hour, working with an air of efficiency and authority she had never seen before, he hired a cart and persuaded the Hospital Mistress to find room for the family living by the river.

'The youngest'll be dead in a matter of weeks, and the mother's in a bad way too, so they'll not take up room for long,' he told her with cruel honesty. 'But we might be in time to save the rest of the family.'

When they returned to the room where they had found Beth he marched in and pulled the man to his feet, ignoring his fuddled protests.

The women and children began to cry in fear and panic as he half-carried his feebly struggling burden out to the waiting cart. Before he could re-enter the room the younger woman slammed the door and started to drag the table against it. Margaret tried to stop her and the woman clawed at her, hissing like an enraged cat; then she shrank back as the rotted wood of the door exploded under the weight of Gavin's foot.

'For pity's sake, can't you see that you're being saved, not murdered?' he roared in exasperation, and the children's sobs redoubled.

'You're frightening them! Why don't you try kindness?' Margaret shouted at him over the din. 'How would you like it if a stranger burst into your home and began to drag you out?'

'I'd like it fine – if I lived in a sty like this!' he retorted, and threw a handful of coins down on the table. The noise stopped at once as the women and children stared at the money. Then, as if by magic, the table was bare and the children were being hushed and gathered together.

Gavin grinned at Margaret. 'You see? Money can do more than kindness,' he said smugly, and ushered his charges out to the waiting cart.

'Mister Brodie'll easily find more tenants to replace them,' she said helplessly when the family had been driven off, clutching their few possessions.

'Not in this room.' He led her back into the building. 'Look at it – the walls are running with water—' His fingers sank into crumbling plaster and with a short sound of disgust he rubbed his hand on his coat and moved to the window. Tall as he was he had to hoist himself up to peer through what glass remained. The breeze ruffled his dark hair. 'The river runs right by this wall. It's oozing in through the foundations.'

He dropped to the floor, then went down on one knee to examine the boards. After a moment he stood up and stamped hard. A plank crumbled under the weight of his foot and the room smelled worse than ever.

'I thought so.' He looked round and his eyes fell on her. 'Give me that thing you've got round your neck – I'll buy you another!' he added as she hesitated. Dumbly she handed over her small headshawl and watched as he wrapped it round one hand then began to rip the floorboards up. The stink in the room was indescribable now, and she clapped a hand over her mouth and ran to the door. Outside, she breathed fresh air in deeply before venturing back into the room.

'Stay where you are,' Gavin rapped as she arrived in the door way. He was examining the large cavity he had made in the floor. Rotten boards were piled by his side.

'A sewer runs right under this floor. It's a wonder these folk didn't fall through the rotted boards. Well, if Mister Brodie won't come and see it for himself we'll just have to take the proof to him.'

Gingerly, he tied a rag round a piece of flooring and dipped it into the hole he had made. It came out saturated with thick stinking slime.

'Now – we're going to pay another visit to the Brodies,' said Gavin coldly.

# Chapter Two

WHEN THE COUNCILLOR'S MAIDSERVANT ANSWERED the door Gavin shouldered it wide and marched through the hall, Margaret at his heels. Straight into the parlour he went, ignoring the maid's cry of, 'But the master has callers—!'

Councillor Brodie and three other men sat round the table; Mistress Brodie and one of her daughters plied their needles diligently on the sofa. Six pairs of eyes looked up as Gavin swept in. Six noses wrinkled as the smell from the rags reached them.

'There—' He dropped his unpleasant burden on the table before Brodie, '—is your lodging house, Mister Brodie.'

The man's face paled and he stood up, pushing his chair back so violently that it crashed to the floor. His wife and daughter squealed.

'Don't go, gentlemen,' the surgeon added smoothly to the other three men, scrambling to their feet. 'You're welcome to hear what I have to say. This rag comes from a bed used by children in a house owned by Councillor Brodie here. A sewer runs under the floor. The river seeps into the building through the walls, and wind and rain have access through broken windows. You can judge for yourself what the stink's like. The children's mother's dying and their father drinks all the money that comes in – apart, I'm sure, from Mister Brodie's rent – to forget the misery of it all.'

Mistress Brodie fainted onto her daughter's shoulder. The colour had flooded back into her husband's face, and his eyes had begun to bulge. His companions were discreetly melting across the room and out of the door.

'I'll have the law on you!' the councillor raved, pointing a shaking finger at Gavin.

'You do that – and I'll see to it that the whole town knows how you treat your tenants. I'll make you a laughing stock in this place.'

'I'll set the militia on you – the pair of you!' Brodie screamed. Dirty mud from the rag oozed over his polished table and the papers strewn across it. Gavin leaned over to prod at the man's fat belly.

'You're welcome to try,' he said with quiet menace, his finger forcing the councillor a step back at each word. The man almost tripped on his overturned chair and only an undignified skip kept him upright.

'I just wish,' Gavin said with real regret as they stepped out of the councillor's gate, 'that I could have pushed him into that sewer. He belongs in it.'

Margaret was almost dancing with glee. 'You did enough! Oh, Gavin – I was proud of you!'

Then her smile faded. 'But your clothes are ruined – and look at my skirt! We're like a couple of tinkers!'

He examined a jagged tear on his coat sleeve and shrugged. 'Mebbe my landlady'll be able to mend it.'

'Come on home – I'll see to it.' She walked on, thinking about the family who would be trying to come to terms with their new life in the Hospital at that very minute, and had got to the end of the lane before she realised that Gavin wasn't with her.

He had perched himself on a low wall and was staring intently at a small and ugly pig that was nosing happily round a pile of refuse. Gavin had broken off a twig from a branch overhanging the garden wall behind him and was twisting it absent-mindedly between his fingers.

She went back to see what was of such interest to him but could find nothing – only the contented pig.

'I've been thinking, Margaret,' Gavin said, his eyes on the black twig with its tight-curled sticky buds. 'I've been thinking it would be a good thing if you and me were to wed.'

'You're daft!'

When she had said that to Jamie by the river he had angrily defended himself. But Gavin, lounging on the wall in the day's dusk, merely said, 'I think I must be. What's your answer?'

'But – why should marriage come into your

head in a place like this?' She indicated the lane, the muck-heap, the rooting pig.

'I didn't plan to mention it here,' he said with a hint of exasperation. 'But I suppose one place is as good as another for the purpose. We get on well enough and I like your sharp way of treating folk, though I realise that most men wouldn't. And there's a lot of sense in that pretty head of yours. I'm ready to settle down – and I have no wish to settle with anyone but you.'

'But I scarcely know you!'

'I've been coming to Paisley with Thomas for a good year now. Besides, we can get to know each other better when we're married, and living in the same house,' he pointed out. 'The more I think of it the more the idea pleases me. You're going to refuse me, aren't you?'

She glared at him. 'If I am I'll do it myself. No need for you to stick your nose in!'

He rubbed the offending feature and grinned. 'You're free to make up your own mind, and you always will be. But as your brother's closest friend I feel it's my duty to advise you to give my proposal some thought. I'm a good catch.'

Then he got up, scratched the pig behind one ear with the branch, and walked on down the lane, saying over his shoulder. 'Come to that, it would be a fine match for both of us.'

It was a ridiculous proposal – unromantic, ill-timed; never, surely, had a woman received a more disinterested offer of marriage, Margaret thought angrily. She ran after him and caught him up as he reached the corner.

'We'd fight – all the time.'

'Well – most of the time, perhaps. I'm counting on that, for I never wanted a dull marriage.'

'If I wasn't happy I'd not stay.'

'I'd hold the door open for you myself. Well?'

Exasperation, disbelief, bewilderment milled together in her mind, together with the dawning realisation that her life would never be the same again, now that Gavin had walked into it. And the further realisation that she didn't want him to walk back out of it.

'Well?' his maddeningly calm voice prompted.

'But Gavin – you've never said you love me!' she almost shrieked at him, stamping her foot. 'Why can't you say you love me?'

His expression, polite interest with just a hint of anxiety underlying it, wavered and crumbled as though it had been a mask, giving way to a look that made her heart flutter and her head spin. She swayed, and might have fallen if he hadn't swept her into his arms.

'And risk the rough edge of your tongue? Oh, Margaret,' he said against her neck, 'are you entirely blind? Don't you know that I've loved you since that night you danced all over my feet?'

'I didn't—' she began to say before his lips stopped hers.

'Don't you know how impatient I've been, and how afraid that you'd send me away if I spoke at the wrong moment?' he asked when he finally lifted his head. 'I thought I'd lost you when William Todd came back from Beith, for the two of you were together so much—'

She ran her finger-tips from the corner of his mouth to where his hair curled on his temple, and the sensation brought a melting joy she had never known before. 'William's one of my closest friends, nothing more.'

Her fingers buried themselves in his hair, sliding round to the back of his head, pulling him down to meet her eager lips again. The pig found a choice morsel and nibbled at it happily, its little eyes fixed on the couple who stood, locked in each other's embrace, at the corner of the lane.

'My mother,' said Margaret shakily, when she was free to speak again, 'will be pleased.'

He grinned down at her, his tawny eyes openly alight with happiness. 'She will. But d'you think our news'll be enough to take her mind off the loss of that fine cabbage we were supposed to bring back?'

# Chapter Three

B Y THE TIME MARGARET AND Gavin married, three months later, Beth Lang had recovered from her ordeal in the slum by the river, and had been taken on as Mary MacLeod's companion.

'It's pleasant to have a young person about the house again,' the milliner said on one of her visits to Margaret's new home. 'I've been lonely since Thomas went off to Glasgow. Though I'm right glad—' she added with more than a touch of malicious pleasure, '—to have you two so near me now.'

Margaret flushed crimson and thumped the teapot down with more energy than necessary. Gavin had agreed to her wish to stay in Paisley, where she could continue her work in the Town Hospital, but only on condition that they took a house fit for a surgeon. Despite her protests, he had bought a house on Oakshawhill, almost the twin to Mary's.

'And that's a nice respectable maid-servant you've got,' Mary went on mercilessly.

'It was Gavin employed her, not me,' her niece

snapped. 'I could have managed the house fine on my own!'

Gavin gave up trying to hide his amusement. 'Poor Ellen has to run morning noon and night, trying to get through the housework before Margaret does it for her. I found the two of them nearly at each other's throats yesterday over who was to get to scrub the kitchen floor.'

'I can't sit still and let someone else clean my house for me!'

'Now, Margaret,' he said with that air of calm possessiveness that both maddened and warmed her. 'You do plenty, what with the Hospital and helping your mother in the shop and entertaining our visitors. That's more than enough for someone in your—'

He stopped short as his wife glared at him.

'—condition,' Mary serenely finished the sentence, setting her cup down and brushing a crumb from the lacy ruffles at one wrist.

'I told my mother in confidence!'

'Tuts, Meg never said a word – it was the smug look she's had on her face for the past seven days that gave it away. Gavin's right, though – you'll have to learn to let other folk take on some of your work.'

A wet, cold October left Colin with a heavy chest cold, and Meg with an agonising bout of rheumatism that forced her to stay at home. That same month the widow who lived with her family in the rooms behind the shop re-married and moved with her family out of the town altogether, leaving the burden of the shop on Margaret's shoulders.

'Colin'll have to find someone else!' Gavin insisted, worried about her health. 'What about the girl that worked there before?'

'Janet? She's gone from bad to worse, married to that lout of a husband,' Meg fretted. 'She's got a family by his first wife to see to, and her own children – not that I'd be able to trust her on her own now.'

'William!' The worried frown cleared from Margaret's brow, to be replaced by a broad smile. 'He's the very one to look after the shop.'

'He'll not come back,' Meg scoffed. 'He's happy working for Matt. He wouldn't even come home for your wedding.'

'But he'll do it for his father's sake. And there's no denying—' the cloud drifted over Margaret's face again 'that Uncle Colin's getting frail now. I'm sure William'll come home – and I'll go to fetch him myself!'

There were moments, during the bumpy carriage ride to Glasgow and the bumpier coach journey to Edinburgh, when Margaret regretted her decision. When they reached the capital Gavin had to carry her in his arms into the coaching inn, where he coaxed some brandy and water between her ashen lips.

'But don't ask me to eat, for I never will again!' she said miserably into his comforting shoulder, her stomach heaving at the aroma drifting from the kitchens.

By the time the brandy was finished she felt a little stronger, and after a night's sleep and a good breakfast the following morning she was herself again and impatient to make the final short journey out to the farm where Matt lived with his wife Mirren.

Their visitors got a warm welcome. Matt, strong and handsome as ever in spite of his greying head, sent a boy to fetch William, who was out in the fields.

'I think he'll want to go back with you, for Colin's sake. But he'll be missed here, for he's a good worker.'

'You should come back yourself, for a visit,' Margaret urged, but he shook his head.

'This place won't run itself. And to me, Paisley was never the same after my father died. I'd see his ghost everywhere. Have you had news of Jamie?'

'The last we heard he was in London, and wondering if he might be sent out to the Americas.'

Matt's big body heaved in a nostalgic sigh. 'There's nothing like soldiering to set a man up,' he said, then grinned at Mirren and added, 'Mind you, there's something to be said for a settled life and the right woman to share it.'

'You're right,' Gavin said from the window-seat,

his gaze reaching across the low-ceilinged kitchen to enfold Margaret in its warmth.

Then he looked out of the window and saw a tall, lithe, well-muscled young man come into the cobbled yard, two farm dogs twisting round his feet as he walked.

'What is it? Is it him?' Margaret saw his change of expression and hurried to the door. Then with a glad cry of 'William!' she was running across the yard.

Gavin watched from the window as William stopped in his tracks; surprise, disbelief, and something else that was controlled so swiftly that Gavin hadn't time to register what it was, chased each other across his tanned face. Then Margaret threw herself into his arms, almost knocking him over, and he caught her and held her close.

In that moment, as he saw his wife's dark brown head blend with William's short, loose curls, bleached by an outdoor life into a tumble of bronze, Gavin knew a stab of uneasiness, and something even stronger. Something that had until then been alien to him.

Jealousy.

'There's nothing in Paisley for me. I'm better where I am.'

Margaret put her spoon down, her face stiff with astonishment as she faced William across the table. 'But your father's not well! He needs you!'

'Did he ask for me to go back?'

'You know he'd never do that. He doesn't even know we're here.'

'That's all right, then.' William kept his head bent over his plate, though he wasn't eating. 'He can get a woman in to tend the shop. There's plenty'd be pleased to get the work. I've my own life to live here.'

'But we all want you to come home, where you belong,' Margaret persisted, and his head was suddenly thrown back, the gold lights in his hair catching the lamp's glow, his eyes angry.

'I don't belong there! I never did!' he said, and pushed his chair back.

'William! Tell him—' she appealed to Matt as the door to the yard slammed behind William, but the older man shook his head.

'He makes his own decisions. I don't know why he's so bitter, but it's deep in him. Best not tamper with it.'

She rose from the table and followed William out to the yard, stumbling as her eyes tried to accustom themselves to the change between lamplight and darkness. A dog growled at her and William's clipped voice silenced it.

'William? Stop this nonsense and come back to Paisley with us!'

'It's not nonsense!' he rapped back in the same tone that had dealt with the dog. 'I'm not one of your Hospital children to be ordered about!' Then he added, his voice changing. 'Why did you have to come here and meddle in the life I've made for myself?'

'I just want you to come back to your father – to all of us—'

She reached out to touch his arm and felt the stuff of his coat slide by her fingers as he pulled back. Then a soft gold light spilled over them as the farm door opened. The glow touched his eyes and gave them the same tawny light that Gavin's had. She saw them move over her, stop at the spot where pregnancy swelled her gown.

Gavin, silhouetted in the doorway, called at her, and William said, low-voiced, 'Go to him, Margaret. Go back to Paisley with him and leave me to my own devices!'

Then he was gone, merging into the shadows, the dogs at his heels, and she was alone.

As Robert Montgomery had predicted, silk was becoming one of Paisley's main cloths, though linen was still of considerable importance. On her return from Edinburgh Margaret managed to get a small incle loom set up in the Hospital so that some of the women there could weave ribbons, another popular new product.

She also found a woman to work in the grocer's shop, and Meg herself was soon back behind the counter, wincing when she had to stoop to ladle grain from the sacks on the floor.

Colin couldn't shake himself free from his chest cold. It settled, and they were all reminded, as

they heard his harsh cough, of his father's chronic
bronchitis.

Margaret persuaded Beth Lang, Mary's companion, to take over her work at the Hospital
temporarily. She and Gavin battled over her decision to return to teaching once her baby was born,
and she won.

'But it's not seemly for a woman to leave her
child to someone else's attentions!' Meg fretted.

'I'm needed at the Hospital. I'll not be away from
the house all that much, and Ellen's well able to
watch over the baby when I'm not there.'

'Isn't it a blessing,' said Mary slyly, 'that you've
got a maid-servant?'

'Since Gavin insists on employing one, Aunt
Mary, I might as well make use of her,' her niece
said sharply, and Mary smirked into the ribbons
and lace of the hat she was making.

It was a relief to Gavin when Margaret stopped
going to the Hospital and the shop every day. He
worked hard, and it made all the difference to him
to find her waiting for him when he came home.

Their marriage was very happy, for all its minor
storms, and they looked forward together to their
baby's birth.

The tranquillity he prized so much was shattered when he arrived home one evening in late
November to find Margaret pacing the parlour
floor, shaking with rage, while Mary sat by the
fire and watched her with a worried frown.

'I'm glad you're back. See if you can talk sense

to this woman,' she appealed to him. 'It's not good for her to get herself into such a state.'

'Gavin!' Margaret clutched at him, her bright eyes and the tension that almost sparked from her body alarming him. 'You'll have to make them see reason! You're a surgeon – they'd surely listen to you!'

'Who? For the love of God, Margaret, sit down and tell me what's amiss?' He pushed her gently down onto the sofa and sat beside her. 'You'll do yourself and the baby no good!'

'That's what I told her. But it's the Society—' Mary began, and he groaned.

'Not the Society for the Reformation of Manners again! Margaret, haven't I advised you to keep well away from them?'

'D'you think that would make any difference? Looking the other way's not the answer!'

'Sometimes it's the only thing a sensible person can do!'

The Society for the Reformation of Manners was a group of well-to-do Paisley people who took it upon themselves to seek out and chastise the sinners in their midst. Compassion and understanding were not emotions that they recognised, and both Margaret and Mary had clashed with them on more occasions than Gavin cared to remember.

'You think we should just let them get on with their foul work unhampered?' There were tears in her eyes. 'Gavin, they're going to flog Janet through the town tomorrow if we don't stop them!'

'That's the woman who used to work for Colin and Meg.' Mary offered. 'It seems she took some cloth from a loom-shop and sold it.'

'But surely that doesn't warrant a flogging?'

Margaret took a deep breath, then said in a flat, calm voice that worried Gavin more than her former hysteria, 'It does as far as the Society and the Council are concerned. Janet's to be driven through the town tomorrow, and given ten lashes at each end of New Street, then another ten lashes at the Cross. Then she'll be put out of the town to fend for herself.'

'And her children,' Mary finished the story. 'That no-good man of hers got out of harm's way the minute he heard that she'd been taken.'

'You've spoken to the Society, Mary?'

'We both have – Duncan and Meg too. But Johnny Brodie's in control of them now – and he's waited for nearly a year to get his revenge for that business over his house down by the river.'

Gavin groaned again. 'Councillor Brodie!'

'They've hired a man from outside for the work.' Margaret's voice was still flat. 'They're paying him three guineas.'

'What? That's more than I'm paid to amputate half a dozen limbs!'

'The Society seems to think it's worth the cost,' Mary said dryly. 'Well, I've done all I can – I'll have to get back home. Take my advice, Margaret

– tell yourself that you can only do your best and no more.'

When she had gone Gavin gathered Margaret into his arms.

'Mary's right – what more can anyone do?'

'You're a surgeon,' she repeated. 'They might listen to you.'

He gave in. 'I've little hope of succeeding, but I'll try – after I've had something to eat.'

She was in bed, wide awake, when he got back. He sat on the bed and took her hand.

'Councillor Brodie's done his work well. Not one of them would change his mind. They as good as told me to mind my own business.' The humiliation he had suffered at the hands of Brodie and his cronies choked him. 'Make up your mind to it, Margaret – you can't always expect the whole town to dance to your tune, and that's a fact.'

Without another word she threw herself over in the bed, turning her head away from him, listening to the sounds of him undressing.

For the first time, they slept without holding each other.

'I wish I could stay with you today, but I'm needed in Glasgow,' Gavin said after a silent breakfast on the following morning. He hesitated, then took her into his arms. Her lips were cool and unresponsive to his kiss.

'Stay in the house today. Don't go out.'

'That won't save poor Janet from her flogging, will it?'

He shook her gently. 'Margaret, nobody can help Janet now. Can you not see that?'

She could, and she would have been happy to stay at home, closing her mind to the day's events. But it was impossible. When the crowd gathered to witness the flogging she was on its outer fringes, watching as Janet was driven up in the back of a cart, her wrists lashed to the rail before her.

The woman, younger than Meg and Mary, looked years older than either of them. Her face was lined, her straggling lifeless hair was grey. Margaret, who hadn't seen her for years, was shocked by the effect life had had on the girl who used to work behind the grocery counter. A carriage bearing some of the Society's members, Councillor Brodie among them, followed the cart.

As the man paid to administer the punishment raised his whip Margaret suddenly came to her senses. Gavin was right – she couldn't help Janet this way. She was only adding to the mob that had come to jeer and gawp and be glad that it wasn't happening to them. She turned, and would have hurried back to Oakshawhill if the crowd hadn't surged forward to get nearer to the cart, closing round her and carrying her with them.

The whip descended. Janet's curses rose to a scream, and to Margaret, fighting to keep her feet as she was carried forward, it became old Hector Lyle's public hanging all over again. She felt her throat constrict and closed her eyes against the faces round her, especially the sight of Janet flinching as the whip came down again and again on her back.

The darkness behind her lids flashed red lightning and threatened to draw her down into its depths for ever. Afraid that she might lose her footing and be trampled, Margaret opened her eyes again and saw a crimson thread of blood run down Janet's chin as the woman sank her teeth into her lower lip. Her face, turned towards Margaret, was knotted with pain as the lash landed for the tenth time. Then the whip was laid aside and a small cup of spirits held to Janet's lips. She sucked at it greedily as the cart jolted into motion down the slope that led to the foot of New Street.

Jostled by the crowd, unable to fight free, Margaret was forced to follow and witness the next ten lashes.

'For God's sake have some mercy!' she heard herself scream at the men in the cart as Janet's thin shawl was torn to shreds and fell, wet and red, from her back. But nobody heard her in the noise of the crowd, half of them jeering at the victim, the other half shouting encouragement to her and abuse to the stony-faced Society members in their carriage.

When at last they reached the Cross, and the

final ten lashes were administered Janet's defiance had gone, and she slumped over the cart's rail, her body jerking as the lash hit it. The man who wielded it was clearly softening the blows, for now that the sport of it was gone the crowd's mood towards him was becoming threatening.

Then it was over, and Janet was released and allowed to fall to the floor of the cart. The militiamen in attendance kept back the crowd as her friends lifted her and carried her away. The Society officials hurriedly left the scene, and the crowd dispersed, leaving Margaret free, at last, to go home.

All she wanted was to go to bed, to hide herself from the day's events in sleep. But when she reached the front door Gavin opened it, his face a mask carved out of ivory.

'Where have you been?'

She dragged her shoulders straight, walked past him to the parlour.

He followed her in and shut the door as she sank down onto a chair by the fire. 'You went to the flogging, didn't you?'

'Of course I did.'

He was white to the lips. 'I knew fine you'd disobey me. I came back as soon as I could – I was out of my mind with worry!'

'I'm not a child! I can look after myself!'

'I wish I could be as sure of that! Listen to me – the woman stole from a weaver. In this town that's a sin, and she knew it. She was punished according to the law and it's not your business to interfere. D'you hear me?'

'I do – and you sound as twisted as Johnny Brodie! I'll not stay in my own parlour to listen to such talk!'

She stormed to the door, anger revitalising her exhausted body. But he was there before her, his hands on her shoulders, his face twisted with rage.

'You'll not mention me in the same breath as that man!'

'Take your hands off me,' she ordered coldly, and his arms dropped to his sides. Choking with rage, they glared at each other. It was Gavin who made the first move towards reconciliation.

'Margaret – you know well enough that if the law's broken there has to be a punishment.'

'So Johnny Brodie can make money from other folk's misery and get away with it, while the likes of Janet are beaten until the blood runs for trying to find the money to feed their children?'

'I'm not proud of the way the law works. There are changes needed, but it's up to the men who run the country to see to that, not you and me. I've got enough to do, worrying about my own wife's well-being, and my child's well-being too—'

She swept away from him, back into the centre of the room. 'Your wife – your child!' she mocked, anger flaring again. 'No need to worry about your possessions, Mister Knox. Your child'll do fine, for he's to be born to folk with enough money to buy food for him. We won't have to steal to keep him alive!'

'Margaret—' He reached for her, but she evaded him.

'I wish you'd stop talking about your precious child as if I've nothing to do with him at all – as if I'm nothing but a – a box to hold your son!'

Hurt grimaced across his face then the anger flooded back again. As he advanced towards her the door behind him opened cautiously and Ellen poked a scared head in.

'Mistress Knox—'

'What d'you want?' Gavin rounded on her and she recoiled before the look on his face.

'A visitor to s – see the mistress. Will I tell him—?'

'Tell him to go to He—'

'Tell him to come in, Ellen,' Margaret ordered grandly.

'You'll do nothing of the—' Gavin began, but the embarrassed visitor had already been scooped into the room by Ellen and was hesitating in the doorway, his country clothes and weathered brown face giving him a strangely alien look.

'I decided I should come home—' he began.

'Oh—! And a welcome sight you are!' Margaret's

anger melted into tears of joy as she brushed past her husband and went forward, hands out-stretched.

Gavin stayed where he was, his eyes as cool as his voice when he said formally, 'Welcome back to Paisley, William.'

# Chapter Four

I T SEEMED AS THOUGH MARGARET'S marriage sailed into a sheltered harbour with the birth of her daughter in March 1771.

There had never been a bonnier, better-behaved baby than Christian, who had her mother's neat-featured face and Gavin's thick dark hair and gold-flecked hazel eyes.

At last Margaret settled happily into domesticity, even deciding to share the Hospital work with Beth so that she could spend more time at home caring for Gavin and their daughter.

With William back, Paisley was its old self. The only person she missed now was Jamie, whose letters were few.

'Kirsty's worried about him,' William said on one of his frequent visits. 'When he does manage to put pen to paper, he says very little. There's something amiss.'

'I've no doubt he'll weather anything that comes his way,' she said comfortably, knitting wires flashing between her skilful fingers, one foot rocking Christian's cradle. 'How's your father today?'

'Keeping to his bed. I was shocked to see how he'd changed.'

'He'll be the better for seeing you. You were right to come home.'

'Mebbe.' Then he changed the subject. 'I've ordered a good stock of snuff for the shop. I hear the men at the Hospital are to be given their snuff penny again.'

Her face lit up. 'Poor souls – a penny a week's not much, but a wee bit snuff gives them such pleasure.'

Two months after William came home Colin Todd died in his sleep. It was as though, as Kirsty said, he had been waiting to see his son home again before he let go.

Margaret paced the parlour restlessly on the evening of the funeral day. Gavin was closeted in his small study, Ellen was entertaining a friend in the kitchen, Christian slept peacefully, and none of them needed Margaret's presence.

She picked up her knitting wires, but tossed them down again almost at once. Her spinning-wheel was discarded just as promptly. She went to the window, but the darkening street outside was empty, with nothing to fix her eyes and her mind on except trees tossing and bending in the rising wind. Finally she fetched her cloak and put her head round the study door.

'I'm going to see William. Ellen'll listen out for the baby.'

'You're going out on a night like this?' The first spatter of rain on the glass underlined Gavin's words. 'Kirsty and Billy are there – he doesn't need you.'

'I'll not be long.'

'If you wait five minutes I'll walk down with you.'

But she had no wish for his company on her errand. 'You get on with what you're doing. I'm able to walk down the hill on my own. I'll not be long,' she said again, and went out before he could argue.

By the time she reached the High Street house the rainstorm had started in earnest and the sky was black. The door had been left on the latch and she slipped into the passageway, a sixth sense leading her to Colin's room instead of up the stairs to the kitchen.

The room was dark, but she could see William, sitting in the wheel-chair, silhouetted against the window. His head turned briefly as the door opened and closed.

'Margaret?'

'I'm here.' She sat down at the table.

'I'm glad you made me come home for – for the end.'

'You'd have come anyway.'

'No.' After a long pause he said, 'I went away because of a quarrel we had.'

Surprise sharpened her voice. 'You and your father? But you've never ever said a harsh word to each other!'

'He didn't – but I did. The thing about words is that you can't take them back.'

'But it was all right in the end, surely?'

'I think so,' he said. 'We never spoke of it again. I was too shamed, and mebbe he didn't feel that there was time for further bitterness in his life. God knows he'd supped more than his fair share of it.'

'You came back, and that's all that would matter to him.'

She heard his breathing check and then change to a soft, uneven rhythm, and guessed that he was crying. Her hands fluttered in her lap hesitantly before folding about each other. Comfort was for hurt children; men needed solitude in their grief.

She waited until, a full ten minutes later, his breath steadied and he scrubbed a hand over his face, then she got to her feet and touched his shoulder.

'I must go home now.'

He turned his head and she felt his lips brush her fingers before she went as quietly as she had come, leaving him alone in the dark.

Lamplight spilled from under the parlour door when she reached her own house again. Gavin was hunched in a chair before the dying fire.

'So you're back.'

'I said I'd not be long.' She knelt on the hearth, sifting powdery ash from the fire with the poker then lifting coals from the gleaming brass scuttle to lay on the embers.

'Did you see him?' Gavin's voice was sullen.

299

'William? Yes, I saw him.'

'And comforted him, I've no doubt.'

She laid down the tongs, sitting back on her heels. 'Nobody can give him much comfort at a time like this. He'll have to get over his loss in his own time and in his own way.'

'That's what I tried to tell you – but you insisted on going to him all the same.'

She got to her feet. 'Of course I did – as I'd have gone to anyone who's suffering as much as he is just now. And if you're going to make such a fuss about it I might as well go to my bed as stay here.'

He was out of the chair and at the door before her.

'Was Kirsty there? Or Billy?'

Irritation began to edge her voice. 'What has that to do with it? Gavin, what's come over you? Every time William's as much as mentioned you begin to jump about like a cat that's fallen into a wash-tub!'

'It's not me that does the jumping – it's you! When he's here you fret about his comfort, when he's not here you wonder if he's all right—' Then his angry tirade stopped as she began to laugh. 'What is it now?'

'It's just you – you should see yourself, like a wee boy that's been left out of a game! Gavin, you're surely not jealous of William? He's like one of my own brothers – the best of them, for Robert was a bully and Thomas too fond of his books for my liking. William was the gentle one, the one I felt safe with. But you're the man I wed, Gavin. If you think of William as a threat, you've as much notion of common-sense as your daughter has of Latin right now.'

Gavin eyed her doubtfully. 'Did he ever ask you to marry him?'

'Never.'

'If he had, would you have accepted?'

The laughter was still in her voice. 'I've no idea, for I never intended to marry, as you know yourself. And as he didn't ask me, the thought was never in his mind either. Oh, Gavin—' She slid her arms about his neck, drew him close and spoke against his throat, feeling his skin warm and pulsing beneath her lips. 'I'll make my own friends where I choose – just as I chose my own husband. And I'm too well pleased with him to look elsewhere.'

Then she squeaked as he lifted her off her feet and turned to the door.

'Put me down – I've just built up the fire!'

'You have that,' he agreed huskily, carrying her out of the room and across the dark hall to the stairs. 'And now you'll have to take the consequences!'

Kirsty's kitchen was warm, noisy and filled with the smell of broth and fresh-baked bread. Meg and Mary, Kate and Robert's wife Annie had come to take tea, and the patch-work rugs on the floor were lively with babies – three-months-old Christian propped up on cushions, Kate and Annie's older children crawling and toddling near their mothers.

301

Margaret took a moment to wonder, as she often did at her own presence in the middle of such a domesticated crowd. Motherhood must addle the brain – but it was a pleasant affliction, she admitted to herself, poking Christian with a gentle toe and watching the smile that was so like Gavin's break over the baby's face.

Then she lifted her head, listening, thinking that she had heard the street door open, a familiar voice calling. But it was impossible to be sure of anything with such a clatter of tongues vying with the whir of Kirsty's spinning-wheel.

So it came as a complete surprise to them all when the kitchen door flew back on its hinges and a tall figure appeared in the doorway. He looked drawn, and considerably older than when they had last seen him, but there was no mistaking the fiery hair, the wide grin, the blue eyes.

'Now then—' said Jamie Todd. 'Here's a bonny sight to welcome a man back home among his own folk!'

'Prison!' Margaret said, aghast. 'Jamie Todd – I always knew you'd fall into bad ways! Haven't I said it time and time again?'

'Not to my knowledge.' Jamie, sprawled comfortably in the Knox parlour, was unrepentant. 'It's not as if it was a real jail, Margaret. Just an Army one. Insubordination, they said.' He rolled the word around his tongue with relish. 'The truth of it was, I got tired of being ordered about by namby pamby officers who didn't know what they were talking about half the time.'

She eyed him closely. For all his joking there was a new awareness at the back of his eyes, deep lines etched into his face, a cynicism that had never laced his smile before.

'There's a lot more to it than that. Something bad happened to you, Jamie.'

For a fleeting second she saw bitterness chill his eyes, then it was gone.

'I'll just say that I wanted to see the world – and there are some things out there that I'd as soon not have seen,' he said lightly, and she knew that that was as much as she or anyone else would get out of him.

'And what do you plan to do next? There's plenty young men in the town talking of going to the Americas to find a new life.'

He stretched his legs out and contemplated the toes of his boots. 'No, I've had my fill of travel for the moment. And it's time the looms were back in my father's shop. After all, weaving's what I was trained to do.'

He hadn't lost the ability to surprise her. 'You'd settle down here and be a weaver?'

'I'm in the mood for that. Paisley has its attractions for me now—' a sly smile sparkled at her '—and that bonny Beth Lang that stays with your Aunt Mary's one of them.'

'Just you watch yourself, Jamie Todd! I've already

decided that Beth would make a fine wife for William.'

'Let William look out for himself, then,' said Jamie, half in fun, half earnest. 'The girl I wanted belongs to someone else now – and a weary traveller's entitled to find his comfort where he can.'

# Chapter Five

'PLEASE GOD, NO!' MARGARET PRAYED aloud as she threw herself out of bed and ran, sure-footed in the darkness, to the crib. By the time Gavin had lit the lamp the baby was in her arms, still making those terrible choking, wheezing sounds that had wakened the two of them.

'Give her to me—' Gavin took Christian over to the light. Her face was congested, her frightened eyes stared up at him, her small fists flailed at the air. 'Go and boil a kettle, Margaret!'

She ran barefoot, terror choking her throat just as the croup was choking her baby. Through her mind, as she poked the glowing kitchen range into life, splashed water into the kettle and swung it on its hook over the fire, tramped a never-ending list of names of infants who had died in the town from the dreaded illness.

Throughout that long night she and Gavin took turns to walk the floor with Christian, filling every pot they could find so that the kitchen became humid with steam to loosen the mucus in the little girl's lungs. Slowly she improved, and by dawn the immediate crisis was over and she slept, exhausted.

It happened again on the next night, and the next. Before their eyes Gavin and Margaret saw their baby sicken and lose ground.

'If anything should happen to her—' Margaret said fearfully one morning when dawn's grey light found Christian slipping into her first sleep of the night, her dark hair wet with sweat, her mouth blue-tinged. Gavin reached out and drew her close.

'Nothing's going to happen to her – nothing!' he said fiercely, but when she looked up at him she saw her own terror mirrored in his tired face.

'Gavin—'

'Sshhh—' he led her back to bed, though it was almost time for him to get up and go to Glasgow. 'I've been thinking, Margaret – some folk say that sea air can be beneficial. I've a cousin living down in Ayr – we could take Christian to spend a few days with him.'

'D'you think it would help her?'

He shrugged helplessly. 'I don't know – but I'll try anything.' Then he lifted her face to his and kissed her gently. 'Leave Ellen to see to the wee one today and go out for a while. You'll make yourself ill if you stay in all the time with her – and I couldn't bear it if something happened to you as well.'

Against her own wishes she did as she was told, turning her steps towards her parents' house. But

Meg was out somewhere, and Margaret couldn't face Kirsty, who had lost a baby to the croup herself. Without making any conscious decision she found herself walking into the grocer's shop.

William was serving a customer. She nodded and went through to the back. The rooms where she had been born and raised were sparsely furnished, for he had few needs. There were a lot of books, two chairs flanking the fire, a rag rug, and little else. The mantelshelf was bare of ornaments.

Shivering, she knelt down to stir the fire into a blaze. The shop door closed and she heard William come into the room behind her.

'Margaret?'

She kept her eyes on the fire. 'William – my baby's going to die.'

He drew in his breath sharply, knelt down beside her so that he could look into her face. 'No!'

'She is – she is—' Margaret insisted, and the tears that had been aching to flow for the past three days finally surfaced in a passion of grief and fear beyond her control.

To her relief he didn't try to stop her. He gathered her into his arms and rocked her as she would have rocked Christian, holding her against his shoulder, letting her sob herself into hiccuping silence before he mopped her face, eased her gently into a chair, and bent to lift the kettle that simmered all day on the range.

Then he wrapped her hands round a cup of tea and made her sip the hot liquid.

She sniffed and gave him a watery smile. 'I've wanted to cry for days now – but I couldn't, in front of Gavin and Christian.'

'Who told you she was going to die?'

'Nobody. I just know. William, if you saw the state she gets into just trying to draw a breath—'

'Hush—' He leaned forward and put a hand against her cheek, his grey eyes holding her own. She felt as though his strength was flowing into her. 'Hush, Margaret. She'll not die – not Christian. She's not the dying sort – and I should know, for I was close to it myself a few years since and it was you that drew me back from the edge.'

'It was Kirsty's skill, not mine.'

'Mebbe, but you gave me a reason to get better – then,' he said quietly, but her mind was on Christian and she scarcely heard him.

'We're taking her to Ayr for a while. Gavin says the sea air might help her.'

He nodded, memories clearing from his eyes. 'Mebbe. It's been a bad summer here. All that rain – the burns are rushing down from the braes and the Cart's risen well up its banks. The air's damp and chill.'

The shop door rattled and he had to leave her. She took advantage of his absence to finish the tea and wash the tearstains from her face. When she heard the customer go out she went into the shop, clear-headed and calm again.

'I'd best get back to Christian. Thank-you for

being such a good friend, William. There's nobody I can turn to as easily as I turn to you.'

A muscle jumped in his face but he said nothing, busily shifting a new sack of meal into position and opening it.

'When I get back from Ayr I'm going to give those rooms of yours a good clean-out,' she added briskly. 'Oh, they're neat enough, but they need a woman's touch. We'll have to think of finding a nice wee wife who'll look after you properly.'

He looked at her, opened his mouth to speak, closed it again – then the door rattled once more, letting in three women laden with baskets, and Margaret left him to his work and went back home, comforted and refreshed.

She never found out what he had been going to say.

Ayr was a revelation to Margaret, who had lived inland all her life. Situated on the Firth of Clyde, it had its own harbour and fishing fleet, rich farmland around it, and beaches where waves rolled majestically in to break on great stretches of sand.

At Gavin's insistence the three of them spent almost all their time out of doors. They collected shells to take home, and when Margaret kissed Christian her skin tasted of the salt-laden winds that blew in from the sea.

All day and every day, no matter what the weather was like, they walked for hours. She and

Gavin talked and talked, played with the baby, grew closer together – and best of all were the nights, when Gavin made love to her in the big comfortable bed, and together they listened to the murmur of waves breaking on the shore, and to the easy, regular breathing of their healthy, contented little daughter.

'You'd think the sky would have run out of rain by this time.' Margaret peered from her parlour window at the dripping trees. The rain, driven by a wind, lanced at a sharp angle, and the few people to be seen were almost bent double as they battled along against the worst bout of September weather in living memory.

Meg, waiting by the fire for Duncan to come and escort her home, bounced Christian on her knee. 'There'll be damage done to roofs and chimney-pots tonight,' she prophesied. 'It's not a night for man or beast to be out.'

'Gavin's supposed to take his turn at the night watch tonight.'

'You tell him to stay by his own fireside – even the robbers'll stay home if they have any sense.'

It was a town rule that all the able-bodied men had to take their turn at patrolling the streets at night. Many of them paid others to do the work for them, and as often as not this led to more law-breaking, for substitutes had been known to turn a blind eye, for a share of the profits, to any crime they came across.

'Here he is—' Margaret said as Duncan's burly figure bowled along the road at a brisk pace and collided with the gate-post.

He refused her offer of refreshment. 'We'd best get back home, for it's getting worse outside,' he said, and took Meg off, the two of them clutching each other as the gale whirled around them.

Gavin insisted on going through with his town watch duties. Well-fed and warmly wrapped up against the worsening weather, he stopped her protests with a kiss.

'You're the one who's always going on about duty,' he said, then the door slammed behind him on a gust of wind, and she was alone.

When Christian was put down for the night Margaret settled by the parlour fire with a novel borrowed from the town's new book-lending club. The wind's whistling round the eaves and the warmth of the fire began to lull her to sleep, and she jumped when Ellen showed William in, his clothes and hair dark with rain. He shook his head when she urged him to take his coat off and get dry.

'No sense in settling down, for I'm off in a few minutes.'

'Off where?' she asked, with sudden foreboding.

'To Edinburgh, for a start. I've come to make my farewells.'

'But why, William? You're settled here again!'

He picked up her book, riffled through it without

glancing at the pages, set it down, fidgeted about the room. 'Now that my father's dead there's no reason for me to stay.'

'But your friends are here! And there's the shop—'

'You're all busy with your own lives, and I'd sooner farm than be a shopkeeper.' He went to the window, parted the curtains to peer out at the wild night.

'How long have you been planning this?'

William let the curtains drop and turned to face her. He looked very tired. 'I've known for a while that I was wrong to come back. I've told Kirsty and Jamie. It's best that I go.'

'But not tonight!' The words broke from her in a cry. 'Not like this, without giving me time to say a proper farewell. You can't be so cruel!'

'Sometimes being cruel's the best way. Goodbye, Margaret—' he said, but she moved before the door, blocking his way.

'William, you've been special to me all my days. It was you I went to when I thought my baby was dying. It was you that gave me the strength to go on. Have you forgotten already?'

'No, for that was the day I knew that I had to go away—' Then, as she stayed where she was, back against the door, his voice hardened. 'Margaret, stop this nonsense and let me by!'

'Not until I find out why you're leaving us!'

For a moment she thought that he was going to pull her clear of the door, and one hand reached behind her back to anchor itself to the handle. Then the anger went out of his eyes, leaving a dull hopelessness echoed in the slump of his shoulders as he walked over to lean on the mantelshelf.

'All right, I'll tell you.' His voice was empty, lifeless. 'You'll not rest until you know, and it's my last chance to say it aloud. And when I have, you'll be glad to see me go.'

Suddenly she was afraid for him. 'William, whatever it is that's bothering you, you must know I'd never think ill of you!'

He turned, looked at her, and said clearly, 'You think not? You see, Margaret – I love you.'

Rain beat at the window. A puff of smoke eddied round his legs as the gale gusted down the chimney.

'It isn't a brotherly love. It's the strong love a man feels for a woman, and it's destroying me. Every time I hear your voice or see you smile or watch the turn of your head it tears the heart out of me. I want to hold you and have you for my own, but I can't do that – I never could. So I'm going out of Paisley, to a place where I'll not be tormented with the nearness of you.'

'But – you never said anything in all the time before Gavin—'

'I told you—' he said harshly, 'I couldn't! That's why I went away. I was contented enough until you came after me and told me I should come back. So I did – just to be near you. I should have had more sense—'

313

He moved suddenly, but she was faster, her hands on his shoulders, holding him.

'William – don't just leave me like this, without—'

His eyes moved to a point above and behind her and she turned, her hands sliding from his wet coat, to see Gavin in the doorway, his eyes dark and expressionless as he surveyed them.

Wet hair was plastered to his forehead and rainwater ran down his face and dripped to his shoulders. As he moved into the room and dropped heavily onto a small chair mud dropped in sticky clumps from his boots.

Margaret was too agitated to think of the picture she and William must have presented to him. 'Gavin – he's leaving tonight for Edinburgh! Tell him he can't just go away like that!'

Gavin's voice was tired. 'He'll not go anywhere tonight, for the river's in spate and that wind would blow anyone off the bridge if they were daft enough to venture onto it in the first place.'

As he reached for the claret, which stood on a small table, lamplight caught the side of his face and she saw a broad ribbon of blood from hairline to chin.

'Gavin!' William was forgotten as she ran to her husband. He put his hand to his cheek and looked at the blood on his fingers with disinterest.

'Pour some claret, for pity's sake, for I'm weary to the bone. It was – a chicken, as I mind. It was trying to roost under a roof and the gale blew it off just as I was rounding the street corner. It struck me in the face.' He took the proffered glass, drained it, managed a twisted grin. 'For a minute I thought it was the Devil himself attacking me, for it's a night when a man can believe in Hell. The poor bird must have got as big a fright as I did.'

She explored the wound with gentle fingers. The panicky bird's beak and claws had gashed his cheek in several places between the corner of his eye and the angle of his jaw. A few drops still oozed from the deeper scratches. She refilled his glass and thrust it into his hand.

'I'll fetch water and some clean rags.'

The front door banged as she was coming out of the kitchen with a bowl of water, but she didn't give it a thought until she got back to the parlour and saw that Gavin, still huddled in his chair, eyes closed, was alone.

'Where's William?'

Gavin started, and looked up. 'I didn't see him go.'

She set the bowl down and ran back to the hall. The heavy front door flew open as soon as she turned the handle, hurling her back into the hallway. Wind and rain surged in, wrapping her skirts about her legs and soaking her. She screamed William's name into the night and the sound was blown back down her throat, almost stifling her. She put her shoulder against the door to close it, but it resisted until Gavin's weight was added to hers.

He shot the bolt across, locking the wild night

out. 'Leave him be. He'll go nowhere tonight, I told you!'

Later, in bed, her head pillowed on his shoulder, she listened to the storm outside and thought of William.

'You don't think he would try to go away in this, do you?'

He cupped one breast, kissed its soft curve. 'Of course not. He'll have had the sense to go back home.'

Reassured, she gave herself up to his loving.

# *Chapter Six*

'YOU'RE NEVER INTENDING TO GO out of Paisley tonight, surely?' the stable-owner asked as his final customer appeared from the storm. 'Man, you'd be daft to try it!'

But William was adamant, and an extra coin or two showed the man the sense of his argument. He led out a sturdy, reliable horse, saddled it, and vanished back into shelter.

The animal was reluctant to leave its stable and William, an indifferent rider, had difficulty in persuading it to move out into the street. The force of the wind, once they were clear of the protective house walls, sent the horse staggering before it managed to brace itself and go forward.

Gavin was right – the Abbey Bridge would be an impossibility in such bad weather. But there were two fords, one at the Sneddon, near the Town Hospital, the other at the Saucel, on the other side of the Cross. William checked a move on the horse's part to go back to the stable and dragged on the reins, turning its head towards the Saucel.

Rain sluiced in sheets against his face, making it difficult to keep his eyes open. He seemed to be completely alone – even the beggars that usually slept against the house-sides had managed to find better shelter that night. The wind shrieked like a pack of enraged ghouls and tried again and again to pluck him from the saddle. He gripped tightly with his knees, determined to get out of Paisley that night.

Clumps of roofing thatch, slates, tatters of cloth and small twigs whipped by him as he rode. His hat was torn from his head and his hair flailed about his face. The wind changed direction and now the rain stung his face like a thousand tiny needles.

He heard the river long before he saw it, roaring defiance to the night as it plunged dementedly between banks that could scarcely contain it. The ragged, racing clouds let the moon through for a minute just as he reached the ford, and William saw that the normally slow-moving river, swelled by weeks of rain and fed by a hundred little burns running down from the braes, had become a mad-dened foam-flecked thing that seemed to be trying to toss the bulk of its water back into the sky.

His terrified mount threw its head up as he urged it down the banking. William's teeth sank into his tongue and he tasted the salt of his own blood.

'By God, you'll go on!' he roared, consumed with terror at the thought of being trapped in Paisley for another night. It was as though the town was a living entity, reaching out to pull him back as he tried to escape for the second time.

The horse backed into a tree and thin branches whipped painfully about his wet uncovered face. Enraged by the stinging pain he caught at a branch and tore it free, more pain scalding through his crooked elbow as he did so; then he used the weapon to whip the horse back into the water, screaming curses that were torn away by the gale the moment they left his lips.

The animal went forward, its hooves slipping in the mud. As the river foamed round its legs it panicked and swung round, scrambling up the soft banking, throwing William off. He managed to get to his feet and found himself thigh-deep in water. Free of his weight, the horse gained the bank and disappeared, headed purposefully back to its stable.

William fought the river's pull, rubbing rain from his face and trying to judge the distance to the opposite bank. In normal weather it wasn't far and the water was no more than knee-deep; in earlier days, before the bridge was built, sturdy women had earned their living by carrying people on their backs across that same ford. Now, swollen and angry, it was an unknown element.

He planted his feet firmly against the river-bed, peered across the tumbling white-flecked water, and saw a light ahead. Someone had set a lamp in a window in the New Town. The sight cheered him. If he could keep moving towards that light he would be safe. He could, if necessary, find shelter on the opposite bank for the night and leave for Glasgow early in the morning before the town was awake. He went forward slowly, tensing his muscles against the pull of the river, testing the river-bed with each step before going on.

Suddenly his foot slipped and the torrent was on him like a hungry dog, bowling him over, bruising him, burying him beneath the surface.

He came up choking and spitting, treading water in a futile attempt to find something solid beneath his feet. He couldn't see the lamplight any longer and he had to fight down panic as he thrashed about, his feet reaching desperately for the river-bed and failing to find it. Then he realised that he must have been carried over the Hammills, the small waterfall between the Saucel ford and the bridge. Now he was in the deep pool where he had often gone swimming as a boy.

Weighted down by his clothing, he kicked out and managed to swim, letting the current carry him for the moment while he concentrated on clearing the pool and reaching shallower water.

But before that happened the Cart wrenched free a mass of flotsam caught between two boulders and hurled it angrily over the Hammils into the pool. A heavy piece of timber hit William with great force on the back of the neck.

His body relaxed, gave up its struggle, and let the river take it, turning over and over as it went.

\*   \*   \*

William Todd was found early next morning, wedged among a pile of debris that had lodged at the Sneddon ford, on the New Town side of the bank.

Jamie came running up Oakshawhill with the news, his boots splashing through great puddles, his face so white that the untidy mop of hair above it looked as though it had been set on fire.

As soon as she opened the door and saw him Margaret knew what he had come to tell her.

# Chapter Seven

GAVIN'S SMART NEW CARRIAGE BOWLED along the road that led from Barrhead to Paisley. On the wide driving-seat beside him Margaret smoothed the skirt of her handsome new green silk gown then braved the sun to look up at her husband, his hands steady on the reins. Happiness enfolded her as snugly and neatly as the long-sleeved gloves on her hands.

Gavin had been visiting a patient, and she had left Christian, now a busy toddler, with Ellen, and gone with him in order to spend some time with Kate, who lived in Barrhead. Beneath the seat, protected from the sun, was a mass of red and pink and white and yellow roses specially picked from Kate's garden; her husband Archie, now retired from the Army, was a keen horticulturist in his spare time.

From the road she could seen burns splashing demurely downhill to join the Cart, neat within their banks and bearing no resemblance whatsoever to the undisciplined torrents of the great storm nine months earlier. White and pink flowers massed the hawthorns, frothy elder-flowers had come into bloom, ragged robins clustered in red clumps by the roadside, creamy-white honeysuckle held out inviting blossoms to the bees and butterflies, who were not slow to sample the heady nectar offered to them.

The air was thick with scented warmth, and even when they came into the town, passing the riverside area where the manufacturers had their warehouses and then taking the turn into New Street, they were bathed in the perfume of the roses near their feet.

'Stop here a minute—' Margaret said suddenly and Gavin drew the carriage up without comment at the gates of the Laigh kirkyard, then jumped down and lifted her from her seat as though she was as light as Christian, instead of a grown woman and almost seven months pregnant.

The Todd family plot was at the back of the graveyard, away from the comings and goings of the street. Colin's and William's graves still had a new look, though the summer had covered them with fresh green grass to take away the stark rawness of brown earth.

Clumsily, Margaret bent and laid a spray of white rosebuds on the mound that covered Colin, then a second spray on William's resting place. She stood for a moment, head bowed. She often came here to talk to William and be comforted by the memory of him. She missed him sorely. She always would.

'Come on,' Gavin said quietly from behind her. 'They'll all be waiting for us.'

They were – Jamie and Billy, Meg and Duncan and Robert. Margaret stopped short in the doorway of the High Street loom-shop, astonished.

'It looks just the way I mind it as a wee girl!'

Almost all the floor space had been taken up by four looms. The floor had been freshly swept, linnets chirped in a cage hung at the sun-splashed window, a great box of the pinks that many Paisley men grew in their weaving shops stood on the sill.

'Now then—' Jamie's grin spilled over them all as he went to his loom, which stood just where his father's had been. He settled himself on the 'saytree', the long bench, and ran his fingers lightly over the wood before him. Then he looked up at the open trapdoor above.

'Are you ready?'

'I'm more than ready!' Kirsty called from the kitchen, where she was seated at her spinning-wheel. 'It's long past time for this house to hear the beat of a loom again. Get to your work and save the chattering till later!'

He winked at the others. 'Aye, mother.'

His foot pressed on a treadle. A set of warp threads lifted and Jamie sent the shuttle flying through the gap to the other side of the machine. Then he moved his foot to another treadle, and another set of threads lifted to form an arch in their turn. The shuttle sped back through it and Jamie warmed to his work, swaying to a steady rhythm beaten out by the thump and clack of treadles and shuttle.

Margaret felt Gavin's arm go round her, and leaned her full weight back against him, secure in the knowledge that he would always be there.

She stood within his embrace, watching as the good strong cloth on the loom began to take shape and grow, inch by inch.

# Bibliography

The Paisley Thread — Matthew Blair

Paisley Weavers, Pen Folk, Etc. — David Gilmour

Statistical Account of Scotland, Volume VII

Vanduara — William Hector

Paisley Weavers of Other Days — David Gilmour

From Cottage to Castle — Andrew Coats

Edwin Chadwick. Public Health Movements 1832–1854 — R. A. Keats

The Paisley Shawl — Matthew Blair

The Paisley Pamphlets — Renfrew District Libraries Services